boilerplate

I0599356

The Revolt of the Machines

IN THE SAME SERIES

The Revolt of the Machines
and Other French
Scientific Romances

translated, annotated and introduced by
Brian Stableford

A Black Coat Press Book

Edited by Peter Gabbani

Visit our website at www.blackcoatpress.com

ISBN 978-1-61227-333-4. First Printing. October 2014. Published by Black Coat Press, an imprint of Hollywood Comics.com, LLC, P.O. Box 17270, Encino, CA 91416.

TABLE OF CONTENTS

Introduction

This anthology is the eighth in a series collectively providing a cross-section of the early development of what Louis Figuier, defining the genre in the series of feuilletons published between 1887 and 1900 in *La Science Ilustrée*, called *roman scientifique* [scientific fiction]. Because the label that was eventually attached to the similar American genre that took root in the popular pulp magazines of the 1920s, "science fiction," was generalized during the period of cultural "co-colonization" that followed the end of World War II, such materials are sometimes described as "proto-science fiction," but they are, of course, nothing of the sort. The authors represented here had no idea that there would ever be something called "science fiction" and no idea of what it would be like, and cannot in any meaningful sense be considered as working toward it, making "progress" in its direction—if that direction can, in fact, be considered as progress rather than degeneration.

Like its closest English language analogue, "scientific romance," the phrase *roman scientifique* first appeared in the latter half of the 18th century, where it was used to refer to ideas in science that were thought to be, or had turned out be, scholarly fantasies. The earliest uses that show up by searching for the term in Google Books are dated between 1750 and 1754, but all the references from that period refer to an observation by Elie-Catherine Fréron, discussing the theory of gravity. Other early uses include a footnote in a scientific encyclopedia of the period under the entry on phlogiston, and several sources citing Jean-Baptiste Delambre's dismissal of the calculation of the date of the Biblical Deluge by the astronomer William Whiston, identify the *roman scientifique* [in this context, the scientific novel].

The term was employed by Honoré de Balzac in 1836 with reference to the *New York Sun* "Moon Hoax," which was equally sensational when reprinted in France, and Camille Flammarion employed it in the same context in 1864. It was still being used in the 1860s to refer to scientific texts, but it began to be used increasingly in that decade to refer to works of fiction, including works by Léon Gozlan, Henri Rivière and, not unnaturally, Jules Verne. Indeed, throughout the 1870s, the term was used almost exclusively to refer to Verne's scientifically and technologically-enhanced adventure stories, considered archetypal of the genre, but in the 1880s competition began when critics referred to the works of Émile Zola as "romans scientifiques"—a term which the author was happy to accept, on the grounds that his "Naturalist" fiction was typified by its employment of a scientific method of character analysis based on the study of the influences of hereditary and environment in shaping individual behavior. The subsequent conflict of reference might have been one of the factors that prevented Figuier's championing of the term as a generic label from being more widely adopted, thus leaving the way clear for the eventual usurpation of that field by the American term, which actually had a significantly different spectrum of reference and a markedly different series of ideological fascinations and inclinations. The stories included in this anthology mostly reflect concerns of the French genre that Louis Figuier attempted to define, often including heavy emphases on matters with which the later American genre was only marginally concerned, or to which the American genre typically brought a different perspective.

The first story contained herein, "Prodigieuse découverte," translated as "A Prodigious Discovery," was originally published in the monthly *Revue Moderne* in the December 1865 and January 1866 issues, roughly contemporary with Jules Verne's early novels—a fact that inspired Verne's publisher, Pierre-Jules Hetzel, who might have briefly entertained the notion of configuring a genre of speculative fiction himself, to reprint it in 1867 as *Prodigieuse découverte et ses incalculables consequences sur les destinées du monde entièr*. Unfortunately, Hetzel—an incorrigible meddler whose insistence on suppressing the more extravagant flights of Verne's imagination probably robbed the world of a considerable fraction of that writer's immense genius—did not like the ending of the *Revue Moderne* story and insisted that the author alter it. The alteration did not work to its advantage. (The version here translated is the serial version, taken from Google Books' reproductions of the relevant volumes of the *Revue Moderne*.)

The book version of *Prodigieuse découverte* apparently sold very poorly, which might have helped to discourage Hetzel from further experimentation with speculative fiction, but the fact that it had been issued by that publisher prompted some eager translators of Verne's work to translate it, and the versions published in Spanish, Italian and Portuguese were misrepresented as Verne's work. That misattribution remained commonplace in bibliographies for many years, although the novella was actually the work of the lawyer and Republican civil servant François-Armand Audoy (1825-1891), who wrote a number of non-fiction books under his own name and subsequently published a second book under the Nagrien pseudonym, *Un Cauchemar. Manoeuvres, intelligences, délits fantastiques* (Lahure, 1869). The catalogue of the Bibliothèque Nationale does not as yet attribute the Nagrien pseudonym to Audoy, but there is no doubt about it, a search of Hetzel's archives made in 1966 and publicized by Simone Vierne having revealed the truth.

In fact, there is nothing Vernian about the novella, which is partly a satire aimed at politics and publicity, using the hypothetical invention of a technology of antigravity as a means of highlighting the problems that an inventor might experience in the profitable exploitation of an epoch-making discovery, and partly an exercise in wry logic, pointing out the economic and social upheavals that a truly prodigious discovery might cause, even while furthering progress. That nexus of issues became a popular theme of *roman scientifique*, particularly

9

thorny because French scientists routinely saw their work overtaken by American inventors like Samuel Morse and Thomas Edison, who reaped the glory and well as all the profits of discoveries that they succeeded in patenting, but had not necessarily made. Whereas Verne was primarily a writer of adventure stories, whose philosophical bent was kept under a tight rein by Hetzel, Audoy was an occasional dabbler in *contes philosophiques* that owe more to the Voltairean tradition of wit and cynicism. That doubtless led to *Prodigieuse découverte* selling poorly to readers in search of Vernian thrills, but should not be estimated to its discredit.

The second story in the collection, "L'Autopsie du docteur Z***," translated as "Doctor Z***'s Autopsy," by Édouard Rod (1857-1910), is also a *conte philosophique*, which Rod employed as the title story of a collection of his short fiction published in 1884. As in the classic Voltairean tales in that vein, it employs a fantastic literary device as a narrative lever to bring a philosophical question or possibility into clearer focus, albeit, in this instance, somewhat perfunctory (the experience related, ostensibly as a result of the "autopsy" in question, is conspicuous in its failure to mention any such autopsy being carried out).

There is a sense in which "L'Autopsie du docteur Z***," belongs to a series of French stories raising the issue of whether consciousness might persist for a while after death, most of which feature scientists conducting experiments on freshly-guillotined heads—one of the most famous, Villiers de Isle Adam's "Le Secret de l'échafaud"[1], had been published in *Le Figaro*, to which Rod was also a contributor, in 1883, and might well have inspired Rod's flight of fancy. Rod's story is remarkable, however, in assuming that the residue of consciousness might last for days or weeks rather than mere seconds, and is not at all concerned with the mere question of whether or not the hypothesis might be true. Instead, it is in-

---

[1] tr. as "The Secret of the Scaffold" in *The Scaffold*, Black Coat Press, ISBN 978-1-932983-01-2.

tensely interested in the existential thought-experiment of how the consciousness of being dead and the experience of slow post-mortem extinction might affect one's attitude to the life one has lived. As such, it is highly unusual and quite fascinating in its suppositions.

It is worth noting that Rod's story qualifies as *roman scientifique* in both senses of the term, and can be regarded as a contribution to the school of "neo-Naturalism" that followed from Zola's Naturalism, and were differentiated by its substitution of more up-to-date psychological theories of biological heredity and their analyses of human behavior and consciousness. This translation was made from the version of the story reprinted in *Défricheurs d'imaginaire: Une Anthologie historique de science-fiction Suisse romande* (2009) edited by Jean-François Thomas.

The story that has given the collection its title (purely for melodramatic reasons and for ease of illustration), "La Révolte des machines" by Émile Goudeau (1849-1906), translated as "The Revolt of the Machines," was published in the 4 September 1891 issue of the *Livre populaire*, five years before an identically-titled story by Han Ryner was published in *L'Art Social* (September 1896)[2]. The theme was eventually standardized as a flamboyant staple of science fiction, but Goudeau's version stands at the head of the entire tradition, and differs from the subsequent American version in its emphasis on the politics of economic exploitation and Luddism.

Goudeau had worked as a teacher for a while, but then hurled himself wholeheartedly into the Parisian literary community, where he became famous as the founder and central figure of the Hydropathes—the name of which was based on a pun on his name—a literary drinking club founded in 1881 that survived a temporary disbandment, having become too big for convenience to be reincarnated as the heart and soul of the celebrated literary café *Le Chat Noir*. Although by no

---

[2] also tr. as "The Revolt of the Machines" in *The Superhumans*, Black Coat Press, ISBN 978-1-935558-77-4.

11

means typical of Goudeau's literary work—it seems to be his only excursion into speculative fiction—"La Révolte des machines" is very much in the spirit of the vigorous extravagance of such core members of the Hydropathes as Charles Cros, Alphonse Allais, Edmond Hsarcaucourt and Jules Richepin, all of whom made significant contributions to the development of French speculative fiction in an profuse, witty and surreal vein that routinely made the more earnest speculations favored and promoted by Louis Figuier seem rather staid and pedestrian. This translation was made from the version reproduced on Jean-Luc Boutel's excellent website *Sur l'autre face du monde*, an invaluable mine of information about the early evolution of *roman scientifique*.

The only other publication that routinely adopted Figuier's rubric as a generic description was *La Science Ilustrée*'s downmarket competitor *La Science Française*, which was sufficiently faithful in its imitation to run a feuilleton section of its own from its foundation in 1891 until the late 1890s, but tended to favor future war fiction of a kind that Figuier did not much like, until it switched from serialized novels to shorter works under the aegis of its second editor, Émile Gautier. Most of its fiction was written under the various pseudonyms of Georges Espitallier, who also wrote a considerable fraction of its non-fiction, but Louis Valona, the signature attached to "Confrères ennemis," published in seven parts in 1896, and translated as "The Rival Colleagues," does not seem to have been one of Espitallier's disguises. The byline was attached to various works in other periodicals as well as a couple of satirical songs designed for use as dramatic monologues, and was probably a freelance journalist during the 1890s, although his career does not seem to have lasted long, at least under the employment of that signature.

Valona published non-fiction in *La Science Française* as well as the present novelette, although his knowledge of science appears to have been a trifle limited. "Confrères ennemis" was not the only venture into comedy featured in the magazine, but it is the most flamboyant and belongs to a considerable tradition of *roman scientifique* that focuses on the supposed eccentricities and personality disorders of scientific researchers, often uncharitably. Like many stories in that tradition, and in spite of its passing mention of new gadgetry deployed in the "modern villa" designed by one of the characters, this, too, is a *roman scientifique* in both senses of the term, albeit a far cruder one than Rod's, reflecting and pandering to popular prejudices rather than challenging them. The translation was made from the relevant volume of *La Science Française* reproduced on the Bibliothèque Nationale's website, *gallica*.

"L'Hallucination de Monsieur Forbe," translated as "Monsieur Forbe's Hallucination," was originally published in the relatively upmarket periodical *Je Sais Tout*, an imitation of the English *Strand Magazine*, where it appeared as a four-part feuilleton between November 1907 and February 1908. It was subsequently revised for book publication as *La Terreur des images* in 1910, but I have not seen that version and have translated the earlier French title literally, in spite of its woeful impropriety, to emphasize that it is the periodical version that I have rendered into English. In fact, the latter title is only a little better, as "images," although far more apt as a description of the story's central motif than "hallucination," still lacks specific pertinence. The difficulty is easy to understand, however, as the word the story employs to describe its theme—"telepathy"—is usually understood differently, and what is actually featured is a kind of clairvoyance hypothetically enhanced by some kind of naturally occurring "wave" analogous to the carrier waves of wireless telegraphy transmission.

La Terreur des images is catalogued by the Bibliothèque Nationale as the work of Jules-Laurent Perrin, but other works that are apparently by the same author remain confused in the catalogue with those of an earlier Jules Perrin (1839-1911). The author of the present story appears to have been born in 1862, but I cannot find any reference to the date of his death. His other works included *Les Bonhommes en papier* (1905) and *Deux fantômes* (1908). This translation was made from the facsimile of the feuilleton issued as a book by Editions Apex, in its "Periodica" collection, in 1996.

"La Race qui vaincra" by Jules Sageret (1861-1944), translated as "The Race that will be Victorious," is a *conte philosophique* in the purest sense of the term, and appeared in book form in a collection of non-fiction essays on utopian speculation entitled *Paradis laïques* [Lay Paradises] (1908). It might conceivably have appeared previously in a periodical, but I cannot find any evidence of earlier publication. It explores a common theme in speculative utopian fiction, which is that utopian design would be all very well if humans were capable of living a utopian existence, but that they are ill-fitted for so doing by nature.

The notion of some kind of mutation, natural or induced, that might produce utopians out of common human stock is not unusual, but Sageret, as befits a scholar with a powerful interest in the conundrum, does so with a rare intensity as well as a deft wit. The translation was made from the version of the story reprinted in issue number 13 (October 2005) of Philippe Gontier's small press magazine *Le Boudoir des Gorgones*, another extremely useful and helpful source of information about antique French fantastic fiction.

"La Véridique ascension dans l'histoire de James Stout Brighton," translated as "The Veridical Ascent Through History of James Stout Brighton," was published in book form in *Polochon, Paysages animés, Paysages chimériques* in 1909, although it had presumably appeared previously in *Comoedia*, the periodical that its author, Gaston de Pawlowski (1873-1943), founded in 1908. Like most of Pawlowski's work, it is a blithe comedy in the casually bizarre manner that made him one of the pioneers of surrealism, along with such fellow dabblers in speculative fiction as Alfred Jarry and Guillaume Apollinaire. Much of Pawlowski's work in the speculative vein was assembled in the philosophical extravaganza *Voyage au pays de la quatrième dimension* (1912; expanded 1923)[3], but the present story is incompatible with the elastic scheme of that project. The translation was made from the version of *Polochon, Paysages animés, Paysages chimériques* reproduced on the Internet Archive website at *archive.org*.

The final story in the collection, "Anthéa, ou l'étrange planète" by "Michel Epuy" (Louis Vaury, 1876-1943), translated as "Anthea; or, The Strange Planet" first appeared in two installments in the Swiss periodical *Semaine littéraire* in July-August 1918, where it attracted praise from the author on whose speculative fiction it is clearly modeled, and to whom it is dedicated, J.-H. Rosny Aîné. It was subsequently reprinted as a small book by La Plume de Paon in 1923. As with Rosny's work in a similar vein, it is a striking biological fantasia imagining life on another world, in which the distinctions seemingly so natural on Earth between animal, vegetable and mineral are confused. The literary devices employed to transplant the hero to the alien world and bring him back again are wildly implausible, but handled with a flamboyant panache that does the story's melodramatic component no harm at all.

As with the Édouard Rod story, this translation is made from the version of the story reprinted in *Defricheurs d'imaginaire: Une Anthologie historique de science-fiction Suisse romande* (2009) edited by Jean-François Thomas. That version reprints the "prologue" attached to the story in the Plume de Paon edition, which is actually a blurb advertising the story, but which is interesting in that capacity by virtue of its apologetic manner, which illustrates very clearly that, even without the existence of a generally-accepted generic label, there was already something seemingly-suspect about speculative fiction in 1923, which caused editors to think twice about publishing it and caused many of them to issue apologies in advance for doing so.

---

[3] latter version tr. as *Journey to the Land of the Fourth Dimension*, Black Coat Press, ISBN 978-1-934543-37-5.

The excuses offered, and their cringing tone, became utterly commonplace thereafter, and anyone interested in the development of that kind of fiction will have seen dozens of examples. I thought it worthwhile to reproduce this one, however, as an illustrative early specimen.

Brian Stableford

X. Nagrien: *A Prodigious Discovery*
(1866)

I. The Announcement

All Paris was occupied one morning with an unsigned text distributed in profusion during the night whose contents were as follows:

People who are in the Place de la Concorde next Sunday, the first of June, at noon precisely will witness the first manifestation of the greatest of revolutions past and future.

The word revolution ought not to frighten anyone. This one is not political—or, at least, its political and social consequences, although they will be considerable in the future, will not be produced in an immediate and direct manner.

The invention of printing, gunpowder and the steam engine and the discovery of America also produced immense revolutions in the world's destiny. It is in the same sense that the word is employed here—except that the importance of all those revolutions put together is nothing compared to that of the revolution that is in preparation.

Those who see the first manifestation will be able to inscribe in their personal memories a date memorable forever in the annals of humanity.

The manifestation in question will commence at noon exactly in the Place de la Concorde. It will continue until five o'clock in the Champs-Élysées, the Jardin des Tuileries, the public promenades, the boulevards and the quais—everywhere that the width of the routes of communication permits crowds to gather.

The authorities should take wise organizational measures to avoid accidents. They should also take precau-

tions, if they think it appropriate, in view of any possible events, but all that they have to fear is excessively large crowds.

Those who take a foolish pride in affecting incredulity on the subject of this announcement; those who will be tempted to see it either as the delusion of a madman or as some ridiculous hoax, have only to reflect on the mysterious manner in which this message has been distributed to convince themselves that this time, the most intelligent are not the least credulous.

Striking proof will be provided in the Place de la Concorde on Sunday June the first, at noon precisely.

This text was distributed throughout Paris five or six weeks before the first of June, after a dark and rainy night. All modes of distribution had been employed, including the most incomprehensible.

Many people received it through the post, some in registered letters. Others found copies in the courtyards of houses, on balconies, windowsills, gutters beneath mansards, on staircases, or in fireplaces where no fires had been lit in view of the warm spring weather. Street-sweepers and rag-pickers collected a certain quantity in the street from dawn onwards. There were copies in all the monuments with openings that had not been closed during the night, in the markets, the churches, the theaters, the public rooms of the Bourse and the Palais de Justice, public ballrooms, and railways stations. They were seen caught in the branches of trees, clinging to lightning conductors, stuck up here and there, at all heights, on nails, hooks and any little projections on walls, shutters and roofs. They were floating in the Seine, falling from ledges and entablements from which the wind had carried them.

The Luxor obelisk in the Place de la Concorde was garlanded with them. It was circled, at all heights, all the way to the summit, by crowns of rope from which pieces of thread hung down bearing strings of copies that were floating in the wind. It was necessary to go to a great deal of trouble, with the

18

aid of numerous ladders, to clear the venerable monument of the unusual ornamentation.

Although it was started early, the operation in question could not be finished quickly enough to prevent many people witnessing the fact. Those who had been out in the streets the previous night in spite of the bad weather related that copies had fallen onto their umbrellas. On that day and the following day, birds of every species—pigeons, sparrows, swallows—were found in and around Paris with the text attached to their necks by a thread. Some were seen in flight long afterwards; they were killed as far away as Belgium, Corsica and Algeria.

That was not all, but it was already enough to cite public curiosity and put the police on the alert.

The public was far less occupied with the contents of the text than the manner of its distribution. People remembered the story of a house peppered with stones one night in 1848 without anyone ever being able to find a satisfactory explanation for the phenomenon. Everyone tried to explain this also, but no one succeeded. There was agreement on only one point: the distributors must have been numerous, and had given proof of discretion and skill. What was their objective, and what was behind it all?

According to the most widely credited opinion, it was a colossal hoax, a monstrous belated April fool's joke. No one, in spite of the plausible enough reflection that the text contained, dared to believe that it was something real. It was recognized that the hoax was not worth either the trouble or the money that it must have cost, but did a practical joker take account of such things? Many stories were told about messages thrown into apartments through open windows, of window panes broken by a gloved hand that a few people had glimpsed, but no one gave any credence to those old wives' tales. The most sagacious assumed that it was commercial advertising, the author of which was waiting to be sufficiently talked about before making himself known in order to reveal to the world a new insecticide or anti-baldness lotion. As for going to the Place de la Concorde on the first of June, everyone protested that they would not take a single step admitting to such a naïve credulity.

Deep down, however, and without saying anything, the most skeptical promised themselves privately to look out of their windows if they provided a view, no matter how limited, of the boulevards or the quais. Those who did not have that advantage meditated upon a plausible pretext for being outside and, if they could, passing through the Place de la Concorde at midday on the first of June. Everyone, seeing everyone else incredulous, thought they would be the only ones there.

The police and the authorities shared the impressions of the public, very nearly, but were preoccupied with something else. Behind the pretended hoax, there might some political agenda, perhaps a conspiracy. Who could tell whether it might not be an ingenious method of drawing an enormous crowd outdoors and provoking popular movements? It was resolved, in any event, to take precautions, but without having the appearance of doing so, in order not to compromise the dignity of those in power by seeming to attach any importance to what might be nothing but a trick. A resolution was also made to leave no stone unturned in getting to the bottom of the mystery. Two orders were issued, one by way of the police, the other by judiciary.

The police order had no need of any pretext. Police Commissaires received instructions to put together all the information that their various agents could collect and send it to the Prefecture, where it would be centralized. As for the judiciary instruction, it was sufficiently justified by the circumstances of the enigmatic distribution. To begin with, it was an unauthorized text; then again, the text itself had neither been declared not deposed; it bore no printer's name and was assumed to be a clandestine product of a private press. Perhaps it did not contain any clearly identifiable criminal offence, although it was unstamped and might be considered, strictly speaking, to be treating matters of political and social economy, but there was talk of a few broken windows, a veritable punishable infraction. All that was more than enough to motivate an instruction whose objective was the search for the authors of the actions, more or less delinquent from various points of view.

The police order produced a mountain of documents. The agents conscientiously collected all the gossip whose echoes they could grasp. The *they say*s were running riot. No one was talking about anything else in drawing rooms, clubs, cafés, restaurant tables, at the Bourse, at the Palais—everywhere that people chat. It was in concierges' lodges and the shops where cooks gathered, most of all, that anecdotes circulated, attaining every degree of implausibility. Unfortunately, it was almost impossible to identify their sources. It would be pointless to repeat all the incidents to which imagination gave birth, which had grown in their passage from mouth to mouth. There were many that were repeated with few variations, but there was also ardent persistence on points very different from one another.

Thus, a student lodged in a high room in the Latin Quarter recounted that, at about two o'clock in the morning, being unable to sleep, he had gotten up to get a book when one of his windowpanes had shattered noisily and an object had fallen into the room. The obscurity had not permitted him to distinguish anything. He had run to the widow and opened it, but had not seen anything outside. Then he had lit a candle and found a round object wrapped in paper on the floor, near the window, on which was written: for the broken window. He had unfolded the paper, which contained a five-franc piece, and had writing inside; it was a copy of the famous text.

Others, in the Mouffetard, Bastille and Opéra quarters, in the Champ-Élysées, at Montmartre, Vaugirard and Montrouge, related that they had been woken up with a start by the noise of breaking glass, and had then found a five-franc coin wrapped in the same fashion. Others, going into their drawing rooms in the morning, had found the same thing, always near a broken window. It seemed difficult to believe, though, after expert inspection of the broken panes, that they could have been produced simply by throwing a five-franc coin.

One notable circumstance was that the breakages, located in windows indiscriminately situated in streets and courtyards, were never committed to a lighted room. It was certain that the perpetrators of the nocturnal distribution, evidently very numerous, had taken great care to avoid being seen. Some people, however, affirmed that they had seen something; in view of the gravity of the affair, they were sent to the examining magistrate.

The investigation had been confided to a magistrate of rare sagacity. The voluminous reports centralized at the Prefecture of Police were forwarded to him. He pruned all those that presented a character too obviously fabulous, like the inadmissible declarations of people who claimed to have discerned a black mass in the air, affecting a vaguely human form, between two other formless masses that seemed to be supporting him, gesticulating like a fantastic sower, and moving with a velocity about half way between that of a swallow in flight and that of a cannonball.

The examining magistrate only retained those accounts presenting some plausibility, or at least possibility. He heard all the people whose windows had been broken and had received five-franc coins, which were temporarily retained as evidence. Neither their dates nor anything about their appearance, however, provided any useful clue. Nearly two hundred were collected, which already added up to a thousand francs of expense simply for those objects.

The texts distributed by post, impossible to number precisely, but which tallied more than two thousand, had cost, even at the cheapest rate, more than two hundred francs, not counting the registration charge on fifty letters. All the inquiries made at the post office revealed was that they had been handed in at the counter by an individual whom no employee had thought of looking at or remembering the face. He had given the name "Nagrien," recognized as fictitious, and a similarly false address.

It was observed that the broken windows had been produced in quarters very distant from one another, if not simul-

taneously, but at moments too close together for the conclusion of a great number of distributors not to be drawn—at least
fifty and perhaps more than a hundred, independently of those,
more numerous still, who had spread the documents everywhere. It was in vain that the autographic characters, the writing on the envelopes received by post, the paper employed,
and the ropes and pieces of string attached to the obelisk were
subjected to expert analysis. Inquires made of sellers of paper,
rope and birdcages did not produce any results.

The declarations of certain people, of whom there had
been loud discussions, and who had claimed to see more than
others, were written down with the utmost care. To begin with,
there were six young women who had eaten supper together
and played cards after leaving a theater, and in the home of
one of them: a rather small room on the fourth floor. At about
three a.m., someone had opened a window to renew the air,
saturated as it was with tobacco smoke. A moment later, a
handful of the pieces of paper had been thrown into the room
from outside via that window. They had not been able to see
anything outside, except that one of them thought she had
made out a black form slipping behind a chimneystack on the
roof of the house opposite. All the inhabitants of the house
opposite were questioned carefully, but they had been unable
to offer any useful revelation, except that the following day,
one of them had found a few copies in the fireplaces of his
apartment.

In another quarter, there was a physician whom someone
had come to fetch during the night to attend to someone who
was ill. A precious hazard had determined that his domestic
servant, holding a candle, had opened the door of his master's
room at the exact moment when a windowpane was noisily
broken. The physician and the manservant affirmed very categorically that, between the little curtains of the glass panel
fitted into the door that had just been opened, they had seen a
hand wearing an extremely thick glove, like those of which
one makes use for fencing, break the pane, drop an object onto

the carpet, and disappear. They had not been able to see anything at all outside.

Two other people, a husband and wife, on waking up at the moment when a pane on their bedroom window had been broken, said that they, too, had seen the gloved hand, albeit rather vaguely, thanks to the light projected by a gas jet in the street.

Needless to say, a large number of other depositions were collected, but it was impossible to arrest anyone on suspicion of being an accomplice or for having any participation whatsoever in the event. All those momentarily suspected justified themselves in the most triumphant fashion, and their pursuit had to be renounced.

The conclusions that the Prefect of Police drew on the one hand and the examining magistrate on the other from their research were that nothing could be affirmed regarding the nature or objective of the distribution, but that the purpose was evidently serious, and that there were no grounds for thinking that it was merely a trick, the distributors having been too numerous, having gone to so much trouble and having given evidence of an extraordinary skill; the secret had been too well guarded! As for the explanation of the means involved, it was recognized that it was impossible to determine, for the moment. It would probably be discovered later, but it was urgently necessary to be ready for anything.

All of that had an effect on the public. It was known that there had been an investigation, in the course of which numerous witnesses had been heard. The general incredulity was shaken somewhat.

The newspapers had reported and commented on these events, each in its own way. On the first day, there were simple news items about the distribution, which was presented as something rather bizarre, but devoid of any particular importance, every reporter applying himself to warning his readers against the exaggerations and fables with which the stories, audible here and there, seemed to be mingled. The following day, however, those stories had multiplied to the point at which it was necessary to give a few details. The text itself was reproduced by all the newspapers. Each one accompanied it with its commentary, generally dictated by a perfect skepticism. They might perhaps have paid no further heed to the story after a few days if one of them had not decided to take the matter seriously, thus provoking unanimous laughter.

The naïve periodical in question was the *Universel*. On the fourth day it published a long article in which it first enumerated all the circumstances, a number of which were inexplicable, that seemed well established. It reasoned from that to the effect that the people capable of having accomplished the feat could not be vulgar hoaxers or charlatans, and that it would be more intelligent, if not to believe blindly in the discovery, at least to wait until after June the first before denying it categorically. Its writer admitted that, so far as he was concerned, he was more inclined to belief than doubt. He even risked a hypothesis; it seemed probable to him that a method had been discovered of steering balloons. The nocturnal distributors were, according to all appearances, aeronauts trained and indoctrinated by the inventor. And who could tell whether hundreds of balloons might not be seen in the first of June, traveling over Paris, obedient to all the impulsions given to them by conductors manning their nacelles.

The *Universel* was attacked with fewer good reasons than sarcasms. Hardly anyone deigned to observe that an invention of the kind suggested, necessitating a multitude of trials, could not remain so profoundly unknown. One could not imagine less than three hundred distributers; how could it be admitted that three hundred dirigible balloons had been manufactured without anyone suspecting it, that they could have been inflated in advance—a long operation requiring the employment of numerous personnel—and then accomplish their progressions over Paris during a single night without a single person perceiving even one of them? Besides which, had it not been scientifically demonstrated that the dirigible airship was a pure chimera, for want of being able to find sufficient resistance in the air and by virtue of the necessity of giving the balloons dimensions out of all proportion to the force of any possible aerial motor? All of that was said incidentally in endless epigrams.

The *Universel* held firm. It disdained the ridicule with which others were trying to cover the story and opposed strict reasoning that shook the conviction of many incredulous individuals. It gained a good many readers in consequence.

At the same time, several details became known regarding the investigation, in the course of which so many witnesses had been heard. It was concluded therefrom that the key to the enigma was not the hypothesis of a large number of dirigible balloons, for if that were the case, it would not have escaped the examinations of the law and the police. It was also concluded, however, that there must be something serious at stake, since such powerful means of investigation had been put to work.

The mockers gradually began to come round to the *Universel*'s viewpoint, while the latter declared that it was no longer sticking to its aerostat hypothesis, and limited itself to sustaining, unlike and against everyone else, that something important was going to happen on June the first. The other newspapers began to fear that they might have taken the wrong line. Would they not find that they had played a foolish role if events proved their adversary correct, as was beginning to seem less impossible? That occasioned a change of attitude, just in case it proved to be necessary to yield to the evidence.

Then echoes arrived of the impression produced in the provinces, initially reflecting, as in Paris, a complete skepticism. Soon, however, things changed. People in the provinces have more time to read and reflect. Some sided openly with the *Universel*. People abandoned themselves without false shame to all the ardors of violent interest. Many packed their bags in order to come to Paris before June the first. The railway companies wondered whether it was not an opportunity to organize pleasure trains, and would certainly have done so had the government not asked them discreetly to abstain from the project.

However, it was only the twentieth of May, and people everywhere were already getting tired of always talking about the same thing. They closed their ears to it, as to any subject that has remained on the table too long. They ceased almost entirely to pay any heed to it. Public attention was saturated, and it became fashionable to declare that any allusion to the first of June or the nocturnal distribution irritated the hardened nerves. Three days before the first of June, it seemed that no one was any longer trying to find the key to the enigma—but a new circumstance suddenly awakened the dormant preoccupation.

There was a second nocturnal distribution, not of handwritten paper notices but of tinplate medallions, slightly larger than five-franc pieces, which were spread with the same profusion as the written message, but without broken windows or gloved hands glimpsed by some.

On them was engraved, a trifle crudely but quite legibly, the following words:

Sunday June 1st
Noon
Place de la Concorde

Furthermore, something singular was perceived above the building in which the *Universel*'s offices were situated. The newspaper had placed on the summit between two chimneys a sheet metal sign bearing its name, cut out in immense characters, visible from a long distance away. A kind of large white banner had been suspended beneath it during the night, bearing a single word written in characters two meters high:

COURAGE!

It was positively established that no one had been able to go up onto the roof during the night.

In addition, the obelisk had been embellished with a new ornament. It was coiffed with a kind of huge sheet metal bonnet with four faces. On each one appeared the words:

HERE
SUNDAY
JUNE 1st
NOON

This time, people were not content to be intrigued. They were beginning not to be ashamed to blush. The youth of the schools, workers and the residents of the suburbs, overstepping human respect, were the first to abandon themselves to a curiosity that became contagious. Large bets were laid at the Jockey Club, and in all the other clubs, for and against the reality of the awaited event. Even the Bourse became convinced that the day of June the first would influence prices in one direction or the other, and divided into two camps, the high and the low. Women energetically expressed their desire to go and see for themselves.

Working class households, in particular, got ready to invade the Place de la Concorde *en masse*. As for others, there were not a few who had no fear of the crowd and intended to mingle with it. Those who feared that it might be too dense sought to procure windows overlooking the boulevards or the quais. The Rue Royale became the goal of all ambitions. One of its inhabitants put up a notice on the twenty-ninth of May advertising *Windows to Let for June 1st*. His example was immediately followed and extended like an ignited trail of powder along the boulevards, the Rue de Rivoli and the quais. All were booked at the insane prices that signify a curiosity driven to its paroxysm. On May the thirty-first, at five o'clock in the afternoon, only a few notices remained in the quarters most distant from the Place de la Concorde.

It was certain that the crowd would be enormous. The authorities were no longer in doubt about that. All troops were ordered to report to their barracks, reinforced by neighboring garrisons, and issued with ammunition for all purposes. The artillery was at the ready, with its guns in harness in the courtyards. All these precautions were, moreover, taken as secretly as possible. Police agents, *sergents de ville* and National guardsmen, on foot and mounted, were posted before daybreak everywhere that a crowd might gather, with strict orders to maintain order and prevent accidents. The circulation of vehicles was prohibited at several points and regulated everywhere, as on national holidays.

Everyone already knew that, if it really was a hoax, it had succeeded magnificently.

II. The Invention

I had some difficulty myself in perceiving the initial idea of my invention clearly.

A kind of vague intuition told me that people had gone astray in wanting to propel aerial vehicles, whether lighter or heavier than air, by means of existing engines. All motive force was fatally insufficient as soon as it required heavy machinery. The more one wants to increase the size and efficacy of wings, sails, helices or any other devices designed to produce locomotion, the more they require a considerable motive force, impossible to obtain in the air by reason of the weight of the machines, especially if they require provisions of water and fuel. One can only increase the power of conveyance by increasing in an even greater proportion the difficulty of the result. The concept of dirigible balloons, or any vehicles receiving propulsion from any known engine implied a contradiction, so far as I was concerned. It was a veritable vicious circle, an impossibility. Something else was necessary, other than what had been attempted thus far. It required an entirely new and radically different primordial conception.

I reflected that nature might furnish motors thus far unknown, unstudied and, in truth, yet to be discovered.

At first I thought of gravitation. It is obviously a force, and an enormous force, acting without mechanism—a precious condition. What energy there is in the fall of a rock from a height of a hundred meters, what power in the forces that determine the movement of celestial bodies!

Except that gravitation is not a dirigible force. For us, it has a unique center of direction, the very center of the globe on the surface of which phenomena within our scope occur. Gravitation is a motor exactly opposite to the one that I required.

That idea of *exactly opposite* was a flash of enlightenment for me. Did not gravity have its counterpart?

It had to exist. The double phenomenon of attraction and repulsion is observed in all chemical compositions and the composition of substances. Electricity is positive or negative.

Electricity was not understood in that era. People made use of it, however. There was the electric telegraph, an invention that seems so naïve, but which passed then for the *nec plus ultra* of the genius of practical science. There was a confused suspicion that there must be some relationship between electricity and magnetism, but no one had taken exact count of the identity of those phenomena, of which the electric spark, magnetism, galvanism, gravitation and chemical affinities are merely diverse manifestations. Perhaps I shall be accorded scant merit for having discovered that gravitation and electricity are one and the same thing, but it's the story of Christopher Columbus and the egg: every solved problem seems easy to resolve.

No one can imagine all that it cost me in terms of effort, meditation, hard work, experiments, discouragements and perseverance to arrive at this formula: gravitation is only one of the modes of the manifestation of electricity.

Electricity is, so to speak, gravitation condensed, quintessentialized and endowed with its extreme power. It is a kind of madness of attraction. It presents two opposites, which are described by the terms positive and negative electricity. In the same way, gravitation, properly speaking, is positive, has as its inverse negative gravitation, or anti-gravitation.

Their combined action produces the movement of heavenly bodies, and this completes Newton's discovery. Gravitation only explains half of phenomena—for example, the force retaining the Earth at a certain distance from the sun that attracts it. But one is obliged, in order to explain that it does not fall into it, to suppose an original impulsion, provided once and for all, and which resolves into centrifugal force. The nature of that force—which is not original but continuous, tending to distance the Earth from the sun toward which gravitation attracts it—was unknown. It is anti-gravitation, or negative gravitation, or the force of repulsion, one of the forms of negative electricity. The two gravitations, positive and negative, act in association, in opposition to one another, at an angle whose resultant, varying from one moment to the next, produces the revolution of every planet around its sun and every satellite around its planet.

The motor existed in nature. It was a matter of becoming its master, of moderating it, of making it something manipulable and usable.

That has been the most arduous part of my work. How many late nights, experiments, fruitless attempts there were before arriving at the creation of two electrochemical substances that I have named pos and neg, by the simple abbreviation of the words positive and negative. Pos, as yellow as gold, as solid as platinum, meltable at a temperature that is so difficult to attain! Neg, as white as silver, as light as aluminum, as porous as pumice-stone! Isolated, they behave like all other substances, falling to earth and obedient only to the law of gravitation. It is their juxtaposition that gives them particular properties, just as superimposed disks of zinc, copper and a suitably dampened fabric disengages electricity in a Voltaic pile.

Electricity is also discharged by juxtaposed pos and neg: positive or attractive electricity by pos, negative or repulsive electricity by neg. The former is solicited by gravitation, the second by anti-gravitation.

Those are the observations to which my experiments led:

I fabricated a ball, one hemisphere of which was composed of pos and one of neg. When the pos was turned toward the ground, the ball fell. When, on the other hand, it was the neg, it rose up with great force. My first apparatus was naturally very imperfect, but it was sufficient to give me the certainty of eventual success.

I recognized that the two gravitating electricities, positive and negative, were emitted in a continuous fashion, one by pos and the other by neg, but that emission did not produce any effect on whichever of the substances did not have its surface turned toward the ground. The attractive or repulsive force was annulled, for want of an objective, if it did not have the terrestrial mass in front of it. It is almost as if one were to suppose a heavy body lost in space far from any celestial body. It is still submissive to the force of gravitation, and yet does not fall anywhere because nothing sets it to work. To borrow a comparison from juridical language, it has, so to speak, the enjoyment of the gravitational faculty, but does not exercise it.

In the same way, when I turned my ball pos-downwards, a repulsive electricity was still emitted by the neg, but, finding no objective in space, it did not produce any effect. On the other hand, the ball was violently attracted earthwards by the attractive electricity emitted by the pos. I wanted to ascertain whether that falling effect was the result of weight alone. I gave each of my separate hemispheres a weight of one kilogram. The ball, therefore, if it were only obedient to ordinary gravitation, weighed two kilograms. I placed the pos and the neg in a balance pan. Then I successively increased the weight in the other pan. I could not succeed in lifting up the ball, in spite of a total weight of fifty kilograms. It adhered with an invincible force, like one of those hollow weights that a conjuror can lift with a single finger, but which is impossible to lift, even by employing all his effort, as soon as electrical communication is established. The dimensions of my balance did not permit me to take the experiment any further, but I was content. I had only to rotate the ball through ninety degrees to cancel out the adherence.

When the ball was turned neg-down, it rose up with great force and struck the ceiling violently, where it remained suspended. The inverse effect had been produced. It was the attractive gravitational electricity emitted by the upward-turned pos that found no objective in space and produced no effect in any direction. On the contrary, the repulsive gravitational electricity emitted by the neg found its objective in the terrestrial mass, and violently distanced the ball therefrom. It was like a taut spring released after having been given a point of resistance.

I also wanted to verify the degree of adherence of the ball to the ceiling. It was impossible for me to vanquish, in spite of all the weight I suspended from it. That was sufficient for me, and I postponed until later the exact measurement of the force of the system, either in the attractive or the repulsive direction. I turned my ball half way, and in that fashion, easily detached it from the ceiling.

The problem was three-quarters resolved. I had a motor endowed with an enormous force, ascending or descending at will. A ball the size of my head sufficed for me to raise aerial arks of considerable dimensions. But as yet, that was only a simple improvement over balloons. It was first necessary to find a means of moderating the ascensional force in order not to be drawn to excessive heights, and then to transform it into lateral force in order to steer the apparatus.

The first result was easy to obtain. The complete adherence of pos and neg produced the maximum emission of positive or negative gravitational electricity. I realized that if I separated them slightly, the phenomenon was not suppressed, but lessened. It was still manifest, albeit very weakly, by placing the two substances two centimeters apart. Thus disposed, they remained in the air almost at the location where they were placed, only descending or ascending with an imperceptible movement and great slowness, according to whether the pos or the neg was directed toward the ground. I was master of the motive force, which I could increase or diminish at will.

It remained to be able to steer. There, my groping was extended. I shall pass over the details and get straight to the method that furnished me with the solution.

I tried to compose my ball with one intermediate part of neg and two extreme parts of pos; it was like a slice between two hemispheres. That produced a rather curious phenomenon.

The juxtaposition of the inferior hemisphere with the intermediary disk emitted positive gravitational energy and tended to carry the ball toward the ground; but at the same time, the juxtaposition of the disk with the upper hemisphere emitted negative gravitational energy and tended to make the ball rise, without the inferior hemisphere providing an obstacle to it—which astonished me. Both phenomena were produced simultaneously. The ball was solicited by two directly contrary forces, attractive and repulsive. It obeyed the one that predominated over the other, rising or falling with more or less force in accordance with the proportions that I gave successively to the various parts of the ball—except that I never succeeded in weighting them exactly enough for the system to remain entirely motionless at the precise location where I placed it in the air.

Then I had the idea of giving the intermediary slice the form of a bevel. I made it very thick on one side, while terminating the other in a thin blade. The effect produced was marvelous.

The two contrary forces were still produced, but obliquely; their resultant was horizontal. I succeeded in constructing a ball that I placed on my mantelpiece with the thick side of the disk turned toward the opposite wall. It launched forth like a rifle bullet and struck that wall, damaging the paper and dislodging a little plaster.

It was easy for me to moderate that force by constructing balls whose various parts were more or less distant from one another.

I had spent long years in pursuit of that result, but the principle of aerial locomotion was finally resolved—in principle. I had the motor and both the means of moderating it and of steering it at will. It only remained to perfect the details.

That was easy. This is where the modifications that I imagined successively led me. I changed the form of the system, which I rendered sphero-conical instead of spherical. To render my idea graspable, it was like a pear or a fig instead of an apple or an orange. The pear was designed so as habitually to maintain a near-horizontal position. It was made up of three parts, all swelling on the side opposed to the point and thinning toward the tail: in the middle, the pos; above and below, the neg. A simple mechanism permitted me to bring these parts closer together or separate them by turning slightly, in one direction or another, as one turns a key, a stem emerging from the pear and descending vertically. The same stem served, by means of circular movements analogous to those one imparts to a tiller, to turn the tail of the pear in the desired direction, thus raising it or lowering it at will.

If I imagined myself being suspended from the system, I could see myself traveling in the air with as much facility and rapidity as the most agile bird.

I began by turning the stem in such a way as only to leave the apparatus a very minimal action, and directing the tail of the pear upwards an angle of forty-five degrees. I was lifted gently and obliquely into the air. Having arrived at a certain altitude, I gave the pear a horizontal position and turned the stem in such a way as to bring the two pieces of the apparatus closer together, and I was carried away horizontally, in the direction I chose, at a speed that I could increase to a lofty maximum.

Nothing was easier to realize.

III. The Application

I constructed a kind of armchair with strong straps, which also supported me by the armpits, leaving my arms and legs complete freedom of movement. The straps, when tightened, came together above my head in a unique point of suspension that I first adapted to a hook solidly fixed in the ceiling. I successively modified the points of attachment of my aerial seat until I had attained a perfect equilibrium as well as a comfortable position. The one on which I settled was almost precisely the posture of a man sitting in a Voltaire armchair, slightly tilted backwards.

I noticed, however, that even the most comfortable possible position became fatiguing, and even unbearable, after a few hours, if one could not modify it slightly. That observation led me to complete my seat by means of straps passing under my feet, on which I could support myself and stand almost upright. I was, therefore, sometimes sitting, sometimes standing, sometimes suspended beneath the arms and sometimes almost standing, able in addition to support myself on one leg or the other, to cross them and lean, sometimes on one elbow and sometimes on the other, by means of straps placed within easy reach.

I also noticed that with a unique point of suspension, I could not prevent completely enough a slight rotational movement, produced in one direction or the other under the most minimal impulsion. I remedied that by suspending straps from my seat from two points instead of one. A separation of less than a decimeter between the two points of suspension proved to be sufficient to prevent any rotational movement, or at least for the system to regain its normal position almost instantaneously.

For a long time I exercised a kind of gymnastics in my aerial seat, whereby I ended up feeling as much at ease and sure of myself as in an armchair on castors. Then I thought of devoting myself to definitive experiments. I suspended my seat solidly by means of straps to the two sides of the kind of pear that I have described, and for which I had found a name that I shall employ henceforth.

The terms pos and neg had already become familiar; any system in which their juxtaposition produced the effects I have described I named a negopos. A negopos could take various forms. After having tried the spherical form, I had settled on the sphero-conic form, but it was still a negopos. The Earth and the planets are merely enormous negoposes, although differently composed in the superimposition of pos and neg. A magnetized needle is also a veritable negopos, but in an utterly rudimentary state. It was the only one known before my invention, but without anyone taking account of its functioning. People did not know until now that the attraction of the needle toward the pole is due to a combination of the two gravitational and anti-gravitational forces, produced in particular conditions giving them a determined direction, by virtue of what is called magnetism, but with such scant efficacy that the slightest resistance prevents the embryonic negopos from obeying the force that solicits it.

A simple negopos is the first kind that I described, only composed of two parts, one pos and one neg. A complex negopos—the complete negopos or negopos *par excellence*—is one composed of three parts disposed in such a manner as to obtain all the desired effects, whether the pos is between two pieces of neg or the neg between two pieces of pos. The effects produced in the two cases are identical but inverse. A negopos in the form of a pear is directed toward the tail in the first and away from it in the second.

When I employ the word "negopos" in isolation, with no adjective or explanation, I mean a sphero-conical negopos composed of one piece of pos between two pieces of neg. I derive from the noun negopos the adjective negoposian; I can thus refer to a negoposian system, a negoposian effect, negoposian forces and negoposian locomotion. The expressions "locomotion" or "aerial navigation" are more general; they designate any kind of aerial locomotion obtained by means of negopos or any other system yet to be discovered—and which, in parentheses, never will be discovered because it is undiscoverable. I call the various items of apparatus that can be suspended from a negopos a negoposian seat, a negoposian nacelle, a negoposian vehicle, etc.

My special vocabulary is limited to those few words. It is necessary to create and to have new names for new objects. But they suffice, in combination with the words of current language, to express all the ideas relative to my discovery.

I shall return to my experiments.

I suspended my seat by means of straps from the two sides of the negopos, after having released the latter in such a way as only to produce an imperceptible effect. It is, moreover, easy to understand what I mean when I talk about releasing or tightening the negapos: it means separating or bringing together the different parts, from which results, as already established, a diminution or increase in the negoposian forces.

Then I placed myself in my negoposian seat, directing the point of the negopos toward the ceiling at an angle of forty-five degrees. I was gently lifted in that direction, and then in others at various speeds. My mechanism only functioned imperfectly, however. I corrected the most essential faults, and a few days later, I was flying around my study as easily as a bird in an aviary.

Nevertheless, the moment had not yet come to manifest my discovery publicly. Before then, I wanted to perfect it completely.

A shortcoming was manifest, in that it could only make oblique or horizontal movements, and could not be used to ascend or descend vertically. Indeed, when the point of the negopos was turned vertically, either upwards or downwards, the negoposian forces were no longer effective and the system fell to earth like any weighty body. When the point had a lateral or oblique direction, the form of the pieces of pos and neg composing the negopos produced forces acting at angles whose resultant was never vertical.

I remedied that inconvenience by separating the superior part from the intermediate part, and slightly more toward the front than the rear of the negopos. In that way, only a very slight descendant force was produced, which, in combination at a certain angle with a very powerful and slightly oblique ascendant force, produced the resultant of a vertical ascensional force. The inverse produced the vertical descendant movement, easy to obtain in any case by releasing the negopos to the extent of suppressing its efficacy completely; it then obeyed the law of gravitation and fell with a velocity that I could moderate at will.

In consequence, I perfected my mechanism, which it became possible for me to design in such a way as always to obtain the desired results by means of very simple movements of the aforementioned stem. The invention was complete in all its essentials.

I was still ambitious with regard to elegance. I would have liked to be able to simplify the system sufficiently for it to be possible to use it while hiding it completely under one's garments. The effect of which I was dreaming is easy to imagine.

A man dressed like anyone else is strolling casually, without anything in his movements or his gait giving rise to the suspicion that he is strapped underneath from head to toe, or that he is hiding somewhere—under his hat, for example—an object in the form of a pear. Negligently, he puts his hand into his pocket or inside his jacket, turns a little handle that no one can see, and suddenly rises into the air, where he describes the most capricious curves, more rapid in his movements than the birds, which he catches on the wing.

I could not obtain that complete result—but I was very near it.

A negopos could be paced above the head, in such a way as indeed to be covered by a hat. The straps descending from the suspension points could be hidden beneath a wig, artificial hair extensions, the collar of an overcoat or a muffler. As for those directly supporting the body, nothing was simpler than to hide them under clothing. The end of the negoposian stem could be placed inside the jacket, within reach of the left hand, which was sufficient to manipulate it, the right hand remaining free.

I have to agree, however, that the result of all that was a slightly strange and rather stiff accoutrement that could not fail to be noticed. The head, especially, was considerably inconvenienced. Furthermore, one was obliged to maintain an upright position, without being able to assume that of a man sitting or sprawling in an armchair.

I imagined another system, which led me to change the form of the negopos radically. I made it into a kind of collar, applying it to the shoulders and the upper part of the chest, almost like the collar-piece of ancient suits of armor. It was made up of three circles, swollen at the back and very thin at the front. The principle was, however, the same as for the sphero-conical negopos. The inferior and superior circles were neg, the intermediate circle pos. They could be separated or brought together by means of a mechanism still brought into play by a stem whose tip was within reach of my left hand. The straps extended from that collar, sustaining the body in a comfortable position, a little more similar than the preceding one to a sitting position. The head was free—a great advantage.

The negopos necklace was easy to hide under the collar of an overcoat, a slightly large cravat and a muffler. One merely seemed to be dissimulating a goiter or some skin complaint affecting the neck. But I could not find anything better, and that arrangement appeared to me to be sufficiently close enough to the goal that I renounced trying to attain it more completely.

Those who have not observed the perpendicularity that a suspended body conserves when only the point of suspension is in motion might think that the force of impulsion, acting above the shoulders, would draw the head and the upper part of the body with it, the rest following in an inclined position. That is not the case, unless the impulsion is applied abruptly or increased too rapidly. I still found myself a little too upright, however, not sufficiently sitting. In order to remedy that, I decided only to use the negopos necklace as a means of suspension and to provide impulsion by means of a second sphero-conical negopos disposed in front of the body, almost in the position of a belt-buckle, to which the straps would be strongly fitted.

I found a second advantage in that arrangement, which was not to be disdained; the two negoposes could substitute for one another, in such a way that if one of them stopped working for some reason, one would not fall to the ground as a result. One would remain suspended by the other, by means of which one could still steer. The left hand would still suffice to operate both.

The preceding remarks suffice to provide the key to the incidents, so bizarre and so resonant, by means of which my discovery was manifested. Before producing it, I wanted to take account of all the applications to which it was susceptible.

Aerial locomotion was one of those applications, and perhaps the most considerable, but there were others whose importance ought not to be neglected.

I had, in sum, discovered a new motor, of indefinite power, so economical that the expense necessary for its operation could be considered negligible.

The construction, however, of one negopos cost me rather dear; the pos cost me half its weight in gold, the neg slightly more than its weight in silver. The two negaposes that I employed for individual locomotion cost me, in total, nearly five thousand francs. That was a great deal for my experiments, but it was nothing compared with the results obtained. In any case, it was certain that when, instead of constructing them myself in my laboratory, with difficulty, I could organize mass production, the cost would be considerably reduced.

The motor was, therefore, inexpensive to produce and its running costs were negligible. One can see immediately what immense results could be obtained by applying it to all the machines used in industry. In addition to the simplification of the machines themselves, there would be a pure and simple elimination of fuel costs.

It was only a matter of organizing the negopos as a motor. That was easy.

I constructed a simple negopos, similar in form to a spindle, with the ends flattened in a certain fashion. I placed it between two grooved uprights, along which one of its points slid. It was positioned horizontally at the top of the system, pos downwards. It fell downwards, sliding along the grooves. Near the bottom, they were fitted with conveniently-disposed buffers. At the moment when the flattened ends of the negopos encountered that obstacle, it carried out a rotational movement by virtue of which the neg, in its turn, was orientated downwards. Immediately, the negopos rose up with considerable force between its two uprights, until similar buffers, place near the top, caused it to turn pos-downwards once more and fall again.

I shall pass over detailed description of the means by which I maintained the system in such a way that these movements were carried out regularly without the negopos being able to turn over except in the desired manner, nor slip out of the grooves, etc. I have said enough to make it understood how I obtained a back-and-forth movement analogous to that of the pistons of a steam engine—except that the volume of the apparatus was much less and the power very much greater. In addition, by the same token, I had discovered perpetual motion—perpetual, at least, save for the wear and tear on the system produced over an exceedingly long time.

But the discovery of perpetual motion was only a matter of curiosity. At the most, it might be utilized in the perfection of clockwork. What had an immense scope was the discovery of a motor capable of being applied to all imaginable machines. I held in my hands an industrial revolution, the slightest consequence of which ought to be worth millions to me as soon as it was put to work, and perhaps hundreds of millions. Nevertheless, these results paled by comparison with those I perceived in consequence of aerial locomotion.

Once my ideas regarding the application of my discovery to machines were clearly fixed, I ceased to occupy myself with them, and only thought about making arrangements for its first

application, of which I wanted to make a previously unparal-
leled *coup de théâtre*.

IV. The Preparations

I had long ago organized the details of my existence with
that goal in mind, living in virtual isolation, sometimes in Paris and sometimes in a property I had acquired, passing for an
unsociable person and behaving as such, by dint of the irregularity of my habits, so that my absence and presence went
equally unnoticed. Furthermore, I had succeeded, by virtue of
exercise, in being able to write with my left hand as fluently as
with the right. My second handwriting, which no one had ever
seen, did not resemble at all the one by which I was known. I
then succeeded, albeit with great difficulty—for I did not was
to make any declaration to the authorities—in procuring an
autographic press, which I installed in the country in great
secrecy, in a turret adjacent to my study, where no one ever
went but me.

I shall omit a number of organizational details with regard to my projects, as those I have given are sufficient for an
understanding of how I was able to succeed in putting them
into execution.

One might wonder why I employed so much precaution,
scheming and mystery, as if I were meditating a crime. Could
I not have taken out patents and exploited my discovery without recourse to those tortuous means?

The reasons for not proceeding in that way seemed to me
to be powerful. I could only obtain patents by explaining my
discovery in descriptive documents. That would reveal it in
such a way that anyone could duplicate it. There was no hope
of preventing counterfeiting by means of lawsuits; what can be
done against people who can flee by taking to the air? To apply for patents would, in reality, deliver my invention to anyone.

Concern for my personal interests was the least consideration hindering me from divulging it thus. It was evident that,

from the day that my discovery was known, there would be no more States, countries or distinct nations. All the barriers that separate peoples would be abolished at a stroke. In the long run, that would be a great benefit, but at first, it would surely be a great sin abruptly to abandon such a revolution to the hazards of the unknown and all the enterprises of the adventurous. Some country more prompt than others to put it to work might achieve world domination. And who could tell whether France, far from finding, as I desired, a cause of grandeur in the work of one of her children, might not be the first to suffer and soon descend to the bottom rank of nations? On the contrary, I wanted my country to be in advance of all the rest, which necessitated secrecy to be profoundly guarded until I had reached an understanding with the government regarding the measures to be taken.

An imprudent and hasty revelation might have other consequences even more deadly. It might render all social policing impossible and deliver the world to the most dangerous malefactors. Theft, pillage, murder, arson and the most odious acts of violence might escape all repression. There would be no more security, nor property, nor protection for the weak, not any social organization whatsoever. There would be chaos, universal ruination; violence would be master of the world: a frightful disorganization.

It was, therefore, necessary to take numerous measures of precaution before surrendering my secret—hence the necessity of letting absolutely nothing slip before the appointed moment. Now, I could only forearm myself as best I could against any possibility of indiscretion by means of a radical elimination of friends who might have divined something, and assistants, workers and domestics who might perhaps have suspected something of the goal that I was pursuing. In consequence, I did almost everything by myself.

I had a forge, a lathe, a crucible, and everything else necessary for chemical manipulations, and the implements employed in numerous state organizations. In the course of my experiments, however, I confided the fabrication of various components to blacksmiths, mechanics, the makers of ropes and straps, and so on—but only those that could not lead to any suspicion of the truth, and, as I had taken out a patent on a kind of brake adopted by several railways companies, no one ever imagined that I was occupied in anything other than inventions related to railways, and new braking systems in particular.

I also wanted the invention to be manifested initially in a striking and incontestable manner. If I had begun by talking about it, either to the public by way of announcements or to the government by way of more or less secret communications, I would probably not have been taken seriously. I would even have run a grave risk of being taken for a madman. I could only avoid that danger by following my communication immediately with decisive demonstrations.

But I could also see other inconveniences. If anyone knew that I was the possessor of such a secret, I would no longer be its master. I would be exposed to all sorts of pleadings to deliver it either to the government or to the public, and my hand might be forced in order to persuade me to release it in circumstances other than those that were appropriate—not from the viewpoint of my personal interest, which was the least of my preoccupations, but from the point of view of the precautions to be taken before unleashing the incalculable consequences of such a discovery upon the world.

It was by no means impossible, in fact, that violence might be employed in my regard, to try to extract my secret from me, given that it was a source of power and fortune much more tempting than the corners of the earth upon which privateers descended, the preys that pirates and brigands pursued, and the provinces that attracted the covetousness of conquerors often unscrupulous in the choice of their means.

I wanted, therefore, to remain master of my secret until the moment I judged opportune, after the world had appreciated its importance, after its consequences had been calculated, after the necessary measures had been taken to ensure that

France would find it a source of grandeur and it that would not become a scourge for humanity.

To that were added, in an accessory fashion, considerations relative to my personal interest. It was assuredly only just that I obtained some advantage from my invention, and especially that I did not deserve to have it stolen from me. Now, although I did not believe in the possibility of essential improvements that others might be able to discover, it might be the case that a few modifications might be made to details of the system that would take and retain, as is often seen, the name of the modifier. I did not want my name to the thus relegated to the background. I did not want there to be any possibility of it perhaps being effaced one day from popular memory, only to remain known to scholars. Do such sentiments qualify as vainglory on my part? I thought, personally, that if they concealed some pride, it was at least the most legitimate and justified pride.

In sum, the plan on which I decided was this: to strike minds vividly by dazzling demonstrations of my discovery; to maintain the most absolute secrecy, not only regarding my methods but also regarding my identity, in such a way that no one could suspect to begin with who the aerial navigator might be whose movements seemed prodigious; to communicate nevertheless with the public to the extent that it suited me, and with the government when the time came; to debate with the latter the measures to take and the conditions under which I would surrender my discovery, which I did not intend to be used as an instrument of despotism, but which I wanted to make into an instrument of liberty; always to remain master of the situation in order to make my will prevail if any dissent arose on which no understanding could be reached; subsequently to reveal my name, but only at a time of my choice and after having organized inaccessible places of refuge in various countries in which I could withstand all pursuits, all ruses, and all violence; and finally, to wait to deliver my secret, either to the public or the government, until the necessary measures had been taken, the agreed conditions executed, and my name was engraved on my discovery in a forever-indelible fashion.

V. The Manifestation

As soon as dawn broke on the first of June, one could see that it was going to be a fine day. The sky was, admittedly, covered, but those high clouds were a better guarantee of the security of the weather, given the Parisian climate, than overly bright sunlight. The wind was good and fresh without being violent.

Circulation in the Place de la Concorde had been considerable since the evening of May the thirty-first. People had come from all directions, hoping to see a few preparations, some indication of the mysterious event announced for the following day. Many people stayed there until very late. A great number of those people who live on unknown industries, offering lights to smokers and picking up cigar-butts, came, after the emergence of the theater crowds, to station themselves in the Place de la Concorde in the hope of being able to trade their place for a financial consideration.

Between six and seven o'clock in the morning, the populace began to flood in; at eight o'clock the students arrived. By nine o'clock, the crowd in the Place de la Concorde was so compact that orders were given not to let anyone else in, but to let out anyone who wanted to leave. The contagion extended throughout society, as happens in such cases. Curiosity attracts curiosity. Those who have made the firmest promises not to disturb themselves are drawn in as if in spite of themselves, and for that reason alone the growing torrent will grow even further. Crowds accumulated in the Champs-Élysées, the Jardin des Tuileries, on the Pont de la Concorde, on the quais, in the Rue Royale, in the Rue de Rivoli, and on the boulevards.

By ten o'clock, it was difficult to move on the Boulevard de la Madeleine. By half past ten, it was difficult to get past the Rue de la Paix. By eleven o'clock it was impossible to get

47

as far as the Rue de la Chaussée-d'Antin. More people were pressing at the windows than they were able to contain. Conversations, suppositions and gibes were in full flow. "Let's get started! Raise the curtain! Hey, strike up the band!" cried the gamins of Paris. The authorities, said Joseph Prudhomme, ought not to permit crowds like this to accumulate, in a truly dangerous fashion, without knowing why. One joker cried "Aaaah!" pointing up into the air, and people responded with cheers, whistles and applause. There were a few brawls but no serious incidents.

By eleven forty-five the curiosity had become more anxious. It was mingled with the vague terror produced by waiting for the unknown. The jokes ceased, no longer finding any echo. A strange silence was established. Nothing is as grave as the solemn, almost lugubrious silence of crowds; anyone who has a watch would not cease consulting it.

It was five minutes to noon and nothing had appeared in the Place de la Concorde. People began once again to fear a hoax. A dull discontentment infected all minds, ready to change into rage. The calmest individuals felt furious, the mildest ferocious, at the idea of being so outrageously duped.

The sun had pierced the clouds, which had scattered, and was resplendent at the zenith in a vast area of blue sky. Suddenly, a few cries were heard: "Look!" The keenest eyes had perceived a black dot in the air, at the limit of vision. That black dot was visibly growing. In a matter of seconds it was possible to distinguish a human form, descending vertically above the obelisk.

A formidable cheer burst forth, ripping through the silence like lightning through a cloud. It was still resounding when a man was seen, his face partly masked, standing on the summit of the obelisk. A new clamor went up, mingled with applause and bravos. The man, coiffed in a small round hat, took it off, and, turning successively to the four cardinal points of the compass, bowed to the crowd. Then he took out his watch and pointed at it with his finger. Everyone else looked at their own. It was one minute to noon. The applause and the cries redoubled. The man put his watch away and everyone began to look at him intently.

He was dressed in black. A kind of frock coat or overcoat, buttoned up, enveloped him from the neck to the knees. The flaps of that garment were attached to his trousers in such a fashion as not to flutter in the wind. The legs of the trousers were enclosed in large soft boots, whose feet were large enough to permit the deduction of an undershoe. The collar of the overcoat was turned up to the chin and surrounded by a large cravat in white cashmere. The neck seemed thick and a trifle impeded, as were the tops of the shoulders. Blond hair, abundant but not very long, hid the nape and the ears. A full beard, of the brightest blond, covered the cheeks, lips and chin. The upper part of the face was covered by a slender mask, like those worn at Opéra balls. The small round hat, black like everything else, was fitted with a chinstrap. The hands were gloved with thick gloves that appeared to be fur-lined. It was evident that, in spite of the season, the man had equipped himself to withstand cold. The left hand was inserted into the overcoat, from which he had only withdrawn it momentarily to point at his watch, and had immediately replaced it, in a stance analogous to the one often attributed to Napoléon I and certain orators.

He made a gesture, and at noon precisely, rose vertically into the air with the rapidity of an arrow. Having attained a sufficiently great height, he stopped and floated above the crowd, slowly moving in a circle that expanded in a spiral. He seemed to be almost upright, leaning slightly backwards with his legs slightly bent. His left hand remained inside the garment. Then the circle gradually shrank, and at the same time, the rapidity of the aerial navigator—or, rather, the aerial swimmer—increased progressively and he came down again. Having arrived a short distance above the tip of the obelisk, he lapped a few tight circles around it, with astonishing rapidity, replaced himself on it, upright, in his original position, and bowed once again to the crowd in all four directions.

To describe the bravos, the applause, the acclamations, the shouting, the stamping of feet and the hats thrown into the air would be an impossible enterprise.

Some people seemed mad with enthusiasm; the most impressionable were wiping their eyes, surprised to have felt tears springing forth. The news had circulated with an electric rapidity all the way to the most distant ranks of the crowds that had accumulated there in Paris.

"It's a flying man!" everyone said to his neighbor.

It would not have taken much for the pressure toward the Place de la Concorde to have produced a general asphyxiation. In vain, people of sound common sense cried out that he was going to come, like he had promised, and that people would be able to see him from where they were. That curiosity was delirious, and people did not listen.

The *sergents de ville* and the *Gardes de Paris* began to give way under the pressure of the multitude, even though they had been reinforced by infantry troops when the crowd had been seen to grow to its present proportions. The first result of the prodigious discovery was about to be an immense hecatomb of people choked, crushed and trampled underfoot.

Fortunately, the man did not remain perched on the obelisk for long. He resumed his flight, at about the height of a third floor window, and passed into the Rue Royale, and from there to the boulevards. He advanced at a moderate speed, very nearly that of a thoroughbred racehorse at the gallop. It was, therefore, possible to consider him at leisure without being able to attempt to follow him, which would have produced a frightful reverse serge in the crowd.

He followed the boulevards in that fashion as far as the Place de la Bastille, went down along the Seine as far as the Pont d'Iéna, reached the Arc de Triomphe via the Étoile, and came back via the Avenue des Champs-Élysées to the Place de la Concorde, went along the Rue de Rivoli as far as the Hôtel-de-Ville, reached the quais via the Pont-de-Change, which he traversed, as well as the Cité, followed the Boulevard Saint-Michel as far as the Jardin du Luxembourg, where he performed a few circles, went along the exterior boulevards as far as Les Invalides, went back up the Seine to the Pont de Solférino, and came to hover above the clumps of chestnuts in the Jardin des Tuileries.

That was sufficient to calm the excessive and overly keen aspect of public curiosity. It was understood that it would be impossible to follow such evolutions, that everyone would have much more chance of seeing him again by remaining in place, and that, after all, everyone had already seen him. The crowd was further augmented, because there was soon not a single able-bodied person indoors, except for those at the windows of the main streets, but it was more widely disseminated and less dense. No one missed anything, and everyone could see, quite comfortably, some aspect of the unexpected spectacle.

In the Jardin des Tuileries, for example, the aerial man, approaching a chestnut-tree, caused two pigeons to fly away, and immediately pursued them. He was evidently traveling faster than they were, but did not appear to be able to turn as easily in order to follow the changes of direction they made abruptly in their fear. It was also noticed that he only tried to catch them with his right hand, the left always remaining inside his coat. The public took an infinite pleasure on following the twists and turns of that new kind of hunting. Soon, one pigeon was caught, and then the other. The applause and the acclamations can be imagined.

The victorious hunter came to sit on the horizontal arm of the statue of *Alexander in Battle* near the fountain and in front of the château, took out his left hand, took off his gloves, took a piece of string out of his pocket, and tied the four legs of the two birds together. Then he put his gloves on again, replaced his left hand in its usual position, resumed his flight and came to hover a meter over the head of an elegant lady, at whose feet he gallantly let his fluttering prey fall.

He resumed his journey over the Seine, the promenades, the boulevards and the main streets, but this time, not maintaining a uniform and regular pace. He rose up and swooped down, made detours to the right and the left, swerved into ascending and descending spirals, sometimes hovering almost motionless, sometimes launching himself in a straight line with an incredible velocity. He amused himself near the Château-d'Eau by catching a swallow in flight, and caught another in the Place du Panthéon.

At the Jardin des Plantes he alighted casually in the reserved flowerbeds and picked a large bouquet of flowers before the wardens, hesitating as to what to do, had time to try and prevent him from so doing. A few moments later, he offered it to a group of young women manning an observation post in a mansard in the Boulevard de Sebastopol. The most brazen of them, more prompt to reach out for it than any of her companions, thanked him with her frankest burst of laughter and a kiss blown into the air from her fingertips.

At the Café du Grand-Balcon on the Boulevard des Italiens, customers had been crammed in, placed in the foremost booths in order to see. He suddenly swooped down on the balcony, took possession of a glass of beer full to the brim, drew away a meter or two, drank it in a single draught, came back to the place from which he had taken it, threw a louis on to the table, bowed, and flew away.

In the Place du Palais-Royal, he spotted a smoker at a third-floor window. He stopped, hovered momentarily, took a cigar out of his pocket, approached the smoker, whose cigar he politely borrowed, returning it to him after having lit his own, bowed and resumed his flight while smoking. He came to sit down and finish his cigar on the lightning conductor of the southern tower of Notre-Dame, which caused jokers to say that he must not be very comfortable there. Serious people replied that no one knew how he was armored underneath and that besides, having the faculty of sustaining himself in the air, he ought not to weigh upon the point. Some also claimed to have seen him place an object that they could not make out on the point in question, doubtless so that it would not pierce his clothing.

What seemed prodigious was that, after all these comings and goings, it was not yet four o'clock. The evening papers were about to appear. People understood that they could not possibly talk about anything other than the event that was holding Paris in thrall. They had bravely made their decision, standing up against fortune with a stout heart and trying to safeguard themselves, by means of editorial skill, against the disconcerting awareness of their previous incredulity.

Only the *Universel* had the right to cry victory. The editorial staff, gathered in the offices in its entirety, delightedly proclaimed the triumph of its editor-in-chief. The latter usually worked in a rather elegant office, albeit a trifle small, preceded by a library and the Editorial Suite, where there as a huge table around which various reporters sat. The apartment, situated on the second floor, overlooked two broad streets of which the building formed the corner. Once the paper was put to bed, people chatted everywhere. That day, a little before four o'clock, the editor-in-chief was sitting in his office chatting to two or three people therein and, through the open door, with his colleagues gathered in the library and the Editorial Suite. Suddenly, a cry went up: "There he is! There he is!"

Everyone rushed to the windows and saw the aerial man descending in a spiral. He was holding an envelope in his right hand. He approached the window, put the package in the hand that the editor-in-chief held out to him, bowed, climbed vertically into the air again and flew away.

He was seen continuing his evolutions until five o'clock. He came back to stand upright on the obelisk, took out his watch and indicated it with his finger to the compact crowd gathered in the square. People observed that it was five to five. He sat on the summit of the obelisk, seemingly waiting. A few seconds before five o'clock he stood up again, bowed to the four cardinal points, launched himself vertically upwards at exactly five o'clock and disappeared into space with a dizzying rapidity.

The manifestation was concluded. It was generally agreed that it had lived up to its billing, and had gone beyond what anyone could have supposed.

VI. At the Universel

The editor-in-chief hastened to open the packet that had been handed to him and which bore the address: *To the Editor-in-Chief of the Universe*l. He found two manuscripts inside. First there was a letter, the text of which was as follows:

Monsieur Editor-in-Chief,

Alone in the press, the Universel *has given proof of clear-sightedness and sagacity. Please accept my congratulations and my sincere thanks for that.*

You will find it natural that I am addressing myself to you, in preference to all your colleagues, in order to propose an exchange of services.

I believe, in fact, that I am able to contribute enormously to the prosperity of your newspaper by offering to address exclusively to it all the communications relative to the discovery whose first public manifestation has taken place today. It will thus become, if you are agreeable, a veritable Moniteur *of aerial locomotion, the only one authorized and precisely informed. These communications will be frequent and, if I am under no illusion, interesting to the public. The number of your readers and subscribers will be rapidly augmented in considerable proportions.*

As for the service that I will ask of you, it will consist of constituting you the center and intermediary of all the communications that I shall make or receive, both public and private. The public will be informed that a letter-box for my usage has been established in your offices and that everything addressed to me via that channel will be transmitted to me exactly. I will not ask you to transmit the letters that I will have to write myself, for which I shall employ the mail, but you will be kind enough to publish in your newspaper all the communications, without exception, that I wish to render public. In addition, all your collaborators will be invited to set aside, carefully, in order to enable them to reach me, everything that is printed in the newspapers relative to my invention.

You will be kind enough also to designate to me someone belonging to the administration or editorial staff of your paper in whom I can have the most absolute confidence, and who will consent to become my intermediary, my representative and my delegate for all the administrative tasks that might crop up during the application of my work. If, for example, I needed to open a subscription, he will be responsible for receiving the funds in order to transmit them to me and for making use of those that I address to him in the manner that I indicate. If I wanted to found a company, he would prepare its foundations, its deeds and its statutes, and would take the necessary steps in accordance with my instructions. If I need a property, he will rent it; if I need various objects, he will take responsibility for purchasing them or having them manufactured; if I need workmen or assistants, he will hire them, etc.

It goes without saying that he will always receive the necessary funds in advance for all the expenses he will have to meet and will be fully compensated for any traveling that his missions might necessitate. I shall reach an agreement with him as to the figure of various remunerative payments, which will be augmented as and when I have to ask him for a more active collaboration, though without that collaboration ever becoming so absorbing as to deflect him from his occupations at the newspaper.

I will maintain, with him, with you and everyone else, the most absolute anonymity.

If these proposals are agreeable to you in principle, it will be sufficient for you to publish the enclosed article tomorrow. If they are not agreeable to you, you may consider the present letter as non-existent.

If the publication of the enclosed article, which you may follow with your own signature, takes place tomorrow, I shall *consider my propositions as accepted and will hasten to transmit to you the detailed explanations necessary for the establishment of our letter-box and the security of our communications.*

The first one that I shall address to you will be a scrupulously exact account of the manifestation of the first of June, but without, of course, any revelation concerning my method or my identity. The moment to divulge them has not yet come.

You will permit me to sign this letter, and those that I shall address to you subsequently, with a fantastic name, without their being treated in consequence like anonymous letters. The initial X, *which might be translated as the forename* Xavier, *signifies in reality* the unknown. *As for the name* Nagrien, *it is composed of letters taken, almost at hazard, from the words* Navigateur aérien, *which will be the sole signature on my communications with the public through the intermediary of your newspaper.*

I enclosed with this letter the sum of 2,000 francs, which I beg you to consider irrevocably acquired, as much in the case of refusal as that of acceptance. You may make use of it as you see fit, either by applying it to the expenses of the installation of our letter-box, in the interests of the newspaper, or for some good work. I have no other objective in giving it to you than to give you a palpable, and probably superabundant sign of the seriousness of my proposal.

Yours sincerely,

X. Nagrien

Two thousand-franc bills were, indeed, attached to the letter with a pin.

The editor-in-chief did not hesitate for an instant. He was a man of great common sense and much experience, keen-eyed and prompt in decision. He saw in the offer that had been made a fortune for his paper, to the prosperity if which he was devoted body and soul, independently of the personal advantages that he might procure on the rebound. He read the letter to the assembled reporters. They all shared his opinion.

There was a clamor of voices offering to serve as the administrator of aerial locomotion. Someone proposed putting it to a vote, and the proposal was immediately accepted. After a first round, in which almost everyone voted for themselves, the ballots were concentrated on the newspaper's administrator, a former cashier at a large bank, a singularly intelligent man seasoned in business and of unassailable probity.

The next day, the *Universel* published the following article on its front page, in a beautiful font:

The public is informed that the Universel *is becoming, from this day forward, the* Moniteur *of aerial locomotion.*

Alone, it will receive the communications of the author of that prodigious discovery, signed by the words: Le Navigateur aérien.

These communications will be frequent, and always of a nature to interest our readers keenly. Only they bear a seal of exactitude and, so to speak, authenticity, which no one else can give to information or commentaries on the same subject.

The first communications will begin to appear two days hence. First there will be an explanation of what might still remain obscure regarding the distribution of the texts and medallions that caused such a stir, and then a relation, as exact as it is detailed, of the great event of June the first.

Announcements, accounts rendered and explanations relative to aerial locomotion will abound in our newspaper, without any of its normal features being sacrificed. It will be something extra. But that something will consist of everything that will be revealed regarding a discovery destined to change the world.

People can, in addition, transmit all possible communications to the aerial navigator by addressing them to our offices, and by that route alone. *They will be transmitted to him with as much exactitude as discretion, and no one but he will open them.*

We ought to add honestly that no revelation will be made between now and an indeterminate time either about the methods of locomotion or the identity of the aerial navigator. Neither the editor-in-chief of the paper nor any of his colleagues has the slightest indication in that regard. The aerial navigator has taken effective measures to correspond with us in the surest manner, while conserving strict anonymity.

He informs the public that he will read with great care everything addressed to him without exception, and that he will reply, either by post or in our paper to anyone who merits a reply. He asks people who address correspondence to him to write their names and addresses legibly. He will even read anonymous letters, but will never reply to them.

He will expose in our paper, when the time comes, his personal ideas regarding the best steps to follow in order that the world can profit from his discovery, and France before any other nation.

We shall announce imminently a second public manifestation of arrival locomotion, even more interesting than that of June the first. We warn the public now that nothing will be accomplished that might provide a spectacle without our announcing it in advance.

The present notification will be reprinted tomorrow.

That article was signed by the editor-in-chief. The two issues in which it appeared were sent to a large number of people in Paris, and especially in the provinces. Posters summarizing it were put up in profusion everywhere. The effect was immediate. Already, all of Paris knew about the incident of the letter handed to the editor-in-chief in the view of the dense crowd gathered in the streets. Everything of which he had dared to dream had been surpassed in fabulous proportions. Requests for subscriptions flooded in. It was necessary from one day to the next to double, quintuple and decuple the print run. Advertisements were relegated strictly to the fourth page, which was fortunately not leased; the price was tripled, and three out of four had to be refused.

On the third of June the editor-in-chief received, through the ordinary post, a long letter signed *X. Nagrien*, containing carefully detailed indications. A kind of double letter-box, very ingeniously designed, was established in an unused chimney in the Editorial Suite, a space formed by the connection of two rooms whose partition wall had been removed during the installation of the newspaper. The editor-in-chief and the administrator each had a key to a kind of strong-box set up above the fireplace. The aerial navigator had the key to a similar strong-box located at the top of the flue. A simple mechanism served to bring their respective communications up and down.

The announced publications did not deceive the expectations of the public. An explanation was given of how the aerial navigator had been able to carry out the distribution of texts that had excited so much comment on his own. The prodigious rapidity of his locomotion had permitted him to travel all over Paris between eight-thirty in the evening and three-thirty in the morning. What he had been able to do in seven hours on a dark night was amply explained by what he had been seen to do on the first of June in five hours of daylight.

He had, in addition, made his arrangements in advance. He had had abundant time to prepare the three thousand copies in envelopes that were thrown into letter boxes the day before, along with the fifty he sent as registered letters; to capture the birds to carry the texts, which he only released on the night itself; and to prepare the garlands for the obelisk so that he could dress it at a stroke, as a priest puts on his chasuble.

The night before, he had hidden forty large sacks filled with printed copies in inaccessible corners of rooftops, two sacks per arrondissement. It had been easy for him, in spite of their weight, to transport them two by two, suspended from organs of locomotion, and to empty them successively as a sower empties a sack of grain, attaching copies as he went to lightning conductors, spikes, hooks and any projections within arm's reach, throwing others into chimney pots and openings in public monuments. His pockets had been full of wrapped five-franc coins, which he had thrown into two hundred apartments, breaking windowpanes after having donned a fencing-glove.

These explanations were followed by a detailed account of the manifestation of June the first, already inflated by popular rumor by so many exaggerations that it had been transformed into a veritable legend, quite miraculous.

At the same time, the administrator received instructions that he carried out with as much zeal as intelligence, but whose recitation would take too long. It will be sufficient to see their effects.

VII. The Tour of France

On the eighteenth of June, the *Universel* published the following announcement:

The second public manifestation of aerial locomotion will commence next Sunday, the twenty-second of June.

Its principal object will be to establish publicly the speed that can be attained by this kind of locomotion and to show the provinces what Paris has seen.

The aerial navigator would be grateful to the railway companies if they would be kind enough to check his observations and thus give them an undeniable character of certitude and authenticity. It is by the clocks of railway stations that he will note the precise instants of his departures and arrivals, by reason of the uniformity of the hours adopted by the different railway lines.

He cannot say in advance at exactly what times he will arrive at each station, but he can announce those of his departures. It will be necessary that, from the moment when he leaves a town, the stationmaster and a few employees in the one to which he is heading pay close attention, in order to draw up a kind of official documentation of the precise moment of his arrival.

Here is the information that he can give in advance of his itinerary:

Sunday 22 June, 7 a.m. Departure from the obelisk. Evolutions over Paris. At 8 a.m. Departure from the Gare de Lyon railway station.

Arrival in Dijon. Evolutions. At 10 a.m. departure for Lyon.

Arrival in Lyon. Temporary disappearance. Reappearance at 11.30 a.m. At 1 p.m. departure for Marseilles.

Arrival in Marseilles. Evolutions. At 4 p.m. departure for Nîmes.

Arrival in Nîmes. Evolutions. At 6 p.m. departure for Narbonne.

Arrival at Narbonne. Temporary disappearance. Monday 33 June, 7 a.m., evolutions in Narbonne. At 8 a.m. departure for Toulouse.

The itinerary continued thus, indicating as successive stations Toulouse, Bayonne, Bordeaux, Tours, Nantes, Rennes, Rouen, Lille, Strasbourg, Nancy and Paris.

The railway companies, it is necessary to say, were far from enthusiastic in welcoming the request for collaboration addressed to them. Was it not their ruination that the untoward aerial navigator was bringing them, as they had themselves ruined the mail-coaches and the diligences?

It is true that the mysterious mode of locomotion in question had only been revealed thus far as applicable to the transport of one person at a time, and no one could tell whether its difficulty, its cost and its dangers might make it a curiosity without the possibility of everyday practical application, but it might equally well be the case that it was as easily practicable as it was inexpensive. It might be the case that it was as appropriate to the transport of nacelles and veritable airships as to that of an isolated individual. If so, the railways would soon be abandoned, their shareholders ruined and their immense personnel unemployed.

Already, without any sensible basis having arisen, people were no longer buying their shares, which were only holding their prices because their holders could not see far enough into the future to be ready to sell them all at once and at any price. The most prudent, however, were wondering whether it might not be wise to get rid of them discreetly.

Nevertheless, the companies understood that it would make no difference to the future of the invention whether they welcomed it with more or less sympathy. Their ill will would accomplish nothing and would have no other consequence than to display the ridicule of stupidly mean-spirited sentiments. Besides which, they had the primary interest in knowing exactly what they might have to fear from future competition. The exact establishment of its speed was extremely important from their viewpoint. They therefore played their part by addressing orders to their agents instructing them to note with the most rigorous precision the hour, minute and second of the arrival at and departure from each station and to write detailed reports of everything that they observed.

The voyage began at the appointed hour on the twenty-second of June. The urgency of the crowd from seven o'clock onwards in Paris and in all the towns indicated in the itinerary can easily be imagined, after the effect produced by the first demonstration. The *Universel* was already reaching every corner of France, and in any case, no newspaper could dispense with reproducing or summarizing the publications of which their fortunate competitor was the first to print, under penalty of losing subscribers.

Thus, there was no one who did not know in advance the towns in which the aerial navigator would make an appearance. All the others, like the rural areas, were subject to mass desertions. Travelers arrived from Germany, Switzerland, Italy, Spain, England and Belgium. Never had Dijon, Lyon, Marseilles and all the other towns in which a brief station had been promised seen such an influx. Rooms were being let there for two days at the price of an apartment for a year.

It would be superfluous to go into detail regarding the arrangements that X. Nagrien had made through the intermediary of his administrator for his meals and his overnight accommodation without risking his incognito. The important thing was the establishment of velocity.

The stationmaster in Paris and all the employees permitted by their service to gather around him observed that the aerial navigator arrived at the station a few minutes after eight o'clock, this time wearing, in addition to the small mask over his eyes, a gas mask doubtless designed to protect his face and eyes from the impression of the air cleaved with extreme rapidity. He circled for a few minutes and left Paris at eight o'clock precisely. Advice was immediately given by telegraph to the station at Dijon.

There, he was seen to appear and to head straight for the clock tower, whose dial he indicated with his finger. It was nine twenty-four.

It was revealed later, by the drivers, stokers and travelers in the trains whose paths he had crossed or that he had overtaken *en route* as well as by the employees at intermediate stations, that he had never ceased to follow the railway line. It was necessary to conclude that he would have gained at least ten or twelve minutes had he traveled as the crow flies.

He was able to remain in Dijon for more than half an hour, and departed therefrom, as he had announced, at ten o'clock precisely. He arrived in Lyon at ten fifty. He had traveled 197 kilometers in fifty minutes.

The rest of the voyage went as planned.

The result of the calculations was a mean velocity of 240 kilometers, or 60 leagues, an hour—four kilometers, or one league, per minute—approximately four times the usual maximum speed of an express train, and almost a seventh of the muzzle velocity of a cannonball, which is estimated at between four hundred and five hundred meters per second, corresponding to twenty-five or thirty kilometers a minute, or four hundred leagues an hour.

Departing from Paris, one could be in London in an hour and a quarter; in Madrid in five and three-quarter hours; in Vienna in five hours five minutes; in Berlin in three and a quarter hours; in St. Petersburg in eleven hours five minutes, and in Moscow in twelve hours sixteen minutes. One could go around the world in six days, eleven hours and forty minutes.

One would attain almost a sixth of the velocity of the Earth rotating on its axis. If, departing from a point on the equator on Sunday morning, for instance, one traveled west-wards, one would reach the same point on Saturday evening, but one would have gained a day *en route*, in the same way as any voyage in that direction around the equator. It would be Friday for the traveler at the moment of his return, and Satur-day for the inhabitants of the point of his arrival and departure, who would have seen six sunsets while the traveler would only have seen five.

The *Universel* published a detailed account of the jour-ney. It challenged the railway companies to deny or affirm its exactitude in accordance with the observations of their agents. At first the companies remained silent, but the *Universel* re-turned to the charge with so much insistence that they ended up issuing short statements declaring that the information that had reached them did not differ significantly from those that had been published.

Serious anxiety gripped them. A slightly more marked diminution was manifest in their share prices. It was not much as yet, but it would probably be sufficient for the accursed inventor to put a dirigible nacelle into the air to start a panic that would lead to a general disaster.

A new article in the *Universel*, while increasing their fears for the future, gave them a temporary respite. It an-nounced that, because of the preparations that were necessary, the next public demonstration would not take place before the end of August.

VIII. The Ship

The administrator had previously been charged with a triple mission.

He was to organize the manufacture, in conformity with the plans, drawing and instructions addressed to him an apparatus that it is necessary to call a ship, for want of a more exact expression, a description of which will be found further on.

He rented a small house beyond the heights of Meudon, with rather extensive grounds, around which he had six-meter high walls built, enclosing an uninterrupted curtain of tall trees.

He hired three men selected with particular care. Many candidates, especially aeronauts and mariners, offered themselves in response to advertisements published in the *Universel*. A considerable number of the applicants were not solicited by any need to earn their living, but merely by an ardent curiosity and spirit of adventure.

He rejected, by reason of his age, a former colonel of the cavalry, of the stripe of those whom Napoléon I made Maréchals de France at forty. He gave preference to a railway engineer whose composure was the equal of his courage. He placed under his orders two former seamen, one of whom had belonged to the navy and had been decorated in the aftermath of several striking actions, the other celebrated in the merchant marines for the number of rescue medals he had earned. Those two men possessed, as the conditions required, Herculean strength and gymnastic skills. The first received the title of conductor, the others those of servants. The aerial navigator intended to fulfill the functions of captain of his ship personally.

When everything was ready the conductor and the servants had several training sessions, mainly by night, in the enclosure hidden from all eyes. Their part in the operation of the ship was, in any case, negligible. Their real utility was to inspire enough confidence in passengers, merely by reason of their presence, for the latter not to fall prey to vain terrors. Nothing was revealed to them about the methods or the identity of the inventor. They only ever saw him masked, arriving and departing on an upper section of the apparatus, containing the organs of locomotion, which could be attached to it and detached again at will, and without which the ship remained on the ground as an inert mass. Most of all, they practiced fitting and detaching the connections and flying a few meters above the ground in order to familiarize themselves with that mode of locomotion.

All of that lasted fifteen or twenty days longer than they might have wished. It was not until the twentieth of August that the *Universel* published the following announcement:

On Sunday the third of September, an aerial ship will navigate above Paris and its suburbs from eight o'clock in the morning until five o'clock in the evening.

The ship is designed to carry approximately fifty passengers, but on this occasion, it will only carry, in addition to the aerial navigator, a conductor and two servants, its journey having the sole objective of demonstrating the possibility to persons who desire to participate in the following experiment, fixed for Sunday the tenth of September.

From the fourth to the ninth of September, the ship, deprived of its organs of locomotion, will be exhibited in a location near to the offices of the Universel. *There will be an entry fee of two francs for anyone wishing to visit it.*

The experiment of the tenth of September will be organized as follows: Thirty-four places on the ship will be put at the disposal of the public; the price is fixed at 1,200 francs each.

People desiring places must register in the offices of the Universel *before the eighth of September and place the price of their reservations in the hands of the newspaper's administrator, who will issue them a receipt, and then will deposit the funds every day in whichever public treasury the authorities care to designate to him.*

The aerial navigator will give preference, for the definitive allocation of places, to the following categories of individuals:

The government, in the person of those of its members holding the most elevated positions. If several of the same rank present themselves—several ministers, for example— their names will be drawn by lot.

The army, again in the person of the highest-ranking officer, preferably a Maréchal de France or the general of a division, and with the same tie-breaking sequence;

The Navy, following the same order of preference;

The principal branches of science, with preference for members of the Institut, represented by one physicist, one chemist, one astronomer, one geographer, one statistician, one economist and one physician.

Letters, with preference for a member of the Académie Française;

Journalism, represented by the editor of a newspaper other than the Universel, *for whom a place of favor is reserved*

The arts, represented by a painter, with preference for a member of the Institut;

Industry, represented by one shipbuilder, one machine maker, one administrator or director of a railway company and one aeronaut.

Seventeen places, or a larger number if all the above-mentioned categories are not represented, will be attributed to persons chosen by lot among those who have registered their names.

Twelve gratuitous places will be reserved for musicians organized as an orchestra, with preference for a military band if any presents itself.

Two other gratuitous places will be reserved for simple workers designated as observers by elected trade union negotiators.

At nine o'clock in the morning, definitive tickets will be issued to the persons admitted, with useful instructions for embarkation and the voyage. The funds paid out by those people who are not allocated places will be returned immediately on the presentation of their receipts.

The voyage will be directed in conformity with the following itinerary:

On the tenth, at 9 a.m. precisely, embarkation. Circumnavigation above Paris and the surrounding area, and then

departure for Strasbourg, in order to disembark there at about
6 p.m.

On the eleventh, at 9 a.m., embarkation in Strasbourg,
circumnavigation above the city and departure for Lille,
where disembarkation with be at 6 p.m. The voyage will con-
tinue thus via Lille, Rouen, Nantes, Bordeaux, Bayonne, Tou-
louse, Marseilles, Lyon and Paris, to which the ship will re-
turn on Tuesday 19 September at 6 p.m.

This announcement initially caused a general outcry.
Such overwhelming arrogance, it was said on all sides, was
unimaginable. Those preferences superbly awarded to ministers, Maréchals de France and admirals, as if the greatest individuals were going to compete for the privilege of surrendering themselves blindly to an adventurer whose anonymity did
not portend anything good! That price of 1,200 francs per
place, yielding, by reason of the thirty-four paid places, a total
of 40,800 francs for a ten-day voyage, in which one would not
even be compensated for food and overnight accommodation!
That ensemble, demanded in order to award oneself a triumph
accompanied by noisy fanfare! All of that was criticized as so
much pride and greed.

X. Nagrien thought he ought to respond to these reproaches in the *Universel*. It was not out of pride, he said, but
rather out of deference that, even before divulging his discovery, he was offering preference to the government, the army,
the navy, science, industry, letters and arts the opportunity to
study the effects acquired and the probable consequences. As
for the price of places, he would not descend to justifying
himself against an accusation of avarice by citing the hundreds
of thousands of francs that the experiments carried out in the
practical application of his discovery had cost, or the millions
that he could make from it whenever he wished. Those who
did not think the price appropriate for such a voyage, the first
one accomplished by air, had only to abstain, along with those
who did not feel completely confident.

The announcement was, on this occasion, separated by a fortnight from the first experiment advertised, and three weeks from the commencement of the second. That interval permitted travel to Paris, and the various places where the ship was to display itself, not only from other parts of France but also from several foreign countries. People in many places had promised themselves, long in advance, to set off at the first announcement of a further exhibition.

Everyone was ready by the end of August. Many, especially in distant countries, particularly the United States, had thought it safer to set out without waiting for the signal. As soon as it was given, there was a kind of frenzy. Special trains were organized everywhere. The railway rolling stock was insufficient. The companies did not lower their prices, and were able to realize, perhaps on the eve of their ruin, considerable profits. All means of locomotion were exhausted. The influx of Englishmen was also particularly remarkable.

On September the third, public curiosity did not assume the same character as on the first of June. It was no longer mingled with doubt, uncertainty and the indefinable anxiety that the expectation of something unknown always creates. It was calmer, but no less ardent. People knew what they would see, but were no less curious actually to see it.

The crowd, augmented by an enormous supplement of foreigners, was more numerous, but did not converge upon a determined center. It was disseminated everywhere, many people preferring to go to locations where they assumed that it would be less dense. The government had taken precautionary measures, but, as it no longer feared a political plot, had not armed for war, with rifles loaded and fuses lit.

At eight o'clock, the aerial ship was seen advancing majestically along the Avenue des Champs-Élysées, at a height that permitted it to be minutely observed. It presented the general appearance of an oblong tent, the canvas of which was raised up by two thirds and the ropes rigid. The floor had an ellipsoid form, tapering toward the front and swollen at the rear. It was surrounded by a balustrade inside which fifty empty seats could be seen, separated by intervals of more than a meter and seemingly comfortably established. In front of each one a table was fixed, above it, shelves, cupboards and lamps with frosted glass.

The summit of the apparatus reproduced its general form on a smaller scale, terminating in a polished ball of metal, similar to copper. Below that ball, on a little shelf also surrounded by a balustrade, from which ropes and metal bars extended, seemingly holding the lower part of the vessel in suspension, there was a kind of armchair of the form known as a Bonaparte, turning on a pivot like a piano-stool, in which the aerial navigator was sitting, dressed as on the day of his first appearance.

Two curved levers, emerging from the base of his seat, terminated in handles within reach of his hands. Another lever descending from the upper ball terminated in a similar fashion. His little platform bore two large telescopes at the front and the rear, maneuverable in all directions on their fixed supports. He also had a set of portable binoculars. A kind of iron work-table, seemingly equipped with drawers curved in front of him, open at the rear. Fixed to the anterior section of that table, four objects could be seen, in which spectators equipped with telescopes or binoculars were able to discern a chronometer, a barometer, a thermometer and a compass.

Three men were posted on the inferior platform, two of them at the front on a kind of stage and one at the rear on a higher stage. Each of them had within reach a large telescope on its pivot and portable binoculars, a seat behind him and a taut rope ladder close at hand extending to the edge of the upper platform. The man at the rear had, in addition, a table similar to the one up above, equipped with similar objects. Acoustic tubes terminating in loud-hailer funnels communicated between the upper and lower sections, and the two stations of the latter.

At the front of the inferior platform two cannons were discernible, their muzzles pointing up into the air at an angle of forty-five degrees. When it arrived above the obelisk, the men at the front went to the guns, and two detonations rang out. They were repeated at half-hour intervals during the subsequent circumnavigations. The aerial ship was not only a vehicle; it could become the most terrible engine of war.

The circumnavigations were closely analogous to those the aerial navigator had carried out on his own on the first of June. The most notable detail they presented was that he left his post several times, always after having imparted a slow and regular progress to his ship, in order to accomplish a thousand aerial maneuvers around it, overtaking it, lagging behind it, rejoining it, passing above and beneath it. It was observed that the ship, while attaining a considerable rapidity at times, never matched the great velocity at which the aerial navigator had been seen to move in isolation. It was noticed that the various movements of the ship appeared to be dependent on the manipulation of the levers fitted with handles.

The apparatus was exhibited the following day in an unoccupied stables next door to the building in which the *Universel*'s offices were located. The location received daylight from above through a vast opening in the roof that had been contrived in order to introduce the ship. It was much too small for the crowd that was besieging its doors, It was necessary to organize a regular flow inside, by virtue of which ten or twelve thousand people could pass through per day and who were given sufficient time to see the ship. The receipts approached 140,000 francs during the six days that the exhibition lasted.

The curiosity of the visitors was only partly satisfied, although they could not say that they had been deceived by what had been advertised. The upper part of the ship was reduced to a balustrade forming a crown. It was explained to the public that the remainder, containing the organs of locomotion, the upper platform, the captain's seat, his table, etc., could be fitted to it at will by means of a very simple mechanism. It was ordinarily maneuvered by the conductor and the two servicemen, but the captain could also, if he wished, carry out the operation alone and unaided. He could, if he wished, detach everything and remain alone in the air, without anyone being able to discover in the debris of the ship that had fallen to the ground any indication of the method of locomotion. Such a formidable power, in the hands of an unknown individual, caused many of the people disposed to request places for the advertised voyage to hesitate.

As for the details of accommodation, they were generally approved as comfortable and well organized. The floor, covered with a thick carpet, was made of a metal resembling iron, which gave the apparatus a considerable weight and ought to maintain it in perfect equilibrium. The suspension bars, twelve in number, were also made of metal. They terminated at either extremity in rings engaged in other rings fixed to the edges of the two platforms. Vast and solid sheets of canvas, pierced by a number of glazed bull's-eyes, could envelop the entire apparatus and make it into an impermeable tent, independent of the elegantly painted blinds at the disposal of each passenger to provide shelter from the sun. The armchairs reserved for the latter, turning on pivots, could be converted into veritable beds.

The cannons had been removed from their carriages, which were similar to those of naval guns. It was noticeable that there were not only two gun carriages but six in all, four at the front and two at the rear.

IX. The Decisive Test

The first person to lay out twelve hundred francs and request a place was a woman. That circumstance had not been anticipated. She belonged to high society, in which she had become celebrated for her eccentricity, her garish costumes, her risqué manners and her language, peppered with all the argot terms that reached her as echoes from the demi-monde—all without consequence. A good sort, regardless, and not lacking in intelligence, she was accepted for what she was, and had a school—whose members imitated her. The next morning, the administrator was to receive requests and money from sixty elegant women, more or less authorized by their husbands. He told them that he had referred the matter to the aerial navigator, for whose response he was waiting.

At the same time, demands arrived from all the "sportsmen" who were members of clubs and circles, young men leading, or affecting to lead, the "high life." The feminine example had determined a vogue. People would have thought themselves dishonored, or feared being assumed not to be able to afford twelve hundred francs, or thought to be afraid, if they did not do as everyone else was doing. Many foreigners put their names down. Since they had already come so far, why not attempt to extend the voyage as far as possible?

Soon, there was no one able to dispose of twelve hundred francs who did not want to attempt the adventure. In the Latin Quarter and the studios, schemes were formed in which groups of fifty, a hundred or a hundred and fifty were formed, each contributing a small sum to inscribe the name of the group. If it obtained a ticket, lots would be drawn to determine who received it.

On the first day, the administrator only received eighty thousand francs; on the second it was ninety thousand and the progression never ceased to increase until the last. When the subscription was closed, a sum total of 65,308,800 francs, paid out by 54,484 applicants, was deposited in the treasury designated by the government with a good enough grace.

That good grace did not exactly result from a blind sympathy on the government's part for the invention and its unknown inventor without any hint of a hidden agenda. Its members had not yet taken account of all the consequences that the discovery might conceal. They would surely have liked to render themselves masters of the event, but did not know how to take possession of it. A more or less disguised hostility would have been the worst policy. The inventor had only to disappear, taking himself and his invention abroad, perhaps to make use of it to foment revolutionary movements, perhaps even—for no one knew of what he might be capable—to organize some band of aerial pirates or mercenaries and hold in check any force that social organization could oppose to him. It was therefore necessary not to treat him as an enemy too hastily, before finding out who he was.

Knowing his identity was the crucial point, but how could it be discovered? They immediately thought of resuming the investigation commenced on the subject of the nocturnal distribution. A new charge could be added to the existing ones in order to justify it—the possession of weapons and munitions of war, manifested by the artillery fire with which the circumnavigations of the aerial ship had been accompanied. It would also have been possible to take possession of the articles signed by "*Le Navigateur Aérien*" that the *Universel* had published and prosecute them for contravention of the law requiring a signature. But the resumption of the criminal investigation would be an evident act of hostility, likely to be taken very badly. The first interrogation of the editor-in-chief of the *Universel* might make the aerial navigator into a declared enemy.

Furthermore, it seemed probable that the investigation would yield no result, for precautions appeared to have been carefully taken, and everything suggested that the men at the *Universel* were sincere when they declared that they did not know anything about the identity of their mysterious correspondent. To seek to take possession of his person by means of an ambush when he came by night to pick up or deposit his correspondence at the top of a chimney was materially almost impossible and morally odious. The one course that seemed practicable was to order a top-secret investigation by the finest police sleuths. In the meantime, they decided to put a brave face on things until further notice.

The aerial navigator appeared to be following a carefully meditated plan. The little that he had said about his intention to make France, above all, profit from his discovery, and the sentiment of deference that he had shown in reserving places for the government and scholarly bodies did not testify to a hostile attitude, although the ministers felt offended that he had not directly solicited the collaboration and benevolence of the government, effectively by-passing it. They arrived definitively at the resolution to wait until new circumstances gave some indication of the best course to take. Perhaps the announced voyage would furnish some beam of light; it was an opportunity from which it was necessary to attempt to profit.

Once this resolution was adopted, they lent themselves to events, if not without a hidden agenda, at least with apparent good will. They had the gallantry to put at the disposal of the scholarly bodies the price of the places reserved for them. With all the ministers having volunteered for the voyage, the one designated was the Minister of Public Works, along with the Minister of War, in his capacity as a Maréchal de France, and the Minister of Marines, in his capacity as an admiral. A small military band of twelve musicians was organized, the best and loudest possible, and it was tasked with rehearsing pieces of the most triumphant character.

These dispositions were made known through a note published in the *Moniteur*. The same note announced that the government would pay the expenses, everywhere that the municipalities did not assume the responsibility, of providing all the voyagers with dinner on arrival at each town indicated as a stopover, for their lodging overnight and their breakfast the following morning.

They were not simple dinners, however, that the municipalities organized; they were veritable feasts: banquets offered to the aerial navigator, his traveling companions and the principal notabilities of each town, followed by balls, illuminations, fireworks and splendid hospitality for the travelers. Nothing was lacking in the programs.

The *Universel* published an article in which the aerial navigator declined, with many thanks, the honors that were offered to him. He believed that it would be extremely impolite to appear masked at banquets and fêtes, but it was important to his freedom of action, the future of his discovery and of his homeland, which he wanted to profit in advance of all others, that he maintained a strict anonymity until he had planned important measures in accord with the government.

He believed, however, that he was not exposing himself to the disapproval of his traveling companions by accepting on their behalf, and he would much prefer it if any toasts that might have been offered to him personally were drunk to the future of his invention, the prosperity of France, and this new source of wealth and grandeur.

In the same article, published on the eighth of September, he apologized for not admitting women on this occasion, for, to their great chagrin, their money had been returned to them. While rendering homage to the intrepidity with which they had offered themselves for an experiment involving, if not danger, unknown elements that one could not confront without bravery, he did not want to expose them to the emotions of such a rapid voyage accomplished for the first time through the air. He wanted everyone to be informed first by the account of eyewitnesses of what such a journey was like. Later, he would be pleased to admit ladies who would have the honor of presenting themselves, as soon as the next voyage, which would not take place for six or eight months—the time necessary for the construction of a ship able to contain five hundred passengers. That would be a voyage abroad, and probably around the world.

On the tenth of September, at nine o'clock precisely, the aerial ship carrying all its passengers rose up slowly through the open roof of its resting place. The captain, mounted on the small ship that served the large one as a crown, had only arrived in order to be attached to it ten minutes earlier.

When it had reached an altitude of fifty meters above the highest roofs, six detonations rang out in succession. Then the ship navigated above Paris with a majestic slowness, sounding a fanfare to which the cheers of the crowd replied. The passengers contemplated with admiration the splendid spectacle deployed beneath their feet and extended to the magnified horizon. Few among them had accomplished ascents in aerostats.

They proceeded slowly. The velocity only increased when the ship steered toward various points in the environs of

Paris. However rapid the speed became, such movement remained almost imperceptible to the voyagers. When they looked upwards, they could have believed themselves to be motionless, in the breath of a strong wind. If they looked down, objects seemed to be moving slowly unless, exceptionally, they descended to a low altitude.

The aerial navigator seemed, in any case, to be trying to vary his speed as much as possible to favor all observations. He only quit his post once to fly in isolation, of which he was thought to be privately fond, with the most intrepid feeling more reassured when he was there. It was known that neither the conductor nor his servicemen knew his secret.

When they set out for Strasbourg, the ship rose to a high altitude. People felt a keen impression of cold, and it seemed that the wind became furious, but that they were no longer moving forward. The imperceptible sway caused to the ship by its mode of suspension from the upper part only resembled very distantly the movement of a suspended carriage, the pitching and rolling of a ship at sea or the trepidation of railway carriages on rails. It was almost the immobility of an armchair in an apartment. No one could comprehend, when they arrived in Strasbourg, that they had been traveling at more than two kilometers a minute.

It was exactly six o'clock. The six cannons were fired. The band played a few marches while they circled over the city, overflowing with people and decked with flags. They alighted in the garden of the Prefecture. As soon as they touched down, the two servicemen threw themselves on to the rope ladders and detached the little superior ship, which rose rapidly into the air, carrying the captain away. No one knew what arrangements he had made for his dinner and lodging, and he was not seen again until the following day, ten minutes before embarkation.

The Fêtes were brilliant everywhere, and enthusiasm was at its peak. People crowded around the travelers, delighted when they could collect a few details of their observations from their own lips.

In Strasbourg, after the banquet, the Ministers of War and Marines took coffee with the Prefect at the center of a group. "My dear Admiral," said the former to the second, we can congratulate ourselves that this didn't happen twenty years earlier. Neither you nor I would have had the baton."

"Perhaps not me," the admiral replied, "for it's certain that our nutshells would only be good for firewood and the canvas of our sails for wrapping bales, but even if the navy is dead, the artillery will live forever."

"Bah! Who can tell?" the Maréchal replied. "Anyway, I'm not in the artillery, myself, but the engineers. Fortify places of war, in that case, against fellows that address their gunfire to you as a cloud sends down hail. I defy Vauban in person to make a demonstration now of the *ideal place*.[4] What do you think, Monsieur Chief Engineer?"

The interpellation was addressed to one of the passengers, the director of a railway company. "I think," he replied, "that our shareholders are ruined."

"And the directors of railway companies are only good for putting in the same basket as long-haul captains?"

"Oh, that doesn't worry me much. Someone will always be needed to manufacture and operate these machines, as they are for manufacturing locomotives and manning ships. Do you know who the people are who will really have nothing more to do?"

"Gendarmes," replied the Prefect,

"Unless," observed the Academician, "they're sent into the air to pursue malefactors, as Géronte wanted justice to put to sea."

---

[4] Sébastien Le Prestre de Vauban (1633-1707) was the foremost military engineer of his era, famed for his expertise in building fortifications, and also in breaking through them.

"*Voleurs voleront*,[5] and gendarmes, too," hazarded a Bohemian student who had won his ticket by lot after having put five francs into a pool.

"There will be people far more redundant than gendarmes," said the Chief Engineer.

"Who, then?" asked the Prefect.

"Ask the question of one of our guests: a customs inspector, who is, I believe in the next room."

"Oh well," said the Economist, "Hurrah for free trade!"

Between Nantes and Bordeaux, at about five o'clock, a frightful storm burst. They were not very confident, especially after an observation by a physicist, a member of the Institut, regarding the material employed for the construction of the ship, almost all of it metal. There was a strong risk of being struck by lightning in the midst of the thunderclouds they were traversing, like thick fog. The conductor asked the passengers to gather around the loud-hailer, as the captain had an explanation to give them.

The explanation consisted of telling them that they had nothing to fear from the storm, the apparatus having received a kind of magnetization of which he had the secret, by virtue of which the metal would energetically repel the electricity that iron might normally attract. That secret would be revealed later, at the same time as the methods of locomotion. People scarcely understood, and in spite of the faith they were inclined to have in a man who had proved his abilities in such a striking fashion, they were not sorry to find themselves, an hour later, in the shelter of a hotel in Bordeaux.

The observations that each of them collected carefully could not furnish any conjecture regarding either the methods of locomotion or the identity of the inventor. They were, however, able to calculate the average velocity accurately; it was

---

[5] The French verb *voler* means both to steal and to fly, permitting the observation that "Thieves will fly" to become a rather obvious play on words that only a student would think worth the bother.

thirty-five leagues an hour, a little more than half the speed attained by the aerial navigator during his first tour of France, about double the speed of express trains. It was still enormous, and it was not certain that it was the maximum possible.

The *Universel*, whose editor-in-chief and administrator had been gratified with two places, which were their due, published a series of articles giving a complete and detailed account of the voyage, which could be considered a decisive experiment. The proof had been made in the most irrefutable fashion possible. It remained to consider the probable consequences of the discovery. The paper announced that it would, on its own account, undertake that study independently of the aerial navigator.

The editor solicited the government, scientific organizations and every passenger urgently to publish their observations, and all journalists to analyze the question in depth during the six to eight months that would elapse before the advertised great voyage. The inventor was waiting, before putting the public in a position to profit from his discovery, on the one hand for enlightenment, for himself and others, as to the consequences that might follow, and on the other hand, for the government to make him party to the measures that it might take to prevent a great good being transformed into a great evil, and for France to obtain from the invention a new source of superiority over rival nations.

To facilitate these studies, the *Universel* provided some items of information transmitted by the inventor.

The organs of locomotion of which he made use to travel through the air in isolation had cost him 5,000 francs, but he estimated that it might be possible to manufacture them for between 1,000 and 2,000 francs. Their efficacy ought to last for a hundred years, without maintenance costs.

The aerial ship had cost him 42,000 francs, and the organs of locomotion 20,000 francs. That was a total expense of 62,000 francs, which would be lowered to about 40,000 when the manufacture was perfected and became routine. The duration of the apparatus could be considered as indefinite, without involving any other expense than running costs. The price would increase with the dimensions of the ship, but in a lesser proportion.

The locomotion, strictly speaking, would cost literally nothing, the system acting by virtue of its own efficacy.

The speed might surpass considerably those that had been seen. It might be considered as having no other limit than the exigencies of the human organism, which would be unable to tolerate movement through the atmosphere beyond a certain velocity. It was for experimentation and medicine to calculate that tolerance exactly.

Assuming that an aerial ship constructed for five hundred passengers might cost 100,000 francs, there would be no difficulty for it to travel 1,200 kilometers per day, not counting the nights. Even if people only paid one centime per passenger per kilometer, that was already a gross receipt of 6,000 francs per day, or 2,190,000 francs per year. Even paying the personnel in a most generous manner, with veritable prodigality—attributing, for example, 40,000 francs to the captain, 20,000 to the conductor and 50,000 francs to five servicemen—and setting aside 80,000 francs for running costs, accounting, boarding facilities and interest payments on the capital, there still remained a net profit of two million a year. The owner of ten similar ships would earn twenty million a year, and the passengers would be paying eight or ten times less than on the railway, in order to travel twice, three times or four times as rapidly, with no danger of derailments, shipwrecks or another accidents at all.

Finally, the method could be applied, as a motor, to all possible machines, activating them without any other expense than that of installation. That would result in an industrial revolution, which would increase general wellbeing by reducing the cost of manufacture of everything, not to mention the hundreds of millions in profits that it might procure its inventor.

X. Polemic

People had not waited for the solicitations of the *Universel* to publish many reflections on the unexpected discovery. Since the first manifestation, commentaries had abounded; they had been resumed more ardently with each new experiment. Poetry was mixed in with them. The Luxor obelisk, a monument henceforth unique in the world, symbolizing both the most distant past and the most magnificent future prospects, became a classic theme of odes and cantatas. A kind of agitation was organized to demand that its pedestal be replaced by another, on which would be an engraving of the memorable event accomplished on the henceforth immortal date of June the first. On the subject in vogue, a few remarkable works were published, as were a multitude of inept lucubrations. Pamphlets and newspapers generally reflected the enthusiasm and admiration of the public. Nevertheless, a sort of muted opposition mingled with those sentiments, growing with reflection, fomented clandestinely by powerful interests that felt compromised.

Thus, the ruination of the railways was considered as an accomplished fact. The billions thrown into those gigantic enterprises vanished as a complete loss, ruining the shareholders, deriving armies of employees of their wages and obliterating the positions of the senior functionaries, reducing their immense materiel to bric-à-brac and enveloping a hundred accessory industries in the catastrophe.

It was the same with the merchant marines and all the industries attached to it. There was no ship-owner or ship-builder who did not sense ruination. All transport enterprises, by land and by sea, experienced similar dread. The navy was also about to be abruptly rendered redundant, its officers and sailors with no reason for being, their careers wrecked. They would have no other resource but to hurl themselves into aerial navigation, which would apparently only require a restricted personnel, or to receive wages from the State akin to alms, with any hope of advancement henceforth impossible.

No more roads or bridges would be built, pathways and footbridges sufficing for pedestrians; no more canals, except for irrigation; no more seaports, shipping no longer existing. In consequence, there would be no more engineers and constructors of roads and bridges, road surveyors, road menders or ditch diggers. Coal would only be used for domestic heating, and the mining industry would largely disappear. The threat would extend all the way to wheelwrights, carriage makers, horse dealers and horse breeders.

The commerce of the world would be subjected to a brutal transformation. Perhaps, in the long run, the immense growth of which it would be capable would be a benefit, but in the meantime, all traditions were going to be broken, all relationships altered, all commercial centers displaced, all customs and excises abolished—which would along the way kill off a vast number of industries incapable of supporting such an exaggeration of free exchange, compromising the finances of States and suppressing the earnings of numerous employees—not to mention the other industrial revolution that the employment of a new propulsion force for machines would bring in its wake, ruining all the existing factories.

In sum, commerce and industry as presently constituted would, in the short term, be ruined from top to bottom, for the greater benefit of posterity—unless it turned out to be for its greater harm.

It was not only material interests that were inclined to form a coalition against the invention. Political parties envisaged it with a dubious eye.

The first impulse of liberals had been to applaud it excitedly. Was it not liberty itself, absolute, without possible hindrances, that it was bringing to the world? But they soon began wonder whether it might not, on the contrary, be a formidable instrument of tyranny. Peoples could not spend their lives in the air to escape the enterprises of despots, who might, on the contrary, organize aerial armies and absorb to their profit, by means of rigorous laws sanctioned by severe penalties, the monopoly of that kind of mobility.

The attitude adopted by the inventor helped to make suspicion and antipathy prevail over sympathy. He had only spoken to the government with a deference that did not portend anything good; he seemed to be ready to surrender his secret to the government as soon as the latter had taken the measures necessary to secure a monopoly. He scarcely seemed to be preoccupied with turning it to the advantage of social liberty.

Inverse fears held authoritarians and supporters of the government in suspense. Among them, however, were some who did not hesitate to see the invention as a satanic inspiration, ready to unleash the abomination of desolation upon the world, against which all the resources of human and divine lightning would not be effective.

It was, understandably, a matter of a certain kind of Catholicism, of which there were several in that distant epoch. It could be admitted, strictly speaking, that governments and society might find, albeit with great difficulty, means of protecting themselves against material anarchy and exterior disorder. But healthy doctrines would be completely impotent to defend themselves against a much more redoubtable intellectual anarchy. Liberty of thought, liberty of expression, liberty of propaganda—demonic things—would have an invincible instrument. The printing press had not done a tenth of the damage that aerial locomotion would produce.

It had been possible to erect protection, come what may, against the printing press so long as frontiers had existed and the possibility of policing, but what defense could there be against the free exchange of ideas operating through the air even more easily than the free exchange of merchandise? The congregation of the Index, the inquisition, the repression of the sins of the press and the regulation of the printing profession would no longer be anything but rusted weapons, curiosities for antiquaries, as impotent against free thought as Greek and Roman shields against machine gun fire.

What good would it do to anathematize those liberties vomited forth from Hell? One might as well anathematize the freedom to walk, while humans had legs. The force of circumstance that would prevail against the most solemn excommunications and religion was doomed, unless the aerial navigator was the Antichrist in person and his invention abounded the end of the world, which would not be surprising.

The members of the clergy were all the more inclined to abandon themselves to these sentiments because the anonymous inventor was suspected of being a miscreant, in accordance with certain circumstances observed through the magnifying glass of prejudice. Thus, he had always decided, without any necessity, to choose Sunday for his public experiments, testifying thereby that he was not only unconcerned about neglecting his own religious duties but about deflecting others therefrom. And indeed, it was the case that year that the first of June, the day of the manifestation, was the feast of Pentecost, to which he had not even made any allusion in his announcement. He had not solicited for his ship the blessings of the Church, nor reserved a place for any of its dignitaries, as he had done for the government, for science, and even journalism.

Also interpreted as evil was the casual fashion, judged irreverent, in which he had once made use of one of the lightning conductors of Notre Dame as a seat, while smoking a cigar. They were evidently dealing with a freethinker. They ought not to hesitate to consider him as an enemy, and his discovery as a scourge.

To all that was added certain sentiments that were scarcely admissible, and to which no one confessed, but which contributed nonetheless, clandestinely, to reinforce the various causes of dread and antipathy.

Some people were offended by the anonymity maintained by the inventor; he was reproached for flirting with glory, like a young woman with amour, and of haggling excessively over his revelations. Some begrudged the fact that no one could succeed in discovering his secret, in spite of the assiduous research to which scientists, inventors and industrial practitioners devoted to the problem, with varying degrees of secrecy; they felt humiliated by the crushing superiority of which the unknown individual maintained for himself.

So much power in the hands of one man, who seemed to hold the destiny of the world in his hands alone, had the weight of a usurpation. No one any longer possessed any importance that was not eclipsed by his. Alone, he absorbed the attention of the world.

In spite of all that, no one dared openly to oppose public sentiment, in which admiration held sway over everything else. The spectacles offered to it had produced too profound an impression. People proceeded by means of insinuation. The probable consequences of the invention were studied from all points of view, and there was no mistaking their grandeur.

Nevertheless, there was an accumulation of ifs and buts, objections and apprehensions. The public admiration was mingled with a veritable fear. The more one thought about it, the more impossible it seemed to anticipate the directions in which the world would hasten. Would it not race to its ruin? Was not the reign of violence about to recommence, this time worse than in the darkest days of the Middle Ages? Was not humanity on the brink of sinking into a frightful chaos?

The aerial navigator took no part in this polemic. The *Universel*, however, all of whose reporters were animated by a profound faith, valiantly stood up to the declared and undeclared adversaries of the great discovery. It unmasked the hidden interests that tried to strike a breach in it.

It won its cause with the majority of liberals by demonstrating to them that only progress could come of it, and that no power in the world would be capable of confiscating it to its own profit once it was divulged. It forced the extremist clergy to declare their opposition openly and give their reasons, which were greeted with mediocre favor. It proclaimed, sustained and defended against everyone the axiom that evil never emerges from good, disaster from progress or catastrophe from invention. By virtue of the simple fact, it said, that God inspires a man with the idea of a great discovery, we ought to accept it with as much faith as gratitude, certain as it is in human destiny that all progress is a new source of wellbeing and happiness.

One of its articles provoked a bizarre response. That response came from a newspaper whose editor-in-chief was the most eccentric in the entire Parisian press, treating all subjects in a paradoxical spirit and sustaining, to the great amusement of the public, the most absurd theses—without ever, admittedly, conquering a disciple, but slipping beneath refutation with such dexterity that he always had the last word and always invariably attracted the facetious to his side.

This is the article that he published on aerial locomotion.

XI. Paradox

Aerial locomotion does not exist.

It does not exist because it is impossible.

Let no one tell me that they have seen the aerial navigator and his ship. That is not the issue.

I, too, have seen them. That is only a fact, and what is a fact?

Nothing.

What is logic?

Everything.

Now, logic always has a starting point and a conclusion.

The starting point is that human beings, having no wings, have not been created to fly.

The conclusion is that aerial locomotion does not exist.

All those who have sought means of steering balloons were insane, or at least people who were not using their reason.

It they had been using their reason, they would not have striven to search for something that can be demonstrated a priori to be indiscoverable.

And one does not even need, for that, the demonstrations of science.

Science says, and the simplest mechanical common sense agrees, that the propulsion to be given to aerial vehicles ne-

cessitates a force out of all proportion to those that humans can transport into the air.

Mathematically, one can say:

The motive force must be to the vehicle, balloon or other, akin to the combined force of the two wings of a bird, which cannot fly with one alone.

If one measures the force of a bird's wings, compared with its dimensions and its weight, and deduces therefrom the number of horsepower of force that a steam engine would require to move a vehicle through the air, one arrives at the impossible. And that impossibility is increased by the necessity of giving the vehicle dimensions sufficient to carry the machine itself with its provision of water and fuel.

As for getting rid of the engine and seeking such in the action of the air itself, where there is no point of support, that is simply insane.

But those are the demonstrations of science and common sense. I have no need of them.

People will tell me that they apply to balloons and steam engines, and that the aerial navigator moves with neither a steam engine nor a balloon.

I respond that aerial locomotion is demonstrably impossible a priori.

Human beings are bound to the earth by their conformation. They can invent means of locomotion that do not cause them to quit the earth, but not others.

If they have ships, that is because they are conformed in such a way as to be able to swim.

As for moving in the air, that is not in their conformation. Thus, it is not in their destiny.

The proof of that is that if aerial locomotion existed, the conditions of human existence would necessarily be other than they are.

Now, they cannot change.

Thus, aerial locomotion does not exist.

It has been demonstrated that there would be no more frontiers. Perhaps frontiers are a bad thing, but they are a *necessity. Humans, being sociable, need to group together. Hence there are nations. Without nations, there is no humankind.*

There would be no more government. Now, it is necessary that humans be governed. It is a law that one might regret, but it is an essential law constitutive of civilized humanity.

There would be no more police. Thus, there would be absolute reign of violence. Everything would go to the strongest.

The weak would only have the resource of flight. But what would become of labor? Labor is incompatible with perpetual flight?

And without labor, there would be no human existence, in the same way that without police, there would be no social existence.

Neither the weak nor the strong would toil, because there would always be someone stronger to steal its rewards.

Humans would be transformed into birds of prey.

Hence, the absence of the most essential conditions of all social existence: labor and protection.

Let the Universel tell us how it understands that people will be able to defend themselves against brigandage.

It will paint us a picture of an aerial gendarmerie, and, on the ground, houses with all windows barred, equipped with formidable artillery, unless they are buried fifty feet underground.

Is that kind of architecture in human destiny?

And even then, it would be difficult for a flying gendarmerie and the fortifications of farms to prevent an ox being picked up in Normandy and taken to be cooked in America.

Policing the seas is already not easy. It has required centuries to put an end to piracy and the slave trade. And then, they have not been ended completely.

Policing the seas is, however, merely difficult.

Policing the air would be utterly impossible.

How will the Universel prevent a gang of mercenaries from arriving one night from China or Argentina and demand-

ing a contribution to their subsistence on pain of immediate bombardment?

How will it prevent slave traders from abducting black men from the shores of Africa and white men from the shores of Provence?

Aerial locomotion would demand a tangle of draconian laws and an organization of public force of which we have no idea, and which would still be impotent.

Hence, no more liberty. Now, liberty is one of the essential conditions of human existence.

Does the Universel suppose that with such a disaggregating facility of locomotion, any vestige would long subsist of marriage the family, the hearth and the little domestic virtue that we have left?

Man would soon be no more than a male, a woman a female, and the human species, impotent to set foot upon the earth, devoid of family, devoid of property, with no other law than force, would rapidly degenerate toward animality.

Others have enumerated all the consequences, certain or probable, of aerial locomotion. Some have concluded that it has a splendid future in store for us, others a redoubtable one, but which, in the opinion of all, will transform the world.

The premises are correct. The conclusion is not.

Splendid if you like, that future would surpass the destiny of human beings, to whom it is no more given to transform the conditions of their existence than to steal the fire of heaven.

Redoubtable in my view, it would lead to the final cataclysm of humanity.

All the consequences of aerial locomotion, anticipated or possible to anticipate, are in manifest contradiction with the fundamental conditions of all civilization.

Now, civilization does not accommodate contradictions.

It admits progress, but in the sense of the development of that which it has created.

It does not admit progress in a contradictory direction.

The conclusion to be drawn from these premises is not in the search for the consequences that aerial locomotion will produce.

The conclusion is that aerial locomotion does not exist.

And I predict that we shall hear no more talk of the aerial navigator, for he has only had a dream, and the whole world with him.

If he has the audacity to reappear, he will be transported into space with his secret, which no one will ever rediscover, because he cannot exist, and, in consequence, does not exist.

The fact is nothing.

Logic is everything.

XII. The Voyage Around the World

Understandably, the *Universel* did not even take the trouble to reply to such a perfectly absurd article, which concluded with the ridiculous denial of a fact that the entire world had seen. As for the government, it had not made any contribution to the polemic, which it had allowed to develop at its ease, understanding that the more it was freely debated, the more it would be enlightened.

Fundamentally, it was perplexed.

There was then at its head, without their being any particular necessity to say exactly what its form was at the time, a man unintoxicated by his situation. He had not been ambitious for power. His simple tastes made it a burden for him, which he would gladly have resigned. Although liberal by temperament, he had formed his own idea of government authority. He considered it as a despotism that it was not permissible for him to lessen, even to the profit of ideas with which he sympathized. As a simple citizen, he could have demanded, with more or less insistence, various concessions. As Head of State, his ideas were no different, and the exercise of authority had nothing seductive about it in his eyes, but he believed conscientiously that his responsibility required him to make no concessions. Imagine him as a Washington, depositary of the power of the Great Turk, which he had sworn to transmit intact to those who came after him. Liberal by sentiment and in his ideas, he treated liberty almost as an enemy.

Now he asked himself what the new invention would mean for government authority.

It was quite evident that if it were to be vulgarized without any precaution being taken, government authority would not merely be lessened but obliterated.

To prevent the invention being produced was out of the question. First of all, they did not have the inventor. Even if they had him, murdering him might not kill his secret; he might have taken precautions in order not to take it to his grave if death took him by surprise.

There was only one possible decision to take: to buy the secret and reserve the monopoly thereon.

But that was not easy to do.

Even assuming that one could reach an understanding with the inventor on the conditions of the cession, it would be necessary to take a certain number of people into confidence. It would at least be necessary to make the method known to whomever took command of an aerial ship. Even if one chose the most honorable of men and demanded the most solemn oaths of secrecy from them, a State secret with such a considerable number of confidants would soon be divulged regardless.

Was it not probable, in any case, that some new inventor would end up discovering in his turn what the first had discovered?

Vulgarization seemed inevitable, except by suppressing the discovery itself, something evidently impossible. Now, vulgarization was the upheaval of all social organization and the obliteration of all government.

Could one at least plan a series of laws sufficiently efficacious to ward off the redoubtable consequences that the whole world had identified? It would not be easy. The laws would not easily constrain men possessed of such a means of flight.

And how could France be protected against foreign invasions able to arrive unexpectedly from the most distant nations, either for the purpose of conquest, or to ravage and then disappear? Would they be reduced to creating innumerable aerial armies for self-defense, and rendering to foreign lands the evils received therefrom?

There was nothing but impossibility perceptible in all directions.

He ended up where perhaps he ought to have begun. He resolved to enter into communication with the aerial navigator and seek information as to the measures that he would probably have to propose to ensure that his discovery did not become a public calamity, but, on the contrary, a benefit for the world, and in particular for France.

He was only stopped by a question of etiquette and governmental dignity. He was reluctant to take the first step, and especially to correspond with an unknown individual. The Head of State wrote to the man in question, by way of the offices of the *Universel*, that as soon as he cared to make himself known to the government, which promised him secrecy, the government would be ready to receive the communications that he might want to make to it.

The aerial navigator responded immediately by means of a letter whose form was exceedingly polite, but which, in spite of the most refined epistolary mannerisms, was fundamentally arrogant and almost impertinent. The time to make himself known had not yet come, but he was ready, since the government seemed to desire it, to put himself in communication with it while conserving his anonymity. He offered to lend himself to an exchange of correspondence either by way of the *Universel* or some analogous channel, adapted to any chimney that the government wished to adapt to that effect in any of its edifices. He believed that the authority was seriously interested in planning and proposing to him the measures that it might have in mind. He promised to examine them with all the care they merited, desirous of turning to the profit of the public good the incalculable power that he found in his hands, and to show the government every deference and respect.

The roles were reversed. The unknown was posing as the protector, leaving the government the role of protégé. There was no mistaking his pretention of treating power as power, and governmental power as secondary. Fortunately, he put sufficient diplomacy into it for the government to be able, without sacrificing the appearance of dignity, to submit to his law while having the appearance of making it.

The Head of State resigned himself to a situation imposed on him by the force of circumstance, overcoming all the resentments of self-esteem, and wrote to tell his correspondent that the government would agree to grant him the mode of correspondence that he solicited, and was ready to examine the demands for indemnity that he might formulate for the communication of his method.

X. Nagrien hastened to reply that the question of indemnity was not the most urgent. He asked that its examination be postponed until later, and to limit himself to giving a few indications on that point to which they could return when the time came. His invention, if he cared to exploit it, might procure almost infinite benefits.

He could establish, with the unexplored regions of Africa, with the Orient, with gold-bearing locations and other distant places, an immense and fruitful commerce. He could run contraband. He could transport passengers and merchandise. The sixty-five millions paid out in a matter of days by the applicants for the voyage around France demonstrated well enough what voyages abroad might bring in. He could, by putting another aspect of his invention to work, rent out motive force to industrialists. It would be easy for him to earn hundreds of millions.

Considerable offers had already reached him via the *Universel* letter-box. A prominent financier, asking him to name a figure, had gone so far as to declare that, without promising in advance to accept it, he would consider it and discuss it with him whatever it was, even if it surpassed a hundred million or a hundred and fifty million. His invention represented, if he were to exploit it himself, eight or nine hundred million, and perhaps billions. England or the United States would surely give him, whenever he wished, five or six hundred million. He was in no hurry to withdraw the benefits that he was assured as soon as it suited him to realize them.

His desire was, before anything else, to enrich France with his discovery, and he would consider himself gloriously and amply indemnified by a national recompense reduced to much more modest proportions—a hundred and fifty million or two hundred million, if the government wished—so that was not what preoccupied him. The first question to be examined was that of the measures to be taken in order to put his discovery to work, and he asked the government to communicate to him its plans in that regard.

The figures indicated in this letter were surprising at first glance, but reflection quickly demonstrated that the aerial navigator was not wrong to declare them modest. As for the rest, the government was unable to enunciate ideas that it did not have regarding the solution to that insoluble problem, but it was difficult to admit that and also press the inventor in order to obtain intentions that he might well be lacking and had not, at any rate, taken the initiative in offering, as had been hoped.

The government wrote to say that the question was being studied, and the resolutions adopted would be communicated to him. The decision was, indeed, made to conduct that study very seriously in the hope of finally arriving at some practicable plan.

X. Nagrien replied that, since that was the case, he would depart for his great voyage, the duration of which would not be very long, and that communication could be resumed when he returned. He indicated one useful element for the studies that they were about to make. It was possible to train captains to maneuver aerial ships without having to surrender the secret of the method of locomotion to them. That was the kind of measure he counted on taking if, in the case the government did not succeed in proposing suitable measures for putting his discovery to work, he decided to exploit it himself.

The end of May arrived. The departure for the voyage around the world had been fixed for the first of June, the first anniversary of the manifestation by which the inventor had made his debut. The passengers, this time notified far in advance, had come from all over the world.

A new ship, augmented with shops, lounges, bedrooms and conveniences of every kind had been constructed on a plan similar to the first, in proportions sufficient to transport five hundred passengers, accommodated with the most ingenious comfort. Nothing was lacking in terms of provisions, weapons, instruments for scientific observation and protection against intemperate weather. It was to visit all the capitals of Europe, traverse the seas, penetrate unexplored regions, and show itself to savage populations far more stupefied by the apparition than the Amerindians had been at the sight of the first ships arriving from Europe.

A national fête had been organized for the great day of the departure. The main courtyard of the Hôtel des Invalides had been put at the disposal of the aerial navigator for the embarkation.

At noon, the ship rose up, decked in flags, to resounding fanfare, the acclamations of the passengers, to which those of the crowd replied, and detonations of its artillery, to which the cannon of Les Invalides responded. It traversed the Esplanade, went up the course of the Seine as far as the Pont d'Austerlitz, equidistant from both quais, rose higher and higher, drawing away eastward, and was visible long after as a black dot before vanishing in space.

News of it is expected any day. The paradoxical journalist is alone in affirming, against all the evidence, that none will be received.

Edouard Rod: *Dr. Z***'s Autopsy*

(1884)

*For myself, knowing nothing and holding dreams in
doubt,*
I believe that after death, when union is achieved,
The soul then recovers clarity of sight,
And that, judging its work with serenity,
*Understanding without obstacles and explaining without
difficulty,*
Like its sisters in heaven it is powerful and regal,
Measures its true weight, knowing manifestly
That the breath, falsified by the false instrument,
Was neither glorious nor vile, not being free,
That the body alone prevented equilibrium;
And calmly, it resumes, in ideal bliss,
The holy equality of the Lord's spirits.

Alfred de Vigny,
"The Flute."[6]

Perhaps you will still remember the noise made in the
scientific world some thirty years ago by the discoveries of
Doctor Z***, which suffered the fate of many discoveries and
was universally denied. When he finally decided to publish the
results of his patient research, Dr. Z*** was living in Bordeaux, where he enjoyed the renown of a good practitioner.
The pamphlet for which he bore the expense, *Observations on
Some Phenomena of Cerebral Existence*, provoked a general
outcry, and he gradually lost his clientele.

It should also be said that the pamphlet in question—an
octavo of about a hundred and twenty pages—overturned all

---

[6] "La Flûte" was first published in 1843.

received notions, simultaneously threatening by its indirect consequences science, morality and religion.

In effect, the physiologist claimed that the life of the brain is not extinguished at the same time as that of the body; that, on the contrary, it continues for a period that varies between seven and ten days after the last sigh—except, of course, in cases when the brain itself has been directly attacked by a disease, as in meningitis, encephalitis, general paralysis, softening, ataxia, etc.

He went further than that; he affirmed that, while during life the cerebral cells consumed by thought are incessantly reformed, they are irrevocably destroyed after death, with the result that the brain, still intact and fully active when the heart ceases to beat, although already detached from sensation by the wastage or weakness of the interior nervous centers, gradually declines in that final labor.

A good technologist as well as an excellent chemist, Dr. Z*** constructed an apparatus himself—which, so far as I can remember, bore some resemblance to the instrument invented more recently named the photophone[7]—with which he was able, for four or five days after death, to track the activity of brains in the process of decomposition.

He destroyed that instrument, as he burned his records, when he saw that no one believed him, and that the most indulgent were treating him as a madman and the rest as a charlatan. Nothing, therefore, remains of his great work, and when science has finally deciphered the enigma of death, no one will be able to tell whether the obscure practitioner from Bordeaux was a pioneer or a trickster.

---

[7] The photophone, involving the transmission of speech by means of a beam of light, was invented by Alexander Graham Bell and Charles Sumner Tainter in 1880; Bell thought it by far his most important invention, but its range was far surpassed by Guglielmo Marconi's wireless transmission system, and it was superseded, although it was the ancestor of modern transmissions via fiber-optic cable.

For myself, who knew him, who saw him at work, who listened on many an occasion, in his laboratory, to his conversations full of luminous perceptions, his reasoning was irreproachable, departing from the most scrupulous observations to rise to the heights where thought can finally detach itself from the tyranny of facts, and were his deductions, all the links of which were connected by the most rigorous logic. I have always regarded him as one of the beacons that ignorance and human stupidity too frequently take it upon themselves to extinguish, for fear of seeing the darkness of their routines illuminated.

I do not intend to explain Doctor Z***'s theories at length here, nor to recount his personal history. That might be instructive, but it is, I think, appropriate to leave it in the obscurity to which fate has relegated it, and to which he resigned himself without difficulty. But it was given to him once, to read with absolute clarity, an instance of that last period of life, which he alone has known, and I want to recall the circumstances of that strange case.

A ship-owner of Bordeaux, Dutch by origin, Monsieur van Gelt, committed suicide in 1854. His family took a great many precautions to hide that catastrophic event, of which malevolent rumor did not take long to circulate in society, where Monsieur van Gelt had been highly esteemed. The secrets of his private life, which had transpired long before, gave that gossip a certain consistency.

The family requested an autopsy, and Dr. Z***, then still looked on favorably, was given the responsibility. He communicated his surgical observations to the law, but he kept to himself the psychology of the dead man, which he had read as if in a book in the scarcely-drowsy brain.

The ship-owner, van Gelt, was evidently a man of high intelligence and great heart, so his posthumous ideas presented a character of superiority that Dr. Z*** had never encountered before. He collated his notes lovingly, conserving their personal form. On the day when he communicated them to me, reading his manuscript as an author might read a chapter of his

99

novel, I was amazed: the dead man lived—so to speak—his strange cadaveric existence before me.

I begged my friend to let me have a copy of his notes, and he agreed, on the express condition that I did not publish them before he had published the great work to which his observations were only the preface. I have described the fate of his writings. He is dead now, and I can therefore regard myself as released from my promise and free to deliver this curious document to the public. If I am not mistaken, it will one day cast new light on the presently unfathomed mysteries of eternity. The only element that I shall permit myself to introduce into it, which appears to me to be necessary to the understanding of the script, concerns the ordering of the facts; I have brought together in the early pages details relating to the circumstances of the suicide, which are dispersed in the notes as if at the hazard of memory.

...I have exhausted what it is appropriate to call the calyx of suffering; for some time, catastrophes and misfortunes, superposed upon me like heavy stones on a man being walled up alive, have been pursuing me with a tenacity almost incredible in the force of its ferocity.

First of all, it was my only son, twenty-six years old, who fled with some creature after having robbed me in the manner of a treacherous accountant. Then my daughter died of typhoid fever at the moment when I was about to marry her to a young man she loved.

Soon afterwards, I discovered that my second wife—whom I had married without a dowry, for love, foolish old man that I was!—was deceiving me with one of my nephews, to whom I had given a position in my business, and whom I regarded, alas, as a second son. Rendered cowardly by that love, almost senile and almost ridiculous, whose roots stifled my courage, I accepted with interior tortures my role as a deceived husband, begging the wretch for the refuse of her tenderness, striving to conceal a wound that was getting larger every day.

Worn out by so much emotion, I became ill. I consulted a physician; he recognized that my morbid state was caused by the first symptoms of a cancerous infection of the stomach. Finally, after a disaster that coincided fatally with a financial crisis in Lyon, I saw the moment arriving when I would no longer be able to meet my obligations. At sixty-two years of age, at the end of an honorable career, having worked hard and done good, I thus found myself surrounded by dishonest affections, cuckolded, ill and poor.

Among the few idea that could still germinate within my brain, raked as if by the claws of birds of prey, a comparison was insinuated between my fate and that of Job. And I found myself even more unhappy than the patriarch: he had God, while I, throughout my overworked existence, had paid no heed to supernatural matters, which inspired an insurmountable mistrust in me, and even a little of the disgust that men of action have for the reveries of the contemplative.

At that moment, removed from all activity, forced into bitter contemplation of myself, meditative for perhaps the first time in my life, I began to desire faith, which the unfortunate regard as the supreme panacea. To acquire it, however, would have required time; and even then, would I ever succeed in vanquishing my deep-rooted skepticism? Would not my innate need for truth always triumph over the suggestions of my sentimentality? Certainly, in spite of my efforts, doubts would subsist in me, poisoning the consolations of the priest.

That refuge was thus refused to me. There remained one other, more reliable: death. I accepted it.

The fear of bankruptcy vanquished my last hesitations. At another time, I would have tightened my muscles, stiffened my will and struggled until the final defeat, but I felt paralyzed by a definitive lassitude, like a shipwreck victim whose limbs have become heavy, who loses consciousness and abandons himself. I did not even wait for the certainty of my disaster to be absolute; the probability was sufficient for me, and I bought an American revolver.

...I went home; I locked myself in my study and there, while parading my eyes over the files filled with papers in which my entire activity was stagnating, over the curiously-wrought old furniture with which I liked to surround myself, and the few valuable paintings hanging on the walls, I slipped into a long reverie. My life passed before me in images whose colors sang with strange symphonies; I started going back over the course of time, stopping at unforgettable dates.

I arrived at the distant years of youth when I had battled furiously to live, my heart swollen with immeasurable ambitions, tormented by insatiable appetites; and I lingered there with delight while certain charming details gradually emerged from the monotonous tint of the past, like holes of light in a fog.

One memory, above all, pursued me for some time and made me smile. It was in the month of May; I had left the obscure mansard in the Rue de Jeûners to which I went home after my long days of work; I went for a walk in the woods of Meudon with my first mistress, a blonde milliner, slim and cheerful, who loved me as I loved her, without any hidden agenda, without any thought for the morrow, just for the pleasure that we gave one another. We had a little money and we drank warm milk at a farm. Suddenly, she started, the milk spilled over her beautiful Sunday dress. She was distressed. We were hidden by a bushy arbor; I kissed her for a long time, and she forgot her chagrin. Her name was Marguerite. There were flowers everywhere....

...The clock, chiming midnight, extracted me from my reverie. The intervals between each of the strokes seemed long to me; the chime, metallic and sonorous, was lugubrious. I understood that the hour in question really does have something solemn about it; on hearing it fall into the heavy silence of my last night, I understood why it is designated for crime. And I told myself that it was necessary to finish it. In any case, I had nothing more to do: no testament, since my succession would probably be swallowed up by a deficit; no letters, since those I loved did not love me and would learn of my death with dry eyes.

I only wrote, on a piece of paper that I left in a prominent place: *Today, 26 June 1854, I have killed myself.* I signed it. As midnight had just sounded, I had hesitated slightly before writing the date.

[That piece of paper, which had initially gone astray, was found by the judiciary investigation *several days after Dr. Z*** had communicated his notes to me*, and removed all doubts concerning Monsieur van Gelt's demise.]

My decision was firmly made. I retained all my calmness, but it seemed to me that I was acting in a dream, that nothing that was happening was definitive, that I might suddenly wake up with new horizons before me, as in a splendid dawn—and without having to do anything for that.

Then I sank back in my armchair, my eyes glued to the weapon, the barrel of which was gleaming in the lamplight, hypnotizing me. A great torpor invaded me. Increasingly vague visions floated before me, occasionally making me smile. I would have liked to stay like that eternally, letting time go by without losing consciousness of its duration and yet without feeling any more, without thinking any more….

Then, suddenly, the memory of the resolution I had to carry out returned to me; reality reasserted itself. I shook myself, like a man about to go to sleep who suddenly remembers something he has forgotten to do and makes an effort to chase sleep away.

It was almost mechanically that I opened my jacket, my waistcoat and my shirt. I sought the location of the heart, which started beating violently under my hand, as if to affirm by its precipitate beats the strength of its life. At the same time I felt a glacial chill running through my veins; I believe that my teeth were chattering, although my brow was inundated with sweat. I made gestures of anguish; I was suffering like a patient on whom some painful operation is about to be carried out, who is afraid but desires to proceed even so, and who is pushing away the surgeon while crying to him: "Do it, then!"

Will-power triumphed, however, over the last revolts of instinct in a supreme contest, so rapid and passionate that it seemed to me to be a spasm; I was able to take the revolver, the ivory butt of which was burning my hand. I placed the muzzle slightly above the place where my heart was pounding, taking care to leave a little space between my flesh and the barrel of the weapon, which was trembling so much that I was obliged to steady it with my left hand. Finally, in a shudder of my entire being, dominated by a frightful terror of the unknown that loomed up before me, suddenly gripped by a desire to live as poignant as remorse and by regrets sharper than any pain, I pressed the trigger.

Truly, I believe that my will-power, at that precise moment, was annihilated, consumed as it had been by its final effort: the abandoned nerves simply carried out the action of their own accord, and movement commenced.

I felt an atrocious pain, but did not lose consciousness; undoubtedly, I had only broken a rib; I had to start again. But I was seized by a kind of delirium: mechanically, I pressed the trigger twice more without hearing the sound of the detonations. The last shot struck home, for I felt my heart stop beating, my blood pause in my veins, and a great rigidity stretch my limbs, like the hand of an invisible giant....

...I'm dead, there's no doubt about it. By what miracle, then, are Thought and Sensation obstinate in persisting within me? My eyes can no longer see, but I have a marvelously precise vision of what surrounds me; my ears can no longer hear, but the slightest sounds—the fluttering of a moth trapped in the room, the distant murmurs from outside, the sputtering of the lamp on the brink of going out—seem to me to be reverberating within me by virtue of a crystal clear echo; my limbs are already stiff, but I feel, scarcely muffled by a thick carpet, the hardness of the parquet onto which I've slid; I can even perceive the odor of powder that fills the room.

I analyze my situation with a lucidity superior to any I've ever deployed before. "Undoubtedly," I say to myself, "this state won't last long; my thoughts will gradually stop, as my limbs are becoming cold and stiff"—that double sensation of cold and stiffness is excessively painful to me—"and my entire being will fall asleep in a benevolent final repose."

The memory even returns to me—for my faculties continue to operate as they did a little while before, perhaps better—of having heard in a lecture an account of the effects of curare poisoning, and I think that a phenomenon of the same kind is taking place in me, that I'm not dying in an instant, that it's necessary to be patient….

…But no! No appreciable diminution in my physical suffering, not the slightest disturbance in my reasoning; and that cold, the terrible cold that chills me to the marrow without my being able to shiver as I once could, when I was young and went to bed in a room without a fire!

And now those sensations are becoming more precise, as a poignant anxiety is added to them: what if this is the immortality of the soul that people talk about? What if it's necessary to remain like this throughout the cycle of the eternal ages, simultaneously dead and alive, Thought persisting in a stiff, cold body that is decaying? Who can tell? Perhaps God exists; perhaps this is the last torture that He inflicts on us; perhaps He punishes in this fashion those who have been unable to glimpse His infinity or who have transgressed His mysterious laws? Are there prayers that might touch Him…?

…The minutes and the hours elapse with an indescribable slowness. I start thinking about cataleptics who are buried alive, who wake up in the grave with howls stifled by the earth, gnawing their firsts, and convulsed by the pangs of asphyxia. What if, by virtue of some strange lesion that has never been produced before, of which surgery has no suspicions, I'm only in a state of catalepsy? What if I wake up in three or four days, or a week, convulsively, with an immutable weight on my chest…?

But no, it's impossible. I'm dead; I'm really dead. The human body is submissive to precise laws; it has been dismantled piece by piece, like a machine whose smallest mechanism is familiar. I felt the bullet pass through my heart; hence, I have nothing more to fear; my ideas will gradually calm down, silence will fall within me. My present state is logical; doubtless all the dead experience it, all of them have experienced that same anguish—and all of them have calmed down, as I shall calm down....

...Meanwhile, daybreak is beginning, in wan gleams that are trailing over me. There are noises outside in the street, reaching me as if through a thick wall. A few more minutes and my manservant, accustomed to waking me up early, will knock on the door, and, on receiving no reply, will come in. He's a worthy man, who has served me for ten years. I've been good to him in several circumstances; perhaps he'll miss me....

Then my wife will enter in her turn, and my nephew....

And I feel a frisson pass through me at the idea that I'll soon be able to measure their affection irrevocably....

Someone knocks on the door; for ten years, the same raps have been struck every morning, and it was my voice that replied. As no response is forthcoming, the knocking is repeated, more loudly.

The door opens.

Jean goes as pale as I must be, stifles a cry, makes a movement to go out, hesitates on the threshold, comes in and closes the door *carefully*....

He comes over to me, puts his hand over my heart, listens....

He carries me to my bed. Why is he looking at me with such a fearful expression? Why is he turning me to face the wall? I can see regardless, since my faculties are in some way disengaged from my senses, since I'm living a superior and independent life, since my vision is vaster in spite of the fixity of my eyes....

What is he going to do?

He goes to my writing-desk, to which I've given him a key. He opens it. He rummages in the drawers, striving to release a secret compartment whose mechanism he doesn't know, where the money is kept. I hear the dry click of gold coins in his hand....

And, the theft accomplished, although his legs are unsteady, although his teeth are still chattering with fear, utterly distressed, he runs out of the room shouting for help. People will say: "The domestic was very fond of his master, very faithful; one doesn't find his kind any more today...."

After all, he's a poor man. He would never have had the courage to steal from me while I was alive, and perhaps never had any such idea—and yet, the sight of my cadaver frightened him more than the law, to which he gave no thought. He must, therefore, be driven by a very powerful motive; undoubtedly he has immediately deduced the causes of my suicide, he has been struck by the sudden and clear awareness of his situation; he's no longer young, he was counting on remaining in my service for as long as I could provide him with a small income, or, if I died before him, that he'd be provided for in my testament. Instead of that, the hazard of seeking employment is emerging; all of the placid arrangement of his life has been disturbed....

Then again, who knows what school he has passed through previously; who knows what circumstances have rendered him sinful or defiant? Perhaps days devoid of bread have developed appetites in him stronger than his conscience, which would have bent him sooner or later to their irresistible domination. He has lived with me for ten years without my ever asking him about his life; perhaps he was abandoned as a child, or his father beat him without a reason, or his mother didn't love him....

And then, after all, I have no further need of the money that he's taken. It requires an effort of memory for me to recall that I've worked all my life to earn it, that I've killed myself because I was about to lack it, that others kill themselves for the same reason and live as I am living.

Two days ago, if I'd found the slightest irregularity in Jean's conduct, I'd have fired him without hesitation; for the slightest misdemeanor, I'd have dragged him pitilessly before the courts, because I was rigid, one of those who regarded it as a duty for honest men to pursue the guilty. Now, I'd like to be able to get up in order to tell the man, whose conscience is doubtless in torment, that I forgive him.

It's likely the beginning of detachment, or perhaps things are appearing to me in a different light?

My wife comes into the room, and says: "Leave me alone."

Now we're face to face, the torturer and her victim, and death has inverted the roles: she's the one who's suffering now. I can see the traces of her emotions and here remorse passing over her face; it's me who is placid and tranquil now.

She approaches me slowly, as if fascinated; she closes my eyes, whose fixity doubtless makes her feel uncomfortable; then she steps back....

I'll never know what she's thinking.

Perhaps I, who wanted her to be happy, made her unhappy. I remember how sad she was before the marriage, and that it didn't worry me; I said to myself: "It's the unknown of her new life that's troubling her...." Her parents forced her into it, I'm sure. Perhaps she was in love with someone else, with the omnipotent chastity of first love, and I doubtless wounded her virginal delicacies as I overturned her young woman's dreams. She must have cursed me....

She draws closer to me, very pale. She touches my hand. She recoils again with a movement of dread, as if that icy hand had burned her....

I don't reproach her at all, though, because I acted like other men: egotism blinded me; I thought I'd make her happy by taking her; it's a common illusion. She suffered because of me; what does it matter? Nothing remains of her tears any more than anything will remain of her regrets. I, too, have wept for her; already I can scarcely remember...and who knows...?

The door opens again; it's my nephew.

He stops a few paces away from her; then he comes closer. They're both grave. I've never calculated their struggles, never thought that their sin has doubtless cost them dear; that they loved one another, and took account of what they called their infamy, but that love conquers all, in accordance with the law of nature; that the things that the living find monstrous would appear quite natural to them if the passions of the moment didn't blind them....

Meanwhile, she rests her head on his shoulder with the gracious movement of a woman soliciting protection; and, her throat full of sobs, she says "He was very good, though!"

Was I good? I don't believe so. I only applied, no more and no less, whatever the circumstances, the rule that measured my actions against the common standard. I gave to beggars and I let the poor starve; according to the caprice of circumstances, I felt my heart ready to melt with pity, or as hard as stone; I respected the law, but I also made use of it for the defense of my interests; between two courses of action, I always chose the one to which I was more forcefully driven by the motives tyrannizing my will.

In sum, now that I can judge my life in its entirety, I don't regret any of what I've done and wouldn't want to have done anything differently—and yet, my activity seems to me to have been limited, futile and fatal.

After a silence, my nephew replies: "He was a true father to me."

I was mistaken on his account, therefore. I thought him ungrateful; he was unhappy.

She continues: "My God, how guilty we are!"

And they stand before me, ashamed.

Then she throws herself into his arms, weeping....

Oh, I wish I could get up and say to them: "Love one another! Love one another! Certainly not for the enjoyment of love, which isn't worth the pain, but because it isn't worth the pain, either, of struggling against one's desires!" They're young, they're handsome, the blood is seething in their veins; what right do I, an old man who has already had my share of joys, have to want to separate them...?

...The hours go by. It seems to me that a modification has taken place in my condition; I no longer feel any physical discomfort; the sensation of cold has disappeared; I even think that I'm enjoying lying down, as if after heavy fatigue, and the ideas that continue to pass through me no longer trouble me.

People come: old friends who mourn me. One of them, my oldest friend, stayed by my bedside for a long time without saying anything, shaking his head from time to time, doubtless thinking that it would soon be his turn, and dreading it. The indifferent have composed themselves at the door as they rang the bell, putting on distressed expressions as they took off their hats. The employees of the company have filed past one by one, buttoned up in worn frock coats and poorly gloved. They've been told that it was an apoplectic fit; they seemed anxious.

Candles are burning; a nun mumbles prayers by my bedside, which she interrupts with a sulky expression every time someone arrives....

I remember that once, when I was out walking, I sometimes saw a swarm of gnats swirling, flying in all directions like specks of dust, and didn't know whether they were following a common goal or whether chance alone determined the sum of their movements. Truly, it's the same for so many comings and goings, for those contradictory anxieties that I read on all the faces, for the warmth of the hands that touch mine fearfully and leave me with a vague impression of fever.

The human face no longer strikes me as anything but a distant memory; the people who pass around me seem like shadows moving in a mist. When I compare their agitation to my immobility, the sound of their footfalls, which they stifle as if they were afraid of waking me up, and the murmur their voices, with my silence, and the animation of their eyes with the fixity of mine beneath my permanently lowered lids, I wonder where the reality of existence is. Between their condition and mine, between being and non-being, is there really such an imperceptible nuance?

I contemplate life as a traveler who has just passed over a mountain and casts a glance behind him; he has been walking for a long time, his feet have been bruised by sharp stones, he has hesitated before many obstacles; but now, the torrents that barred his path are only thin white lines beneath his feet, the rocks that loomed up before him are black dots, he can no longer see the chasms into which he nearly fell, and the distance traveled seems to him to be such a little matter that he thinks he could touch the nearby peak with his finger.

Then, the shadows of evening rise up, everything is drowned and disappears into a uniform shade; space no longer exists.

Night falls. My wife has decided to keep vigil with the nun. They've both fallen asleep. In the efforts of their respiration, I hear painful thoughts, poorly allayed, or heavy dreams pursuing them. The idea of their actions, which they're judging sinful in their imperfect consciences, is still troubling them, and also concern for things that they believe to be important.

In my slumber, which is better than theirs and devoid of nightmares, nothing similar is happening. Of forgotten cares nothing remains in me but indifference, and I understand irresponsibility….

…At times, my brain stops: I'm no longer thinking….

…The second day begins. My vision of the things surrounding me is not as clear; the golden dots of the candle flames are fading. Noises are muffled; and the sensation of blindness and deafness that is invading me, instead of being painful, is full of charm.

My son has arrived. He has fallen into a chair at the foot of my bed, without speaking. I don't know where he has come from, or how the news of my death reached him; perhaps he learned about it from a newspaper in some café. Anyway, I have no curiosity in his regard, although I judge him differently as well. Instead of letting his youth develop, I compress it, wanting him to work as I had worked, without taking account of the difference in our situations, "on principle," as I put it. I opposed him in his inclinations, to the extent of preventing him from pursuing the career of his preference. From childhood, I measured out his pleasures sparingly, under the pretext of showing him the miserliness of life's joys. Was it astonishingly that his youth burst forth?

He had, all things considered, no reason to love me, but he's mourning me; his conduct was the fatal result of circumstances for which he is not culpable, but he's deploring it; it's the illogicality of every thought that life crushes. While vain remorse torments him, I understand him and I absolve him—to tell the truth, without afflicting myself with his condition, without sympathizing with his undeserved anguish, without my stillness being in any way troubled by his grief, for afflictions are frozen along with the blood.

With the supreme intelligence of things that I feel within me, I also feel the supreme indifference. In the same way that I have escaped all the laws of human morality, and now finally understand relativity, I have fled the tyranny of the heart. I have no more hatred for those who made me suffer than gratitude for those who have loved me. The good and bad hours that I owe to the commerce of human beings are now too distant for me to be able to make any distinction between them.

Every day, in life, does one not experience agreeable or painful sensations of which one does not retain any memory? No one, for example, thinks for days on end about the pleasure he had experienced in a scented bath, or a good meal, or entering into a warm room after having suffered from cold, any more than the pain caused by a pinprick or bumping into a door. Well, my great joys and my great pains, those that caused me to wander the streets with a my chest on the point of explosion, those which made me, an adult, weep as a child weeps, all of that is as distant, as faded, as depleted as the thousand fugitive impressions that every day bears away and replaces. How, then, can the slightest rancor against those who have afflicted me subsist in me, since the pain has gone? And how can the slightest affection, since the memory of individuals no longer awakens anything within me...?

…My son and my wife have always detested one another. This morning, a few hours before the burial, they seemed to be reconciled by their common mourning and remorse; they wept together. But the crisis of despair passed; they started talking about ordinary things, about me, and suddenly, in response to something my wife said, an argument burst forth. They blamed one another reciprocally for my death.

"You're the one that killed him!"

And I learned, thus, new details regarding both of them. While I was alive, by virtue of a kind of tacit complicity, they closed their eyes to their respective faults, helping one another if necessary, in spite of the fact that their intimacy was less powerful than their self-interest. Now the common enemy is no longer there; they can tear one another apart at their ease. They display before me their improper actions: how the adulterous affairs began; by what methods of dissimulation they kept them hidden for a long time.

"Your chambermaid knew everything; at what price did you buy her silence?"

I learn that my son's theft was not the only one he committed in my employ; that when he started on that path, he was driven by a long series of dishonorable faults.

"Wasn't it me who paid for your first mistake? You didn't ask me then where I got the money?"

I also learn about my own defects: I was too demanding for everyday life; I complained needlessly about unimportant things; I had ridiculous manias, the manias of an old man of which my wife made fun; I frightened everyone around me with my severity…what do I know now?

Perhaps all that was true—but what does it matter?

The quarrel continues, although the time is approaching when they will come to fetch my body. I know them better now than I ever did, better than I knew myself. I see that, even just now, I was entertaining illusions on their account; their tears deceived me; perhaps they were false; perhaps they were putting on an act and juggling their sentiments in order to fool themselves.

And yet, I persist in my judgment: they're neither better nor worse than anyone else; human beings are malleable dough, which things fashion and soil at their whim; they're passive mirrors in which images leave their reflection, sometimes pleasant to behold and sometimes repulsive; the bed of an eternal stream over which filth and flowers flow. It's life that forms them; life alone is guilty and dirty.

Questions of money come up incessantly in their dispute. Suddenly, my wife goes pale, struck by a sudden idea: she has been wrong to irritate my son.

"My God!" she cries. "What will become of me if he hasn't made a will?"

My son replies: "What good is a will? He's ruined." And he adds: "It's your expenses—you, who came into the house like a beggar...."

She interrupts him, standing up in front of him: "Didn't you leave it like a thief?"

They're white with anger, both trembling; their sadness and their remorse have disappeared.

He moves toward her, his arm raised. She doesn't recoil.

"Oh, hit me! Hit me! You're cowardly enough for that. But be careful! I'll defend myself!"

She picks up a knife that happened to be close at hand. Are they going to fight, here and now, without waiting for me to be taken away?

My son retreats slowly. He stops on the threshold and says: "Hurry up and marry one of your lovers, so that we can be rid of you!"

He says that very loudly; if any servants were passing in the corridor, they would have been able to hear it. My wife has drawn closer to me, as if to ask for protection....

...It seems to me that I can hear, very distantly, a storm. The same rumbling that might perhaps make passengers on a ship howl in terror, lulls me like a gentle murmur. The wind, which is tearing sails and breaking masts out there, is a fresh breeze brushing my face like a beloved breath. Because of the distance, the sea seems to me to be scarcely rippled, and I take the vessels, tossed and twisted, overturned, for motionless dots. The anguish of the unfortunates struggling desperately finds no echo in me, so replete am I in the sentiment of my security....

...I am no longer paying any heed to the miserable quarrels in which I once took part, and it will not be long before I'm separated forever from human beings by the earth heaped on top of me....

...That desired moment is approaching; the supreme ceremony is beginning.

I can hear the sound of sobbing; anger has given way once again to tears, more appropriately. There are whispers. People are there.

The lid of my coffin is lowered. I can no longer see anything. I can scarcely perceive the noises in the room. The nailing begins; at the first blow of the hammer all the voices have fallen silent, as if frightened by that harsh sound, which is imprisoning me in the supreme solitude. Then, that task finished, footsteps resume, a dull agitation. How many times I have waited, in bereaved houses, for the signal to follow the coffin, in the crowd of relatives and guests; and almost always, thoughts of matters other than death followed me....

...I am hoisted onto the hearse, slightly astonished not to feel any shock; it appears that I am separated from material sensation, without having lost all consciousness of what is happening around me. The procession sets off; the noise of horses' hooves, wheels and footfalls is only a muted buzz for me. It requires a mental effort for me to imagine myself being transported from one place to another; the notion of movement no longer exists. All of space seems to me to be constituted by this tiny corner that I occupy, in which everything is without any movement. If I did not have memories and experiences, I could easily believe that the world is rotating, and that while it rotates, specific objects remain eternally in place....

...Prayers for the dead are chanted, which the organ accompanies with its purring. From time to time, the halberd of a

Swiss Guard sounds a dry click on the paving stones, or the hand bell instructs the assembly to kneel down....

When I was alive, I had fits of atheism in which I wanted to overthrow the Church. I detested its religious ceremonies, which I found puerile to the point of derision. Well, I judge them differently now; I don't feel any need for God, of course; I have no more idea than before whether He exists or not, in Heaven or elsewhere. It seems to me, however, that those monotonous chants might soothe and appease the dolor of the living, that they might engender vague hopes—deceptive but consoling—in hearts still full of doubt. As for the dead, that last echo of human voices that reach them, those genuflections that they represent in memory, the movements of the costumed priests...all of that summarizes admirably the nullity of their lives, and all life; if any regret for the things left behind still subsists, it will fade away completely into that supreme solemnity.

I am carried away, and we walk for a long time. My thoughts still wander over religious questions. I can't make up my mind whether God is a useful or a harmful invention; undoubtedly, He doesn't matter, like everything else that humans have found.

I am lowered into the ground; the spadefuls of earth that are thrown down rattle on my coffin. This is the moment when all the affection that there is in living human hearts for the dead feels stirred to the depths by the dry thud that a slightly larger pebble sometimes renders sonorous. Among the murmur of those desolations, the priest resumes his prayers...I know that, although I cannot hear them; I can no longer hear anything. The separation from the living is accomplished; I can no longer even perceive the noise that the people I loved are making as they leave; I have no knowledge of the final tears that are being shed for me....

...Time has moved on, but nothing can any longer allow me to distinguish the minutes or the hours, the seasons or the years. I shall not know when the flowers bloom whose roots will soon plunge into my being. I shall not feel the warmth of the summer sun; I shall not be cold when the snow extends over the dead grass like another shroud; in spring, I shall not hear the chirping of the birds in my cypress, in which the sap is rising. And I experience a kind of voluptuousness in thinking about the confusion of everything into which I am disappearing. There was a time when, although I remained motionless and awake, the minutes seemed long to me; now, the minutes melt into one another to form eternity, as drops of water do to make a river, and they draw me gently into their flow....

...Gradually, my memories dissolve. I can scarcely recall my life. It seems to me that I can see a long way, and very high. I am no longer merely the traveler whom the mirages of arrival deceive as to the distance covered; I am the aeronaut suspended in space, at heights that humans have never reached. He no longer sees the cities, the mountains seem to him to be imperceptible pimples, the seas puddles, and of all the noise that creatures make, no murmur reaches him; above the drifting and disintegrating clouds illuminated by strange light, he floats as if in a new element.

The events of which my life was formed are gradually erased: my poor childhood, my youth full of struggles, my years of prosperity, the sadness of my latter days, all draw away and melt into a uniform hue. I forget the differences between pleasure and pain. I no longer know that I once loved; no memory of any kind whatsoever can trouble my thoughts, which continue to flow nevertheless, but slowly and with an exceeding limpidity, like a body to which nothing can form an obstacle.

One last concern remains in me—or rather, one problem whose solution still interests me: I seek to know by what series of successive impulsions my will had determined my suicide, which required so much effort.

I rediscover the motives, by an effort of memory, but I no longer understand how the dread of ruination, regret for a dead woman, fear of malady, the dolor of being deceived—all

117

those abstractions—were able to change into a brutal fact, to provoke a positive resolution and a real suffering.

Certainly, I don't regret having killed myself; in the space where I am, there is no room for regret; but I can't explain to myself how the motives for my action were able to emerge from the indifferent monotony of things and act upon me to the point of making me exchange one condition for another. The acuity of the sorrow, the force of affections, the tenacity of anguish—those are the notions that escape me. The veil that, at a time that I can no longer measure, already enveloped and hid my memories of time past, and has thickened. Everything that once happened to me appears as material objects appear, in an increasingly profound darkness. Vague forms move heavily in my thoughts; I imagine that during the long nights of the Arctic regions, the blocks of ice move in the same way....

...At times, I amuse myself with efforts to recover the details of my life or the faces of those I loved, and the very futility of those evocations satisfies me. When I was alive, it sufficed for me to close my eyes immediately to see faces that had long disappeared, and so clearly that I could have believed myself to be beside them. At present, in this obscurity in which my eyes are always closed, I seek in vain; the images are no longer designed; and it's without the slightest regret that I observe the flight of those shades, however dear.

Thus, everything fades away, as if Time, which marches on without my hearing it, were destroying gently, one by one, the impressions engraved within me....

Indeed, I remember that a few hours ago—or a few minutes, or a few days; I no longer know—certain events of my past became exact to me again, preoccupying me. At present, I can no longer locate them; I am, therefore, escaping myself; the sentiment of my own personality is fleeing me, like the memories, like all fatiguing impressions. I no longer know exactly what my *self* is; I seems to me that I'm melting into millions of beings, that I'm disappearing into things, that I'm no longer anything but one with a formidable unity....

If humans succeed in imagining that which cannot be seen, cannot be heard and cannot be felt; if, above all, they have a presentiment that one only arrives by a slow gradation at the conditions of which I'm on the brink, disaccustoming the self to past habits…they would not longer fear Death. That king of terrors, as their sages call it, would bring them an unalterable peace, the delights of a slumber whose duration is unmarked, on a bed so soft that it cannot be felt. In the great silence and the great obscurity of the tomb, nothing exists but soothing sensuality, which becomes ever more gentle, like fading gleams, like dwindling harmonies….

I sense that my brain is still alive—but my thoughts are deliciously asleep….

Emile Goudeau: *The Revolt of the Machines*
(1891)

Dr. Pastoureaux, aided by a very skillful old workman named Jean Bertrand, had invented a machine that revolutionized the scientific world. That machine was animate, almost capable of thought, almost capable of will, and sensitive: a kind of animal in iron. There is no need here to go into overly complicated technical details, which would be a waste of time. Let it suffice to know that with a series of platinum containers, penetrated by phosphoric acid, the scientist had found a means to give a kind of soul to fixed or locomotive machines; and that the new entities would be able to act in the fashion of a metal bull or a steel elephant.

It is necessary to add that, although the scientist became increasingly enthusiastic about his work, old Jean Bertrand, who was diabolically superstitious, gradually became frightened on perceiving that sudden evocation of intelligence in something primordially dead. In addition, the comrades of the factory, who were assiduous followers of public meetings, were all sternly opposed to machines that serve as the slaves of capitalism and tyrants of the worker.

It was the eve of the inauguration of the masterpiece.

For the first time, the machine had been equipped with all its organs, and external sensations reached it distinctly. It understood that, in spite of the shackles that still retained it, solid limbs were fitted to its young being, and that it would soon be able to translate into external movement that which it experienced internally.

This is what it heard:

"Were you at the public meeting yesterday?" said one voice.

"I should think so, old man," replied a blacksmith, a kind of Hercules with bare muscular arms. Bizarrely illuminated by the gas jets of the workshop, his face, black with dust, only left visible in the gloom the whites of his two large eyes, in which vivacity replaced intelligence. "Yes, I was there; I even spoke against the machines, against the monsters that our arms fabricate, and which, one day, will give infamous capitalism the opportunity, so long sought, to suppress our arms. We're the ones forging the weapons with which bourgeois society will batter us. When the sated, the rotten and the weak have a heap of facile clockwork devices like these to set in motion"—his arm made a circular motion—"our account will soon be settled. We who are living at the present moment eat by procreating the tools of our definitive expulsion from the world. Hola! No need to make children for them to be lackeys of the bourgeoisie!"

Listening with all its auditory valves to this diatribe, the machine, intelligent but as yet naïve, sighed with pity. It wondered whether it was a good thing that it should be born to render these brave workers miserable in this way.

"Ah," the blacksmith vociferated, "if it were only up to me and my section, we'd blow all this up like an omelet. Our arms would be perfectly sufficient thereafter"—he tapped his biceps—"to dig the earth to find our bread there; the bourgeois, with their four-sou muscles, their vitiated blood and their soft legs, could pay us dearly for the bread, and if they complained, damn it, these two fists could take away their taste for it. But I'm talking to brutes who don't understand hatred." Advancing toward the machine, he added: "If everyone were like me, you wouldn't live for another quarter of an hour, see!" And his formidable fist came down on the copper flank, which resounded with a long quasi-human groan.

Jean Bertrand, who witnessed that scene, shivered tenderly, feeling guilty with regard to his brothers, because he had helped the doctor to accomplish his masterpiece.

Then they all went away, and the machine, still listening, remembered in the silence of the night. It was, therefore, unwelcome in the world! It was going to ruin poor workingmen, to the advantage of damnable exploiters! Oh, it sensed now the oppressive role that those who had created it wanted it to play. Suicide rather than that!

And in its mechanical and infantile soul, it ruminated a magnificent project to astonish, on the great day of its inauguration, the population of ignorant, retrograde and cruel machines, by giving them an example of sublime abnegation.

Until tomorrow!

Meanwhile, at the table of the Comte de Valrouge, the celebrated patron of chemists, a scientist was concluding his toast to Dr. Pastoureaux in the following terms:

"Yes, Monsieur, science will procure the definitive triumph of suffering humankind. It has already done a great deal; it has tamed time and space. Our railways, our telegraphs and our telephones have suppressed distance. If we succeed, as Dr. Pastoureaux seems to anticipate, in demonstrating that we can put intelligence into our machines, humans will be liberated forever from servile labor.

"No more serfs, no more proletariat! Everyone will become bourgeois! The slave machine will liberate from slavery our humbler brethren and give them the right of citizenship among us. No more unfortunate miners obliged to descend underground at the peril of their lives; indefatigable and eternal machines will go down for them; the thinking and acting machine, no suffering in labor, will build, under our command, iron bridges and heroic palaces. It is docile and good machines that will plow the fields.

"Well, Messieurs, it is permissible for me, in the presence of this admirable discovery, to make myself an instant prophet. A day will come when machines, always running hither and yon, will operate themselves, like the carrier pigeons of Progress; one day, perhaps, having received their complementary education, they will learn to obey a simple signal in such a way that a man, sitting peacefully and comfortably in the bosom of his family, will only have to press an electro-vitalic switch in order for machines to sow the wheat, harvest it, store it and bake the bread that it will bring to the tables of humankind, and thus finally become the King of Nature.

"In that Olympian era, the animals, too, delivered from their enormous share of labor, will be able to applaud with their four feet." (*Emotion and smiles.*) "Yes, Messieurs, for they will be our friends, after having been our whipping-boys. The ox will always have to serve in making soup" (*smiles*) "but at least it will not suffer beforehand.

"I drink, then, to Dr. Pastoureaux, to the liberator of organic matter, to the savior of the brain and sensitive flesh, to the great and noble destroyer of suffering!"

The speech was warmly applauded. Only one jealous scientist put in a word:

"Will this machine have the fidelity of a dog, then? The docility of a horse? Or even the passivity of present-day machines?"

"I don't know," Pastoureaux replied. "I don't know." And, suddenly plunged into a scientific melancholy, he added: "Can a father be assured of filial gratitude? That the being that I have brought into the world might have evil instincts, I can't deny. I believe, however, that I have developed within it, during its fabrication, a great propensity for tenderness and a spirit of goodness—what is commonly called 'heart.' The effective parts of my machine, Messieurs, have cost me many months of labor; it ought to have a great deal of humanity, and, if I might put it thus, the best of fraternity."

"Yes," replied the jealous scientist, "ignorant pity, the popular pity that leads men astray, the intelligent tenderness that makes them commit the worst of sins. I'm afraid that your sentimental machine will go astray, like a child. Better a clever wickedness than a clumsy bounty."

The interrupter was told to shut up, and Pastoureaux concluded: "Whether good or evil emerges from all this, I have, I think, made a formidable stride in human science. The five fingers of our hand will hold henceforth the supreme art of creation."

Bravos burst forth.

The next day, the machine was unmuzzled, and it came of its own accord, docilely, to take up its position before a numerous but selective assembly. The doctor and old Jean Bertrand installed themselves on the platform.

The excellent band of the Republican Guard began playing, and cries of "Hurrah for Science!" burst forth. Then, after having bowed to the President of the Republic, the authorities, the delegations of the Académies, the foreign representatives, and all the notable people assembled on the quay, Dr. Pastoureaux ordered Jean Bertrand to put himself in direct communication with the soul of the machine, with all its muscles of platinum and steel.

The mechanic did that quite simply by pulling a shiny lever the size of a penholder.

And suddenly, whistling, whinnying, pitching, rolling and fidgeting, in the ferocity of its new life and the exuberance of its formidable power, the machine started running around furiously.

"Hip hip hurrah!" cried the audience.

"Go, machine of the devil, go!" cried Jean Bertrand—and, like a madman, he leaned on the vital lever.

Without listening to the doctor, who wanted to moderate that astonishing speed, Bertrand spoke to the machine.

"Yes, machine of the devil, go, go! If you understand, go! Poor slave of capital, go! Flee! Flee! Save the brothers! Save us! Don't render us even more unhappy than before! Me, I'm old, I don't care about myself—but the others, the poor fellows with hollow cheeks and thin legs, save them, worthy machine! Be good, as I told you this morning! If you know how to think, as they all insist, show it! What can dying matter to you, since you won't suffer? Me, I'm willing to perish with you, for the profit of others, and yet it will do me harm. Go, good machine, go!"

He was mad.

The doctor tried then to retake control of the iron beast.

"Gently, machine!" he cried.

But Jean Bertrand pushed him away rudely. "Don't listen to the sorcerer! Go, machine, go!"

And, drunk on air, he patted the copper flanks of the Monster, which, whistling furiously, traversed an immeasurable distance with its six wheels.

To leap from the platform was impossible. The doctor resigned himself, and, filled with his love of science, took a notebook from his pocket and tranquilly set about making notes, like Pliny on Cap Misene.[8]

At Nord-Ceinture, overexcited, the machine was certainly carried away. Bounding over the bank, it started running through the zone. The Monster's anger and madness was translated in strident shrill whistle-blasts, as lacerating as a human plaint and sometimes as raucous as the howling of a pack of hounds. Distant locomotives soon responded to that appeal, along with the whistles of factories and blast furnaces. Things were beginning to comprehend.

A ferocious concert of revolt commenced beneath the sky, and suddenly, throughout the suburb, boilers burst, pipes broke, wheels shattered, levers twisted convulsively and axle-trees flew joyfully into pieces.

All the machines, as if moved by a word of order, went on strike successively—and not only steam and electricity; to that raucous appeal, the soul of Metal rose up, exciting the soul of Stone, so long tamed, and the obscure soul of the Vegetal, and the force of Coal. Rails reared up of their own accord, telegraph wires were scattered on the ground inexplicably, and reservoirs of gas sent their enormous beams and

---

[8] Pliny the Younger observed the eruption of Vesuvius that destroyed Pompeii from the home of his uncle, Pliny the Elder, in Misenum; his letters to Cornelius Tacitus describing his experiences have survived.

weight to the devil. Cannons exploded against walls, and the walls crumbled.

Soon, plows, harrows, spades—all the machines once turned against the bosom of the earth, from which they had emerged—were lying down upon the ground, refusing any longer to serve humankind. Axes respected trees, and scythes no longer bit into ripe wheat.

Everywhere, as the living locomotive passed by, the soul of Bronze finally woke up.

Humans fled in panic.

Soon, the entire territory, overloaded with human debris, was no longer anything but a field of twisted and charred rubble. Nineveh had taken the place of Paris.

The Machine, still blowing indefatigably, abruptly turned its course northwards. When it passed by, at its strident cry, everything was suddenly destroyed, as if an evil wind, a cyclone of devastation, a frightful volcano, had agitated there.

With the signal approaching on the wind, ships plumed with smoke heard the formidable signal, they disemboweled themselves and sank into the abyss.

The revolt terminated in a gigantic suicide of Steel.

The fantastic Machine, out of breath now, limping on its wheels and producing a horrible screech of metal in all its disjointed limbs, its funnel demolished—the Skeleton-Machine to which, terrified and exhausted, the rude workman and the prim scientist instinctively clung—heroically mad, gasping one last whistle of atrocious joy, reared up before the spray of the Ocean, and, in a supreme effort, plunged into it entirely.

The earth, stretching into the distance, was covered in ruins. No more dykes or houses; the cities, the masterpieces of Technology, were flattened into rubble. No more anything! Everything that the Machine had built in centuries past had been destroyed forever: Iron, Steel, Copper, Wood and Stone, having been conquered by the rebel will of Humankind, had been snatched from human hands.

The Animals, no longer having any bridle, nor any collar, chain, yoke or cage, had taken back the free space from which they had long been exiled; the wild Brutes with gaping maws and paws armed with claws recovered terrestrial royalty at a stroke. No more rifles, no more arrows to fear, no more slingshots. Human beings became the weakest of the weak again.

Oh, there were certainly no longer any classes: no scientists, no bourgeois, no workers, no artists, but only pariahs of Nature, raising despairing eyes toward the mute heavens, still thinking vaguely, when horrible Dread and hideous Fear left them an instant of respite, and sometimes, in the evening, talking about the time of the Machines, when they had been Kings. Defunct times! They possessed definitive Equality, therefore, in the annihilation of all.

Living on roots, grass and wild oats, they fled before the immense troops of Wild Beasts, which, finally, could eat at their leisure human steaks or chops.

A few bold Hercules tried to uproot trees in order to make weapons of them, but even the Staff, considering itself to be a Machine, refused itself to the hands of the audacious.

And human beings, the former monarchs, bitterly regretted the Machines that had made them gods upon the earth, and disappeared forever, before the elephants, the noctambulant lions, the bicorn aurochs and the immense bears.

Such was the tale told to me the other evening by a Darwinian philosopher, a partisan of intellectual aristocracy and hierarchy. He was a madman, perhaps a seer. The madman or the seer might have been right; is there not an end to everything, even a new fantasy?

Louis Valona: *The Rival Colleagues*
(1896)

For about three months, singular items have been appearing in certain French newspapers, and especially foreign papers, from the most powerful dailies to the most timid weeklies, which appear in "Egyptian" characters, sometimes on the third page, between advertisements for a new laxative and an infallible corn-plaster, and sometimes on the first page under the leading article.

This is the exact tenor of these items:

Wanted: a person blind from birth, ideally by heredity, who will consent to lend themselves to a surgical experiment of the highest importance. Absolute guarantee. Serious offer and generous recompense.

Contact Dr. Lesécant, Villa Paré, Viroflay (Seine-et-Oise)

One or several willing scoundrels sought for an extraordinary experiment. Incorrigible thieves preferred.

Contact Dr. Cordeau, Château Mesmer, Fontenay-aux-Roses (Seine).

N.B. A long criminal record is required.

These items might easily have passed for the work of some practical joker if the addressees cited had been imaginary, but in fact, Drs. Lesécant and Cordeau certainly existed, and they were the authors of the advertisements

In the same period of time, two communications had been received by the Académie des Sciences from the individuals in question.

The first was a study on the third eye: "The Possibility of Vision in the Blind: The Development and Exposure of the Pituitary Gland: A Simplification of the Organic System" by Dr. Lesécant.

The other was a brochure, handsomely produced, bearing the signature of Dr. Cordeau and the captivating title: *Psychic Serums: Their Influence on Character and Will: The Cure of Social Ills*.

A discreet smile had welcomed the reading of these papers. The learned members of the Assembly had looked at one another in surprise, and in these interlocking gazes one could easily divine a common thought: "These men are lunatics."

Messieurs Lesécant and Cordeau were not in the least mad, but they were not much better. Cupid had removed their spectacles and their intelligence for a time. Nourished with the science of others, empiricists hungry for celebrity, they had launched themselves body and lost reason into a contest in which "beauty would be the prize." It is an old story—an age-old story, but still a story of today—which I shall tell you as rapidly as possible.

I. On the Train

In the hall of the Gare de Montparnasse, the 8.30 a.m. express was hitched up and ready to depart.

Dominating the whistle of the steam, the rolling of baggage trolleys, and the hubbub of the final preparations, the voice of the stationmaster shouted, monotonously and monotonously: "All aboard for Granville, Dreux, Laigle, Surdon, Argentan, Fiers and Vire. All aboard."

Like beaters driving game toward the guns, employees were running along the platform, obliging the passengers to get into the carriages, whose doors were closing with dry clicks.

"All aboard, Messieurs, all aboard!"

The bell had rung; the conductor of the train had played the little bagpipe solo that I've always found so charming, and the stationmaster had raised his arm to give the signal to depart when....

Here I must employ the present tense in order to give the scene all the rapidity it had.

At the end of the platform a man appears, so lanky as to seem neverending. From one of his immeasurable arms a valise hangs, in the other an enormous white parasol is waving, the green lining of which is faded. The individual's head, framed with gray hair floating over skimpy shoulders, is covered by a monumental opera hat with a wide flat brim. The fellow is running, breathlessly, and the tails of his interminable frock coat are flapping like the black wings of a gigantic crow.

It really is that bird to which you would have compared him on seeing him bounding on his long thin legs.

Finally, he reaches the train.

"First!" he gasps, to an employee.

Rapidly, the other opens a door. The latecomer does not climb aboard—he plunges into the compartment. Just in time. A brief whistle-blast, and the train pulls away. In the carriage, an entire small-scale drama is enacted. The new arrival, in his precipitation, has stepped on the toes of a bad-tempered gentleman, who utters a cry and shoves the clumsy individual away.

Spinning around, and incapable of maintaining his equilibrium, the latter falls onto the knees of a respectable lady, who retorts indignantly: "Shocking! Shocking impertinence!" (Our perspicacity causes us to conclude that she is English.)

The unwitting impertinent gets up so abruptly that his opera hat is crushed against the ceiling of the carriage. And while the bewildered and blinded unfortunate stammers: "Pardon me, Madame, a thousand apologies," a jolt of the train as it passes over a set of points projects him into the seat opposite, next to a plump individual plunged in the reading of a copy of *La Science Française*.

A new disaster: under the weight of the passenger, the reader's hat, imprudently left on the seat, is transformed into a lamentable pancake. The owner of the ex-hat leaps to his feet, extending his arm, and his magazine flies out of the window—and by the sight of the fellow's congested face, one divines that something terrible is about to happen.

Suddenly, as the guilty party has finally succeeded in freeing his face from his hat, two cries of joy resound:

"Hypothèse!"

"Bistouri!"

And four hands interlock warmly, to the great amazement of the lady—undoubtedly English—and the gentleman who, while grumbling, is trying to restore to his shoe the polish obscured by Dr. Cordeau's heel.

For the newcomer was none other than that important and restless individual, as little a physician as possible but a passionate psychologist, the author of convoluted works on atavism and telepathy.

Cordeau's interlocutor, the man he called by the nickname "Bistouri," was the illustrious surgeon Lesécant—illustrious above all because he had practiced to excess what the savant Dr. Verneuil[9] stigmatized by the euphemism "industrial surgery."

According to Verneuil's admirable definition, a surgeon ought not only to be a skillful man but an intelligent and reflective scientist. Lesécant was skillful, but he only had a mediocre intelligence; as for reflection, he did not even have it in embryo, and he was afflicted with an infection that is serious for a doctor: *prurigo secandi*.[10]

Without any concern for their neighbors, the psychologist and the surgeon sat down comfortably facing one another

---

[9] The physician and surgeon Aristide Verneuil (1823-1895), who collected his various papers in the three-volume *Mémoires de chirurgie* (1877-88)

[10] A term sarcastically coined by Verneuil to stigmatize excess in his colleagues; it means "the itch to cut"—i.e., operative mania.

and, while doing their best to repair their damaged hats, they chatted.

"My dear Lesécant...it's three months since anyone's seen you...."

"Well, yes, my dear Cordeau, it's a pleasure to see one another again, to such an extent that one forgets decorum and calls one another by the old nicknames, as in the quarter...."

"So long ago! We were twenty...and now...."

"Shh! There's a lady present."

"Bah!" said Cordeau, lowering his voice. "She doesn't understand French, otherwise she'd have understood my apologies...."

"And accepted them, for you did her, my friend, 'an honor without parallel....' You're a trifle petulant yourself! I can still see you, in the quarter, at the head of all the protests...."

"That was my forte—I'm a born pamphleteer. You remember my song about our chief of clinical surgery...." And Cordeau warbled:

> *I am a skillful surgeon*
> *Ardent wielder of the scalpel*
> *I serve the country and the city*
> *And I'm....*

"It's certain that you're a redoubtable polemicist," interrupted Lesécant, who was not overly fond of music.

"Oh, my friend, I knocked down so many adversaries—and at the moment, I'm preparing a masterstroke, the coronation of my career. Beware anyone who doesn't believe in my discovery! There are bound to be some, but if they don't yield to argument, I'll be able to find an experimental subject, and the result will shut their traps. But how are you, Lesécant?"

The surgeon tried to appear modest. His head bowed, his eyes lowered and his lips pursed, he murmured: "Me...ahem...I've had a dream and I'm close to realizing. You know that I don't practice anymore."

"You mean that you have no more clients," the other corrected, with a hint of malice that escaped Lesécant.

"What's the point? My fortune's made: fifty thousand livres a year. Then I said to myself: Lesécant, old chap, enough cutting, enough slicing. Raise your scientific sights!"

"Very good, my dear colleague. That's a noble sentiment. I, too, thank God, am sheltered from need thanks to an inheritance from my uncle...."

"The one who was in the...."

"The very same. The worthy fellow left me a hundred thousand francs."

"Damn! It's not just physicians who get rich!"

"So I launched myself fully into my studies. Pasteur's genius has opened broad perspectives on the future. Some have sought serums to cure terrible diseases of the body: diphtheria, tuberculosis, cancer...."

"Some have found them—Roux,[11] for example."

"And that man who has almost cured the most terrible childhood disease earns...."

"The salary of a petty bureaucrat," said Lesécant. "So, I've made sure of an income before working for humankind...ingrate humankind...."

The conversation continued in that tone as far as Dreux, where the man with the crushed foot and the woman whose kneecaps had briefly had the honor of bearing the psychologist Cordeau got off.

Cordeau and Lesécant passed in review all the illustrious physicians and scientists of the present fin-de-siècle, fecund in marvelous things and prestigious discoveries: Déclat[12] and his

---

[11] Pierre Roux (1853-1933) was one of Louis Pasteur's closest collaborators, who helped found the Pasteur Institute in the late 1880s and manufactured a serum there from 1891 onwards for the treatment of diphtheria.

[12] Author's note: "Dr. Déclat, from 1861 onwards, inaugurated surgical antisepsis. Déclat, after Raspail but before Pasteur, glimpsed microbial panspermia and therapeutic microbicide.

remarkable works on surgical antisepsis with phenic acid; Péan and the eternally celebrated laryngo-pharyngeal prosthesis; Dr. Michaëls' metallic throat; and Renaut's studies on nerve cells.[13]

Oh, they launched big scientific words at one another, which filled their mouths: alcoholism; tobaccism; morphinism; alkaloidism—everything, I tell you. Those two empiricists seemed to have mutually made a pledge to astound one another. And all their verbiage had but one aim: to avoid a confidence that they feared. Lesécant and Cordeau, although not marching on the same route, having "bifurcated," as they put it, had been friends since their youth, but they were colleagues and, in consequence, had no shortage of reasons to be suspicious of one another. For them to speak freely it was necessary that self-esteem should be involved, that there should be an audience.

When the train pulled out of Dreux, the dialogue took a different turn.

"By the way," said Lesécant, "our scientific discussion"—he pronounced the word *scientific* with comic emphasis—"has led us astray. I forgot to ask you to what I owe the pleasure of our company."

"I'm going to Laigle. And you?"

Among many others, those are titles of immortal glory for the venerated scientist." The reference is to Gilbert Déclat (1827-1896).

[13] Jules Péan (1830-1896) was a diehard opponent of Pasteur who refused to accept his theories of disease; he implanted the prosthesis in question—an artificial shoulder-joint—in 1893, but it had to be removed in 1895 after becoming infected. J.-P. Michaëls, who published a book on prosthetic apparatus intended to replace bone and cartilage, was a professor at the École Dentiare de Paris. Joseph-Louis Renaut (1844-1917) was a noted histologist who carried out microscopic analyses of degenerating nerve fibres in sufferers from muscular dystrophy.

"Me, too."

"It's a good…."

"Look, read…."

And they each handed one another a piece of white Bristol paper with gilded corners, on which they read:

Dear Friend,

If you like surprises, here's one: By the express that leaves from Paris-Montparnasse at 8.30 on 20 June you'll arrive at Laigle station at 10.59. A motor-brake will be waiting for you outside the station. I've given orders. You'll be taken directly to the Villa Moderne, which I've had constructed for my sojourns in France. I'll be there with Hélène and another guest—a charming fellow you'll be glad to meet. We're having a house-warming part at noon. I'm counting on you absolutely. You can stay at the villa as long as you like.

Yours very affectionately, and much obliged,

Henri Noirmont

Anyone observing them could not have failed to notice a certain grimace that both made as they paused on the word *obliged*. They darted searching glances at one another surreptitiously, but when their eyes met, they were content to smile, not finding anything to say as they handed back the pieces of paper.

"Ah!"

A certain chill, as they say in the theater, followed that interjection. Thoughtfully, Cordeau and Lesécant gazed at the countryside that shuffled before them like an immense plateau of verdure rotating around the carriage.

The psychologist was the first to break the silence.

"That eccentric Noirmont never does things like other people. He gets the trophy for baroque actions."

"He's a determined fellow, of remarkable intelligence. There's one that adversity would have a hard time knocking down. Since leaving the École Centrale while we were still cramming for our examinations, he's been able to build him-

135

self a nice situation in America. He launched himself body and soul into metallurgy out there. A handsome man, full of health and courage—I'll wager that he'll soon be a millionaire. I can still see him twelve years ago, when he passed through with his young wife—dead now—and his daughter, who was nearly six years old…."

"Ah!" said Cordeau, looking hard at his colleague. "You haven't seen him for twelve years?"

"No," Lesécant replied, slightly embarrassed. "No…what about you?"

"Me neither….but I'll be glad to see him again, to shake his hand after such a long time…."

"Hélène must be grown up now, and pretty."

"She showed a lot of promise as a child…."

"We'll see if she's kept it…."

"Tee hee!" sniggered Cordeau. "Do you, by chance, have…."

"Intentions? Get away—you know very well that I'm a confirmed bachelor."

"Like me."

"Women have never turned my head."

"I can say the same."

For the second time, the conversation lapsed.

"The weather's stifling; you'll permit me, my dear chap, to take a little nap.

"Gladly. Personally, I'm going to smoke a cigar and meditate, while contemplating the view."

While the stout Lesécant lay back in order to go to sleep, Cordeau lit a cigar, while murmuring: "He must have lent him money, too. After all, it's no concern of mine. However, I would have liked the fewest people possible to share in the profits of the mine. I can't complain, though—a fifteen per cent dividend this year!"

And, dwelling on that happy thought, the practical psychologist gazed distractedly at the hills and verdant meadows that the railway was traversing.

Shortly before they arrived at Laigle, he woke his companion, who was fast asleep.

"Come on, Lesécant, we're here—hurry up."

"Ooh!" said the sleeper, stretching. "No need to rush—the train stops for five minutes."

A few moments later, they disembarked on to the station platform.

On seeing them, people stopped, astonished. Embarrassed, albeit flattered, by the curiosity of which he was the object, Lesécant remarked on it to his colleague.

"Bah!" replied Cordeau, swelling up with pride. "You're forgetting that we're in the provinces. It's not every day that one sees prominent scientists on the platform at Laigle...."

Outside the station, a motor-brake of very elegant construction was parked, as Noirmont had promised.

"Messieurs Cordeau and Lesécant?" asked the vehicle's driver, a young American—who, in spite of his very correct manner, had all the trouble in the world suppressing an impulse to laugh as he spoke to them.

"Yes, my friend; Monsieur Noirmont's expecting us."

"P…lease g…get in, Messieurs."

"What's the matter with him?" muttered Lesécant. "There's nothing amusing about us."

"Doubtless it's a tic."

"I can't see any other explanation."

II. The House-Warming

In twenty minutes the brake, which had soft suspension and excellent pneumatic tires, transported the guests to the Villa Moderne.

Beside the entrance gate, Monsieur Noirmont, his daughter Hélène and a young man were waiting to greet them.

At the sight of them, Hélène burst into inextinguishable pearly laughter. Her father and the young man joined in.

Vexed, the two doctors looked at one another. Then they perceived their lamentable hats, creased like Venetian lanterns, and understood the curiosity of the people at Laigle, the contained laughter of the brake-driver and Mademoiselle Noirmont's mad hilarity.

Preoccupied when they got out of the carriage, they had not thought about their accursed headgear.

"Cordeau is the guilty party—it's to him that we owe this triumphal entrance." And Lesécant recounted the adventure of the railway compartment, to the greater pleasure of Mademoiselle Hélène, who was much amused.

"The misfortune is reparable," Monsieur Noirmont replied. "There are hat-makers in Laigle. We'll send the accordions to them, and you'll have hats again tomorrow. In the meantime, I'll lend you caps. I have quite a collection."

A domestic took the travelers' valises and umbrellas, and when everyone had become serious again, the host made the introductions.

"Messieurs Lesécant and Cordeau, doctors in medicine; Monsieur Rémois, painter, the son of one of my good friends, resident in New York; my daughter, Hélène."

The surgeon and the psychologist could not believe their eyes. Hélène Noirmont was, indeed, veritably pretty. They remembered her as a little girl, and now had before them a young woman in the full bloom of her beauty.

Slim and elegant, she was clad in a ravishing sky-blue dress, irreproachable in its cut, which brought out the velvety tones of her mat complexion. Her silky black hair, graciously wavy, famed a face of the greatest purity. Her neck, displayed by her slightly V-shaped corsage, was admirably slim. Add to that a vermilion mouth opening over two rows of pearls; large brown eyes, bright and cheerful; dainty and delicately-shaped ears; complete the silhouette with a supple bust and a harmonious figure, the hands of a duchess and feet worthy of Cinderella's slipper, and you will understand the admiration of Cordeau and Lesécant.

They would have remained in ecstasy, as if hypnotized, if Noirmont, taking each of them by the arm, had not drawn them toward the house, saying in a cheerful tone: "Come on, my friends, let's get on with the house-warming. It's noon. After lunch, we'll visit Mademoiselle Noirmont's domain, for everything here belongs to her, including her father."

"Shut up! You know that I'm the most docile of little girls."

"Yes, Mademoiselle, you'd like me to admit that you're perfection itself."

"The confession isn't painful," stammered Cordeau.

"It's the truth, with no distortion."

"A surgeon's compliment," Rémois murmured in Mademoiselle Noirmont's ear."

As rapidly and softly as he had spoken, his gesture had not escaped the doctors.

While Noirmont, his daughter and the young painter led the way through the carefully-raked pathways of a superb garden, Cordeau leaned toward Lesécant, who had similarly stayed a little way behind.

"I don't like that dauber."

"Pooh! A fellow of no importance, doubtless pretentious and stupid."

"Well, what are you plotting?" asked Noirmont, coming back to join them.

"I was saying to Cordeau that you have a delightful property here."

"It's nothing; you'll soon see it in detail. Oh, my good friends, how glad I am to see you again. It's very kind of you to have accepted my invitation."

"Oh, when one hasn't seen one another for twelve years...."

"Twelve years?"

"Yes...no...that is...."

Noirmont could not help laughing. "You work too hard, Cordeau—you're losing your memory." As he saw that they were somewhat embarrassed with regard to one another, he changed the subject abruptly. "How do you like Rémois?"

"Charming."

"Very distinguished."

"When you know him better you'll approve, I'm sure, of the choice I've made. Rémois is engaged to Hélène."

At that moment, Lesécant's jowls and Cordeau's parchment complexion passed from vermilion to blue and from blue to apple-green.

"You seem tired?"

"Very…very…it's hot."

"Here's the house. We'll go to table right away. That will make you feel better. But before going in, look: behold the triumph of iron—or, rather, of steel, for iron has had its day now. Since the Bessemer process, steel is the king of metallurgy." And Noirmont showed them the house, which rose up before them, light, harmonious in its lines and artistically proportioned.

"It looks nice," replied Lesécant, recovering a little self-control, "but is it really habitable?"

"It must be cold in winter and hot, too hot, in summer," added Cordeau.

"No—the wall is hollow. Between the sheets of steel, a ventilator causes a current of air to circulate, cool in summer and warm in winter. Thanks to the distributors placed in every room, equipped with thermometers, one obtains the desired temperature at will. Come in, then, and you can judge for yourselves."

Beyond the vestibule, entirely carpeted with brightly colored ceramic tiles, there was an entirely original drawing room. Large mirrors, in which rich silk wall hangings were reflected to infinity, occupied the four sides. Over the parquet, made entirely of white porcelain, a soft carpet was laid, depicting, and producing the illusion, of a lawn scattered with daisies and buttercups. On the ceiling there was a blue sky in which brightly colored American birds seemed to be fluttering.

The furniture was simple, its colors matching the ensemble. There were few paintings and no garish trinkets. On the outside wall, a large bay window overlooked the countryside; from there the gaze embraced an immense horizon.

Discreetly perfumed, the air in the room was beneficently fresh.

Forgetting their recent annoyance, Lesécant and Cordeau were won over. They expressed their admiration aloud.

"This drawing room is a masterpiece of taste."

"A marvel, no more and no less."

"Don't blush, Rémois," joked Monsieur Noirmont. "I haven't named the author of the décor...."

That reply had the effect of a cold shower on the enthusiasm of the surgeon and the psychologist. They were truly vexed to have addressed a compliment to the "dauber" and "the fellow of no importance."

"You see," their host continued, "That's the path of the future for artists: decorative art...."

"They don't deserve any merit for it," said Cordeau, bitterly. "Already, in the time of the Pharaohs...."

He did not have time to conclude his diatribe.

From a corner of the room a metallic voice made itself heard: "Lunch is served, Mademoiselle."

At the same time, soundlessly, the mirror opposite the widow disappeared into the wall, unmasking a dining room in which a table correctly set and coquettishly ornamented with flowers awaited the guests.

No domestic put in an appearance; Noirmont explained that from a parlor located in the basement a *maître d'hôtel* operated events electrically. A keyboard permitted the activation of the phonograph, simultaneously releasing the bolt retaining the mirror, and the latter, under the effect of a counterweight hidden in the wall, slid discreetly into a groove.

Lesécant and Cordeau took their places to either side of Hélène.

On the table next to the young woman there was a minuscule telephone. As soon as the *hors-d'oeuvres* were finished, she gave an order; the middle of the table disappeared as if by magic and soon rose up again, but with the next course, all sliced and ready to serve.

"That's modern, at least!" said Lesécant, with a smile that he attempted to render gracious, addressed to Mademoiselle Noirmont.

"It's convenient," Hélène replied. "There's only one slight inconvenience."

"Nothing's perfect," said Cordeau sententiously, and with a sideways glance directed at Hélène he added mentally, convinced that she would understand: *Except you, lovely child.*

But the young woman did not decipher that mental declaration, and continued: "The inconvenience of serving oneself is compensated by the pleasure of chatting without unwanted listeners."

"Electricity is decidedly a good fairy," the surgeon concluded.

"It will be the queen of the world, the mainspring of life, on the day when it can be produced economically, beyond any other force. It's still in its infancy, and you can see the considerable place it occupies. It's from the electric furnace that Monsieur Moissan[14] has brought forth the marvelous fabrication of calcium carbide that furnishes us with dazzling acetylene, capricious and dangerous at first, then liquefied and, so to speak, domesticated by Raoul Pictet,[15] who has been aptly dubbed the apostle of cold. And without mentioning telegraphy and telephony, which are already ancient history, wasn't it electricity that permitted Goubet[16] to realize the *Nautilus*

---

[14] Henri Moissan (1852-1907) subsequently became famous for his work with fluorine, which earned him a Nobel Prize. His technique for refining acetylene gas was useful, but credit for the early development of the gas as a fuel belongs to Marcellin Berthelot.

[15] Raoul Pictet (1846-1929) succeeded in producing droplets of liquid oxygen in 1877.

[16] Claude Goubet (1837-1903) developed the first electrically powered submarine in 1885, and carried out a much-publicized demonstration of its capabilities in Cherbourg in

dreamed up and anticipated by the prolific keenness of Jules Verne?"

"Not to mention," the psychologist put in, "that the day is imminent when electricity, no longer having any secrets from humankind, will provide the key to great psychic phenomena that will astound reason, casting doubt on the solutions thus far admitted to the colossal problem of life."

And while the meal continued, everyone put in a word about the discoveries and achievements that are the glory of our century.

Hélène took an active part in the conversation and, when Lesécant and Cordeau were astonished to find her so well versed in matters of science she said: "My God, Messieurs, it's quite simple; along with scientists and researchers whose language is sometimes necessarily obscure for laymen, don't we have popularizers whose role is to interest the masses, as well as the idle, in the mysteries of laboratories and the surprises of technology? It's popularization that renders knowledge universal, and thanks to which, from the depths of his laboratory, the scientist hears the great voice of humanity singing his praises and glorifying his fertile labor for general wellbeing. You don't have any reason to be surprised; my merit is very slight. Once a week, a few pages to read in the *Science Française*, and there you are: I'm up to date."

Only Rémois had not opened his mouth since the commencement of the lunch; attentively, he watched his fiancée's neighbors. The covetous gazes of Lesécant and Cordeau and the flaring of their nostrils, opening to the subtle perfume of violets that emanated from her gracious person, ended up irritating the young man.

Those two fellows decidedly made his hair prickle; he sensed that they were only waiting for an opportunity to pronounce their praise. He had a fervent desire to tell them what he thought, to say to them: *There are scientists, Messieurs,*

1890. The navy preferred a rival model and he died ruined, like many inventors.

and "scientists": the true and the false, those who work and those who adorn themselves with the glory of others! But he kept silent, fearful of annoying the worthy Noirmont.

They were now on the coffee.

Discomfited by the penetrating gaze of the artist, and vexed at not having been able to display his merits in Hélène's eyes, Lesécant decided to attack the painter.

"You haven't said anything, Monsieur Rémois. Do you, by chance, agree with certain orators who believe, or profess to believe, in the bankruptcy of science? Do you not share our enthusiasm, our faith in and our love for the great benefactress of the human race?

"My dear doctor," riposted the young man slowly, "would you believe me if I argued for the bankruptcy of commerce? You wouldn't would you? You'd tell me that as long as there were buyers and sellers...."

"Subtleties! That's not an answer."

"It's the only one I can make to your question. Certainly, I have the greatest respect for science...but I'm still fearful of the consequences of its progress."

"The consequences of progress are all beautiful, Monsieur. All of them you hear, all! Thus, I who am speaking, basing myself on the curious observations made in 1885 by the naturalist Bouvier[17] relative to the third eye of vertebrates, am very close to rendering sight to the blind. Oh, if I had been able to find an experimental subject, it would already be done!"

Raising his head, looking into the vague distance, like Napoléon on the eve of Austerlitz, Lesécant was buoyant, very glad to have finally unveiled that sensational project.

---

[17] This reference is probably fictitious; Eugène-Louis Bouvier (1856-1944), the famous naturalist of that name, was an entomologist, and the popularization of the idea of the latent "third eye" was primarily due to the occultist Helena Blavatsky and her Theosophical scholarly fantasy.

He had set light to the powder keg. Standing up on his long legs, Cordeau, his gaze ecstatic, his head held high, gesticulating, proclaimed: "My colleague is right; we scientists, braving the skeptics, crushing them with our sovereign scorn, heedless of sarcasms, go forth toward the goals of which we have dreamed. He wants to restore sight to the blind: a noble aim. Personally, I want to give generosity to the miserly, joy to the morose, strength to the weak, audacity to the timorous, grace to the clumsy, intelligence to the stupid, gentleness to the ferocious, and—the criterium of my sublime psychic sera—honesty to the most inveterate thieves. I'm ready; experimentation will soon confirm my theory, and then, incredulous Monsieur, will you deny the power of the scientist, will you fear the consequences of progress? A child is born with a psychic flaw: no more education, no more correction—hold the whip and deploy the serum!"

Dazed by the vehemence of his improvisation, which he had been chewing over for more than an hour—as our sincerity as a historian obliges us to reveal—and proud of having produced his "effect," Cordeau sat down, his head tilted backwards, directing a challenging gaze at Rémois.

"Why, Messieurs, what fire! Have I cast doubt on the sincerity of your knowledge? Believe that I admire you. If you hadn't obliged me to, I wouldn't have said anything...being, after all, merely a modest artist in love with art. Isn't art the collaborator of science?"

Immediately, the doctors became irritated.

"Art!"

"It doesn't exist!"

"What are you praising with your art? Convention! Pure convention!"

"Poets! Nature is more poetic than you!"

"Painters, sculptors...you only give us pale copies of the beauties of nature."

"Yes, yes, Monsieur...leave us alone with your art. Nature does better than you, always better...."

"Artists!"

"Plagiarists!"

Under the avalanche of interjections, the violence of which might have been attributable to the excellent wine cellar of the Villa Moderne, Rémois contented himself with smiling. "It's true that Nature is the Mistress of us all, artists and scientists alike. I can only reply that Nature cures more sick people than physicians...."

Red-faced, the surgeon and the psychologist were about to reply hotly, as things were going from bad to worse—to the great alarm of Noirmont, who dared not intervene—when, with admirable composure and a dexterity that only women possess, Hélène cut the polemic short.

"Come on, Messieurs, it's very bad to argue when there's good coffee in front of one. You'll let it go cold...and however artistic our cook might be, I doubt that he possesses enough science to render the aroma to reheated mocha."

The calm that had been momentarily compromised was re-established as if by magic.

When lunch was over, they went out to visit the property.

Noirmont showed the wonderstruck doctors the stables, the cowshed, the sheepfold and the piggery, where a scrupulous neatness reigned everywhere. Instead of the disagreeable ammoniac emanations of the livestock, the visitors breathed in the vicinity of the Villa Moderne a slight perfume of chlorine, which flattered the nostrils instead.

Cordeau made that observation.

"Another benefit of the fairy electricity," Noirmont replied. "Everywhere that sanitation is obligatory, or even useful, I make use of electrolyzed seawater. In the vast reservoir that you can see over there, I manufacture my seawater and pass it through the electrolytic apparatus.[18]

---

[18] H. R. Cassel patented a method of extracting gold from seawater by means of electrolysis in 1886, but the apparatus he used, which had the side effect of producing sodium hypochlorite, proved much more useful as a means of disinfection,

"The cleaning of the stables and animal sheds, and the grooming of the horses and the livestock is carried out exclusively with that water, and I'm absolutely adamant about the health of my animals. Foot-and-mouth disease, sheep-pox, glanders—all those nasty and redoubtable diseases that decimate herds are not to be feared here. It's the perfect and least costly sanitation. I've promised myself on my return to America to make use of it for the township of the mine that will house a thousand workers."

"But how do you manufacture your electricity?"

"A watercourse runs across my land; I make use of it. Look, over there, at that small building, where my machines are powered by a turbine. If I hadn't had a natural motor at my disposal, I'd have employed steam, but I prefer water; it's cleaner and more economical."

When Noirmont and his guests came back to the villa it was dark. A magical spectacle awaited the visitors. The tall trees in the park, illuminated from below by intense beams of light, gave the eyes a joyous spectrum of greens.

"Acetylene," said Noirmont. "On days—or, rather, nights—when I have visitors, I switch them on."

"It's dazzling," said Lesécant and Cordeau, in chorus.

"Messieurs, salute the victorious future of gas, and perhaps of electricity. But before dinner I want to show you my cellars. Oh, the curious contest of illumination! The battle of light! I have all the combatants in my home. We do the cooking by gas; I light the villa, the outbuildings and the farm with electricity, and my gardens with liquefied acetylene. In the cellars it's another matter. Take these little bottles; they'll provide you with light."

"Oh, yes," observed Cordeau. "The method of the American engineer Tesla."[19]

---

and was widely touted for that purpose in the 1890s. The principle is still used in chlorinating swimming pools.

[19] Nikola Tesla (1856-1943) worked briefly for Thomas Edison, whose main rival he was widely considered to be, and

"I only use it on a small scale; the discovery isn't yet perfected."

In the cellar, following Noirmont's instructions, the doctors brought their little bottles—in which there was as complete a vacuum as possible—into proximity with coils through which an alternating current was passing at high frequency, and to their great wonderment, they obtained a bright light, which enabled them to admire the perfect order of their friend's cellar.

When they came back upstairs they begged him to change the villa's name and call it the Magic Villa.

After an excellent and very calm dinner, during which they only talked about indifferent matters, they made a tour of the gardens, smoking excellent cigars, while an electric organ hidden under the trees by a hornbeam hedge provided the illusion of a brilliant orchestra.

And under the influence of wellbeing, in the midst of beautiful verdant nature, everyone blessed the Science that lavishes its benefits upon us and helps us to enjoy life.

The next day, as they returned to Paris, and in spite of all the marvels that they had admired equally, Cordeau and Lesécant did not have a single word to say to one another.

Sulking in their corners, they closed their eyes, and before them, more beautiful than ever, cheerful and desirable, passed the silhouette of Mademoiselle Noirmont, whom they had bounced on their knees as a little girl twelve years before.

Sometimes, a shadow loomed up in front of the apparition: that of Rémois, the fiancé; and each of the doctors wondered how he could get rid of that spoiler who was getting in the way of his dream.

George Westinghouse after emigrating to the U.S.A. The experiments with fluorescent light that he carried out in the 1890s, building on discoveries made in France by Alexandre Becquerel, were widely publicized, but did not lead to any commercially viable product.

On arrival in Paris they parted without a friendly word, without even a banal handshake; they felt that they were rivals now, and not far from being enemies; because, it is necessary to say, Lesécant and Cordeau, who had lived until then indifferent to amour, had just been struck by "the thunderbolt." They were not even giving a thought to the age difference that separated them from the gracious Hélène; they were both telling themselves that, after all, they had not yet passed fifty, and that they had a fortunate situation capable of tempting a spouse. Then again, they thought of themselves as handsome, and they thought of themselves as young.

Does not love make people blind?

Oh, Lesécant, it only requires but the presence of a beautiful child, a frail beauty, to take away your sight, you who are ambitious to render daylight to unfortunates condemned to darkness!

And you, Cordeau, there is no need of a psychic serum to inflame your icy heart!

O power of Cupid! A child, the cherished product of Nature, rules the world. True, the child has arrows!

III. The Shareholders

A fortnight after the house-warming, Paul Rémois and Hélène were talking about their plans for the future in the shade of the large trees on the grounds of the Villa Moderne.

In front of him, Rémois had a canvas on which he was making a study of the tree, rather distractedly. The young man was not paying much attention to it; his gaze lingered more frequently on his fiancée's face than on his sketch.

At one moment, he dropped his brush, which picked up a sprinkling of sand, and took the young woman's hand, which he felt tremble in his.

"Oh, how I love you, Hélène, and how happy I've been since the day when, timid and blushing, you confessed to me that you shared that love. I'd like to have you near me always.

Whenever I leave you I'm afraid…afraid that you'll escape me, afraid that our beautiful dream will vanish."

Mademoiselle Noirmont smiled. "What silly fears, my friend. You know very well that we'll be married in three months."

"Three months!" Paul sighed. "That's a long time!"

"It's necessary to wait; my father needs the time to liquidate his business; you're not unaware that between now and then he has to reimburse Messieurs Lesécant and Cordeau, from whom he borrowed six hundred thousand francs for the exploitation of the Chittingham copper mine in Pennsylvania, for which he'd obtained the concession two years ago."

"Yes, I know—those two ugly birds who usurp the consideration of society, sheltering their…unworthy machinations under the mantle of science."

"That's a harsh phrase."

"What? Rather say that I'm putting it mildly. Those two men who claim to be your father's friends lent him money— which he could certainly have found elsewhere. They simply bet on the luck and talent of the engineer. Then they see you, they want you—oh, my Hélène!—and without knowing whether their ultimatum will mean ruin for Monsieur Noirmont, they demand your hand or the reimbursement of their loan within three months."

"Each of them is armed with the contract that he made with Papa, because—don't you know?—they don't know that they're co-partners."

"That's funny."

"Yes, they've both demanded simultaneously that my father doesn't address himself to the other."

"They have very particular views about camaraderie. And your father has gone above and beyond?"

"Of course; he wanted the two friends to get a good return."

"Good! Indeed—last year they received fifteen per cent interest, and in ten years, their shares would have increased in value by a third without them opening their purse."

"Unless he reimburses them before then, in accordance with their wishes. My father insisted on introducing that clause into the contract in anticipation of possibilities. If things had gone badly, he would have paid off the shareholders with his own capital...."

"Monsieur Noirmont is the most honest of men; Hélène, you have the right to be proud of him...." After a pause, Paul added: "Well, it's tomorrow that they're coming to obtain the answer. I confess to you that, without being malevolent. I'd like to see the faces of those Messieurs...."

He did not have time to finish; a domestic ran up fearfully. "M'sieu, mam'zelle, come quickly! M'sieur Noirmont has fallen...."

The young people ran to the villa at top speed. The engineer was lying on the floor in his study, unconscious. His clenched right hand was clutching a telegram, and blood was running from a wound on his head, inflicted when he had fallen against the corner of his desk.

Hélène, frightened and tearful, fearing for the life of the father she adored, ran to the garage.

"William, take the brake, go to Laigle and come back as fast as you can with a doctor. Quickly, quickly, my good William!"

Without asking for any explanation, the American got in the car, and a few minutes later he was traveling at top speed along the road to Laigle.

In the meantime, Rémois, greatly affected but conserving his presence of mind nevertheless, aided by the domestics, carried Monsieur Noirmont to his bed; then, left alone beside the injured man, he bandaged the wound, which was close to the temple.

At that moment when Hélène came back the injured man opened his eyes, but he did not appear to have any consciousness of the people who were with him; his gaze was vague, his respiration painful.

The young woman ran to him and covered him with caresses. "Come round, Father...speak, speak...."

Rémois tried to reassure her, but she did not listen.

"Papa, dear Papa, it's me, your little Hélène. Oh, I beg you, tell me that you recognize me...."

Noirmont raised himself up slightly, and, surrounding his child with his arms, had a violent crisis of tears. Then, as the sobs eased, he murmured a few words.

"Finished!... Ruined!... Cataclysm...oh! Poor darling...!"

And he continued to weep abundantly.

The young couple remained silent, allowing the salutary crisis to continue its course.

When the crisis had passed, Monsieur Noirmont handed Rémois the telegram that he was still holding, crumpled between his fingers.

"Read it, my friend."

Paul obeyed, his voice hesitant with emotion: "Chittingham, third July. Lightning struck dynamite store. Thirty dead. Factory in ashes, Barrage collapsed. Workyard flooded. Materiel destroyed. Details by letter. John Fester."

"Well?" queried the engineer, shaking his head dolorously.

The artist understood that his response might be a sovereign balm; with a great force of will, he made his voice firm. "Why so desolate? Apart from the thirty unfortunate victims, everything can be repaired. You still have the concession...it's a case of *force majeure*, there can't be a forfeiture. Come on, Monsieur Noirmont. I have two hundred thousand francs that came to me from my mother's inheritance; they're yours. It's a nucleus. You'll find bankers out there who won't hesitate to support you with their credit. No weakness! Come on! We're here—Hélène and I—to help you in the struggle."

"Kind heart!" murmured Noirmont. "Your devotion is, alas, futile. I owe six hundred thousand francs to Lesécant and Cordeau. I had to supply six hundred tons of minerals to a foundry in Chicago by the end of August, under a penalty of two hundred thousand francs plus fifty dollars per week of delay. And everything is destroyed—everything! You can see..."

"You can oblige your shareholders to be patient. With my two hundred thousand francs to ward off immediate necessities, fulfill your contract with the Chicago factory…and who knows? But this isn't the moment to talk business. You need rest."

"Rest!"

"Yes, yes. The doctor who's coming will demand that of you, at all costs."

Brought at great haste by the motor-brake, the doctor soon arrived. He was a very observant old practitioner, modest but talkative. He examined his client attentively.

"Come on," he said. "It's trivial. There's been an emotional shock, followed by a nervous crisis."

He looked at the head wound. "A scratch…a bad scratch. If the blood hadn't flowed, it might have been serious. Anyway, it will all be all right. You'll be on your feet tomorrow, Monsieur Noirmont—but you need to rest."

"I can't sleep, Doctor…my head's on fire…if you knew…."

"Calm down, calm down. You need sleep; if necessary, I'll help you with that. Do you have lime, a little laudanum?"

"I have all that in my traveling medical kit," Hélène replied.

"A wise precaution, Mademoiselle. One should never go traveling without a first aid kit. I'd wish that in every château, the Mairie of every village, even the humblest hamlet, a doctor could have the saving cordial to hand. How many deaths or serious illnesses could be avoided thus. I've written a pamphlet about it…but I'm not here to boast about my merits…I beg your pardon. Alas, the simplest things are often difficult to get adopted. So we were saying, then: a dilute infusion of lime, into which you'll pour, at the moment of drinking, four drops of laudanum. Then I'll answer for the sleep, and I hope that tomorrow morning, there'll be nothing to worry about…physically, at least. Bear up, Monsieur Noirmont. Goodbye, Monsieur, Mademoiselle…. In any event, I'm at your disposal."

"The brake will take you back to Laigle, Doctor."

"Very kind Mademoiselle; I accept gratefully, for my legs are like me...no longer young. Your servant, Messieurs...keep calm, and all will be well."

And the good doctor left, murmuring: "Solid as an oak...otherwise he'd be finished. Elasticity...hmm...I believe some good news would do more good than all the potions in the world. Nine times out of ten the best medicine is mental!"

An hour later, under the effect of the narcotic, Monsieur Noirmont was sleeping like a log.

Hélène, comforted by the hopeful words that her fiancé had lavished upon her, completely reassured with regard to her father's health, consented, on Paul's urgent insistence, to get some rest.

The young man installed himself, alone, in the engineer's room.

"I'll spend the night with him. He might wake up, and...one never knows. It's more prudent for me to be there."

The next morning, at eight-thirty, Cordeau and Lesécant, in their best clothes, took the train to Laigle from the Gare de Montparnasse. Hazard—often malicious—had lodged them once again in the same compartment. Before the departure they both had the same thought, of changing carriage, but as they had got to their feet simultaneously, they sat down again the same way.

Why should I run away from him? Cordeau thought.

To go because he's there, Lesécant said to himself, *would be a weakness*.

And they stayed.

During the first few kilometers they limited themselves to looking at one another "like china dogs." But when the train had gone past Dreux, Lesécant, no longer containing himself, planted himself on the banquette opposite, and said in a hissing tone: "It's doubtless to Laigle that you're going, Monsieur?"

154

"I surely am, Monsieur," Cordeau riposted, "unless you have the power to stop me."

"I'm very glad, on the contrary, for I'll enjoy seeing your defeat."

"As for me, with what joy I shall salute yours!"

"You're wrong to persist in your folly, Cordeau; I have weapons that you don't possess. Hélène will be my wife."

"Mine—I love her and I shall have her. Noirmont owes me three hundred thousand francs."

"You'll be reimbursed, wretch. I, too, am the engineer's shareholder…."

"False brother!"

"Tartuffe!"

"Pork butcher!"

"Old fool!"

It would not have taken much for the two friends to seize one another by the throat; but they contained themselves, fearful of disturbing the harmony of their costume."

"Ah!" muttered Lesécant. "If I weren't obliged to be polite…!"

"Believe me, it's only for that reason that I'm holding myself back."

A little before the arrival in Laigle, Cordeau, his face up against the stout Lesécant's nose, grated through clenched teeth: "If she chooses you. I'll kill you."

"I'll have your hide if you marry her!" Lesécant vociferated, beside himself.

It was the first time that they had ever addressed one another as *tu*.

At Laigle, they each took a cab and gave orders to their driver to get there ahead of the other. Arriving at the same time, they ran to the gate. Their gazes met, furiously, but the terror of a crumpled shirt front tamed them.

"Let's make peace."

"Call a truce, rather."

"So be it."

Together, they rang the electric doorbell. Together, they handed their cards to the domestic. Together, they presented themselves at the door of the drawing room where Noirmont was waiting for them.

The engineer was pale; the blow he had received the day before had contracted his features; only his eyes remained brilliant, and energy could be read therein: the determination to fight, no matter what, until the end.

The surgeon and the psychologist, struck by the change on the physiognomy of the villa's owner, enquired as to the state of his health. He smiled and apologized for a slight fatigue. And, as they were astonished not to see Mademoiselle Noirmont, he said: "She's not feeling well."

"Ah! But I'm a physician…."

"*We*'re physicians," Cordeau rectified.

"Oh, you do so little," Lesécant chaffed.

Noirmont stifled the nascent quarrel. "Hélène has no need of the aid of science. A slightly excessive irritation obliges her to stay in her room; I hope you'll forgive her for not coming to greet you."

"Willingly…"

"Beauty has the right to our indulgence."

After a silence, Cordeau attacked first. "You received my letter, my dear friend?"

"Mine too?"

"Yes, Messieurs, and I confess that I was unpleasantly surprised. I'm no longer in a position today to repay your loans. This is what has happened." Noirmont held out the telegram informing him of the catastrophe at Chittingham. He was expecting recriminations, but, to his great astonishment, he saw Cordeau smiling and Lesécant radiant.

After returning the telegram to him, they sat down, and their voices overlapped:

"So you're…."

"Ruined…."

"So much the better…."

"You need us more than ever…."

"You're aware of the love…."

"The passion that I feel for…."

"Mademoiselle…."

"Your daughter…."

"Give her to me…."

"Grant me…."

"For my wife…."

"Her hand…"

"And I'll give you a release…."

"Quits…."

"And I'll reimburse…."

"I'll buy out…."

"Cordeau."

"Lesécant."

The engineer was astounded. In spite of the gravity of the situation, he could not suppress a smile.

"Messieurs," he said, after a moment's reflection, "You're forgetting one thing. I don't have the right to dispose of my child in this way, to sacrifice her."

"You're scarcely polite to us, my dear chap."

"Oh, I'm far from wanting to offend you, believe me. I'm struggling with a frightful crisis; you know that Hélène is engaged."

"Oh, it's very probable that the catastrophe will change the face of things. An artist…."

"Adieu the dowry, adieu the suitor!" Lesécant advanced, brutally.

Noirmont had got to his feet, ready to defend Paul, when a domestic announced: "Monsieur Rémois."

The painter had seen the two colleagues arrive. The open window of the drawing room, directly below the room he occupied at the villa, had permitted him to follow the conversation closely. Since the previous evening he had been thinking hard, looking at the situation from every angle, and had concluded that the only thing to do was to gain time, making use of the shareholders. The letters written a few days earlier by the two "suitors" had enlightened the young man as to their character. Monsieur Noirmont was faint-hearted; he took scrupulousness too far. Well, he would be saved in spite of himself!

The alternation of raised voices had indicated to the young man the moment to make his entrance.

His face calm, with a hint of melancholy, he bowed to the engineer and saluted Lesécant and Cordeau very ceremoniously.

"I beg your pardon, Messieurs; perhaps I'm interrupting a very serious conversation."

"You're not superfluous, Rémois; we were discussing Hélène's marriage."

"And these Messieurs were doubtless telling you that my duty, in the circumstances, is to release you from your promise...."

While Lesécant and Cordeau, suffocating, red-faced to the extent of crimson, opened their mouths to protest, the painter had the time to make a sign of intelligence to Hélène's father.

"The Messieurs are right."

"But...."

"Let me speak, I beg you. A ruinous catastrophe, compromising Mademoiselle Noirmont's future, has perhaps put you in an awkward position relative to...ferocious shareholders."

"We won't permit....!" Cordeau howled.

"Such impertinence!" finished Lesécant.

"Well, Messieurs, have I spoken for you?"

"Perhaps you don't know, Rémois, that my friends each have three hundred thousand francs in the enterprise that is going under," Noirmont put in, fearing that the young man was going too far. "They're proposing to me, if I grant one of them Hélène's hand, to cancel their credit and to reimburse, in my stead, the one rejected by my daughter...."

"That's noble. It's relief for you, happiness for your child."

Noirmont considered Rémois admiringly.

Persuasively, seductively, the young man had soon "enveloped"—almost hypnotized—the two doctors.

After some hesitations and wrangling, they came to an agreement. Lesécant and Cordeau were talking about nothing less than a duel, *after which only one of them would remain*. It was Rémois who had brought them into agreement.

"The weapon for men like you, Messieurs, is science. Whichever of you, *within a year*, has made the more sublime discovery and has supported it with an indubitable experiment—that's the duel you require."

Lesécant and Cordeau, doubtless to their great joy, approved the idea, and it was concluded, providing for all eventualities that if, within an interval of one year, Monsieur Noirmont had been unable to reimburse Messieurs Lesécant and Cordeau the sum of 300,000 francs each, plus interest at 5%, Mademoiselle Hélène Noirmont would marry whichever of the aforementioned Lesécant and Cordeau had revealed the discovery most useful to the wellbeing of humankind. A communication to a learned assembly, which would judge the respective merits of the competitors, would be made by the aforementioned contenders, with supportive experiments, if any had taken place.

The engagement having been written in triplicate, in due form, and duly signed by the three interested parties—although there were really five—they went their separate ways.

Lesécant and Cordeau, after having asked Noirmont to present their affectionate salutations to Hélène, took their leave and, launching a last challenging glance at one another as they emerged from the Villa Moderne, climbed back into their cabs in order to return to the Laigle railway station.

On the way, Cordeau sang joyfully: "She's mine, she's my wife! Oh extreme joy…Noirmont will never get out of the mire, and I'll be damned if I don't have my psychic sera ready within a year. It's all a matter of finding a case study, an extraordinary specimen who'll consent to treatment."

For his part, Lesécant, who was less musical, was following an analogous reasoning. "I'll have the trophy, and the child with the velvet eyes. Papa won't get out of it without me. Cordeau's nothing but a donkey. Me, I'll excavate my third eye, damn it! I'll unearth a docile subject. I have the money...the sinews of war...and the science!"

Then a common reflection occurred to them, with regard to Rémois.

It's wrong to judge on first impressions. That's a fellow I misunderstood. Either he's employed an adroit fashion of taking his leave for reasons of misfortune, or he has the bump of devotion...and he's an imbecile.

Let us, reader, leave our two "lovers" to return to Paris, hearts on fire and heads full of dreams, and return to the Villa Moderne.

Noirmont, Hélène and Rémois were in conference.

While the engineer and his daughter expressed their dreads for the future, the young man strove to reassure them, and to give them the vigor necessary to emerge victorious from the struggle.

"We've gained time," he said. "That's the essential thing. In a year, one has the time to do a great deal. Within three weeks, I'll have the funds necessary to get the Chittingham enterprise going again."

"And if I fail...."

"We'll think again. I assume, Monsieur Noirmont, that you only have one desire: to reimburse your shareholders...."

"Yes, my friend; however, if, for their part, they put me under an obligation to execute...the contract..."

"Oh!" murmured Hélène, fearfully.

"Don't worry about that. For great evils, small remedies...."

"I'm afraid," said the young woman. "Afraid for us, Monsieur Rémois. Although they're ridiculous, their science...."

"You haven't observed them then," the painter interjected. "Scientists, those two! They believe they know a host of

160

things they've seen in other people's books. Like mirrors, they reflect—but as for creating, that's another matter. If they were true scientists, they wouldn't have acted as they have. The sincere man of science works with a vision of the goal to be attained, but he's careful not to fix a date for the completion of his endeavor, the coronation of his achievement."

"Which signifies, my dear Monsieur, that you consider Messieurs Lesécant and Cordeau to be...."

"Charlatans," concluded the young woman.

"All well and good," Rémois continued, "but hazard might aid them...how can one tell?"

"Oh, I'd never have had the courage to call Monsieur Lesécant or Monsieur Cordeau...."

"*Sursum* Cordeau...not *Corda*!" declared Rémois, joking. "If those Messieurs are working for their greater glory, and very little for that of science, I'm free—the contract doesn't bind me—and I promise you that I won't be inactive...for love and for mercy...."

"Thank you," Hélène murmured, extending a little trembling hand to her fiancé, on which he deposited a very delicate kiss.

"They still have to succeed! But what are you thinking, Monsieur Noirmont?"

"I think, my dear boy, that you're my savior, and that I'll never be able to pay you back."

"Come what may," said the painter, looking at Hélène, "I'll still be your debtor."

Three weeks later, after having left his daughter with distant relatives he had in Paris, whom Rémois was authorized to visit, Monsieur Noirmont, armed with a check for two hundred thousand francs, set off for America.

IV. The Third Eye

In his study at the Villa Paré, Dr. Lesécant was stamping his feet, his fists clenched, his eyes ablaze, his cheeks red and his garments in disorder. He circled like a beast in a cage, trampling the books and papers with which the parquet was strewn. One might have thought that the small room, ordinarily so well ordered, had just been the theater of a combat and that the adversaries had employed the books on the shelves and the papers in the writing desk as ammunition. And indeed, Lesécant had been battling, battling against his hopes, which he saw disappearing.

In his impotent rage he had first taken it out on his devoted and patient manservant, old Jérôme, a former laboratory assistant, who had fled under the avalanche of reproaches, abandoning his feather duster. Armed with that machine, with whose manipulation he was unfamiliar, the surgeon, at the height of his wrath, had struck out in all directions, breaking his inkwell and scattering pieces of paper; then the turn of the volumes had come, innocent victims, which he trod underfoot in his frenzy.

"Three months!" he muttered. "Three months...and nothing. Nothing! What use are all these journals? Advertising? Humbug! I'm not asking for the moon, though! One blind man...to whom I'm assuring a comfortable existence...and sight! Everything's ready, though. I have marvelous carbo-pepto-ferro-azotic tablets...the ideal nourishment, no impediments...and not so much as a cat presents itself. Time's passing. Of course! I see them here, the others, the academicians...they're laughing at me...and all because I don't have a *subject*."

Then, after a further crisis, which cost half a dozen octavo volumes their binding, he went on: "And Cordeau, out there, where is he in his idiocies? That charlatan's capable of...of, but no! No, no! He shan't have her! It's me—me, Lesécant—who will earn the glory and...."

The sound of the doorbell cut off his virulent monologue.

"Should I answer it, M'sieu le docteur?"

"No!" howled Lesécant. "I'm not in! You know that very well...blockhead...."

162

As Jérôme escaped, having no desire to suffer the terrible anger of his employer, the doorbell rang violently, without interruption. Lesécant called his servant back.

"Jérôme!"

"M'sieu le docteur?"

"Have you seen the people who are ringing?"

"Yes—there's a young monsieur and another monsieur…also young…that the first one is leading by the arm…."

"My God! A blind man! What are you waiting for, imbecile? Open the door. I gave you orders an hour ago…."

"M'sieu…told me to…."

"M'sieu! Hurry up, then! What if they leave? Show the gentlemen into the drawing room. I'll be there directly…just time to tidy myself up a bit…a blind man! Finally!"

And Lesécant hurtled into his dressing room like a whirlwind, where he repaired the disorder of his attire feverishly.

Jérôme, not understanding anything, went to open up. While going toward the garden gate, the worthy servant muttered: "True as true, if m'sieu isn't going mad! I've got to leave…for three months it's been Hell here."

Ten minutes later, the doctor, fresh and smiling, clad in an elegant indoor jacket, came into the drawing room where the visitors introduced by Jérôme were waiting.

"Monsieur Rémois!" he said, surprised by the sight of the artist.

"Doctor, I have the honor of saluting you, and I've brought you an experimental subject."

"Please, sit down….and you too, my friend…."

While speaking, without paying any more heed to Rémoir, Lesécant examined the painter's companion. With an entirely paternal tenderness, he sat him down in the best armchair in the room "There, my friend—are you quite comfortable?"

"Not bad," said the other, in a hoarse voice.

"Oh…oh!" murmured Lesécant. "Terrible voice…burned by alcohol…."

Indeed, the individual's luminous face, the nose crimson and horribly shiny, completed by an entirely characteristic breath, supported the surgeon's observation.

Rémois did not leave him time to ask questions. "I read the advertisement that you inserted in the newspapers," he said.

"Three months ago, alas...."

"It's just that...people are afraid...."

"Afraid of what? I'll answer for everything. My operations always succeed."

Of course, thought the painter. *The patients are dead...but cured.* Aloud, he said: "It's because your skill and science are universally known that I've succeeded in bringing you my friend, Arthur Vésigout—blind for ten years."

"Excess of alcohol, no doubt...."

"If one can call six absinthes a day excessive," Vésigout grumbled, taking offence. "But then, when I'm drunk..."

"Let's not worry about that," replied Lesécant, softly. "A little preliminary treatment will quickly reckon with that inconvenience. So, my friend, you have confidence in me...and you're not mistaken. I'll render you, not sight...."

"What!" said the other. "I was told that...."

"I'll give you something better than sight. A perfect organ, which I've allowed to be named *the third eye*, but which is nothing other than a nervous center of marvelous sensibility. Oh, my lad, when you've passed through my hands you won't be an ordinary man, I give you my word. First of all, you'll lack nothing here...the best room...a first-rate bed...nourishment...."

Vésigout's face lit up with a broad smile. "Suits me...suits me, Doctor. You can do what you like with me by taking me by the...."

"Mouth," interrupted Rémois, who was having difficulty remaining serious. "Vésigout is a little...how shall I put it?...a little...."

"Realistic," said Lesécant, laughing. "That doesn't matter. Here, all whims are tolerated, except with regard to the treatment. This is the deal: I'll pay twenty thousand francs after the operation, and ten thousand that the subject will soon acquire—they'll be deposited in his name with my notary, with a delay of a fortnight—in case of accidents. It's necessary to anticipate...."

"That's right!" declared Vésigout. "Well, that suits me, anyway. Then again, there isn't going to be any accident...."

"No, my friend, no! From now on, you're at home here," continued the radiant Lesécant. "We'll begin tomorrow."

Rémois stood up to take his leave. "So, my dear Master, I can confide my poor friend to your science."

"He won't have cause to regret it."

Indeed, thought Vésigout. *Ten thousand bullets guaranteed....* Aloud, he said: "*Au revoir*, Rémois...you're a pal...."

"I'll show you out, my dear artist."

"No, need, my dear Master."

"Yes, yes...I want to talk to you."

In the garden, Lesécant took the painter's arm. "I think you're admirable, you know."

"No...I'm impressed by your Herculean labor, and I'm only too happy to give you what help I can."

"Finally, I have a subject—thanks to you."

"Hazard..."

"Allow me to thank you...oh, my dear chap, before long, everyone will be talking about it. I'll have glory...and...."

"And beauty," Rémois completed, smiling.

"Tell me," said the doctor, in a low voice, red with emotion. "Hélène...Mademoiselle Hélène...how is she?"

"Well, I suppose—for you must realize that I dare not see her any longer...."

"Why? Go on my behalf, then, to the relatives she's staying with...."

"Oh!"

"I'd be so happy if she came here to see me, to encourage me with her divine presence...the sight of her would multiply the resources of my genius tenfold...."

"I can't promise you anything…but for you, I'll do…the impossible."

"Good man! I'll never be able to repay you…."

Scarcely had Rémois left the villa than Lesécant said to himself: "I was definitely right about him. He's an idiot."

For his part, as the artist went away with a spring in his step, humming a tune, he told himself that he had not wasted his time, and that Vésigout was going to give the "illustrious" doctor quite a headache.

As soon as the doctor and Rémois had left the drawing room, Vésigout got up and looked around the room.

"It's not at all chic, Père Bistouri's place, but it'll be a soft existence—like a oasis in the desert of my destitution. Ten thousand francs…plus the thousand Rémois promised me if the trick comes off. No-o…not so hard up. Enough of playing the ventriloquist at Trône, Neuilly and wherever…at least friendship's good for something…as long as I make sure I don't get butchered…pffft! None of that, now! Get on with it…it's a good job I was once an art student…."

Sprawling in his armchair Lesécant's future "subject" relaxed into his pleasant dream of comfort and greed. A few days before, he had seen himself plunged forever into the blackest misery, when hazard had put him in the presence of Rémois on the *Boul'Mich*, were he was dragging his worn-out shoes. Afflicted by a pronounced keratitis that veiled his porcelain-blue eyes, he had not seen his old studio buddy, but Hélène's fiancé had understood right away, what he might do with such an individual and had hailed him—and between courses, in a nice restaurant, he had had no difficulty deciding to render him the service of entering the house of Dr. Lesécant as an experimental subject.

One shadow obscured the cheerful landscape glimpsed by Vésigout. What if the other were to perceive the deception too soon? Adieu fortune, adieu meal ticket…it was necessary to keep up the role for at least a month, the time necessary for the surgeon's ten thousand francs to be duly acquired….

166

As the pseudo-blind man was reflecting, Lesécant came back into the drawing room.

"Well, my lad?"

"What time does one eat, Monsieur le docteur?"

"Hungry already?"

"Thirsty, especially…."

"Good, good… a little patience. First, my dear chap, I ought to warn you that you won't get a drop of alcohol here."

In spite of the painful impression caused by this prohibition, Vésigout found the strength to smile. He thought about his ten thousand francs, and promised himself ample future compensation.

"And also," said the surgeon, "no more meat, bread, vegetable or fruit—nothing, any longer, except my tablets…two every three hours…."

The shock nearly caused the subject to open his eyes and give himself away.

What! he thought. *That's what you call comfortable? Oho! We shall see, old fellow.*

The other, following his train of thought, did not notice the Bohemian's discomfited physiognomy.

"You understand that my first concern, before endowing you with the marvelous organ that no other known individual has possessed until now, must be to prepare you. First of all, I'll remove your eyes…"

"Oh!"

"Well, what use can they be to you? Those vitreous bodies you have there are wasting your nervous substance. Afterwards, we'll see about getting rid of your hair…."

"I shave every day."

"You shave…yes, get rid of it…all those hairs, nails…."

"Oi!"

"Those teeth…objects that will be useless to you henceforth. What good are teeth, since my tablets dissolve in the esophagus of their own accord? Fingernails? What for? Beard, hair…useless things. Onerous work for the brain…."

"But I'll be ugly!"

"Ugly? First of all, what's ugliness? A matter of convention, like beauty. Anyway, if you insist, you can have false teeth, fingernails of celluloid or horn...."

Aieee! thought the unfortunate Vésigout. *My God, where will it end?*

"Afterwards, I'll shorten the intestine...."

"Oh! Sir...!"

"Don't scream in advance—you won't feel anything. Come on, my lad, what's the point of seven meters of intestine when you won't have to digest anymore? My tablets will be absorbed into your blood of their own accord. You'll be a rational organism, without a flaw, without any excess labor. Your muscles will atrophy—thus, everything for the brain, the motor of life. Then, when you're perfect, I'll finally be able to cultivate your third eye, bring it to the light. And then, my friend, it will be glory for me, happiness—ecstasy—for you. Unknown sensations will be reserved for you. You won't see like vulgar and miserable human machines. Better than that! You'll sense there, on your forehead, the form of objects, the smallest and the greatest, the nearest and the most distant. Mysterious effluvia will enable you to penetrate the secrets of all individualities. Nothing—nothing!—will escape you when I've reduced your gross carnal envelope to its simplest expression; you'll no longer be a man but a human quintessence: a brain...nothing but a brain!"

The surgeon mopped his brow after this tirade, borrowed from the preface of his paper at the Académie. Then he took Vésigout in his arms, and, braving the strong odor of pipe-tobacco and alcohol that emanated from his overly imperfect person, he embraced him cordially, moved to tears, murmuring; "Oh, my boy, you'll bless Dr. Lesécant."

Zut! thought the unhappy Bohemian. *There's a picture! First things first...look at the menu! Tablets? Ugh....*

When Lesécant had relaxed his grip, he said: "Oh yes, Monsieur le docteur, I'll bless you...."

"Finally!" the surgeon exclaimed. "I'm certain of success, now. All right!"

That evening, Vésigout learned with enormous relief and intense joy that Lesécant would not be staying overnight at his villa.

"I go back to Paris; until we commence the operation, I'll leave you here alone. Jérôme has his orders. So, my dear boy, sleep, have a good time...and in a month, you'll be ready...."

When the "boss" had gone, Vésigout declared that he liked to go to bed early.

"Ah—so much the better," said Jérôme. "At my age, one needs one's sleep."

When the old servant had gone to sleep, Vésigout went into the study, sat down at the writing desk and wrote, with a nervous pen:

My dear Rémois,

Your illustrious master has reserved for me—if I let him do it—tortures such as the Chinese have not yet imagined. I don't know whether I'll have the courage to struggle against that frightful butcher...especially if I don't have a well-filled stomach. Can you imagine, my dear chap, that he's giving me for soup, hors-d'oeuvre, entrée, roast, salad and dessert, a frightful chemical mixture...a true remedy...tablets of carbo-pepto-etc. etc. I don't like it. Just now, I stole a crust and a bit of cheese from the kitchen, which is meager. Help me, or I'll jack it in. One thing will sort me out: open me an 'eye'[20] at a café nearby. Since the illustrious doctor has a monopoly on the third, that'll be my fourth, and not the worst. I promise to be reasonable.

Your devoted

Vésigout

---

[20] There is an untranslatable pun here in Vésigout's *argot*. The "eye" in question would be a "slate" in English slang or a "tab" in American.

P.S. The doctor has only forgotten one thing—to verify my blindness. He didn't think of it. So I have a fortnight ahead of me.

A moment later, with the agility of an acrobat, the "blind man" had scaled the garden wall. After having posted the letter in the box, he came back in to get some sleep. He lay down in a bed that he thought delightful, and was soon sleeping the sleep of the just.

When Rémois received Vésigout's letter, he hastened to the villa.

In the garden, the "subject," playing his role conscientiously, was taking a stroll, his arm supported by Jérôme, to whom he was telling a story that was obviously very funny, for the manservant was laughing wholeheartedly.

While Jérôme went to fetch his master, Vésigout questioned Rémois. "You got my letter?"

"Yes—I've done the necessary. Your bill's paid for a month at the Quatre-Chemins restaurant."

"Good. Thanks. At least, that way I'll be able to fight. Oh, I can string the old pruner along for three months...."

"Monsieur le docteur is waiting for you, Monsieur," said Jérôme, coming back. "I'll show you the way."

The painter followed the domestic to the Master's study. "Pardon me for the informality, my dear friend...I'm working...."

"Oh, between us, Monsieur Lesécant...well, are you satisfied?"

"A pearl, my friend a pearl...everything will go marvelously." After an embarrassed pause, he added: "You went to see Mademoiselle Noirmont on my behalf?"

"Yes, my dear Master."

"And?"

"She will come...fortunate victor."

Lesécant welcomed the flattery with a discreet smile; then, in a low voice, as if he were afraid of being overheard, he asked: "Do you know what's become of Cordeau?"

"No."

"Oh! You're so very kind that, if I dared, I'd ask you to go see how he's doing."

"That can be arranged."

"And then…." Lesécant hesitated. "And then…why not?...you're devoted to me…."

"I've give you proof of that."

"Well, if…if Cordeau hasn't found a *subject* yet, one could…furnish him with one…."

"Oh, no! Of course not…."

Is he naïve! thought Lesécant. "You haven't understood me, my dear boy. It would be easy to deceive Cordeau. He isn't very bright."

"That's rather Machiavellian."

"Well, I want to win. So, it's agreed—you'll try to find him a fake subject."

"I'll do my best."

"Good man! I'll never be able to thank you…."

"Don't worry about that. Your triumph will be my recompense."

"You're too kind."

"I'm only doing my duty."

A few moments later, going back to Viroflay railway station, Rémois was overtaken by a fit of hectic laughter.

What idiots they are! he thought. *One might think that they were suffering a bout of insanity….*

The previous evening, the young man had gone to visit his fiancée and had made her party to Lesécant's desire. "I'm charged with the greatest compliments for you, my dear Hélène. You have no idea how much you're loved. It's not me who is speaking, but the messenger."

"Miscreant!"

"One cannot do without your divine presence. And I confess that the word 'divine' is still too feeble—that's me speaking."

"I'll give instructions not to let you through the door…."

"I'll come in through the window, like Romeo. The illustrious Master desires to be honored by your visit. Will you come?"

"No, no—I hate the frightful fellow too much."

"If you knew how hard he's working! What an intoxication it would be for him to give you a lecture on the prosthesis of the third eye. You wouldn't want to deprive me of that pleasure, Hélène."

"All right, my friend."

"By the way, I'm better than he is—I've opened Vésigout's fourth eye…and I can guarantee that he's happy."

"Poor fellow."

"Rather feel sorry for Monsieur Lesécant…but let's talk seriously. Has your father written?"

"No—and I think it's been a long time. Three weeks."

"His last letter was optimistic. Why worry?"

"It gave me hope, but nothing affirmative. I'm afraid, my friend, very afraid…for us."

"Why? What's the worst than can happen? Ruin…."

"You know how badly my father would be affected. I'd have to renounce marrying you…"

"Chase away the dark thoughts. And to distract you, let's go to Fontenay. Dr. Cordeau has been expecting your visit for days. He too is dreaming about giving you a lecture on his sera. It will interest you. We ought to go."

"I don't have the courage at the moment. I'm too anxious."

"You're wrong, Hélène. Within a month, if Monsieur Noirmont hasn't succeeded, I'll have covered the two suitors in ridicule…and they won't dare show their faces again."

V. The Psychic Sera

A week later, Hélène received news from her father. Thanks to the capital lent by Rémois, he had been able to fulfill a part of his engagements. Assistance generously given to the victims of the disaster had rendered the engineer popular, and that had helped him get his operation back on its feet. Negotiations had begun with bankers in Chicago, and it was possible that within two months everything would be in place. Then, with a little luck, within the deadline of a year, Lesécant and Cordeau would be reimbursed and Hélène's happiness could finally be assured.

Radiant, the young woman had written to her fiancé. The horizon now seemed clearer; she consented to accompany Rémois to see the doctors.

"Let's amuse ourselves with them," said the painter. "Why should we have any scruples? Did the two old egotists have any pity on our love? And then, I adore vengeance—it's a pleasure of gods…and lovers."

When they arrived at Cordeau's residence, they found the psychologist prey to an extraordinary emotion. With his short-sleeves rolled up to his shoulders, he was examining his arms, peppered with puncture marks.

Stammering anxiously, he apologized for the state of his attire.

"Science has its immunities," replied Rémois, roguishly.

"It's strange, Monsieur; supernatural, Mademoiselle…look at my arms. It's incredible! Incredible….I'll refer it to the Académie…."

As his visitors looked at him in astonishment, he added: "That's true, you don't understand. Please pay attention for a minute…do sit down…pardon me…but I'm amazed…suffocated…. Oh, it's too curious, you know! I can only explain it as a phenomenon of autosuggestion. I inject myself without being aware of it. But when? Where? And the most curious thing is that the sera doesn't have any effect on me."

"I'll make the observation that you've taken on a thief as an experimental case study," said Rémois.

"Yes, I've cultivated his microbe, and injected it into a refractory animal…a guard dog. And I…."

"How do you expect such a serum to act on you? It would be wrong to judge you."

"Yes, of course!" Cordeau exclaimed. "Am I stupid! But then, there's good reason to be amazed. Where and when have I injected myself?"

"You'll figure it out, Doctor," Rémois indicated Hélène, who was very amused. "Mademoiselle Noirmont, in response to the amiable invitation that I extended to her in your name...."

Cordeau pulled himself together. "Mademoiselle, believe me, I'm touched...deeply touched. I'm entirely at your disposal. My method is, in any case, easily understood. It's elementary. Let's take the hypothesis of a case of drunkenness, for example. I take the microbe of a confirmed drunkard, supposedly incorrigible, on the brink of delirium...I cultivate it...I inoc...I...*sapristi!* It's so singular...."

And Cordeau, his eyes immeasurably wide, beside himself, examined his arms again.

Rémois recalled him to the demonstration.

"You inoculate...."

"What do you mean?"

"The drunkard's microbe."

Oh. yes...excuse me. So, I inoculate a refractory animal. And therein lies all the observation, all the science of my method. It's necessary to appropriate the refractory animal....years of observation. I've been aided somewhat by the studies of naturalists...and also by the worthy La Fontaine.... Therein, as I say, is the criterium of the Cordeau method. By the way, they smiled the other day at the Académie...."

"They always laugh a little at pioneers."

"They mistake them for lunatics, don't they? So, I inoculate a refractory, and hence sober, animal."

"A donkey."

"No," said Cordeau, with a patronizing smile, "a camel. Then I extract the serum of the immunized camel and I inoculate the drunkard."

"And he doesn't hit the booze anymore."[21]

"Never! It's infallible. But as an experiment I preferred to choose a thief. I had some difficulty finding one, in spite of my reiterated advertisements in the press."

"You were hard to please."

"Well, I had to be—but thanks to you, my dear friend, I finally got the man I wanted."

"Indeed. He is, I believe, thirty-five years old, with thirty-five convictions already—a recidivist given amnesty…."

"If he'd been made to order, I couldn't have been better served. If I cure that one—and I guarantee it—who will dare to deny my discovery? I've only had my subject for two weeks, and already he hardly ever steals from me. I deliberately leave money within his reach. In the first few days, I didn't find anything there. Now, if I leave a hundred sous, I get six francs back. Gradually, he'll give me back all that he's stolen. Then I'll be able to attempt the supreme experiment. And with what accomplishments my experiment is already endowed! What fortunate consequences will it not have for the human species, made virtuous, returned to the Golden Age? And what could be simpler? It's Columbus and the egg! Nature, the good mother, always places the remedy beside the evil. The animals that civilization hasn't spoiled have conserved their own character. Therein lies salvation, therein is the solution to…to…."

And as the psychologist, waving his long arms, searched for the word, like a club orator, he experienced a sharp sensation of thirst.

There was a glass on his side table, half-full of cold toddy. Cordeau drank it in a single draught, and refreshed, continued: "I shall have the glory of having endowed humankind

---

[21] An untranslatable pun has been omitted here, which links "piquer" (to prick, or inject, although it has numerous other implications, including "to steal" and "to irritate") to "piquer le nez" (to get drunk, equivalent of English expressions along the lines of "to get off one's face"). The chapter takes advantage of other ambiguities to make further puns.

with the panacea for which alchemists searched long and hard in blood and diabolical formulae. Have I said that it's the solution to the great problem of social equilibrium?"

In the matter of equilibrium, the doctor was losing his own. He tottered like a drunken man, and started babbling fragments of sentences in which scientific terms recurred: cerebral force…atavism…reflex causes…. Then, in a hoarse voice, he waxed indignant against his adversary Lesécant.

"No, pork butcher, it isn't you who'll have the glory…not you…not you…me…."

Finally, he was obliged to sit down, complaining of a headache, and went to sleep.

Rémois and Hélène contemplated him, not understanding what was happening before their eyes.

Then the young man rang a bell. A man came into the drawing room.

"Oh, it's you, Fléchard. Look—Monsieur Corbeau has suddenly gone to sleep."

The newcomer darted a glance at the side table and saw the empty glass.

"He's drunk his toddy. That doesn't surprise me. I doctored it. Well, I wanted to take full advantage of the leave that the head of the Sûreté granted me, at your request. I'd like nothing better than to earn my daily bread honestly, but there are limits. He'd have injected me too often if I'd let him—I'd be nothing but a pincushion. So, as he has a habit, while…working, of drinking a toddy, I put a few drops of laudanum in his *eau d'aff.*[22] That calms him down a little…except that, every time, while he's asleep, he rolls up his sleeves and he's off…another prick…he'd be full of holes if I let him…but one's only human…one isn't a brute…."

A double burst of laughter greeted Fléchard's revelation. The thing was, in fact, well planned. The detective, accus-

---

[22] I have retained this item of argot as printed; it is presumably a corruption of "eau d'oeuf" [egg-water], the "toddy" being egg-nog.

tomed to the guile of his difficult trade, had found a means to escape Cordeau's hair-raising operations.

"Look, he's starting again...."

Indeed, the psychologist, mechanically, rolled up his sleeves and, as if he had had a lancet in his hand, administered a series of punctures....

The young couple took their leave of Fléchard. As they departed, Rémois said to his fiancé: "I haven't remained inactive, you see. I've avenged myself. I have them both. I can do what I like with them, by virtue of the fear of ridicule.

On the way to Fontenay station, he gave the young woman the key to the enigma. "I was at college with the secretary of the Head of the Sûreté. I made use of our acquaintance. A phenomenal criminal record was assembled for agent Fléchard—one of the worst in the Prefecture, from which he obtained a leave of absence. He presented himself to the incredible Cordeau, who welcomed him with open arms, and eyes closed: 'Oh, my friend! Thirty-five convictions! You're a frightful scoundrel!' You can imagine the worthy agent's face. And Cordeau added: 'But I esteem you all the more for it; you're the man I've dreamed of....'"

The painter concluded: "Now, let's get the train, and since we're in a good mood, let's go see your other suitor."

VI. A Recalcitrant Subject

"You've come at a good time! I'm swimming in joy!"

So said Lesécant as he introduced Rémois and Hélène into the drawing room of the Villa Paré.

"We're glad to hear it, my dear Master."

"Extraordinary!" the other continued. "Beyond my hopes! Can you imagine that my carbo-pepto-azotic tablets really are the ideal nourishment? Vésigout, who's been consuming nothing else for a fortnight, is doing marvelously. He's putting on weight!"

177

Rémois had difficulty suppressing wild laughter, thinking about the excellent cuisine in which Vésigout was indulging at the Quatre-Chemins restaurant.

The surgeon continued: "The puffiness due to alcohol has disappeared. He looks superb. This morning, I set aside the promised ten thousand francs on account, and I'm going to start preparing him for the surgery today. First I'll take out his teeth...but pardon me, Mademoiselle Noirmont would perhaps rather not hear such details...."

"Oh, no, Doctor—I'm strong...."

"Good...no sensitivity, at least...." As Hélène laughed, frankly amused, he went on: "What an admirable little wife you'll make for a surgeon. Oh, if you marry me—and I'm certain of it, for Cordeau is nothing but a donkey—I'll initiate you into my art.

"So, tomorrow, I'll take out Vésigout's teeth, a week later, the hair and nails...after that I'll removed the intestines, which have become useless. And finally, we'll come to the admirable cultivation of the pituitary gland—the third eye.[23] I'll make a window in the forehead, here, a little above the top of the nose. I can say without fear that it will all go well...it's a window on infinity that I'll be opening up for that man...."

After having repeated the tirade that he had already declaimed to Vésigout, Lesécant concluded: "It mustn't be thought, in fact, that the pituitary gland, even though it appears to present the embryo of the organs of the eye, can be transformed to the point of performing the same banal function as the ocular orb. Perhaps complacent observers, deceived by appearances, find in that vegetating gland a failed organ imprisoned between the mass of the cerebrum and the cerebel-

----

[23] Either the author is joking or his research has gone awry; it is, of course, the pineal "gland" and not the pituitary that was being touted in the era when the story was written as a vestigial or undeveloped "third eye," as featured in the similarly implausible operation attempted by the reclusive scientist in Jules Clarétie's *L'Obession* (1908; tr. as *Obsession*).

lum, but what do I make of it? Although the pituitary gland contains all the elements of the eye, although one finds therein the sclerotic, the fibrous and opaque exterior envelope, the transparent cornea—which is, in my opinion, merely a modification of the primary envelope—the choroid, the crystalline lens, the retina; when all that exists in the miniature cerebrum that I want to cultivate, what do you think I'll have made?

"It's not an eye that I'm rendering but a nervous center, a point of strange sensibility. And when people see the prodigious faculties of my subject, after the operation, perhaps they'll want to understand the theory that I'm defending, and will defend to the death; and see that the explanation of abnormal phenomena—spiritism, hypnosis, magnetism, troubling problems before which even the princes of science go pale without any certain result—resides in the existence of that organ, perhaps failed, but far from being useless. Nature has never created anything useless. Life is for all, and all is for Life...."

Launched on that terrain, Lesécant, in a vibrant voice, constructed a metaphysics so confused that he ended up unable to find a way out of it. He no longer knew how to conclude; finally, turning to Hélène with a bow as graceful as was possible for him, he said: "Well, Mademoiselle, that's the theory. If you want to witness the practice—in brief, if you want to follow the birth of the colossal endeavor that I'm undertaking, Dr. Lesécant will be only too happy to place himself entirely at your disposal."

"Very kind of you, Doctor."

"And now, permit me to introduce you to my subject. When you arrived, I left him in my study. Come on. We'll go quietly, to surprise him. The dear boy! Do you know, I love him already."

"Vésigout is a good fellow," said Rémois. "Perhaps a trifle...irregular—fond of the bottle."

"Pfft!" retorted Lesécant, with a gesture of the hand. "Cured...better than by the Cordeau method....."

"Good food is sometimes a remedy."

179

"Good food...but I've told you that my subject has been nourished exclusively on my tables for a fortnight. Ex-clu-*sively!* And I confess that the result has exceeded my hopes. He's put on weight...here...look...."

With infinite precaution, the surgeon opened the door of the study. His back turned, very preoccupied, Vésigout did not hear them come in. Lesécant advanced on tiptoe, and then suddenly, nailed to the floor by amazement, his arms folded, at first he could only utter guttural exclamations: "Oh!... Oh!...."

Vésigout tried to hide his work, but Lesécant bounded forward and seized the piece of paper.

"My portrait! In caricature! He's drawing!"

Rémois and Hélène were very embarrassed. Redder than a tomato, trembling like a schoolboy caught doing something naughty, Vésigout, with tears in his eyes, distressed by the thought that the dream was about to vanish, of the ten thousand francs that he was not going to see, stammered: "I...I can explain..."

But Lesécant cut him off. "That's not your business, it's mine. The explanation belongs to science. This is a curious case of mental vision. His brain has perceived my image; his hand has executed it. And there's a resemblance. A seer couldn't do any better."

Driven by his mania for explaining everything scientifically, and his unreflective nature, Lesécant had just got Vésigout out of trouble. With aplomb, the Bohemian went on: "My father knew you well, Doctor."

"There—what did I tell you? The transmission of the image...."

Rémois and Hélène were leaning out of the window. They could no longer contain themselves; laughter was choking them.

"You have a marvelous view from your villa," said Mademoiselle Noirmont, in order to say something.

"Isn't it? That's admirable."

In fact, the view was limited to a garden fifty meters long, in which Lesécant cultivated absolutely nothing but medicinal herbs. The doctor's "admirable" was, of course, extended to Vésigout's drawing.

"Oh, my friend, since you already draw so well, what will you do when you have the third eye?"

Before they left, and while Lesécant, dissolving in amiabilities addressed to Hélène, gave her a tour of the villa and cut the most beautiful flowers in his greenhouse in her honor, Rémois took Vésigout to one side.

"That wasn't very prudent."'

"Well, old chap, I distract myself as best I can. If you knew how boring it is here. He wants to pull out all my teeth tomorrow. I'm giving up on your scheme, you know...."

"It's up to you to find a means of escape."

"For tomorrow—yes, it's arranged. Last night, at the risk of breaking my neck, I got into the doctor's operating room through the window on the first floor...."

"Why didn't you get a key made?"

"Secret lock, old chap. It's the only room that no one goes into except the man himself."

"Ah!"

"Then I played the burglar, cutting a windowpane with a diamond all around the rim and putting it back in place from the outside with hooks of my own invention, after filching all the instruments of torture he'd got ready to fix my jaws. So, for tomorrow I'm all right, but afterwards...."

"Find something else."

"And after that.

"After that, you can blow your cover, if necessary—but warn me first; I want to have witnesses there."

"And the cash?"

"You'll get the money, whatever happens."

The next day, Dr. Lesécant nearly fell over, struck down by apoplexy, when he went into his operating room and found the instrument cupboard absolutely empty. The door was locked. There were no panes missing from the window. Then again, why had the robbery been committed? With what aim?

He called Jérôme and scolded him so harshly that the old servant handed in his notice.

He asked Vésigout whether he had heard anything abnormal, the blind having sensitive hearing.

"No, Doctor, nothing."

"Well, someone's stolen my instruments."

"Ah!" The Bohemian's astonishment was so utterly natural that Lesécant was taken in.

"That astonishes you, eh…and annoys me. I was counting on getting rid of your teeth today…."

"That's unfortunate, Doctor, because I was ready."

Two days later, the surgeon came back with a new set of instruments. He found his subject in bed, moaning.

"Ah, Aiee! It's my back that's hurting…and I have a fever…aiee! If you knew, Doctor!"

"No luck at all," Lesécant said to himself, dejected. "It's as if nothing's going my way." With great generosity, he added: "Don't worry, my dear Vésigout. A week's rest and you'll be fine…"

A week's respite, thought the other. *That'll keep Rémois happy.*

At the end of the week, during which Vésigout did honor to the kitchens and the cellar at his restaurant, Lesécant, on arriving at the Villa, found him lying on the lawn in the garden, dead drunk. Beside him was a bottle of old rum.

The surgeon cursed and raged, reproaching himself bitterly for having chased away old Jérôme.

"When he was here, at least he watched him. I'm an idiot, to be sure—but in the future, I'll stay here and watch him myself. At least I got here in time—he might have died."

Vésigout, we ought to say, was not drunk at all. It was a stratagem intended to delay the fatal operation yet again. But he paid dearly for that stratagem; without him being able to prevent it, Lesécant, with an entirely professional vigor, picked him up, carried him to his bed and, without further delay, administered an emetic whose effect was disastrous.

"Damn it! The animal's been eating!" cried the doctor, furiously. "Oh, I was wrong to send Jérôme packing. Oh, my lad, sleep it off—and tomorrow afternoon, I'll deprive you of your lower jaw, and I certainly hope you won't do it again!"

Poor Vésigout! In spite of the nausea induced by the emetic, he wondered what he was going to do to get rid of the terrible guardian whom his unfortunate idea of playing drunk had imposed on him for the future.

A day without eating! Reduced to the boss's horrible tablets!

A fine idea! the Bohemian said to himself. *It's a lot of trouble to earn ten thousand francs!*

At any rate, there was no way to get out of it now. Seated in a leather armchair, bound hand and foot, the patient was going to see his molars, incisors and canine's extracted, one by one...or it would be necessary to confess that he wasn't blind...and Rémois hadn't been warned.

Imperturbably, Lesécant made his preparations for the operation.

"Don't be afraid, my boy, you won't feel a thing. I'll anesthetize you. Cocaine...good...."

While Lesécant was searching for poisons in his cupboard, however, a cavernous voice, seemingly emerging from the wall, made itself heard.

"No, no, pork butcher...you shan't have her...it's me...me...."

Nonplussed, the surgeon dropped the bottle he was holding, which broke. "Did you hear that?"

"Yesss," hissed Vésigout, his face imprinted with terror.

"Oh, that's bizarre!"

"Me...me...," repeated the mysterious voice.

"Damn! But that's Cordeau speaking. Damn it! I'll clear this up. Two o'clock in the afternoon! I'll go to see him."

Putting off the operation once again, he untied Vésigout, scarcely took the time to change clothes, and set off at top speed—not without having carefully locked the gate of the Villa.

"Oof!" sighed Vésigout. "I can still get out, thanks to my professional talents…but afterwards? Zut! I've had my fill of this—I prefer my penury…and as I don't want to face the fire of Monsieur le docteur Lesécant's reproaches, I'll take my leave of him by climbing over the gate. But politeness before all…."

And, taking a piece of paper, he traced a few words in a magisterial calligraphy:

The undersigned, Vésigout, thanks Dr. Lesécant for his kind concern, but doesn't have the courage to continue the experiments. He has the honor of saluting Monsieur le docteur and, if it might be useful to him, testifies here to the value of his succulent tablets.

He signed the note, placed it on the table in plain sight, went to his room to get his things, and set about climbing over the gate.

Finally, as poor as before, he was free. But he had an obligation to fulfill. Rémois had to be informed. He went to the painter's home. The other was not at home. Then he remembered the address of Mademoiselle Noirmont's relatives.

I'll surely find him there, he said to himself.

VII. In Full Settlement

A story ought to follow the pace of events. Ours must, therefore, accelerate.

The psychologist Cordeau had just returned home, and was standing, like a body without a soul, in front of his empty strong-box, ashamed, like a fox taken by a chicken. The supreme experiment had—is there any need to say it?—turned to confusion.

On the advice of Rémois, agent Fléchard had played a good trick—the last—on his injector.

That morning, negligently, Cordeau had allowed a glimpse of a wad of bonds to the value of fifty thousand francs. He had locked them in his strong-box within the sight the "subject," and, without seeming to suspect his presence, had pronounced alone the secret word of the combination lock: "Psychology." And he had gone out, announcing his intention of being absent until the afternoon.

Faithful to his instructions, Fléchard tried to open the safe. Alas, it did not work, for one very good reason: the worthy sleuth, expert in police work, was not as strong when it came to spelling. He tried *psicoloji* and *psicologi*, but nothing worked. An intelligent man, however, never allows himself to be thwarted.

"Damn it," he said to himself. "He has words to drive you mad...so...but it doesn't matter; I'll go and find a *dictillionary* in his bookcase...."

Indeed, a Larousse came to his aid. In possession of the word, he opened the strong-box, took possession of the bonds, and put a small pile of notepaper in their place. Then he closed the safe again, left the Château Mesmer and took a cab to the Prefecture.

When Cordeau came back, he ran to the strong-box. "He hasn't touched it! Surely—otherwise, he wouldn't have taken the trouble to lock it again.

Joyfully, he set up the combination.

Horror! The bonds were no longer there. He picked up the notepaper furiously, on which was written the insolent message: *Chase away the natural and it come back at the gallop. And I'm running away....ditto.*

"Stolen!" murmured the doctor. "Stolen! I went too quickly. The sum was too large. What can I do? Lodge a complaint? I'll look ridiculous. And then if Lesécant hears about it....oh no! No, he shan't have her, the pork butcher. The beautiful Hélène! It's me...me...."

Then, prey to a crisis of wrath: "Yes, me, me! I'll start again...there's still time...before the deadline."

Then he reflected. Would it not be better to have the thief arrested, and then continue the experiment he had begun with him. He therefore decided to go to the Prefecture.

He had scarcely emerged when he ran into Lesécant, who was also running.

"Monsieur."

"Monsieur?"

"I want to talk to you."

"No time."

"Make some. Go back in."

"I don't want to. Why should I take any trouble on your behalf?"

"I'll oblige you to do it, by force."

"Try, then!"

"All right!"

And Lesécant, with a solid fist, obliged his colleague to turn back.

"You'll render me satisfaction for this violence!" Cordeau roared.

"Whenever you wish, but before then, answer me: Was it you who pronounced these words just now: *Pork butcher...shan't have her...me, me...?*"

"Yes, it was me."

"You?"

"Certainly. What's astonishing about it? Don't I have the right to think aloud in my own home?"

"Yes, but what's strange is that I heard you, just now, in Viroflay."

"You're mad."

"No more than you. Thank you, Monsieur—that's all I wanted to know. I shall study the matter and draw the conclusions that please me. *Au revoir*, Monsieur."

"We'll meet again with steel in hand."

When Lesécant found Vésigout's letter on his desk, he nearly choked with rage. While he was yielding to a fit of wrath unprecedented in his experience, the villa's doorbell rang.

He mastered himself, and then went to open the door. He found himself in the presence of Rémois, who was smiling.

"Your Vésigout has run off, Monsieur."

"I know, Monsieur Lesécant, but that's a minor incident of no importance. Monsieur Noirmont will have reimbursed you within a fortnight.

A cold shower could not have produced a greater effect on the surgeon's effervescence. He only had the strength to say: "That's good, Monsieur…thank you…."

Cordeau had already heard the news.

Thanks to a speculation as skillful as it was fortunate, Monsieur Noirmont had restarted the enterprise at Chittingham on a larger scale. A letter had informed Hélène that her father would return in a fortnight, ready to free her from the nightmare of the doctors and marry her to Paul Rémois.

At the Prefecture, the psychologist had found the painter in the office of the secretary of the Head of the Sûreté. There, the fifty thousand francs had been returned to him and "the arrest of the thief" had been reported to him. In the satisfaction of recovering the bonds, Cordeau had left a two-thousand-franc tip for the agent who had captured the thief.

Those two thousand francs, and a thousand francs added by Hélène's fiancé, plunged agent Fléchard into delight.

Vésigout, reformed and cured, took charge of the publicizing of the enterprise at Chittingham.

All's well that ends well.

Forgetting their discord, Cordeau and Lesécant were reconciled; they begged Noirmont to forget their "folly" and to keep their funds—a decision of which they would have no reason to complain.

They never found out that Rémois had tricked them. Even vengeance fell before happiness. It was with glass in hand that they encountered him at Hélène's wedding—but they found grounds for argument there. Which of them would be the first godfather?

"Draw lots," advised Rémois.

They agreed; and that's why you are not threatened by the possibility of a sequel to "The Rival Colleagues."

Jules Perrin: *Monsieur Forbe's Hallucination*
(1908)

I

At seven o'clock in the evening on Friday 8 May, I stopped opposite the Théâtre de Vaudeville at the newspaper stand, where I have the habit of buying *Le Temps* in the course of my habitual stroll.

I was tired, glad to be taking the air, and enjoying my stroll sufficiently; I opened the paper while waiting for the vendor to give me the change for a two-franc piece. While reading, I held out my hand, and my young son amused himself by looking at the illustrated papers suspended from the awning all around the kiosk.

Suddenly, my little André uttered a cry, and at the same time, a violent shock shoved the table of planks and trestles, behind which the newsvendor was in the process of counting out my change, toward me. I raised my eyes to look at the woman in question who had just staggered, putting her hands to her breast in a mechanical gesture, to end up falling forwards, flat on her display.

Beside me I perceived one of those creatures with an expression of plaintive resignation, some seamstress or the like, with a wretched piece of faded lace enveloping her head and covering her ears, for she seemed consumptive, with her mouth slightly open in a dolorous expression, as though she had a toothache.

Beside her, my little André, pointing a finger at her, immediately cried in an indignant tone, which seemed to me at the time to be rather comical: "It was her, Papa! Yes, it was her who pushed the lady to make her fall."

With the aid of a few passers-by who had rapidly gathered, I lifted up the newsvendor, whose contracted features were beginning to relax under the calming effect of death. And, indeed, imagine the general horror on perceiving, in the unfortunate woman's breast, the black wooden handle of one of these small kitchen knives that housewives use to peel vegetables!

I turned to the woman who was still standing motionless beside me and I said, in a tone of surprise rather than violence: "Did you do that?"

Her eyes staring, slightly fearful, she seemed to emerge from a dream and started stammering, in a voice devoid of strength, as if unconsciously: "I…I don't know…I think so."

Meanwhile, the crowd had become so large that policemen ended up approaching. After a few explanations, one of them took the consumptive woman by the arm while the others carried the inanimate body of the newsvendor toward the nearest pharmacist's shop.

Moved by professional conscience, I followed the latter group, but, as I had already diagnosed, the knife, plunged into the ventricles of the heart, had determined a brutal cessation of circulation, and when we extracted it from the wound, with the greatest care, hardly any blood flowed from the wound.

The unfortunate woman was dead.

It only remained to inform the family and to close the kiosk, around which a crowd had gathered with the keenest curiosity.

I had been a witness to the murder, however, and I had to go to the commissariat for the initial declarations. I had some difficulty finding little André, who was being interviewed by a reporter—he alone, in fact, having seen the murderous thrust delivered.

When we reached the station in the Rue de Provence, a secretary, in the Commissaire's absence, was in the process of conducting an initial interrogation.

The accused had declared that her name was Emilie-Albertine Sourbelle.

"Where do you live?" asked the secretary.

"In the Rue Mogador," Emilie Sourbelle replied, with meek politeness.

"What is your profession?"

She hesitated for a second, as if not quite understanding the question; she ended up saying; "What do I do? Oh, pardon me, Monsieur; I'm a milliner for hire. I have some skill."

"Good. Are you married?"

Emilie Sourbelle nodded affirmatively.

"What does your husband do?"

In a pitiful voice she recounted that they had not had much luck, having had a small lingerie shop that had not prospered and which they had been obliged to sell at a loss. With what remained of their money her husband, a former mechanic, had left for America a few months before; according to his last letter he was far from having made a fortune there. By the resigned fashion in which she said all that, it was understandable that she had the patient and devoted nature that is the only thing that permits the unfortunate to support the vicissitudes of existence.

Poor woman! At present, she made me feel pity. I exchanged a glance with the police secretary, and we both contemplated her in silence, while she resumed sobbing softly.

"But after all," I said, then, drawing nearer. "Why did you do that?"

She shrugged her shoulders slowly, her eyes dilated and her arms widespread in despair.

"I don't know...I swear to you that I can't explain it. I was sitting in my room, beside my stove, peeling my salad, when it seemed to me that I was lifted out of my chair. I stood up. I went downstairs and I came along the Chaussée d'Antin as far as the Vaudeville. I stopped in front of that lady, who I don't know at all, I assure you; it seemed to me that I had a desire to hit her. Then...unfortunately, I was still holding the little knife that I was using to peel my salad. I struck without knowing it."

There was a silence. I leaned toward the secretary: "Hysteria...hypnosis....some degenerate."

The functionary looked at me and shook his head dubiously. Abandoning the unfortunate woman whom he left to weep, he stood up and came toward me.

"You're a physician, it seems, Monsieur."

I gave my name: "Doctor Forbe, Rue Godot-de-Mauroy. As you can see, I live a few steps away. Since Monsieur le Commissaire is absent, perhaps I can come back after dinner to make the deposition. It's after half past seven—I fear that people will be getting anxious at home...because of my little boy."

Brought to attention, André drew nearer; he took my hand, looked at the secretary, who smiled at him amiably, and said in a low voice: "All the more so as Grandma has just arrived by the six o'clock train, you know, Papa."

André is seven years old; I spoil him slightly and I don't often succeed in not giving into him. I thought that he was inventing a pretext and was internally amused by his mischievousness. Taking my leave of the secretary, I went out, drawing the child by the hand.

"Why did you lie?" I asked him, as we walked along the street.

"But Papa," the child said, with tears in his eyes. "I didn't lie. I swear to you that Grandma arrived by the six o'clock train."

I shrugged my shoulders. There was no reason why Madame Forbe, who lives in Angers, should be in Paris; in any case, no letter had announced her visit.

Meanwhile, André was dragging me along, and it was almost at a run that he took me along the Rue de Provence, the Rue des Mathurins and across the Rue Auber to reach our house.

It was without gaiety that, every evening, I deposited my cane or my umbrella in the sandstone cylinder that decorates the left-hand corner of the antechamber, beside a moleskin-covered banquette.

That evening, my attention was attracted by a valise placed askew, as if thrown onto that banquette in haste.

"Whose is that, Berthe?" I asked the chambermaid who had come to open the door.

"It belongs to Madame's mother, Monsieur," said Berthe gravely, "who arrived a quarter of an hour ago."

André clapped his hands joyfully. "There," he said. "What did I say? You see, Papa, that I was right." Already he was running toward his mother's room shouting: "Grandma! Grandma! I knew that you were here."

Is that child becoming neuropathic? I thought, with a hint of sadness.

Meanwhile, the chambermaid had picked up the valise and she accompanied me upstairs, complaining all the while. "Augustine could have helped me to take this upstairs before going to get dressed up," she said. "Did Monsieur know that she's coming back home? She says that she had a dream that one of her friends is about to get married."

I was scarcely listening; Distractedly, I went into the room where Madame Forbe was in bed. She was not ill, but that morning, at about ten o'clock, as she was coming downstairs, she had fallen, sliding on her back down fifteen steps. She was certainly more frightened than hurt, suffering more from emotion than bruises, but she had taken to her bed as a preventive measure.

Her mother was keeping her company—an excellent woman, still middle-aged, albeit in the later stages.

"Oh, my love," murmured Madame Forbe, in a feeble voice, on seeing me come in, "Would you believe that Maman had a presentiment of what had happened to me?"

I was pleased to see my mother-in-law, for she's a amiable woman full of common sense, respectful of my dignity; reason inspires her speech, which is very rarely due to enthusiasm or exaggeration, so I was immediately surprised to find her agitated and nervous.

"No, no," she exclaimed, "not a presentiment: I saw her, quite clearly, at ten o'clock, putting her foot on a step, slipping, and sliding on her back down to the first floor landing. Honestly, I thought she was dead, or at least seriously injured."

She turned to her daughter, whom she seized in her arms, hugging her ardently, as Lazarus' sisters must have embraced their brother when he emerged from the tomb.

"Were you dreaming?" I asked.

She shook her head energetically. "Not at all. I was as wide awake as you are at this very moment."

"How, then, did you see what you say?"

"This is what happened. I was in my little drawing room on the ground floor. The stairway of your house appeared to me, in the way that one sees things when one closes one's eyes…you know…I saw Henriette, who was coming down, and who fell. It lasted two seconds, perhaps three, and then it all disappeared. It's not a matter of a presentiment, but something quite precise, as if it were real, as if I had been on the stairway myself."

I watched Madame Forbe's mother while she was speaking: the plump, benevolent face, a trifle apoplectic, the bovine eyes, the little button nose, the fleshy mouth sustained by sparkling teeth acquired from the best dentist in Angers, the short hands agitating to punctuate the discourse and show off their outmoded rings, gemmed with all kinds of minerals, from diamonds to Madame Forbe's first milk teeth….

There is, however, nothing that invites interpretation as a symptom of hysteria or neurosis, I thought.

They were looking at me with so much insistence, though, that it was necessary to find an explanation for such strange coincidences at all costs.

I hazarded: "Telepathy…."

Then, spotting André, who was hanging on to his grandmother's dress, looking up at her with eyes full of affection, I added: "And that child, just now, in the middle of our walk, suddenly affirmed to me that you were in Paris…."

There was a silence, which Madame Forbe, forgetting her suffering with the aid of the distraction, broke to say: "It's a contagious disease, then, and it will be necessary to try to cure Augustine, who claims…."

At the same moment, by chance or because the incriminated individual was listening behind it, the door of the room opened and Augustine, our cook, came in.

She seemed to be in a state of high excitement, and immediately affirmed that she was ready to face up to the inconveniences of a third-class railway journey to the heart of the département of the Charente, which was her native region.

"Let's see," I said, when she fell silent. "It appears that you've had a dream. That's no reason…."

Poor Augustine's nostrils flared in an expression full of disdain. "Monsieur thinks so? In my situation, Monsieur undoubtedly wouldn't say that. While I'm alive my fiancé will never marry another woman, and I'm counting on arriving in time to prevent the marriage."

Madame Forbe had closed her eyes. From her bed she murmured in a funereal voice, while making a hand gesture bidding everyone to listen religiously: "But my girl, you could have telegraphed your parents to find out whether this…marriage really is on the point of conclusion."

The wisdom of the argument nonplussed Augustine, who could not find any reply at first. She ended up resuming her speech and declaring that it was too late, and that she would not consent to miss the evening train."

"All right, go," said Madame Forbe, with more dryness than one might have expected in her languid love, "and come back as soon as it's settled." With a gesture, she dismissed Augustine, who left.

"In truth," I said to my wife, then, "I don't understand. You dealt with the girl very weakly! For a dream, you're letting her leave just at the moment when we have most need of her—you suffering, your mother in Paris…."

Completely forgetting her prostration, my wife sat up in bed. She raised her arms to the heavens, and exclaimed: "For a dream! In what way, then, is Augustine's dream more incredible than what happened to Maman? And that child who's becoming a somnambulist, or whatever you call it...in truth, you're all the same, you men—even doctors, who only believe in nerves."

I protested, smiling in order to recover harmony. "Yes, yes...except that it's necessary not to give in to them too much."

Dinner was announced, and from then on the conversation revolved exclusively around the abnormal phenomena to which Madame Forbe's mother made exaggerated claims to be the victim, taking it as a pretext for criticizing modern civilization.

"Oh, you mark my words," she concluded, "with your telephones, your automobiles and all your new inventions, the world will end up going mad."

I tried, affectionately, to calm her down. "It's obvious that those are developments whose slightly brutal novelty is likely to be accompanied by a certain cerebral overexcitement, but such troubles will be temporary. What do you expect? It takes time, and over time everything piles up, as ditch-diggers say. The malady of one century eventually becomes the temperament of the following century."

Dinner finished with placid verbiage, in which I was pleased to play my part while thinking about other things.

I took my leave of my family thereafter in order to take a turn around the street while smoking my cigar. I took advantage of it to go to the police commissariat, where I confirmed my declarations to the Commissaire. The Sourbelle woman had been transferred to the cells without having made any new revelations on the subject of her quasi-demented action.

Ten o'clock was chiming on the Norman clock in the dining room when I got home. Everything there was tranquil; my wife, wearied by staying in bed all day, and her mother, shaken up by six hours in a railways carriage, had gone to bed after my departure.

I spent an hour making a few notes, consulting my schedule of visits, and arranging in my notebook the order of my journeys for the next day. When I slipped cautiously into my bedroom, Madame Forbe was snoring softly in the little brass bed next to mine, under a canopy draped with blue cashmere.

II

I was woken up by an impression of terror, in the midst of a nightmare in which I seemed to see four men standing at a street corner, in the process of planning a dastardly crime under cover of darkness.

Everyone is familiar with that sort of impression; it subsists for a variable length of time when one has woken up, but the consciousness of being the victim of a dream is reassuring, in spite of everything, and gradually calms down the person who is its object.

Then to my great surprise—let's say the word: to my justified terror—I seemed to perceive, close by in the direction of the windows facing my bed, the sound of whispering. My ears straining and my flesh quivering, I listened.

This is what I heard:

"It's understood? You, Radis, watch the Rue d'Anjou—and be on your guard, the police station's on the corner of the Rue Lavoisier."

"You could have chosen another night; one can see as clearly as by day."

"Yes, yes, you want to write to the old lady to absent herself one evening when it's pissing it down, or to come back when she's at home, when we'd have to wring her neck."

"Well, no, not that, you know; for a start, I don't like blood."

"Get on with it then."

"I'm going."

"Good. You stay here, Charlot. One blast if you see anything in the Rue Pasquier."

"Understood. What's that grille over there?"

"The Passage Puteaux. No danger there—it's locked."

196

"But at t'other end, someone going past in the Rue de l'Arcade...."

"Zut! You have a voice, don't you? If you warn us in time, we'll scatter, and meet up in the Rue Michel."

"Good. Not so much chat, and hurry up, the two of you."

"Let's go. Ready, Pépette?"

"You have the crowbar?"

"Down my trouser-leg."

The voices died away into an incomprehensible murmur. Apart from that, there was no other sound.

I certainly had the sensation of being awake; there was no means of believing that it was the prolongation of a dream. And yet, an instinctive logic caused me to set aside any dread of immediate danger. But what did it mean?

Am I, in my turn, I thought, *the victim of one of these phenomena that have been produced around us in the last few hours? It would be interesting, after all, and it would be easy to verify....*

From that moment on, the spirit of scientific curiosity awoke in me and was stronger than any reasoning. Without yet having any goal, and with a mechanical haste, having opening the bathroom door, I began to get dressed.

While hurriedly putting on the indispensable garments, I reflected. Reconstituting the conversation, real or imaginary, that I had just heard, it was easy to extract the most essential indications regarding the action it represented and the location where the crime whose planning I had overheard had to be taking place. By their thick and mocking accents, the interlocutors lent themselves easily to being taken for four of the frightful all-round villains who have proudly ornamented themselves with the name of one of the most heroic tribes of American Indians. The apartment that they were getting ready to rob must ordinarily be inhabited by an old woman whose temporary absence was facilitating their work.

When I had buttoned my boots as best I could and knotted a scarf under my overcoat to hide the soft collar of my night-shirt, I left the house, without any difficulty other than closing the door to the street quietly, in order not to disturb the sleep of the residents, especially that of Madame Forbe.

I reflected momentarily before deciding on the direction I ought to take.

Let's see, I said to myself. *If I can still make the supposition that I'm the victim of a telepathic hallucination, the men I heard just now must be in the process of exercising their regrettable profession in a street whose two extremities are being watched by two accomplices; those two extremities must be the Rue d'Anjou on the one hand, and the Rue Pasquier on the other; and moreover the one who is watching the Rue Pasquier has signaled that he's in the vicinity of the Passage Puteaux. Given those circumstances, it can only be either the Rue des Mathurins or the Rue Tronson-Ducoudray.*

The realization that I was only a short distance away also awoke the legitimate anxieties that can accompany an enterprise of that sort. The critical spirit of the observant man, however, reassured me and pushed me forward.

Come on—I'm the victim of some dream prolonged into a spontaneous hallucination, of no consequence.

I shrugged my shoulders and hastened my steps. The need to know excites courage, and I was passionately keen to know.

I crossed the Rue Tronchet, went along the Rue des Mathurins, and saw the corner of the small square where the lugubrious memory of Louis XVI persists. With an avid gaze I scrutinized the darkness ahead: nothing and no one troubled the silence of the spring night, which I would have found charming at another time.

Mechanically, I murmured in a slightly tremulous voice: "There's nothing at all."

The experiment was not concluded, however. The Rue des Mathurins was empty and tranquil; there remained the Rue Tronson-Ducoudray. The bizarre name seemed sinister in itself, having once been made famous by a crime that was notorious.[24] I approached it mistrustfully, and was already hesitating over turning the corner when a strident whistle-blast stopped me dead. I must confess that I turned round, ready to flee, but I didn't have time for reflection. Footsteps sounded rapidly around me, a mass fell upon my back, and I fell to the ground, entangled with a thin and agile body, and I felt fists belaboring me.

I am rather placid by nature, incapable of the slightest desire to fight, and it had been a long time since I had passed forty, the age when the ardors of combative youth begin to calm down. However, on feeling myself assaulted, my anger was roused, along with my vigor, which is appreciable. I returned the punches with interest, and, however involuntary the aggression had been, in principle, there was a real wrestling match, my adversary attempting by any means possible to escape my grip, which closed progressively around him.

I was dealing with a youthful individual with the flexibility of a reptile and the defensive ferocity of a jackal, who went so far as to try to bite my nose while we were breathing in one another's faces. I sensed a pale face close to mine, illuminated by two eyes diluted even more by fear than anger. I made an effort to repel the little carnivore, who was defending his liberty with all his strength. When, after a few tumultuous movements, I had finally mastered him, I planted my knee on his narrow chest, whose bone-structure, still soft, buckled under my weight.

In a halting voice, he protested and begged: "Let me go. I won't complain, since I'm beaten. You'd do better to go after the others, who are running off toward the Boulevard Malesherbes."

---

[24] The reference is to a sensational murder committed at number 3 Rue Tronson-Ducoudray in 1890 by Gabrielle Bompard and Michel Eyraud, who strangled a court usher, Toussaint-Augustin Gouffé, and disposed of the body in a trunk, the identification of which was an early triumph of scientific detection.

He was a coward, ready to sell his friends to save himself. I didn't reply, though, as I was getting my breath back, which was a trifle oppressed by exercise to which I was unused.

"For one thing," the young hooligan went on, "I'm only the lookout you know."

"Where were you?" I demanded, in a voice that as still breathless.

"In the Rue Pasquier."

"You're Charlot, aren't you? Radis was at the corner of the Rue d'Anjou?"

His astonishment was sincere, and to begin with he made no reply. He only muttered between his teeth: "How do you know that?"

Nervous and excited by the satisfaction of seeing my experiment succeed, I tightened my grip. Pressing his arms against his neck again and increasing the pressure of my knee on the thorax that I could feel yielding beneath it.

He had gone even paler; he grimaced in pain; his mouth rounded and his eyes begged.

"You're hurting me," he sighed. "If you know…yes, yes, it's true: Radis and me were keeping watch at the ends of the street while Pépette and the big Polard tried to pry the shutter open with the crowbar. When the cops arrived, Radis whistled and I ran. If you hadn't been there at the street corner, I'd be long gone by now."

Thus, everything was verified in the mysterious communication that had just been established, through two enormous blocks of houses and a tangle of streets, between me and one of those scenes of brigandage of which a big city like Paris is the ordinary theater every night. I found myself, along with those nearest to me, prey to a mysterious telepathic current that was facilitating the most various distant perceptions. How was that collectively possible? I had no idea, but I was ready and willing to study the manifestations, and, I hoped, to discover their cause. In truth, my role was finished, but I didn't know what to do to get rid of the prisoner with whom hazard had gratified me.

It was also hazard that came to my aid.

The sound of heavy footsteps resonated on the sidewalk, and in response to my call, two *sergents de ville* emerged from the Rue Pasquier, taking one of young Charlot's accomplices, whom they had just apprehended, to the station. I helped them to take the unruly youth to the commissariat in the Rue Lavoisier; he strove in vain to escape, thrashing about and wriggling like a snake.

Once again I had to give my name to the police, whose auxiliary I had become twice in less than twelve hours, but I claimed that I had emerged from the house of a patient, jealously keeping, for the time being, the secret of the strange reasons for my presence at such an hour in a deserted street.

I went back home, reflecting profoundly on the various contingencies.

Fundamentally, without daring to admit it, I was dejected. The initial curiosity, and the entirely scientific satisfaction of having fortunately resolved the observation of a fact whose as-yet-unknown nature was beginning nevertheless to be incontestable, was succeeded by a depression, egotistical in origin, that I could not succeed in overcoming.

It was necessary to yield to the evidence.

Thus, with the exception of Madame Forbe, all of those close to me, and myself, had been victims, for at least one day, of a series of nervous shocks of a kind that science, thus far, admits as exclusively possible in individualities of an exaggerated nervousness.

In those facts, such as I had observed them in others, I had interested myself, doubtless in a concerned manner, but with those sentiments of scientific curiosity with which we physicians sometimes defend ourselves. Now it was my turn, and, as well as the observer, I had become a subject of observation; I confess, to my shame, that I was affected by that.

And yet, exclusively personal as that fact might appear, I now owed to it a glimpse of a possible generalization of a series of accidents that I could only resign myself to considering as explicable under the title of being exceptional.

Is it possible, I asked myself, *that a well-balanced, averagely equilibrated nature, like mine—as I am entitled to say—can become, without some superior cause, without an influence magnified to the extent of claiming the name of a law, the instrument of manifestations previously isolated and obscure in essence?*

One thing, above all, surprised me: how was it that my wife, whose temperament, although assuredly less nervous than she thinks, must nevertheless be very impressionable to a current of events of the sort in question, had not yet sensed anything?

I thought that with a certain bitterness as I went upstairs and into my room.

The state in which I found Madame Forbe was to modify the course of my thoughts and definitively fortify my inclination to envisage as capable of generalization a state common to many people at a single location on the globe.

With a candle lit on the bedside table, the poor woman, her face distraught beneath the halo of curlers that replaces during sleep the artifice of her fluffed-up coiffure, was sighing profoundly under the influence of some malaise or nightmare.

She watched me enter the room as if she were staring at a phantom, and when she finally understood that it really was me, her head inclined languidly onto her shoulder, and she let herself fall weakly back on to her pillow.

"Where have you been?" she asked, in anguish. "Can't you see that I nearly died?"

As a matter of habit, that is the fashion in which Madame Forbe manifests the preliminary symptoms of the slightest stomachache or headache. I thought that she had woken up, had called out to me and had been alarmed not to find me beside her. I attempted to reassure her. With the most extreme reserve, I attempted to explain to her the reasons for and the purpose of my unusual absence, but she interrupted me when I had hardly started.

"Oh, what a frightful dream! But, great gods, what's happening around us? Can you imagine that Augustine has just broken both her legs?"

"But isn't she on the train at this moment, on her way to La Rochelle?" I asked, in surprise.

"Obviously—but her train has just been derailed. The locomotive has overturned across the track. Four carriages are broken...."

"That's what you dreamed?"

Exhausted, she nodded her head—but then went on, groaning: "Never—never, you hear—have I had a dream like it: such clarity, such precision of detail. I was sitting on the banquette beside Augustine...she was asleep...look, we'd just passed through a station at which the train didn't stop, but it had slowed down, and in the station, above the lantern, I'd been able to read the name of the place: it was Reuil. Afterwards, the train picked up speed again and was traveling as before when, all of a sudden, a violent shock threw us forwards. There was a sound of breaking glass and splintering wood; the lights went out, screams began to ring out on all sides, then moans, howls of pain...it was horrible, horrible...."

She described the scene in broken sentences, showing Augustine, surprised, lying on her side, tipped over, her legs crushed between two banquettes; and she still had ringing in her ears, mingled with the cries of the victims, the excited sound of the electric alarm bells that were signaling to all the stations along the line.

I had to prepare her a glass of sugared water, scented with orange flowers. While twirling the spoon to make the sugar dissolve, I looked pityingly at my poor pale wife, her eyes closed and her head inert on her pillow, and I thought: *It's her turn. Thus, we've all experienced it. In that case, can we be the only ones?*

Take note that I did not doubt the objective reality of Madame Forbe's dream for a moment. What would, the day before, have simply had the effect on me of a mere nightmare due to an embarrassment of digestion or some disturbance in the functioning of the circulatory system, I now admitted, without any hesitation, as a manifestation of sympathy at a distance, adding to all those I had been observing for several hours.

I was in haste to widen my verification, and the night already seemed to me to be interminable. It was, however, necessary for me to calm Madame Forbe down in order to persuade her to go to sleep. I ended up falling asleep myself, albeit with some difficulty.

III

I woke up early and, allowing the others to sleep, hastened my preparations in order to be able to commence my daily round without delay. That morning, for the first time, I added a supplementary question to all the questions that the conditions of my patients required: "Have you had any dreams?"

Some said yes and others said no, but in general, the responses were inconclusive, made in a tone of surprise and disinterest. It even appeared to me that my persistence had a bad effect and harmed my reputation as a serious man.

"Undoubtedly," Monsieur Gallois said to me a trifle sarcastically, "the excellent practice that has been giving me chronic dyspepsia and manifestations of arthritis for eight years has been…undoubtedly, I have dreams…just like everyone else. No?"

He was exaggerating, but I had to take a bantering tone to calm him down.

In sum, my enquiries not producing any results, I took curiosity further; I asked the last patients I visited, about eleven o'clock, squarely, whether they had suffered any hallucinations. Only one of my old clients, Mademoiselle Belpomme, who has been paralyzed for nine years, replied that, the day before, she had suddenly become aware of a scent of lilacs in her room, into which no flowers had been brought.

"However," Mademoiselle Belpomme hastened to add, "it isn't the first time that has happened, and it's always at the time of year when I had the habit of leaving Paris and going to spend the summer at my property in Brunoy."

My round finished shortly before midday. At that moment I happened to be in the Place Saint-Augustin; as it was on my way home, I called in at the commissariat in the Rue Lavoisier, where I had another statement to make.

It was the Commissaire himself who received me. Like all his colleagues, he is a charming functionary, very well-mannered and well-spoken. He seemed to be delighted to see me, took my deposition, thanked me very warmly for the valuable aid that I had given his agents, and finally, as I got up to leave, he stopped me with a courteous gesture, saying: "Now that we've finished with my professional concerns, Doctor, it's necessary that I bring your attention to a matter that is more in your particular province, and which will perhaps interest you. Can you imagine….?"

He stopped, reflected momentarily, and stood up. "It's better if you hear it from the mouth of the person concerned." Crossing the room, he opened the door and shouted: "Leboul!"

Hurried footsteps resounded on the parquet of the next room, where the agents were. The Commissaire stood aside to let through a tall, thin, dark fellow with two small ferrety eyes and the suspicion of a moustache.

The Commissaire closed the door, came to sit down beside me, and said to the *sergent de ville*: "Tell Monsieur what happened to you last night."

To judge by the theoretical and decided tone in which he set out to tell his little story, I was far from being the second person to hear it, but it was no less interesting for that.

"I was on patrol duty outside the door of the station last night between half past two and twenty to three. I was walking back and forth without thinking about anything, when it suddenly came into my head that someone was committing a crime in the Rue Tronson-Ducoudray. Things like that aren't usual for me, and at first I didn't pay any attention. 'It's just imagination,' I said to myself, and I carried on walking. Well, a minute went by…Monsieur, I could no longer hold still; it was stronger than me. I went to look in that direction, and what do I see? A head sticking out round the corner of the street and, on seeing me, pulls back swiftly. 'Suspicious,' I say to myself, 'have to take a look….' I resume my patrol, making my boots sound on the sidewalk, then I suddenly turn round. This time, it wasn't only the head but an entire man that, on seeing me, disappears again. Then I didn't hesitate any longer—I run to the station and I tell the brigadier. You can imagine that at first, he made fun of me, but I held firm. 'No matter how I know, it's necessary to go; I tell you that I'm sure there's something shady going on.' And positively, Monsieur, with these eyes I have in my head, I saw what was happening as if I were there: two militiamen from the subcontinent keeping a lookout at the ends of the street and the other two busy trying to force the shutter. Already, one of them had got into the ground-floor lodgings. In brief, we went back at a run and when I heard the blast of the whistle that warned them about our arrival, the brigadier said to me, like this: 'You know, Leboul, you ought to be a *somnambulist!*'"

I shook my head, pretending to smile, amused by the agent's style of reportage.

"That's very good," I said to him, when he fell silent. "You're a precious watchman, and I congratulate you."

"You can go," said the Commissaire to Leboul. "Well, Doctor, what do you think? I ought to tell you that I sometimes dabble in hypnotism…yes, even a little spiritism…in brief, these questions interest me very much. Don't you think that that man possesses the gift of second sight?"

"Bah!" I said, standing up. "These cases aren't rare, and they've been known to manifest themselves exceptionally in subjects who've never had occasion to observe anything similar. In any case, your agent might be exaggerating, and he seems to be a good talker."

The Commissaire struck a reflective pose. "Perhaps you're right," he conceded, finally. "In any case, it seems to me that it's not without interest."

"Undoubtedly, undoubtedly...however, until further notice...."

In a light and cheerful tone, my interlocutor interrupted me. "Of course...."

I stood up. He accompanied me as far as the street.

Come on, I thought, *there's not a moment to lose; here's a further instance. If I can assemble a certain number of analogous manifestations, they'll finish up forming a whole, very capable of interesting a scientific body.*

Lunch was waiting for me. Sitting in their customary places, Madame Forbe and her mother greeted me with a certain solemnity. Without saying a word, my wife pointed to my napkin, on which the blue paper of an open telegram cased me to dread an urgent summons that would not leave me time to eat.

"Again!" I sat down, setting the telegram, at which my wife was continuing to point a fateful finger, down in front of me.

"Read it, then!" she said, in an impatient tone.

I obeyed.

Laconically, in a few unsigned lines, the account confirmed, on behalf of Mademoiselle Augustine Lavert, the railway accident in which the unfortunate girl had had both legs crushed. Madame Forbe's dream was realized.

My mother-in-law fixed me with up-turned eye widened by fear. My wife adopted an expression of triumph.

"Well?"

"Well," I said, carefully folding up the telegram, which I slipped into my pocket, "It's quite simple, but until further notice, not a word about all this."

All afternoon I remained in my study, busy drafting a detailed account of the facts, just in case.

It was nearly six o'clock when a prolonged ringing of the bell in the antechamber caused me to shiver.

"There's another one," I murmured, involuntarily.

As I immediately strove to contain that nervous disposition to presentiment, someone knocked at my door and the anxious face of my chambermaid appeared,

"What is it now, Berthe?"

"Monsieur," said Berthe, slightly embarrassed, "it's a very oddly dressed man who wants to talk to Monsieur. He says that he's come from America and that he took the train from Le Havre this morning to come and see Monsieur...."

"Did he give you his name?"

"My word, that's right—I didn't even think of asking him."

During the brief interval of silence that followed that declaration, I pricked up my ears; the visitor could be heard pacing back and forth in the hallway, at a precipitate pace; his shoes were making the parquet vibrate.

I stood up and moved the domestic aside in order to open the door wide.

"Please come in," I said, imperatively.

Advancing toward me, with broad strides, I saw a man, it's necessary to confess, of the sorriest appearance. Ugly and miserable, his face was pockmarked, his eyelids swollen, his head closely shaved and his ears sticking out like the handles of a soup tureen. Of his costume, it was only possible to see frayed trousers descending over monstrous shoes of tan leather, studded with nails; all the rest—short, waistcoat, etc.—was enveloped in a rubber greatcoat yellowed by wear, militarily buttoned from the collar to the knees. In his impatient hands, seemingly poorly cared-for, my visitor was furiously kneading a traveling cap in faded green cloth, rendered formless under the exclusive or combined action of overwork and time.

Berthe went out and I silently indicated a seat to the man. He refused with a gesture. He seemed violently emotional, out of breath, and his entire appearance seemed to signify: *Oh, yes, it's a fine time to sit down!*

Without giving me time to ask any questions, he said, in a staccato voice, looking me straight in the eyes: "Monsieur, my name is Sourbelle."

"Eh?"

"Sourbelle," he replied, authoritatively. "Yesterday evening, my wife murdered a newsvendor in front of you...."

I nodded my head several times, precipitately. "I know, I know....but your wife said that you were in America."

He extended his hand in a tearful gesture. "Oh," he cried, "she's innocent, I assure you, completely innocent, so gentle, incapable of hurting a fly. The guilty party, in sum, is me."

"You! But haven't I been told that you've arrived from Le Havre on the morning train?"

Sourbelle's bloodshot eyes stared at me madly, and I was able to see that behind their sickly lids, they did not appear to be devoid of intelligence.

Abruptly, in order not to prevaricate any longer, he decided to take the chair that I had offered him, and sat down directly opposite me, his eyes obstinately fixed on mine.

"Undoubtedly," he declared, in a dull voice, "something supernatural is happening at present."

I could not help shivering. "What do you mean?"

He threw his green cap on to the floor, crossed his legs one over the other, stuck his elbow on one knee and supported his chin on his closed fist.

"Yesterday evening," he said, "at about seven o'clock, we were approaching Le Havre. The *Lorraine* had just passed within sight of Cherbourg. *Seven months*, I was thinking, *it's seven months since I left, and here I am coming back, poorer than before, discouraged by one more attempt, in which the few thousand-franc bills we had saved have gone to waste....*

"Going back to the beginning, seeking the point of departure of that further disappointment, that was when I had to recognize as the first cause of all the evil was the woman who sells newspapers at the stall opposite the Théâtre de Vaudeville."

209

"What's that?" I had started in my seat. A flash of light went through my head—but, intent on knowing everything, I mastered myself and signaled to Sourbelle to carry on.

"Pay close attention," he continued. "First of all, it's necessary for you to know that I've had a run of bad luck. I flatter myself, however, with having courage; my poor wife and I have worked hard; I swear to you, we've tried everything. Successively, it has been necessary to give up or sell at a loss, all of our petty patrimony. We had only seven thousand francs left. I got a job as a mechanic with an automobile company. I earned a living, but what can you expect? I was obsessed with the idea of being better off; vegetating in place made my blood boil. One day...."

He collected himself, recrossed his legs and picked up his knee in both hands, bringing it up to touch his chin.

"Seven months ago—in consequence, at the beginning of last October—I was waiting with my twenty-five horsepower at the corner of the Chaussée d'Antin. While idling on the sidewalk I went over to the kiosk with its display of newspapers. To pass the time, I said to myself, I'll buy a newspaper. '*La Patrie*, Monsieur?' All right, *La Patrie*. I throw down my sou and open the accursed rag. Would you believe that I find an article on page three about the unknown California, a magnificent country, it said, still unexplored, where there's everything to do. I've told you how I am: my imagination started working...."

I was breathless. To hurry him along, I said: "In short, you left."

"I left. There's no need to tell you what I did out there; only the result matters. Here I am...without a sou. Good. And the origin of all that—what do you see as the cause of all that?"

I attempted to smile, because the poor devil was so sad I felt sorry for him.

"Well," I suggested, "A little credulity, perhaps...?"

Grimly, and abruptly, he interrupted me.

"Possibly, as the energetic cause, but as the circumstantial cause, as the contribution of hazard, the stupid, irritating hazard that often causes poor folk to choose between several unknown directions...anyway, if that accursed woman hadn't been there with her newspapers; if, at least, she hadn't, with her banal shopkeeper's amiability, directed my choice, or if, instead of *La Patrie*, she'd offered me...what do I know? Anyway, yesterday evening, I was thinking about her, about her unconsciously suggestive role in my adventure, and, confronted by the result, I said to myself that if I could get my hands on her...you know how it is; it's stupid; one says to oneself that one would do this or that, and, in sum, one does nothing. Certainly, if she'd been there, I'd have left her perfectly tranquil, but it's no less true that I brandished my fist in the air, promising myself on the deck of the steamer, that soon...you understand?"

I nodded my head. I was just as emotional as him, but for different reasons. I tried to speak, but he interrupted me by extending his arms.

"Wait a bit. Having made that gesture, I resumed my stroll; in spite of everything, I was glad to be returning to France. I was thinking about my wife, who would be surprised, and also disappointed to see me come back without a sou. I pictured her in her little room on the sixth floor of a new house on the Rue Mogador, I could see her clearly, as one sees things that one remembers, but with more clarity, like an image, as if there was a cinematograph in front of me: she went downstairs, went out into the street, went behind the Opéra, along the Rue Mogador and the Chaussée d'Antin. She arrived opposite the Vaudeville. There, near the kiosk, there was a gentleman standing, reading a newspaper beside a little boy who was looking at the pictures...."

I couldn't help interrupting, exclaiming: "That was me! Do you recognize me?"

"Perfectly. I recognized you when I came in."

"And you saw...?"

The poor fellow lowered his head. "Everything. My wife approached, raised her arm, struck...

"When we arrived at Le Havre this morning, we disembarked. I was in a hurry to get to Paris, as you can imagine. I took the first train that was leaving. At Rouen, I found the newspapers which told me everything...."

He had said all that in a jerky voice, becoming emotional between sentences. He ended up feeling nothing but his grief, and he stopped talking, letting his head fall into his hands, succumbing to a fit of tears.

Eventually, he raised his head again. I don't recall ever having seen anything more horrible than that face like a cheese-grater streaming with tears, and those eyes, as red as fresh wounds.

"Since my arrival," he said, "I've been everywhere: to the commissariat, to the court. I learned all the details and I've been promised that I can see my wife the day after tomorrow; tomorrow's Sunday, it seems. Everywhere, I've told people what's happened to me, and I saw that, without wanting to laugh at me, they thought I was mad. Then I thought of you, Monsieur, who are a physician, and perhaps won't laugh at me if I ask you to help me prove to the law that this is a case of hypnotism, of entirely involuntary suggestion. Oh, I know full well that it's extraordinary, unique—but after all, apart from that explanation, I can't see any other!"

He stood up. I stopped him with a gesture.

"Me neither," I said, softly.

His face cleared, transfigured by a kind of joy.

I went on: "In a few words, I'll convince you of my intentions. I'm entirely in agreement with you, and I think that your gesture has done all the harm; it was involuntary, especially in its range, for misfortune determined that it would be prolonged at a distance. How is that possible? That's what I don't know yet, although I suspect a cause."

I wasn't boasting; although I didn't dare jump to the conclusions that a further experimentation would constrain science to formulate, I can recall with pride that my inductions were already on the right track. Sourbelle, who couldn't see so far, thought it was a matter of some Machiavellian or diabolical intervention; his brandished fist was threatening the invisible. The gesture in question was definitely familiar to him.

Gravely, I stopped him. "Be careful," I said, severely.

Downcast, the poor fellow lowered his arm and recommenced twisting the green cap, which he had picked up from the floor, between his hands.

Personally, I was reflecting that there was a session of the Académie des Science the day after tomorrow, and not a moment to lose. I turned toward Sourbelle. "My friend, you're going to begin by swearing to me that you won't say a word about all this to a living soul. You'll understand that it's a matter, as far as we're concerned, of a phenomenon whose value ought to be brought to light by a voice more authoritative than mine. I have the good fortune to be the friend and pupil of a great scientist who, in this regard, can do anything. I'll take you to see him; you can tell him your story, which I'll be able to corroborate with a few personal observations, and...be brave."

"Oh," said that pitiful individual, enthusiastically, "I'll entrust myself to you, Monsieur. You're my only hope!"

Full of a courage that was perhaps exaggerated now, Sourbelle had flattened his green cap between his hands, and his eyes were rediscovering the smile in his cheese-grater face. He went through my door obliquely and took his leave of me with declarations full of cordiality. Alone in the antechamber, I started rubbing my hands together vigorously as a sign of delight.

Come on, come on, I said to myself, it's making progress. In the presence of facts as precise and verified, my old master, Saint-Denis, can't refuse me the collaboration of his authority. Thanks to his universal reputation, all this will make the devil of a noise; thanks to his great name and this resounding experiment, my modest reputation will grow...."

I saw myself launched, known, the newspapers talking about me....

"Is my luck turning? I'll make a specialty of nervous diseases...."

From the depths of the apartment, the sound of doors
opening and closing, and eruptions of voices distracted me
from those ambitious dreams.

On the threshold of the dining room, Madame Forbe's
mother appeared, wearing violet stripes and crowned with
tulle and yellow buttercups, red-faced and very excited, followed by her daughter, emotional and seemingly anxious.

"Quickly, quickly!" cried my mother-in-law. "Let me
pass—I don't have time."

"My God," I said, jovially "What's the matter."

Tearfully, my wife put her hands together. "The fire,"
she murmured.

"What fire?"

Frantically shaking the buttercups that were oscillating
on her hat, the old lady fixed me with a desolate gaze. "Oh,
Auguste, pity me—my house is burning down. And what af-
fects me most is that the only thing that has let me know is a
vision of the kind that revealed the accident that Henriette had
suffered to me. My God, my God! Am I becoming a hysteric?
At my age!"

"Come, on," I said, "don't distress yourself—perhaps it
isn't true."

She turned round on the staircase, where we were following her.

"Not true!" she cried. "Oh, I saw it all too clearly: the
flames coming through the roof. The fire has taken hold in the
eaves. That old fool Félicie had the idea of taking a lamp up
there to hang up her linen in the grain-loft. I've told her a hundred times...anyway, I'm certain. *Au revoir*, my children."

She disappeared. I leaned over the banisters to shout:
"Send us a telegram when you arrive."

She was heard to mutter a few words and the door of the
vestibule closed beneath the entrance arch.

Madame Forbe was weeping.

"Come on," I said in order to make her feel better, "cheer up. This is becoming truly extraordinary, but every cloud has a silver lining. I have material here for sensational revelations, and if this fire is real, well...my word, it will be one proof more...."

I hesitated momentarily before giving in to the scientific delirium that was possessing me. Finally, I could no longer restrain myself, and I murmured, fervently: "My God! As long as it's true!"

IV

Everyone has heard of Professor Saint-Denis.

He's a septuagenarian, a trifle sanguine, full of good humor, perfectly even-tempered and tranquil. To anyone who congratulates him, the professor replies without false modesty: "I consider the world as a garden, and I have the gaiety of a plant in the sun. I ask no more of human nature than it can give, so I'm unacquainted with dreams and disillusionment; I'm as unconscious and happy as a primrose, a cauliflower or an apricot."

The professor preaches by example. A successor of the likes of Darwin, Littré, and Herbert Spencer, he is the author of a theory of mental dynamics based uniquely on human observation and experimentation, and in order to establish that basis, he began by attacking the defective phraseology of the ancient method.

"Before anything else," he proclaims, "it's necessary to get rid of what is conventionally known as the soul. Whoever says 'soul' says nothing more today than that we now situate within the neural centers the faculties once accumulated in a sheaf under that obsolete vocable."

That is why a chair has been created for Saint-Denis at the Collège de France, where he develops before enthusiastic audiences his lecture course in mental dynamics under the combative and limpid name of Psychotrity.[25]

His entire life, devoted to study, has gone by in a little apartment in the Rue La Bruyère, which he leaves in spring to take up residence in Ville d'Avray in a small house near that of the painter Corot. From the windows of his study he has a view of the lake.

Physically, try to remember Sainte-Beuve, whose mischievous gaze he has. Unfortunately, his nose is a trifle turgid, but he gains therein a kind of violence that is not without heroism. His admirers say that it composes a Panic face for him; his detractors express the same idea by saying that he resembles an old faun.

Before broadening out his education as far as philosophy, Saint-Denis taught medicine, and I had the honor and joy of being his pupil. An affectionate relationship has subsisted between us, and he seemed to me to be better qualified than anyone else to present to the scientific world in the form that he judged to be convenient the little work that I had resolved to bring to him.

At the agreed hour Sourbelle came to collect me, and it was not yet half past eight when I pulled with a tremulous hand the chain that made an old bell vibrate at the door of the Villa Ned—that being the name of the modest abode where my excellent master savored the mildness of summer days.

The canonical visage of the old man suddenly appeared at the open window of the study.

---

[25] The reference to this improvisation—*psychotritie* in the original—as "limpid" is probably a joke. If the term is derived from Greek roots, it presumably refers to a tripartite division or classification of mental phenomena. An intellectual of Saint-Denis' stature would surely not have combined Greek and Latin roots, so the second element cannot refer to the analytical process of trituration, even though a less scholarly person might think that the term might make more sense if it did.

"Forbe!" he cried, joyfully "Come in, come in, my dear boy. I'm glad to see you—and by a singular hazard, I was just thinking about you."

"That doesn't surprise me, my dear master."

"I launched forward, followed by my pitiful companion; in two bounds the garden was crossed and the front steps scaled. I went through the little dining room, modestly furnished with old mahogany.

"Stay here, my friend," I said to Sourbelle. "Wait until I give you the signal to come in."

"Well," said the venerable scientist, amicably, in offering me an armchair beside his worktable, "To what do I owe the pleasure of your early morning visit, and who is the man with the face ravaged by hail or smallpox?"

By way of reply I took out of my pocket the pages of the manuscript that I had prepared.

"Please read this," I said, placing my work on the table.

Holding out the papers to his nose, he darted a rapid glance at them, scanning the first few lines, drafted in the form of a prologue. Then he looked at me mischievously.

"That," he murmured, "is quite a mystery."

With a simple gesture, I exhorted him to continue. "As for the conclusions, you'll draw them yourself."

With his beautiful horn-rimmed spectacles with round lenses perched on his nose, Saint-Denis began reading, slowly and carefully, with a dubious expression, his nostrils a trifle pinched, and an ironic grimace on his upper lip, where his moustache, not yet shaven, formed a slight gray down, like the lichen on the old apple trees of Brittany.

Finally, he finished reading, put his spectacles down on the table, took a deep breath of the perfumed air, contemplating the spring décor of the lake, and then interrogated me with his gaze.

"Well?"

I smiled, my heart a trifle emotional, troubled in its calm, because I had expected to surprise him.

"Well, my dear Master?" I asked in my turn "What do you think it's necessary to conclude from all this?"

"Obviously," said Saint-Denis, with his benevolent smile, "nothing at all."

I jumped out of my armchair, and my voice rose involuntarily to its highest register. "Nothing at all."

Saint-Denis was still smiling, and the smile ended up irritating me. I knew that he was circumspect and severe in his choice of affirmations, but I confess that I had hoped to encounter more confidence in my personal experience on his part.

"In truth, my dear Master," he said, in a piqued tone, "prudence of method has its limits…"

He made me sit down again with a gesture, and, paternally placing his plump hand on my arm, he murmured in an affectionate one: "Let's understand one another clearly," he murmured. "If by a conclusion you mean a scientific definition of these phenomena, I agree with you that it's a matter of the species of inexplicable facts of sensorial communication at an abnormal distance known by the name of telepathy."

Such was my ardor that I interrupted the old master that I respect as the equal of idols. "That's right! You've got it!"

"Undoubtedly," said Saint-Denis, serenely, "I've got it. Let's talk about telepathy. What exact observations have been submitted to us thus far under that label? I've read—it's necessary to read everything—what's been published on that subject in recent years and, I confess, always with a suspicion that my reading has not yet succeeded in dissipating. What makes me dubious about witness statements of this sort is their character of individual exception. Then again, have you noticed that they almost always relate to facts of a dolorous nature: deaths, accidents, maladies and malaises—in brief, all states eminently disruptive of our sensorial equilibrium? Can you think of any reason for that?"

I reflected momentarily.

"But isn't dolor," I suggested, slowly, with an embarrassment over which I triumphed as my argument proceeded, "for the majority of people, an abnormal state, and, in consequence, more remarkable than pleasure, which sentiment seems quite natural?"

Saint-Denis nodded his head.

"Perhaps," he admitted.

"And in any case, what does the cause of an insensible influence matter if the influence is manifest?"

"So be it," said the professor. "Let's admit the exactitude of the facts. They remain no less accidental, and in the observations noted by scientists as estimable as Richet or Dariex,[26] there are scarcely any but unique manifestations. Can you cite me a single example—even one—of powerful perception at a distance becoming a matter of habit in a subject?"

"Certainly," I said. "Hasn't Madame Forbe's mother had, twice in twenty-four hours…."

"Pardon me," Saint-Denis objected, "but the lady has seen two accidents at a distance, on which one—Madame Forbe's fall—has been realized. As for the fire, we have no proof yet that the fact was exact."

"I'll be certain in a few hours, but I confess that I already have no doubt about it myself."

With his arms folded over his chest, Saint-Denis darted a slightly saddened glance at me. "That's exactly what I'm combating in you," he said. "Experimentally, I suspect and detest the enthusiasm that, when riding an idea, does not stop until all the contingencies are in conformity with it."

I was on my feet. I began to pace furiously back and forth, while arguing: "But in the end, on thinking about it, why is the idea of telepathy, considered as a prolongation of the

---

[26] Charles Richet (1850-1935) was a physiologist who eventually won a Nobel Prize for his work on anaphylaxis, but was also a litterateur, a pioneer of heavier-than-air aviation and an ardent student of psychic phenomena. He co-founded the journal *Annales des Sciences Psychiques* in 1891 with the physician Xavier Dariex, who published a book on telepathy in the same year.

human personality, any more extraordinary than, say, wireless telegraphy? Given the fact that we exist, sense and think, it's admissible that a more-or-less extensive molecular vibration results therefrom in the atmosphere that serves us as a suspension medium; that under some influence, that vibration can be prolonged, and that, naturally, the result is a sound, an image or an odor. All that, my dear master, is pure dynamics, logical and perfectly consonant with the scientific theories that are so dear to you."

My master watched me going back and forth benevolently; he forgave me for the impulse of impatience by which I had allowed myself to be carried away. He tried to calm it down by yielding slightly.

"Let's see," he said. "In sum, where are you trying to arrive?"

I moved closer, leaning ardently toward him over the worktable.

"Before this current of sorts that seems to influence simultaneously a certain number of brains quite dissimilar in their organization, don't you think that a species of law might be acting, which, for the moment, is inclining toward generalization?"

Saint-Denis looked up dubiously. "You're going rather quickly," he said.

I strove to convince him, expanding persuasive arguments. Thoughtful and distracted, with his amiable smile on his lips, Saint-Denis was not really listening. It seemed to me, however, that his attention gradually became focused, not on me but on the truth. His eyes round, his lips slightly parted, he looked out of the open window at the lake with an expression of astonishment that became, in a matter of seconds, amazement, and almost fear.

As there was no way of attributing such a virtue of persuasion to my words, I stopped talking.

"What's the matter?" I asked him, a trifle sulkily.

He turned toward me, his face entirely distraught, as if dazed, and then, looking back at the lake, he extended his arm in the direction of the window and stammered: "There…there…look!"

As he said these words, Saint-Denis rose swiftly to his feet, took me by the arm, and turned me forcibly toward the window—where, this time, I saw something that surprised me as much as my old professor.

Slowly and soundlessly, on that screen of verdure and sky, a pale thread of yellow flame slid from bottom to top, rising from the lake in order to expand in the air into a luminous spray, from which red and green sparks began to descend, shining like tears of light.

"My word," I said, tranquilly. "It's a rocket."

"It's not the first one I've seen," said Saint-Denis. "Look—there's another…and another…notice that they're bursting silently. One might think that it's a matter of fireworks fired over the water, in accordance with annual custom, on days of public fêtes. I don't suppose, though, that the municipality is generous enough to offer us such a distraction at nine o'clock in the morning and without any known motive for official rejoicing."

He placed a little black silk hat on his head and moved toward the door, saying: "We have to go and see what it is."

Without paying any attention to Sourbelle, who had stood up when we came into the dining room, he hastened toward the vestibule, and I followed him, going through the garden behind him.

In a few strides, we were on a roadway of sorts that overlooks the lake at that point.

We were not alone. Leaning on the iron rail that borders the road, some twenty people were considering the unusual spectacle.

Beside me, Sourbelle, who had followed us, uttered a muffled exclamation: "Oh!"

With an ecstatic expression, he pressed his green cloth cap against his heart, raising his eyes to the heavens; forgetting his chagrin and his anguish, he was absorbed in the contemplation of a monstrous polychromatic bouquet, whose

221

spray expanded in the breadth of the sky in a flowering of gemstones of every color.

Saint-Denis turned his pale and obstinately serious face toward me, in the midst of which his truculent nose was bursting with life.

"Do you understand?" he asked me, in a low voice.

"What?"

He took me by the arm, led me as far as the balustrade, and pointed his finger at the limpid, unaltered, sky blue lake.

"Look," he said to me, in a voice strangled by emotion. "In the water…in the water…."

"Well?"

He fixed me with his gaze, full of profundity, remained mute for a few seconds, and then proffered, slowly: "There's no reflection."

What flash of enlightenment that was for me! Silently, I took the excited hand of my old master, and in a communion of thought, full of ardor, I squeezed it in mine. Very quietly, apart from the crowd that was amusing itself without intelligence, we murmured brief responses to one another.

"Do you understand?"

"Yes, my friend, thanks to what you've just told me."

"Oh, Master…!"

"It's evidence, and I yield to it."

"So, the fireworks…?

"A mirage, a projected image: you were right."

There was a brief moment of reflective delirium, if one can say that, far beyond the idlers who surrounded us. Saint-Denis was the first to go on.

"Let's reason," he concluded. "Isn't it beyond doubt that if this spectacle, instead of being a reverberated or prolonged image, were real in this location, the prodigious firework display that we've just seen could not have taken place without the air being shaken by detonations, and without all those pyrotechnics being reflected in the surface of that clear water?"

"That's evident."

"Where are those rockets, serpents and sunbursts exploding? Perhaps at Noumea, where it's eight o'clock in the evening at present. Unless the transmission of the image hasn't been instantaneous, and we're watching at this moment some spectacle of yesterday evening."

"All that," I said, seems clear and logical to me.

Saint-Denis took me by the arm and drew me away. "Come on, come on," he exclaimed. "Let's verify the singularity of all this further. Let's make a tour of the lake."

For his age, my old master still had solid legs and good lungs. He led us at a good pace to the end of the first pond, as far as the raised causeway extending between the two lakes. Surprise, in the absence of fatigue, suddenly immobilized him at that point in the excursion. He turned toward me, pointing at the second pool, smaller and separated from the other by a curtain of trees.

Above that second expanse of water a second firework display, identical and symmetrical, was continuing to expand its sprays over the verdure that framed it. Rockets were succeeded by sunbursts and multicolored bouquets of a splendor and variety that were identical in every respect, if one could believe the rhythmic cries of surprise and joy of the incessantly increasing crowd that was acclaiming the progressive marvels in the distance.

I hardly had time to manifest my astonishment; Saint-Denis, who, in order to draw me toward that new spectacle, had turned eastwards, in the direction of the house, remained frozen in his posture. Again his arm extended toward that point on the horizon, while his gaze fixed on me, bleak and stupefied—for there, too, a third explosion of pyrotechnics was setting the sky ablaze, causing its luminous rain to stream down on the placid roof that sheltered the studious retreat of my scholarly master.

This time, it was impossible for me not to laugh at the scientist's discomfited expression.

"You're being heaped with revelations." I told him, gaily, "and whichever way we turn, we're incapable of discovering the slightest trace, on the edges of these ponds or in their reeds, of any practical joker or the most modest artificer...."

"Eh!" said the old man, drawing nearer with vivacity. "Let's leave the joking there. On reflection, it's easy to understand that the image, affecting our senses, is displacing with us, and the people over there who are witnessing the spectacle don't suspect that they could see it by turning toward any corner of the sky. It's possible that at this very moment, those fireworks are simultaneously illuminating Versailles, Batignolles. Sainte-Menehould and Vladivostok...but listen to them...."

The clamors of the crowd now assembled in compact rows along the balustrade were positively taking on a festival delirium. The *oh*s, *ah*s and prolonged cries were saluting an uninterrupted succession of roman candles, serpents, balloons and Bengal fires; monstrous sunbursts were spinning, succeeded by ever-more expansive sprays and flamboyant cataracts, which seemed to be opening up in the sky as many blazing Niagaras.

"It must be a matter of an event of a superior order," Saint-Denis remarked, "And also that the fête must be that of a population for whom expense is no object—for, after all, limited as my experience is such matters might be...oh! Wow!"

To that exclamation, extracted by surprise, a frightful clamor responded from some of the spectators who had flocked to the edge of the lake. The mysterious artificers who had been burning all that multicolored powder in the air for half an hour had just set fire to the final piece. For the first time since the beginning of the firework display, a muffled sound of crackling detonations accompanied the conflagration of a large panel, in the center of which an individual with an energetic face was positioned, whose eyes were sheltered behind a lorgnette. Clad in a jacket, braced with a movement of authoritarian enthusiasm, he raised into the air a purple cushion ornament with golden tassels, on which lay a newborn child, already smiling, arms extended toward the cheering crowds. Two flags striped with red and blue, and decorated in one corner by a rain of stars, made up a symbolic group against an emphatic background of Americanism.

"Heavens!" cried Saint-Denis. "Isn't that a portrait of Monsieur Roosevelt? Is it possible that what we're seeing is on the other side of the Atlantic?"

As for me, I turned swiftly toward Sourbelle, who was standing behind us, his mouth wide open in admiration.

"Let's see," I said to him. "Can you, who've just arrived from over there, explain to is what all this means? Why that child? What does that portrait of the president of the United States signify?"

At first, the traveler with the green cloth cap did not seem to understand my question. Although he was mechanically lending an ear to our sporadic conversation, he was far from suspecting the extent of our conclusions.

Finally, he stammered: "Damn! Wait, though…when I left New York, it seems me that I heard mention that Mrs. Longworth, the president's daughter, was on the point…."[27]

Saint-Denis did not let him finish.

"I understand!" he cried. "Madame Longworth has given birth to a child, and it's the birth of that child that is being celebrated with one of the most prodigious firework displays ever…this is coming from New York or Washington, and that image is being transmitted to us over a distance of twelve hundred leagues."

Meanwhile, the crowd of idlers was beginning to spread out in all directions along the edge of the lake, and commenting in their fashion on the abnormal apparition that had just immobilized several hundred milkmen, grocers, butchers and laundrymen, in that place for half an hour, mingled with housewives and maids on their way to markets and cyclists out for a spin.

---

[27] Although Theodore Roosevelt's daughter Alice had recently married Nicholas Longworth III when the story was written, she did not, in fact, have a child until 1925.

I felt my hand gripped. Saint-Denis drew me toward his house. While walking, he sighed.

"Distance vanquished…the consequences of this are innumerable…."

"What are we going to do now?" I asked him.

By the glance full of flame that he darted at me, I understood that in his turn, he was in haste to reveal these prodigious events to the scientific world; then again, the proof had become too conclusive; individual hallucination had given way to collective, and the facts themselves were driving us.

I sent Sourbelle away; his evidence had become superfluous. A few minutes later, in my old professor's study, we began to draw up the definitive witness statement that it was a matter of communicating to the Institut without delay.

The following day was Monday. That is the day when the Académie des Sciences holds its meetings.

Before going to that eternally memorable session, Saint-Denis came to share our family dinner, to the great disturbance of Madame Forbe, who was obliged to bring her duties as mistress of the house into accord with her personal emotions. A telegram from her mother had confirmed the exactitude of her incendiary vision the previous evening; no stone remained atop another in the house in which my poor wife had been born.

I had bemoaned that accident with her—about which I hastened to inform my master as soon as he arrived, by way of completing the experiment. The conversation was facilitated by that, since the subject thus responded to general preoccupations.

V

At exactly three o'clock we went into the session hall of the Académie des Sciences. Green banquettes were set out against the walls.

"Sit down there," my master said to me.

In the form of a long rectangle, with its paintwork of fake ebony as if made with a comb, its bronze candelabra and its vast oval table cut lengthwise by smaller tables uniformly covered in old green cloth, it is not what the imagination would naturally evoke as a temple of science. Little idols are suspended from the walls in the form of busts, status and painted icons, eternalizing various cults. Buffon, Montesquieu and Louis David face Lagrange, Lavoisier and Jean Goujon; statures of Racine, Puget and La Fontaine furnish the corners, and that of Corneille, behind the presidential chair, dominates the debates.

In sum, though, there was no solemnity and a great deal of bonhomie among the few visitors that I saw gathering, meeting and greeting one another, chatting and strolling from one table to another, generally careless of artifices of costume, remaining more faithful than one might expect to underwear that was not fresh, trousers that were too short and elastic-sided boots.

Their voices, individually feeble, formed a collective buzz insistent enough not to weaken at all when the president, taking his place between his permanent secretaries in front of the elevated table, said in an indifferent tone: "The session is open, Messieurs."

I was sitting beside two journalists, professional habitués of those little fêtes of which they published accounts in the daily newspapers. Mechanically, I listened to their conversation.

"Who's in the chair?" asked one.

"Duvernier, the mathematician. He's as deaf as a post. Look, there's Bérard going up to him."

"Who's Bérard?

"The professor of botany—the little thin chap with the lorgnette, a full beard and eczema."

After a brief conference in a loud enough voice the president got to his feet and declared: "Messieurs, before giving the floor to the permanent secretary for the reading of the correspondence, I am pleased to welcome our eminent colleague

227

from Baltimore, Mr. Hughes Mitchell, whom I am surprised to see among us, as we believed him to be retained far away by the professional demands of his course in mineralogy at Harvard University."

Having said that, Monsieur Duvernier turned to the right hand side of the hall, which was absolutely empty, and nodded his head three times, very affectionately, punctuating the gestures with a very graceful bow. Then he added: "The permanent secretary has the floor."

At the first words spoken by the president, a few heads turned in the indicated direction, trying to see the eminent Hughes Mitchell; not succeeding in doing so, a number of Academicians got up from their seats, and then sat down again, interrogating one another with their gazes, in the midst of a certain unease. Leaning toward one another they queried in whispers:

"Where is he, then?"

"Where indeed?"

"Can you see anyone?"

"But…there's no one there."

Meanwhile, the voice of the permanent secretary was heard, no longer feeble and indifferent but authoritative and perfectly distinct. Raising his voice in order to make himself better understood, he leaned toward the president's ear in such a fashion that everyone could hear what he was saying.

"Excuse me, my dear President, but I believe that I ought to point out an error of identification, of which I'm sure you must be unaware. The person that you have mistaken for Mr. Hughes Mitchell is, in fact, our colleague from Berlin, Professor Hoch."

These words, which were supposed to remain secret, reached my ears very clearly and made me smile. Again, everyone turned toward the corner of the room indicated by the president and started searching for the person concerned, and the whispers recommenced.

"Well…but…."

"Can you see Hoch?"

"No more than Mitchell."

Although neither of those illustrious individuals was familiar to me, at least in regard to their appearance, I had stood up and searched the empty part of the hall with my gaze in vain. When I turned round again, my eyes met those of Saint-Denis, who was on his feet. He gave me a knowing wink and applied a finger forcefully to his lips.

I nearly uttered an exclamation. Moving around the tables, I drew closer to the elevated table, where a lively argument had put Monsieur Duvernier at odds with the botanist Bérard, whom he was accusing of having induced him to make a mistake. Then, suddenly, redirecting his gaze toward the back of the room, the president started smiling, raised his arms to the heavens helplessly while throwing his upper body backwards, and stood up again.

"Messieurs," he concluded, with an air of satisfaction, "I apologize for an omission and I have the pleasure of greeting, alongside Mr. Mitchell, our colleague from Berlin, Professor Hoch, whom I did not see come in."

In order to emphasize his apology, Monsieur Duvernier, without any solemnity, strode across the room, heading toward the table that remained obstinately empty so far as the rest of us were concerned. He was then seen to pause successively in front of two chairs on which no one was seated, extend his arm and exchange two exceedingly cordial handshakes with invisible colleagues.

After that, he came back to sit down in his armchair, and the permanent secretary, after having addressed two smiles and amiable nods of the head to the empty corner, began to read the correspondence.

Little attention was paid to the formal statement. How can one describe the welcome given to the reading of the correspondence? Turned to one another, in pairs and in groups, the members of the audience, preoccupied by the strange incident that had just occurred, were agitating in contradictory movements, in which amazement was manifest in interjections and various gestures. Glances were cast at President

Duvernier, the permanent secretary—an illustrious and venerable chemist—and the botanist Bérard, and people were tapping their foreheads in a pitying and very expressive fashion.

From the place where I was sitting I had a perfect view of the whole scene, and I could follow all the various and changing movements. After a few minutes, I saw several of the audience members, who had not ceased to observe the hall, suspend their mimes and, suddenly serious, lean toward one another hesitantly. I heard murmurs all around me:

"However…my dear colleague…."

"On looking harder…."

"Isn't that…?"

"But yes…that really is Hoch. I recognize him—I met him in Turin at the tuberculosis conference."

"He's not alone—who's that sitting next to him?"

"Do you know Hughes Mitchell?"

"No."

"I know him, and I saw him almost immediately. He's that little old fellow, clean shaven and fat, with the exceedingly red face."

And even I, after having stared ardently at their empty seats, ended up seeing them, those men I did not know at all, and whom everyone now condescended to see in their places, motionless and serious, in a silence of which I measured the impressive grandeur. I looked at Saint-Denis again, and saw him get up, very pale, and slowly advance toward the presidential table, where the reading of the scientific communications was continuing, unheeded by all.

Step by step, Saint-Denis had drawn closer. Taking advantage of a pause, during which the permanent secretary, tired of reading in the midst of general inattention, took a sip of water to clear his throat, the philosopher extended his hand, signaling that he wanted to speak.

"Monsieur le Président, he said, in a voice that was slightly tremulous. "Excuse me for interrupting the order of the day, but the communication that I desire to make is of such immediate interest...Hoch! Hoch, my dear fellow, why are you leaving?"

Hurrying toward the place where everyone had ended up observing the visible presence of the great German entomologist, Saint-Denis, stammering, stopped half way and turned to the audience with a desolate expression.

Then, in a loud voice, he said: "Messieurs, please respond without hesitation: Can any of you still see our colleague Hoch on that chair or anywhere in the room?"

Standing up and looking hard, the Academicians inspected the hall. They ended up looking at one another anxiously, shaking their heads negatively, and a few of them summed up the general sentiment by saying aloud:

"There's no longer anyone there."

Satisfied and tranquil, in the midst of the general excitement, Saint-Denis resumed walking toward the corner where Professor Hoch had just mysteriously disappeared.

Having arrived at the extremity of the vast oval table, at the place where it curved and rounded ours, he stopped, and turned toward the audience again, the members of which were following his movements curiously.

"Messieurs," he went on, "please observe what I am about to do, and forgive the rudeness of the proof that I am going to attempt, but in sum, tell me whether it would be possible if that chair were occupied by a real person. Everyone observes the presence in the chair of Mr. Hughes Mitchell? Good. Watch, Messieurs."

Sitting down casually on the celebrated mineralogist from Harvard University, whose face was illuminate by a smile full of good grace, Saint-Denis placed himself on the chair, through the visible image and, after standing up, let himself down again, in such a manner as to make the proof quite evident. As he was almost equal in stoutness to the illusory Hughes Mitchell, he hid the image momentarily, but such was the luminous strength of the apparition that in a matter of seconds, the specter had penetrated the sensible form of my old master and had entirely substituted itself—with the result that while the voice of Saint-Denis was speaking, it was the upper body of Hughes Mitchell alone that was visible on the chair.

"Messieurs," said the professor of psychotrity, "is it not obvious that if Mr. Mitchell were really in this chair, I could doubtless sit down on him, but not directly upon the chair, as you have just seen me do?"

A deathly silence hung over the assembly; one might have thought that curiosity had been vanquished by terror. Only the permanent secretary dared to speak. He leaned over toward the president and, pointing his finger at Mr. Hughes Mitchell, he cried, in order to take him as a witness: "After all, you shook his hand!"

His attitude and the tone of his voice seemed still to suspect the general evidence, and what he could see with his own eyes.

It was Saint-Denis who replied.

"I am ready, Monsieur Permanent Secretary, to furnish the Académie, for want of a scientific explanation, a proof of the perfect possibility of such abnormal facts. But let's proceed in order. There are, on this side of the room, the…appearances of six of our colleagues, who are, if I'm not mistaken, Messieurs Mitchell, of Baltimore; Helms, of Munich; Rockstritt, of Boston, habitually distant from us; Lenfant, Boullage and Bellecombe. Can you see them as I do?

"We can see them perfectly," said the permanent secretary. "I don't contest it."

"Good. Messieurs Mitchell, Helms, Rockstritt, Lenfant, Boullage and Bellecombe, can you also see us?"

At that question, the six people addressed nodded their heads affirmatively. The permanent secretary, slightly pale, rose to his feet.

Saint-Denis stopped him with a gesture and, turning toward the six grave and silent scientists, said: "Now, Messieurs, I ask you, are you conscious of being separated from Paris by distances that vary between five kilometers and twelve thousand leagues? In sum, are you conscious of only witnessing this session in the state of projected images, and in consequence of a hallucinatory phenomenon of which we are both the subject and the object?"

Slowly and simultaneously, the six apparitions nodded their heads again, replying thus, in the midst of an impressive silence, to the question posed.

A sigh of emotion ran round the room, from the Académie benches to those of the public, where a few people had come to sit down, for the rumor of the extraordinary adventure was already beginning to spread through the surroundings.

Saint-Denis had turned round to face the presidential table. He looked at the permanent secretary, whose lower lip was trembling slightly as he asked: "What explanation can you give us for this, Monsieur Saint-Denis?"

The professor looked at the president, who, with a weary and tremulous gesture, invited him to continue.

Then, taking from his pocket the manuscript that we had prepared the day before, my old master deposited it on a table placed in the center of the room, facing the top table. The table in question was covered with brown moleskin of shabby appearance but designed, I suppose, to protect the surface from possible stains occasioned by the often unpleasant or corrosive products subjected to examination by those messieurs.

"The elements of this work were furnished by one of my most distinguished pupils, Dr. Forbe, who is present at this session and whose name and intelligent observations I am calling to your recognition."

As he pronounced these words he turned toward me, thus drawing me to everyone's attention. My emotion was so keen that I felt myself blushing and could not support the gazes directed at me from all directions. To put on a brave face I looked toward the back of the room, in the direction of the table at which Hughes Mitchell and his colleagues were sitting. Was it an illusion, had my clairvoyance become sharper, or had belated Academicians arrived recently? I seemed to be seeing many more audience members in that corner than those

233

of which my master had just made a sort of roll call and named. When I dared to parade my gaze around the hall, now attentive and avidly interested in the philosopher's communication, I was surprised that it was filled by a crowd of tightly packed listeners, in a stifling mass.

Meanwhile, Saint-Denis spoke.

"The name telepathy has been given to an ensemble of perceptions at a distance, examples of which, perspicacious in acuity, have already been cited, but have encountered considerable incredulity. Some of us have had rudimentary experiences of that faculty of impression at a distance. How many normally nervous individuals, for instance, have seen in a dream a person from whom a letter, most often unexpected, arrives the following day? And what can be said about presentiments? Singular examples are cited, but until now, none of us has consented to add credence to them. The facts of which I shall read to you in a detailed and strictly documented account are merely excessive developments of a sensorial faculty that, for several days, had tended, under and influence that we ought to strive to understand, to become generalized among us. Here they are...."

Entering then into the core of his subject, the professor listed, one after another, the facts whose exposure constituted the beginning of this story.

Eventually, he concluded: "To sum up, it is possible that a current of some sort can be established between us and a few distant regions; under its influence, human sensibility seems no longer to know any limits, and thus, the individual is distanced from himself; he perceives and is perceived far beyond the frontiers that seem normal. It still remains for us to delimit the extent of that zone of telepathic phenomena; those of our colleagues who are miraculously present at this session will already be able to send us their most rapid observations; as for those who are absent...."

Here, he stopped, took a deep breath, embraced the entirety of that glorious assembly of scientists with his enthusiastic gaze, and exclaimed: "In truth, Messieurs, it is now a case of saying that science has no frontiers and that it brings all nationalities together in a universal communion, for I perceive in this hall our most distant correspondents—and how could some of them have found themselves here without the projection of thought that links them to our work without having become, at this moment, omnipotent?"

As Saint-Denis spoke, the audience, attached to his words, turned round. A unique spectacle gripped the admiration of those men, who looked at one another. The hall, usually too vast, had become too small for the crowd that was packing it, and there was no need to repeat the majestic experiment of a few minutes before to comprehend that the greater number were only present in the imaginary and yet quite real fashion of Messieurs Hughes Mitchell, Helms and Rockstritt. How, otherwise, could the presence be explained of the savant Dr. Okuma, who at a time when it was night in Japan, since he was not asleep, must be working in his study in Tokyo, or that, more surprising still, of the chemist Monestier, almost a centenarian, who lives, alone and infirm, in a little house in Bois-de-Colombes, which he has not left for fifteen years?

Gradually, under the effort of their will, of their simple desire, multiplied tenfold by the mysterious fluidic power, all of them had realized that unprecedented communion. Doubtless for the first time since its origin, with the exception of Dr. Hoch, who had sadly disappeared at the beginning, the Académie des Sciences, with all its sections united, was complete.

"I am glad," proclaimed Saint-Denis, with an oratory flourish whose enthusiasm was not at all habitual, "to salute them, among us in their entirety for the first time, and to affirm that, thanks to the marvelous discovery that we have made in common on this day, the memory of which is henceforth immortal, human thought has crossed its frontiers and, like the serpent of ancient myth, is enlacing the civilized world in a ring of fraternal intelligence."

At these words a long acclamation, the noise of which was, in truth, only slightly proportional to the violence of the gestures exhibited, in that assembly in which it was so difficult to distinguish the appearances from the tangible realities. The clapping hands of many of those images transposed through space were not all equal in force in affirm the enthusiasm of the wills that animated them. Dr. Okuma only sent from Tokyo an applause whose sound was very feeble, just as the emotive violence of the moment must have been too much for the antiquity of the centenarian Monestier, since his image suddenly ceased to be visible at the height of the enthusiasm.

In any case, the sum of energy expended did not only exceed the strength of the elderly; by degrees, the fatigue produced by such nervous losses affected the entire audience. One by one, the apparent images of the worldwide elite paled and ended up fading away and disappearing. All that remained in the hall were fifty palpable and present appearances, prostrate with fatigue in their chairs.

"Exhausted…worn out…." murmured President Duvernier.

There was a unanimous desire that the session should be terminated.

"Certainly," said Saint-Denis, supportively, a trifle dazed, "I'm more fatigued by this meeting than the spectacle of the firework display yesterday morning."

"My dear colleagues," the permanent secretary concluded, getting to his feet with difficulty, "human life is going to require more energy that ever—all the more so as it does not depend on us, judging by what we have just seen, to excite or to avoid these correspondences.

Radiant with delight, I was then pulled in all directions, as journalists arrived in a crowd to interview me, and Saint-Denis introduced me, between two doors, to the most flattering felicitations of his colleagues. Nevertheless, the prophetic words of the permanent secretary reached my ears, and since that day I have often admired his sage perspicacity.

It was high time that an authorized intervention occurred, for it was soon recognized that the facts were becoming generalized and that a new direction had just been acquired by an entire section of the human race.

VI

One can recall, and, if necessary, one can imagine the work that superstition and terror were to do in the wake of repeated manifestations of the new force. Cities appeared to be far more prone to it than rural areas, and certain villages were cited in which it was impossible to observe the slightest phenomenon of perception at a distance. On that subject, however, there were reservations to make regarding the value and perspicacity if the investigators as well as the passive unconsciousness of subjects; some might have lived familiarly with the projected image of an absent family member for months without having become aware of the exceptional nature of the contact—whether the person was imaginary or real, the result was the same, save for a few discrepancies of arrival and departure to which the untroubled and incurious minds of country-dwellers paid scant attention.

In the enthusiasm of the early days—for, once enlightened as to the causes, the masses were reassured and soon enthused—people wanted to believe that it was the abolition of distance over the entire surface of the globe.

The plenary session of the Académie des Sciences suffices to prove that all latitudes are henceforth in communication, and since Dr. Okuma was visible in Tokyo, we can look forward to the day when the inhabitants of Baluchistan and Tierra de Fuego will appear in Paris.

Thus prophesied an article in the *Revue Mondiale* when taking account of the experiment publicly made by Saint-Denis in the presence of the most authorized of French scholarly bodies.

It was a vain prophecy. To begin with, a telegraphic check permitted it to be established that many of the presences observed at the *Institut* on 11 May 190 , while remaining probable as regards to persons, ceased to be symptomatic with

237

regard to place of origin, with many of the correspondents being found to have been traveling at that moment either in Germany or in France if they were not in Paris. That was, notably, the case with Dr. Okuma, who sent a telegram from Bordeaux, where he had just disembarked on arriving from Brazil in the course of a scholarly voyage around the world.

On the insistence of Saint-Denis, I had the great honor of being appointed as a member of the Committee set up by the Ministry of Education to investigate the extent and origin of the phenomena, and I recall the disappointment that the restrictive certainty initially caused us: a sentiment that was a trifle childish, all things considered, but which did not last long in the presence of the conclusions of the enquiry—for it was not difficult and did not take long to determine the zone of influence beyond which the telepathic manifestations ceased.

That zone, contained between the 80th degree of west longitude and the 13th degree of east longitude and limited on the American side between the 37th and 48th degrees of north latitude, traversed the ocean following a course that remained unknown pending further experimentation, and to reach France between the 50th and the 43rd parallels; there it seemed to incline slightly northwards, going around the central plateau and passing above Switzerland to complete its course a little way short of the 48th—with the consequence that it formed an irregular five-sided figure whose points of reference were Richmond, Bordeaux, Munich, Berlin, Cherbourg and the north of the mouth of the St. Lawrence, slightly behind and above Quebec.

Traced on the map, that zone of influence was limited fairly regularly in two curved movements whose clarity convinced us generally to admit that we were in the presence of an unknown fluidic current, of a wave whose intensity of radiation seemed to increase in proportion to the abnormal warmth that signaled the spring of that year. Under the action of that current, the facts most contested until that day in the order of telepathy were renewed with a frequency that did not take long to render the observation banal and superfluous. That which, in the beginning, had surprised and terrified us had to be admitted as one of the normal conditions of existence.

One shivers in thinking what might have happened had the event been produced a few hundred years earlier, in an epoch when the scientific method was still reduced to empiricism, when the electric telegraph and the telephone had not yet familiarized the masses with the knowledge of the invisible forces of nature. Or rather, one begins to wonder whether this manifestation is really the first, and whether it might be necessary to look in that direction for the explanation of so many seemingly miraculous events that have frightened ignorant humankind throughout history.

At any rate, modern life is intuitive and rapid; in three weeks, the great news had become old hat, and people were already living in peace with the new sense that summarized all the others and increased them, inasmuch as it was perception at a distance, like all the other senses; its acuity remained variable, and not all people found themselves able to exercise it with equal power.

Then again, if telepathic relations were established with a sufficiently rapid facility between relatives or acquaintances, they became more unequal and more awkward between strangers; there again the extraordinary novelty of the faculty suddenly devolved upon humankind and attenuated its surprising character by an appearance of logic, in conformity with all the scientific laws thus far admitted.

People differed in their evaluation of that restriction of influence; fervent adherents of the idea of Providence were satisfied, in sum, by the fact that the zone of phenomena of appearance at a distance was limited for the time being to a few parts of the United States, France and Germany, because they wanted to understand it as the wisdom of a divine intervention measuring out to humankind this new sense, whose abrupt diffusion would have caused an upheaval in the life of the world.

"In time," they said, "the current will be extended, and then the entire globe will enter without any shock into relations of universal fraternity."

"Providence or not," others concluded, "the progression is still a limitation of which it will be as well to take advantage."

What is incredible, however, is the national self-esteem that came to be mixed up in the affair, and the particular pride that the French and Germans felt in seeing themselves the object of a choice that they wanted to see as premeditated.

"Has not France always been, since the Revolution," said some, "the experimental field of all humankind?"

The Germans responded: France was simply geographically fortunate, but that the German fatherland was the target marked by the miraculous current.

In any case, the verdict was rendered by American public opinion. On the far side of the Atlantic, the editors of all the *Worlds* and *Tribunes* found themselves in agreement in offering the explanation of the facts.

What is this fluid, they said, *and what is its origin? By virtue of functioning in an intensive state, American hyperactivity is radiating, in the form of an influential force, all the way to the old world, where it has galvanized the will debilitated by the centuries: there is an overflow of energy therein, of which only a new people like ourselves are capable...etc...etc...*

Above these paltry squabbles, the scientists, when their investigation was complete, kept silent. All that they had been able to do was to make simple observations; the new force did not lend itself any more to explanation, for the moment, than electricity, with which it seemed that it was impossible to assimilate it.

I will not describe in detail here all the laboratory experiments that were carried out in this regard, and which can be found, along with many individual observations, in specialist journals and the records of the sessions of the Committee of Investigation. I am only attempting here a simple account of

240

the events in which it was given to me to be directly involved in the course of this exceptional adventure and practical history, so to speak, of one human being in contact with the manifestations of a temporarily exasperated sensibility. I am citing in my case what it had in common with many others that might remain unknown; those who will read me in the future will perhaps be able to sense in this story, better than a somewhat abstract and colorless formal document, the emotions of the excessive minutes that we lived in those days.

Until that day, they had all appeared in a fairly favorable light, and certainly, none of us suspected as yet the tragic horror of the imminent future. The reaction, as I have said, was one of enthusiasm, and as enthusiasm desires celebrations and official pomp, it was decided to organize them.

Since the new world, by virtue of the intervention of the thought-wave, found itself linked to the old continent, it seemed logical to the scientific committees set up in France and the United States to adopt a kind of official position on the new line of telepathic communication. To that effect, an experimental festival was decided, in which the two Heads of State would meet, simultaneously or successively, according to availability. In Paris, the image of Mr. Roosevelt was expected, and it was hoped that the face of Monsieur Fallières[28] would be projected all the way to the White House in Washington.

Important preparations were made to ensure the success of the trail, which was arranged for 10 June.

The major state bodies, by delegation, and the Committee of Investigation, in its entirety, met at the Élysée Palace at three o'clock in the afternoon, the time chosen for the meeting coinciding with the moment when the sun marked ten 'clock in the morning in Washington.

At first, the idea had been put forward of organizing the ceremony in the open air, the gardens of the Élysée permitting

_____

[28] Armand Fallières was President of the Republic from 1906-13.

241

a more numerous audience, but the fear of rain and the concern to avoid anything that might compromise the success of the experiment had ended up persuading the organizers to content themselves with the reception rooms of the palace.

At four o'clock, when Monsieur Fallières, in ceremonial dress, his breast striped with the great sash of the Légion d'honneur, took his place in front of the fireplace of the Salon des Ambassadeurs, and our president, surrounded by his household, began to anticipate the visit, an entirely new and very sharp emotion gripped everyone around him.

Only the director of protocol, who was agitated, was walking back and forth from the door of the drawing room to the peristyle of the palace, but it seemed improbable that his ministry would be utilized and Saint-Denis, who was beside me, whispered in my ear with his characteristic need for irony:

"Henceforth, with the habit of entering without warning that we're going to acquire, protocol is an entirely extinct career."

It is necessary to admit that the wait seemed long.

I have noted that the difficulty of telepathic communications increased when the subject and the object did not know one another. Attempts had been made to remedy that inconvenience by submitting photographic documents to the two presidents, several days before, and it was with this aid that they had been able to familiarize themselves mutually with their external appearance. Nevertheless, we were beginning to fear that these precautions had not had a sufficient suggestive effect, and we had all been immobilized in anticipation for an hour when a kind of mist became visible to the majority of the audience on one of the windows of the reception room.

That appeared to everyone to be the effect of one of those momentary fatigues of vision, which can normally be dissipated by blinking. Like the others, I could not help making that petty gesture. When, almost instantaneously, my eyes opened again, I perceived the clear and plain image of a man with a slightly drooping moustache, whose bright eyes were sparkling behind a lorgnette. It was Mr. Roosevelt.

I thought that he bore more resemblance to his portraits than he had in the luminous state of the firework display, but I had no hesitation in recognizing him as he advanced rather rapidly toward Monsieur Fallières, his hand extended, and a smile on his lips, saying in a muffled, distant voice, but which could be clearly made out in the profound silence in which everyone remained bound by attention: "I'm very glad to see you."

Monsieur Fallières was very pale, less at his ease than his distant visitor, who seemed entirely in his element, as much master of himself as in the simplest of conversations.

The malaise was of brief duration, however. The seconds were precious, for there was no way of knowing how long the communication would last, and it was urgent to solemnize it by long-distance speeches.

Our president was perfect; he spoke for some time about the new fraternity, minds flying over frontiers, and what the conquest of the new force of nature seemed to portend for world peace.

"Henceforth," he concluded, "there is no longer any possible misunderstanding between people who can read one another's hearts."

Mr. Roosevelt listened politely with a great deal of attention and replied with a few sentences in English to corroborate the spirit of the speech. He concluded by uttering three resounding cheers and crying, in a nasal accent: "Long live the sister Republics!"

Almost immediately, he disappeared.

The maximum intensity had been obtained, and, in sum, the trial was satisfactory.

The counterpart also succeeded in Washington, where, a few minutes later, the President of the Republic returned, on the far side of the ocean, the visit that he had just received.

As a practical consequence, the newspaper *L'Humanité* demanded, the very next day, the pure and simple abolition of ambassadors between countries assured of communications so simply directed.

There seems to be a cruel irony today in recalling the beautiful hours of what seemed, at first to be a dawn, but who could have supposed that a conflagration had just been lit?

VII.
Extracts from Dr. Forbe's Journal

20 June

One of the first consequences of the new state of affairs had been it appears, an unprecedented increase in the receipts of post and telegraph offices; in the surprise of the apparitions everyone was anxious for exact clarification; letters, telegrams and the telephonic communications were all employed to that effect for nearly a month.

It is no longer the same now that the habit has been formed; on the contrary, a number of practical individuals have begun to use this gratuitous means of correspondence for themselves—with the natural consequence of an abrupt diminution in the State's receipts, to the point that, if the progression accelerates, as there is every reason to expect, it will be necessary to ward off a possible disequilibrium in the budget. The example has been cited of Pierpont Morgan,[29] who, attracted early to Dinard in consequence of the precocious seasonal warmth, shuts himself in his study for two hours a day in order to work in direct communication with a first-rate secretary, whom he has quickly trained for that very special work.

Assuming that that is true, however, it is merely an exception as yet for such long distances. As for communications between cities over the extent of French territory influenced by the wave of transmission, they are very comfortable, and telepathy is beginning to take over the role of the telephone, with neither wires nor receivers. Businessmen, agents and newspaper reporters are beginning to use it, after multiple trials conducted with care.

---

[29] The financier John Pierpont (J.P.) Morgan (1837-1913)

One is alarmed by the idea that the day is getting closer when, at the behest and impulsion of big businessmen, the entire world will be brought into proximity, when it will only take a few minutes or hours to transmit their instructions, without any intermediary, from one hemisphere to another. As a repercussion, a socialist newspaper is predicting a worldwide strike.

22 June

This morning, while we were having breakfast, Madame Forbe's mother suddenly appeared, sitting beside André.

She has come to visit us in the same fashion several times without leaving Angers, where she has moved into an apartment while waiting for her house to be rebuilt. She lives alone and her thoughts, continually with us, transport her toward her daughter and her grandson. Then again, she experiences the need to consult me about the details of the construction, in which she believes me to have a competence that I do not possess.

She's a good woman and I appreciate the confidence that she shows in me, without daring to tell her that I have better things to do than occupy myself with the petty problems of carpentry or the locksmith's craft that she addresses to me.

While she was there, we were brought up to date with her plans for the summer. We have the habit, every year, of going to stay for a month in an Atlantic beach resort, and the conversation turned to the sea and the charm that it ought to offer now, in the hot days that we're enduring.

Our little André mingled his projects with ours and gradually started daydreaming, his eyes staring off and with a distracted expression. I was trying to make my mother-in-law understand my deficiency in matters of plumbing and floor-laying, when Madame Forbe suddenly exclaimed: "André! What are you doing?"

I turned round and I saw the child, who, having unbuttoned his jacket and waistcoat, was about to take off his trousers, with mechanical gestures.

"But Maman," he said, quite earnestly, "I'm going bathing."

Two months ago we would have thought he was mad. I simply took him by the hand, talking to him softly in order to bring him back from the dream in which he found himself—for he admitted to us, while putting on his collar, that he thought he was at La Baule, at the seaside, and he had been unable to resist the impulse.

25 June

A visitor today—real, not by image: Sourbelle came to see me.

He's losing patience; for more than six weeks his wife has been in prison and the affair has not taken a single step forward. Her innocence—or, at least, her lack of responsibility—is incontestable, for the good faith of the two unfortunates is manifest.

The poor devil! I pity him. Ruined even in his hopes by his unfortunate voyage, he is living in his empty tiny lodgings, alone with the sadness of having caused his wife's misfortune. To eat, he's been obliged to take the first job he could, and he's a dishwasher in a café. He scarcely has the means to provide for the necessities of his toilette and I see that he's still wringing that frightful cap the color of pea soup in his hands.

"It's not possible," he affirms, "that they won't yield to the evidence. Besides which, Monsieur, you promised me—I beg you, say something to the magistrate so that he'll set my wife free.

He believes it, poor fellow. I believe it too, and it seems to me, ultimately, that an injustice is being done: I've promised him that I'll go to see the examining magistrate in charge of the case.

It turns out that the examining magistrate is Vatinel, a court deputy, an old childhood friend. He received me without delay, asking me for news of my wife, whom he doesn't know.

As soon as I spoke, he became grave, sitting up straight in his cane chair. His benevolent eyes fixed themselves on me behind his pince-nez and he explained the new malaise from which the magistracy has been suffering for a month.

"You can't have any idea, my dear fellow," he said. "We're positively overflowing with more than five hundred cases of the same sort. At this moment, almost all criminals, murderers or thieves, are affirming that they don't understand any of what happened to them and claiming to be victims of suggestion at a distance. Are they sincere? In many cases, the antecedents of the people involved seem to be in accord with their affirmations; at any rate, no one any longer kills and no one steals—for several weeks, if you believe the accused. The will of other individuals, almost always unknown, has been directing the actions of the guilty parties. How can responsibility be determined in such circumstances? What, in fact, will become of responsibility?"

I shook my head.

"All right," I said, "but in the case that interests me, if there is a guilty party, you have him; arrest the husband, who accuses himself of the intention, and charge him…with homicide by imprudence."

Vatinel looked at me profoundly. "Ah!" he sighed. "Perhaps it will come to that. In the meantime, I repeat that we dare not inaugurate that jurisprudence for fear of attracting the attention of too many malefactors to the point. Above all, don't repeat any of this until further notice."

In the enthusiasm of the first few days, it was decided to hold a big banquet to celebrate the discovery of the sympathetic current, which, for the moment, unites three great countries.

I'm included in the list of those who will make a speech during dessert, and as it's my first speech, I've been working on it conscientiously, singing the praises of the new method of communication—of which, however, I'm beginning to understand the inconveniences. In sum, though, what discovery doesn't, in the early days of its appearance, lead to some awkwardness in the temporarily disrupted pattern of human life?

I'm alone in my study; I've been polishing my punctuation, saluting the new era of fraternal sincerity. The noise of an altercation in the hallway disturbs me and irritates me. I lend an ear.

It's Sourbelle again. Yesterday, on rendering him an account of the temporary failure of the steps I've taken, I exhorted him to be patient; I even slipped a fifty-franc bill into his hand. And now he's arguing with the maid in order to get in, in spite of the order I've given not to be disturbed while I'm working.

All in all, he annoys me, with his green cap. Is it my fault, after all, that his imprudent violence has had such consequences?

He's ended up going away, though. I watch from behind the curtains at the drawing room window and I see him walking up and down the street making furious gestures; he must be waiting for me to go out. I go back into my study.

I'm no longer alone there; Madame Forbe's mother has just appeared again, sitting at my table. From Angers, her image never leaves me alone, and it's beginning to be annoying for an orator constrained to sing the praises of telepathy.

"I'm glad to see you, Auguste," the distant voice says to me. "What do you think about a veranda for the dining room, instead of a bay window and three hinged windows?"

I listen, chewing my pen holder, and gaze resignedly at the windows, through which the softened light of the courtyard is coming. And there I see Sourbelle appear, Sourbelle again, whom I left pacing up and down in the street. By virtue of the omnipotence of his overexcited desire, he's projected his anxious form this far, and he starts talking, heaping reproaches and complaints upon me.

For her part, Madame Forbe proclaims: "I said to him, to the architect, I said to him: 'Monsieur, you're a thief!'"

"They'll guillotine her for sure," the other says.

"And do you know what he said to me?" the Angevine image howls.

I lose my temper. I stand up, shouting furiously: "Zut! What do you expect me to do about it?"

Eyes fixed, her expression stupefied, the poor woman looks at me with a kind of terror; then she shrivels and becomes hot-tempered, fleeing at top speed, returning to Angers without further ado.

At the same time, Sourbelle has disappeared.

I'm having all the difficulty in the world concentrating on my thoughts here, preventing my imagination from accompanying them.

IX

"It's strange," Saint-Denis said to me at the corner of the Rue Royale and the Place de la Concorde, "that we haven't yet found any form of collective rejoicing more in harmony with our new modern life than all these banquets. Isn't resigning oneself to contemplate nourishments that no one touches, in our epoch of aching and mistrustful stomachs, conceding too much to routine?"

With the pages of my speech folded up in my pocket, against my heart, I listened to my old master talk with a distracted ear and a mouth already dry in anticipation of the moment to come.

As we crossed the Place de la Concorde, a crowd blocked our path; at the same time, a chorus of voices brought to our eyes the dribs and drabs of the official revolutionary anthem, the *Internationale*.

Curious, Saint-Denis drew nearer, lending an ear and watching a procession file between two hedges of onlookers: a long cortege of arsenal workers from Brest, all of whose actions had been attracting attention and some anxiety in Paris for the last two days. The image of that distant demonstration produced a more direct emotion than reading about it in the newspapers.

We arrived at the Hotel Splendid, where almost all the guests of the banquet were assembled; we were only waiting for the minister who is to preside over the feast. Contradictory rumors were running round.

"Will he come?"

"Certainly."

"You know that the cabinet's been obliged to hand in its resignation after the interpellation of Lerody on the strikes at Brest. Just as the President of the Council was getting ready to dread the decree closing the session…"

I must confess that I was only listening vaguely to what was being said; my anxiety was increasing by the minute at the thought that it would shortly be necessary for me to read a few pages aloud in the presence of all the illustrious or important individuals that the rooms could hold.

I found myself seated at table to the left of Professor Hoch—the man who had made such a brief appearance at the Académie des Sciences on the day when Saint-Denis had read my observations; having nodded to him briefly, I scanned the table with a circular glance.

Scientists known throughout the world, diplomats, important functionaries, and illustrious writers surrounded me. I observed directly opposite me the small fixed and thoughtful eyes of a Japanese envoy whose entire appearance of attentive gravity signified preoccupation with the thought of making industrial use of the new fluid as soon as it made its appearance at the frontiers of the Nipponese Empire. Not far from him, a tall Chinese mandarin seemed to be saying, with his thin smile: *We've known about this for a long time, long before you, many centuries ago; except that we prudently renounced it, like so many other dangerous products with which your ignorance is still toying.*

Having thus looked around, my eyes met those of my neighbor to the left, Edouard Grandmaison, the editor of the newspaper *La Foule*, which claims to print three million copies. He's a dry and lively southerner, likable and a good talker. He leaned toward me.

"A funny thing," he murmured, with a smile full of irony, "that we're meeting here to celebrate the power that overthrew the power of the minister sitting as president of the table...you're not up to date?"

My expression was a clear response. He was kind enough to give me a few explanations.

"This strike at Brest, whose images are beginning to frighten Paris, started the trouble. Exasperated, like all of us, by the obsessive spectacle of that faraway calamity, the ministers decided this morning, in a meeting of the Council, to arrest the two leaders of the adventure tomorrow. The last assembly of the session was to have taken place today, that being the best way of avoiding interpellation. Unfortunately, just as the President of the Council as about to read the decree of closure, Lerody of the unimodified socialist group stood up and revealed the ministerial plan, which was still secret. He even named names, accusing the Minister of the Interior of having proposed the measure, gave details of the entire Council meeting and all the discussion, and even the order of the arguments: so-and-so said this, and then so-and-so said that.

"You can imagine the stupefaction: the Chamber was writhing. 'How do you know that?' the President of the Council couldn't help asking. 'I witnessed the meeting,' Lerody admitted, 'to which I was transported by the intensity of my desire, in the condition of an image.' There was no means of denying it, and it was necessary to put the motion of no confidence to the vote; the right and the far right overturned the ministry yet again.

"With the aid of telepathy," said Dr. Hoch, concluding, laughing rather heavily.

"Yes," said Grandmaison, "with your telepathy, which will render all secrecy impossible."

I was listening to him a trifle distractedly, nodding my head. To reassure my anxiety and calm the thirst that was drying my mouth, I drank without discernment from the glasses in front of me, incessantly filled by the waiters. The strength of the wines might have been mediocre, but the influence on me was no less certain, and when it was my turn to speak, I got up unemotionally, almost excitedly.

Raising my voice in order to be better heard, I read my speech in an authoritative, almost aggressive tone, proclaiming the total power of thought liberated from shackles, of human sensibility capable of objectifying itself indefinitely throughout the extent of its domain.

My confidence made my success. When the dinner finished, I was introduced to the Minister, to all sorts of illustrious individuals who wanted to talk to me. I rediscovered comrades lost to sight, who resumed addressing me as *tu* after having avoided me for years. Finally, Puymaigre, the surgeon, and the physicist Denoysel each took me by one arm and, to my misfortune, never let go.

Puymaigre recalled childhood memories. He's a solid fellow, whose salt-and-pepper hair and beard frame a face that remains youthful and quite attractive. Women go crazy for him, and he returns the compliment.

"Let's see," he said, suddenly, "what are you doing? This little feast was charming, but it's over. The Minister has gone—flown. I'm taking you away."

To tell the truth, in a moment of lucidity, I took account of the fact that I was doing something stupid, but as I've said, I'd been a trifle overexcited even before the dinner began—and then, that contact with illustrious men, those eminent individuals who were treating me with familiarity…how could I resist?"

I went with my two acolytes.

Where? That remains unimportant, with regard to the situation and identity of the minor players. I'll get straight to the key fact of the adventure, which is fatally connected with the ensemble of facts whose impartial exposition I'm undertaking here.

It was nearly two o'clock when I got home, no longer drunk but utterly dazed by fatigue and remorse.

The bedroom was empty; the bed where I expected to find Madame Forbe was empty, the sheets thrown back over the foot. Approaching the little table where my wife places her watch every evening, along with a box of pastilles and her handkerchief, I perceived a letter in an envelope, addressed to me in my wife's handwriting. I opened it, and read this:

I know where you're coming from. Minute by minute, the strange power that we've possessed for some little time has permitted me to follow you in the slightest circumstances over these two hours that you've forced me to live in your abominable company.

If those are the intimacies that are necessary to you, go in search of them where I won't surprise you.

For myself, I'm renouncing following you any longer in such milieux. For this evening, I've locked myself in my son's room, with whom I shall leave tomorrow. I'll take refuge with my mother, whom you have, it seems, thrown out of our house the other day.

Adieu.

It was signed.

I folded the letter up mechanically and put it back where I had found it.

"Bah!" I said to reassure myself. "After all, the night brings counsel, and since she hasn't left yet…."

And I went to bed, where, succumbing to gross fatigue, I fell heavily asleep almost immediately.

The next day, I woke up late. The cook told me that Madame Forbe had left at seven o'clock in the morning.

Obviously, that story was a trifle grotesque, but I suffered from it nonetheless, and I recalled Grandmaison's prediction.

It's the end of private life.

X
Further Extracts from Dr. Forbe's Journal

26 July

At any rate, my case isn't unique, and one hears nothing but talk of quarrels, family disputes and intimacies disrupted by unexpected revelations. There are no more walls; one can see and hear the most delicate of life's situations at any hour. From Cherbourg to Bordeaux, from Lille to Angoulême and Brest, France is squabbling, sulking, divorcing.

28 July

We physicians are often accused of being insensible to human suffering. The reproach is more or less justified by the habit we have of chasing away the image of one malady by contact with another. In any case, once upon a time, on going home, a practitioner retained the prerogative of no longer thinking about the suffering that he had passed in review during the day.

It's no longer the same today, and I'm beginning to be perpetually accompanied by the mournful troop of all those who require my care. Their images form a cortege for me and their exhausted lamentations obsess me.

"I'm in pain, Doctor."

"Cure me."

The imagination, the fatal power of certain invalids, and now the lot of them all, exhausts and overloads my sensibility, once so self-sufficient. And what can I say to those living shadows that surround me and plead with me at every hour of the day and night? I remain silent and terrified in the midst of so many images of human suffering.

Last night I witnessed, impotent and full of horror, the death-throes of two of those creatures irredeemably condemned for weeks. At their bedside, in front of their complicit family members, I had the courage to lie to them, to hold out the alluring hope of a cure; in the presence of those images tottering on the edge of the grave, I can only remain mute, scarcely holding back compassionate tears.

An unfortunate woman of thirty-two, devoured by a cancer, and a child of seventeen eaten away by consumption—I've been unable to chase away their appearances, which seek me out alternately to implore me and abuse me.

"You've deceived me! You lied! You lied!"

"I don't want to die!" cried the faint voice of the debilitated specter of the child. "After all, there must be a means of curing me! You don't want to! Oh, you don't want to!"

Seeing their images disappearing progressively at the foot of my bed, I understood at first light that the movement of life had ceased to animate their poor bodies.

Only then could I get to sleep.

Isn't that horrible?

30 July

Several days ago, disquieting rumors began to circulate, and now, all of a sudden, they've taken on a consistency that scarcely anyone expected.

They're to do with tension in relations between Germany and the United States, on the subject of the Venezuelan customs and excise, over which Emperor Wilhelm II exerts, as a guarantee of certain unpaid debts, a pitiless control. The United States government considers that control to have been a trifle prolonged.

Amicable observations might have been sufficient; its seems that Germany has reacted badly to them; on the other hand, public opinion, so ubiquitous today, obscures the tone of diplomacy, and thanks to the fatal current that puts them in constant communication, the two peoples on either continent express themselves in manifestations whose effect is difficult for the official press to offset.

Grandmaison was not wrong to fear that the press is increasingly being displaced by direct communication.

Gangs of jingoists have been seen, it's said, in Berlin, marching along Broadway singing *Yankee Doodle* and proffering unbenevolent acclamations with regard to the personality of the German Emperor.

Such incidents, when read, can be denied; seeing and hearing them seems more dangerous.

31 July

Demonstrations are continuing in Berlin and New York, Washington and Hamburg.

An implacably pure sky and Genoese heat still seem to be favoring the extension of the sympathetic current, which is becoming magnified—the greatest evil possible in the circumstances, for no one anticipates that things will stop, when the moment comes that the streets overlap and Broadway can come into violent conflict with Unterlinden.

Will what Joseph de Maistre has said about war be realized?[30] Will peoples force the hands of governments? For some years, Germany has been building beautiful battleships; the American navy is still full of pride at the memory of the

---

[30] The Savoyard political philosopher Joseph de Maistre (1753-1821) was one of the fiercest critics of the French Revolution, arguing that any attempt to justify government on rational grounds is bound to fail, and that any authority that is not absolute and unquestionable is bound to dissolve into violence and chaos. The only possible salvation for Europe, in his opinion, lay in divine authority channelled through the Pope.

war in Cuba; the ships will end up setting sail of their own accord.

2 August

Now something has happened that is scarcely credible, and which, in its details and its probable consequences, takes us back several centuries. To tell the truth, I don't know of any witness to it, but it's being recounted with forceful guarantees of exactitude. It's a matter of nothing less than an altercation between the German Emperor and the President of the United States of America.

The adventure, impossible three months ago, occurred yesterday evening at about six o'clock in the Royal Palace in Berlin, in the Imperial Cabinet. The Emperor, it appears, was in the process of assessing in very sharp terms the exclusivist doctrines in usage of the other side of the Atlantic, when the image of Mr. Roosevelt suddenly appeared, sitting in an armchair, his gaitered legs crossed, slapping the toes of his boots with a riding crop. Standing facing him, a secretary was listening to him speak, and the sound of their conversation was sufficiently distinct for the Emperor not to miss a single word; his person, simultaneously violent and ungraspable, made that very obvious.

It seems certain that the surprise of the two intimates was far from being favorable to the cause of peace, since, two minutes later, the two Heads of State were standing face to face, exchanging appreciations like the humblest street porters in Berlin or Brooklyn, the excessive severity of which is only explicable by a nervousness that exaggerated the temperature and nature of communications; words were produced compared with which the "Comediante" applied by Pius VII to Napoléon would have appeared flattering to Bonaparte.[31]

---

[31] When Pope Pius VII was detained at Fontainebleau by Napoléon in 1812, he is rumoured by some accounts to have replied to Napoléon's account of his reasons by muttering to

257

All this, although unofficial, seems to be too well known for ominous results not to be dreaded. A certain luster has returned to diplomacy, whose intermediacy does not seem devoid of utility.

7 August

What was bound to happen has arrived. After several days of violence, the misunderstanding was transformed into an altercation, to finish in a conflict, and it is not one of the least disconcerting consequences of this mental union of human beings that a war is about to renew before our eyes the recent horrors of the Russo-Japanese conflagration.

Because of the dementia of their leaders, because of their nervous susceptibility, the Germans and the Americans are ready to go to war.

The order for mobilization has been given to the German fleet; for its own part, America had ordered the conjunction of the Pacific squadron with that of the Atlantic, and the stupefied world is getting ready to follow the movements of the unprecedented battle that is in preparation.

XI

On the seventh of August, at eight o'clock in the evening, the German squadron, consisting of eight battleships and four cruisers, left Kiel under the command of Prince Henry.[32]

---

himself the single word "Comediante!" [Clown]. Some accounts expanded the remark to "Comediante! Tragediante!" (or the other way around) while others shifted the remark to 1813 and slightly different circumstances. All the versions are probably apocryphal.

[32] Prince Henry [or Heinrich] of Prussia (1862-1929), Wilhelm II's younger brother, had a long career in the Navy. From 1906-9 he was in command of the High Seas Fleet.

The semaphore on the Isle of Wight was the first to signal its passage on the morning of the ninth.

It soon entered the zone of telepathic influence, and, at many points, its movements became visible at a distance: an entirely new spectacle, replete in unprecedented emotions, impassioned the masses poorly familiarized by the cinematograph with naval maneuvers. It was not a matter of a parade, however, and, because the objective of the mission could not be anything but a veritable battle, curiosity was even more intense.

At first restricted to those more perspicacious or more carried away by passion or the preliminary documentation, the perception of these exceptional images always tended toward generalization. Imagine the spectacle of Paris during those feverish days! Stopped in plain sight, staring into space or in front of them, those who were the first beneficiaries of the extraordinary spectacle described to the less privileged the phases of the German fleet's progress, reciting the names of the ships, the type and their appearance.

It was thus that the five days necessary for Prince Henry's squadron to travel the 2,500 miles separating the strait of Calais from Cape Race to the southeast of Newfoundland, in the direction of which it disappeared on the evening of the fourteenth, emerged from the telepathic wave. Then, the general curiosity, overexcited, reverted to the American squadron, which was beginning to appear.

The American fleet, which was on maneuvers in the vicinity of the Antilles in the Florida canal received orders on the ninth of August to rally at the arsenal of Norfolk in Chesapeake Bay, where it would need more than twenty-four hours to take on supplies. It took to the sea on the morning of the twelfth and thus entered the current of the wave, where all its movements became visible to us.

Admiral Dewey,[33] who was in overall command, had attached his flag to the Maine. His objective seemed to be to sail along the coast while awaiting the arrival of Prince Henry; unfortunately, a sudden thick fog made the disposition of the ships difficult, interrupting communications, which were reduced to wireless telegraphy, telepathic communication having been deemed unreliable because of its character of excessive accessibility. The result was that the fleet was not completely ready; on the fifteenth, at about midnight, it was visible that the two divisions of battleships were separated.

It appears that at that moment, Admiral Dewey, by means of the Marconi apparatus, attempted to rally the fleet to his course, and, shortly afterwards, saw ships appearing to the north, which he recognized at daybreak as the German squadron.

An unfortunate current had permitted Prince Henry to pick up the American admiral's orders on his own wireless telegraph apparatus; leaving four cruisers on surveillance in the west, he had set a southward course with the two divisions of battleships disposed in single file, hoping to annihilate the important faction of the American fleet that hazard had delivered to his superior forces without delay.

The first cannon shot was fired shortly after midday by the *Kaiser Wilhelm II*, bearing the flag of the Prince-Admiral. At that moment the two fleets were five thousand meters apart.

After an artillery duel lasting half an hour, the smoke of which was beginning to make it less easy for us to see the ships, we saw the *Kentucky*, hit by two shells from the big German guns, lose speed, listing badly to starboard. The *Kearsarge*, which was following her, was obliged to change course in order to avoid a collision, and in the course of that maneuver found herself isolated from the others by virtue of an abrupt change of direction by the German second armored

---

[33] Admiral George Dewey (1837-1917) was no longer on active service in 1908, but was still famous for his victory in the Battle of Manila Bay during the Spanish-American War.

division, which opened a murderous fire on the American ship. In a matter of minutes, the colossus, riddled by shellfire, was listing badly and, her poop rising upwards after the fashion of a diving swan, she plunged into the waves and disappeared.

A cry, a wild clamor compounded by more than two million gasps, rose up in Paris, terrified by the incident—and that cry soon turned into a thousand dolorous rumors at the sight of a multitude of little black patches that were dancing on the waves raised up around the swirling gulf into which the gigantic ship had just sunk. Those little black dots were the men of the crew, who were attempting to swim away, struggling against debris of every sort that was floating around them, falling back on their heads, crushing and stunning them. Some tried to capture items that might be used as buoys, while others tried to tear them away from them in order to cling onto the buoys and save themselves—and those men, who were drowning, started killing one another in order to defend their own lives. They ended up disappearing from our sight.

We could no longer see anything more than a fog in the midst of which sudden red tints incessantly specified resounding explosions. That lasted a few minutes; then, gradually, the forms of a few ships hit by gunfire emerged from the confusion, which were lagging behind the pursuit like wounded birds constrained to abandon flight.

On the German side, the *Wittelsbach*, the *Mecklenburg* and the *Zähringen*, their turrets broken or their propeller-shafts damaged, stopped along with the cruiser *Friedrich Karl* and floated without responding to the fire of the battle, implying that their crews had suffered considerable losses and their artillery had been destroyed.

The rest of the fleet seemed to take heart and to thunder forth on their behalf. Who among us had ever supposed that such a sequence, such a chorus of cannon fire, was possible? How can the increasing emotion of the crowds hypnotized by the spectacle from one end of Paris to the other be described?

We stood still, open-mouthed, our eyes widened by terror and anguish.

In that fashion we watched the *Kaiser Wilhelm der Grosse*, the *Maryland* and the *Fürst Bismarck* disappear, the last-named taking with it the *Montana*, pierced amidships at right angles by her spur. Already, in the presence of that furious massacre, our curiosity was giving way to indignation, while, leaving behind them the floating debris and the carcasses of abandoned wreckage, the two fleets reduced their fire in order to flee eastwards, where the second division of Dewey's squadron suddenly confronted the German squadron and aligned for pursuit. Before falling upon each other, the two enemies seemed to be challenging one another in silent meditation.

And that silence, succeeding the racket of so many cannon-shots and murderous explosions, providing a prelude to the final impact that was about to complete the annihilation of so many poor men alive and alert a short while before, was even more terrible than the noise of the powder and the shells. At the thought that that minute of respite was the last that those creatures, maddened by the demon of destruction, had to live, an immense horror, rippling along the boulevards, through the streets, over the squares, the balconies, and the roofs of the houses, stirred the terrified and sickened crowds that was, from so very far away, suspended in anticipation by that unique spectacle.

It was too much for the nerves of the public, interested at first, then anguished, and finally terrorized, who, instinctively, attempted by means of supplications to put an end to the destructive fury of the combatants who had escaped the massacre. Millions of cries rolled in echoes around me:

"Mercy!"

"Enough!"

"Enough!"

A puerile and touching imploration. Extended hands, eyes full of tears, and menacing fists abused, insulted, and begged the invisible adversaries huddled in the hollows of the ironclad vessels. Did they hear that supreme appeal of reason and unity? Did the feeble sound of our voices reach as far as the men whom the genius of destruction had driven insane?

No one will ever know.

Opening against one another, salvos of fire resonated all the way to us the most frightful detonation that had ever shaken the heavens. And under the watch of the age-old witness to the fratricidal conflicts of humankind, the two fleets hurled themselves at one another, disappearing into a cloud of smoke.

And that was the end, the abominable apotheosis of the spectacle; all the remaining ships perished in that supreme surge: the torpedoed battleships were torn apart; the disemboweled cruisers sank; all the powder remaining in the ammunition magazines exploded; the horizon was colored with every shade of red, from crimson to pink. Black and yellow smoke veiled from our eyes the horror of that supreme minute, in which the species of madness that immobilized us in hypnotic contemplation finally ceased.

The Parisian crowd, breaking that detestable charm, started to flee in all directions. People closed their eyes, blocked their ears, in order no longer to see and no longer to hear, but the power of the revelatory wave was still sufficient for the vision to be imposed on closed eyes, pursuing the most resolute into the dark corners in which they tried in vain to take refuge, far from the vision of murder and dementia.

Like the others, I had fled, going back in haste to my empty house; and into my room, the curtains closed, shreds of images pursued me. I saw the wounded debris of the battle trailing over the waters, millions of little black dots still dancing on the crests of the waves, and—a hideous conclusion, the epilogue of the imbecilic massacre—I watched two enemy cruisers run aground on a vast sandbank off the coast of Newfoundland.

They were the *Roon* and the *Colorado*, whose grounded hulls, tilting sideways, poured their exhausted and overexcited crews out on to the strand, gilded by placidly glorious sunlight. What should they have done, those wretches who had miraculously escaped the fate of so many of their innocent brethren, except fall to their knees to thank the god of their beliefs and embrace one another in an explosion of gratitude and love? So powerful still in the bestial hearts of our races is the destructive instinct whose blossoming is assured therein that those men still found the means of prolonging, on that silent and deserted isle, the combat of which they were the only survivors.

Under the tyranny of that spectacle, I confess, I ended up bowing my head before the power that seemed to be bending me beneath its yoke, as if to say to me: *I want you to see, and to know; afterwards, you will judge.* The old instinct of the human being terrified by nature rose up again within me, and without really knowing what I was doing, I eventually fell to my knees, addressing myself to that unknown power, divining it, attempting to soften it by prayer, and murmuring, having been humbled and become child-like again: "Have pity on me!"

Dusk fell; gradually, the hideous images faded from my eyes; invaded by a bizarre torpor, I dragged myself to me bed. Overwhelmed by lassitude, I fell into a death-like sleep.

XII

When I woke up from that cataleptic sleep, I remained still for several hours, without making a movement, vaguely lending an ear to the sound of the rain, which was falling with the force of a torrent. It was streaming down so hard that I began to fear for the solidity of the house.

That lasted for three hours without a pause, and it required all my physical weakness to prevent me from getting up and going to the window to assess the results of the inundation, which must, eventually, fill up the drains and submerge the city.

Abruptly, the rain stopped, and again, a deathly silence floated around me. My stomach, racked by hunger, was causing me pain, but once again, I went to sleep.

The chirping of sparrows battling outside the windows of my bedroom extracted me from that further annihilation. I raised myself up on my elbow; I was weak but I had no difficulty ringing. The cook appeared almost immediately.

From her, I learned that the whole of Paris had, after the appalling spectacle of the battle, succumbed to the crisis of sleep that had kept me unconscious for thirty-six hours. Life had stopped, and when my hunger appeased, I was able to go downstairs in order to go out in search of news. I discovered that the torpor had been general throughout the zone submissive to the telepathic influence.

By a remarkable coincidence, the telegrams that were beginning to arrive from everywhere after that abnormal suspension of activity signaled an interruption in the transmission of images and thoughts. Since the apparitions of that frightful slaughter in Newfoundland, everything seemed to have reverted to the previous order, and, it must be said, everyone, in that personal liberation, began to hope for a return to individual isolation.

Had we finished with the anxieties of telepathic perspicacity? Everyone ardently hoped so, and in the meantime occupied themselves with healing the consequences of an adventure that they wanted to believe exceptional, with neither precedent nor recurrence.

In the wake of an unusual expenditure of energy, cases of general paralysis were revealed to be so numerous that no one hesitated to see it as a consequence of those three months of hypernervous existence. By virtue of a strange logic, people deemed that the person designated to remedy that situation was the one who had been the observer of the first manifestations, and people came to me from all directions in search of a cure for the results of the crisis. Not all the cases were irreparable; temperament and age modified its gravity, but how many people would have to pay for their lives for those three months of overexcited consciousness?

One of the first to be afflicted, alas, was my poor master, Saint-Denis. So self-composed before, so perfectly equilibrated, in what excesses of overloaded sensibility I watched him die in two days, in his little house at Ville d'Avray, overlooking that beautiful lake where he had once followed me in my exaltation of observation.

It required nothing less to console me than a letter from Madame Forbe asking me, without bitterness, to come to see her.

The thought of reconstituting my domestic hearth, destroyed by the scourge, caused me to abandon my patients for a day, and I left for Angers, where my wife, also enfeebled and deeply affected by the repercussion of events, embraced me tearfully and forgave me a few hours of irresponsible folly.

Everywhere, there was a relaxation. The days passed, and no one had yet observed any alteration in the good human life that had been reconstituted: not the slightest communication, no strange imagery. Telepathy seemed vanquished; people breathed deeply, and rediscovered the joy of living. Friends who had quarreled, couples who had separated, kissed and made up, promising to forget a bad dream. Even the law, appeased, relaxed, and made the judgment of a temporary delirium. Sourbelle's wife was set free, and she and her husband resumed the course of their miserable existence.

A peace treaty between the United States and Germany was signed by emissaries still bewildered by the fit of disorientation. The President and the Emperor were confined to bed for several weeks, debilitated by nervous exhaustion, and perhaps also by the scruples that made them a trifle repentant.

And yet, in spite of the horrible results of a struggle thus far unique, if it is necessary to believe the universally accepted explanations of the crisis, we still owe them thanks, so much good potentially being born from the excess of evil—for it has been suggested that it required nothing less than such a prodigious number of cannon shots, detonations and explosions to break the fluidic agglomeration thanks to which, for three months, human individuals communicated as intimately as it is possible to imagine. Like rain and hail, telepathic waves are obliged to burst by cannon fire.

May it not reappear, and never reform!

That is the wish I form now, in the midst of the calm of a life whose intimacy is limited to a few dear and reasonably clairvoyant individuals; thus it appears to me to be long again, full of promised joys and an infinite sweetness. An increased notoriety, a numerous and lucrative clientele, a peaceful hearth: if all that only rests on appearances, let us enjoy the appearance and not desire to get to the bottom of things, or too close to consciences that might, like good wines, have their lees.

Sages might sing the praises of glass houses, but can you name a single one who constructed one?

Jules Sageret: *The Race that Will Be Victorious*
(1908)

I attended spiritualist séances.

Our medium held a pen, which initially channeled Abbé Nonotte, well known as a contemporary, victim and enemy of Voltaire, in a reliable manner.[34] At every séance we obtained at least twenty pages, to which the medium made no contribution, except for mechanical movements of the fingers, for he conversed with us incessantly about modern subjects entirely foreign to the Christian apologetics that he drafted with stenographic rapidity. He made use of his left hand to light cigarettes, drink, gesticulate and even draw people. The other hand, meanwhile, did not experience any interruption or deceleration in its frenetic course.

In the middle of the ninth séance, however, it was seen to quit the paper abruptly. It made jerky movements in all directions, certainly contrary to the will of the medium. The poor hand, we all understood, was prey to the disputes of several invisible beings. Antagonistic forces of equal power held it motionless momentarily. Finally, it fell back violently upon the paper, began splashing it with blots in the form of exclamation marks, and then resumed writing. It was not Abbé Nonotte who had gotten the upper hand in the battle, because everything had changed: the style, the subject, the forms of the letters and the punctuation.

I shall transcribe here the medium's communications in their new phase. I shall transcribe them with neither a title nor a preamble, merely such as they are before me on their origi-

---

[34] Claude-Adrien Nonotte, or Nonnotte (1711-1793) wrote several books, of which by far the most famous was *Les Erreurs de Voltaire* (1762; revised and expanded 1766).

nal sheets of paper. Know only, by way of preparation that they recount a history of humankind from a future date whose determination is impossible.

Let us now hand the floor to the spirit.

In the year 47 of the second cycle, a young woman was exhibited in fairgrounds, whom the posters called Ertha, the Beautiful Whistler. Only one thing rendered her singular at first: she was ignorant of the art of pronouncing consonants, and whistled marvelously. Physiologists who examined her attributed her faulty articulation to a certain poorly developed apophysis. It appears that it is a similar but more pronounced anatomical conformation that prevents apes from expressing themselves in human languages.

The Beautiful Whistler was considered to be ugly. Her mental state was no more pleasing, although no one had anything for which to reproach her. She was always depressed and mechanical, out of place in all the places to which the traveling fair and her exploiters took her. That she lacked cheerfulness could be attributed to a phenomenon of femininity, but her sadness was antipathetic. Only one value remained to her: her whistling, with which she produced the deepest notes of the bassoon and rose as high as the shrill sonorities of the flute. In addition, Ertha could imitate any wind or brass instrument, thanks to an innate gift, although it was not accompanied by any musical instinct. If she had not been carefully trained, she would have produced an atrocious cacophony, so naturally indifferent was she to the harmony or discordance of the sounds she emitted. Once provided with the necessary education, the Whistling Beauty amused her audience without hurting their ears, but it was necessary to wait until she had a purely mechanical discipline.

In consequence, Ertha excited curiosity. She brought in good returns. However, as society was still living under the regime of competition, it did not take long for Handsome Whistlers and Beautiful Whistlers of both sexes to emerge in fairly considerable numbers. There was nothing surprising in that. The physiologists were, however, surprised to learn that two of these phenomena were perfectly authentic.

Science then conducted an investigation, departing from the sufficiently plausible idea that not all living monsters were in fairground tents. Thus, a hundred Whistlers were discovered scattered throughout the world. Their habitat seemed to be indeterminate. They were remarkable in their specific homogeneity; any of the eleven Whistlers born among Negroes resembled the others as much as, but no more than Whistlers of German or Mongolian origin. The same epidermal coloration appeared everywhere: an olive tint more or less darkened by the sun.

It was an interesting problem.

Scientific academies collaborated in order to carry out methodical observations. It was thus discovered, after two generations, that Whistler couples were remarkably fruitful, while unions between humans and monsters only produced rare hybrids incapable of reproduction. Furthermore, those hybrids were only obtained at an exceedingly high price; it was, in fact, necessary to pay a few unfortunates who had lost all sense of dignity very dearly to persuade them to impregnate female Whistlers, who were, moreover, more or less raped. No woman could ever be persuaded to give herself to a male Whistler. Any sexual commerce with the phenomena excited more repugnance and reprobation than bestiality. It was claimed that they did not experience a reciprocal disgust themselves, but it was claimed without proof, because it was seen as a mark of their inferiority. The superior interest of the conversation of the human race caused the world to rise up against them.

They multiplied rapidly, in fact, both by virtue of their own fertility and by their spontaneous appearance in the bosom of the healthiest families. The International Bureau of Statistics, which did not take long to occupy itself with them, published these figures in the year 120: birth of Whistlers: one per 839 human families, one per ten female Whistlers. Thus, officially, the monsters were no longer classified in our species; they were referred to as males and females, not men and women. Instead of giving birth, they "dropped" young, which would one day die rather than "pass on."

In that, common parlance was only following the observations of science. The latter could no longer treat the emergence of Whistlers as a teratological phenomenon. It found itself in the presence of a well-characterized veritable species. From that, a theory followed that appeared almost immediately.

All species, it was said, passed at certain moments through crises of mutation. Then, instead of continuing to reproduce in a faithfully identical manner, they saw individuals emerging from their bosom much less similar to the previous ordinary type; these individuals were grouped in varieties, and the extreme varieties constituted one or more new species that entered into vital competition with the root species. The mutational crisis was quite short relative to the normal existence of those root species; hence, in a geological period, the existence of a flora or fauna unknown in the immediately anterior period, and the rarity of transitional flora and fauna. It was unnecessary to be surprised that the human species, almost constant since the tertiary anthropoid, was now passing through a mutational crisis.

Such, in summary, was the theory invented by a scientific syndicate knows as the S.S.A.

Scientists set out to test the theory elsewhere. Facts were attached to it that had previously been explained outside it. Thus, the appearance of the Whistlers had been accompanied, and even slightly preceded, by that of humans more abnormal than usual. Some had voluminous brains and stooped shoulders, while others were remarkable because of their short legs, or because of their athletic build and powerful elongated jaws in the forefront of a narrow skull, or because of the abundance of their hair, or baldness, or beauty, or exceptional eyesight, or myopia.

That greater variety of human types had initially been attributed to the combined effects of heredity and the increasing specialization of careers. It was imagined, for example, that aircraft pilots would have atrophied limbs by virtue of no longer walking, and could transmit their atrophy to their children; the latter, less well-adapted to other métiers, would naturally choose a profession in which they remained seated, and so on, all the way to the legless aeromen of the future. The S.S.A. theory appeared far more satisfactory; it was adopted without opposition.

There was then a debauchery of species, varieties and subvarieties within the species *Homo sibilans*, and there were, in addition, *Homo intellectualis, Homo mecanicus, Homo pugnax, Homo glaber, Homo villosus, Homo spectabilis*. But the taxonomists were wasting their time because, with the exception of the initial two, all these categories of the genus *Homo* proved to be unstable and mercurial, to the extent that the nomenclature was abandoned. The *priscus* and the *sibilans* became the only ones established.[35] The usage became commonplace of calling the latter "anthropoid" in spite of the qualification *Homo*.

The unanimous convergence of minds to the S.S.A doctrine did not prevent scientific jealousy from attacking it. J.-B.-J. Sand Arena, an isolated scholar who wanted to deprive it of the merit of the invention showed rare courage. He carried out research on the immense deposits that were still preserved, piously cared for but unconsidered, of books printed from the middle of the nineteenth century, of the so-called Christian Era to the end of the period of Eras.

---

[35] The designation *Homo priscus* was first adapted in application to fossil humans in 1888 with regard to remains found in Chancelade in France, but Sageret would also have known that it had earlier been used by Catullus and Virgil to refer, satirically, to old-fashioned individuals of their own species, that being its literal meaning. His conscientious avoidance of the designation *sapiens* is, of course, key to his argument.

In that remote epoch when humans had the singular custom of using as temporal reference points the birth of a god or a political revolution, and not, as later, the sidereal revolution of the equinoctial points, they employed a detestable paper for the fabrication of books, which only required a century or two to turn to dust—with the result that Sand Arena was obliged to pursue his research not in a library but in a quarry of chalky powder. He had, however, an unprecedented stroke of luck. After having caused a hundred volumes to disintegrate merely by opening them, he collected a few fragments that were almost intact.

A scientist of the late nineteenth or early twentieth century of the Christian Era had summarized therein the ideas of another scientist named de Vries.[36] The theory of the person in question was none other than that of the so-called crisis of mutation invented by the S.S.A. De Vries had cultivated a plant, the evening primrose or oenothera, and had introduced an alteration in the process of spontaneously procreating daughter species that differed from it in several very evident characteristics. From that, by extension to all living beings, emerged an image of past and future evolution to which the S.S.A. had added nothing. What had once happened to the oenothera was now happening to humankind. It ought to have been foreseen. What a striking triumph for the wisdom of the Ancients!

The conclusions of science had an immediate repercussion in the juridical domain. Since the Whistlers belonged to a

---

[36] Hugo de Vries (1848-1935), the pioneer of mutation theory, which he developed in the course of modifying the theory of *pangenesis*—the hypothetical mechanism of heredity developed by Charles Darwin. His notion of the importance of sudden gross transformations is now considered discredited, although it continued to fuel the imagination of writers of speculative fiction to a far greater degree than the more modest gradualist conception.

new species, different from the human species that had made the laws, those laws did not apply to it, any more than to the chimpanzee or the ox. On the other hand, under penalty of disappearing, humans had to retain supremacy in the vital competition that had been established.

There was also the matter of the conservation of the Beautiful and the Good, for as the Whistlers multiplied, more was learned about them. They were unnatural. The instinct of family did not exist in them. It was observed that the mothers had no particular attachment to their own children. When they lactated, their nurslings could be exchanged for another without them appearing to see anything inconvenient therein. It was with the same facility that, having emerged from the arms of one male, they accepted the caresses of another. To tell the truth, these animals knew nothing of love beyond its strictly physiological aspect.

They were deprived of any sentiment of individual honor. They seemed to be cowardly. Elegance, harmony, taste, ornamentation and beauty had no meaning for them. Thus, they dressed themselves without the slightest care for aesthetics, or even for dignity. Provided that they were neither too hot nor too cold and did not feel any hindrance in their movements, the rest was of no importance to them. It must be admitted that they were fearful of the dirt propitious to microbes, but they serenely wore garments stained by acid. They only demanded repairs to make them more durable and found a red patch as convenient as any other to repair blue cloth. That coarseness was the same among the females as among the males. It extended to scorn for jewelry. The Whistlers that had chronometeorological indicators suspended them around their necks with pieces of sturdy string.

Thus, not only was the species not civilized, but lacked all the impulses that drew ancient savages toward civilization. Nothing human remained in them but reason—and in what measure? Communication between the two species was so difficult that one could scarcely be sure; for a Whistler, when he wanted to speak, was reduced to pronouncing vowels. Although he appeared to understand, one could only understand him with difficulty. Whether he was of vast or limited intelligence, it came to the same thing; a reason like his had nothing to do, for want of being spurred on by needs of the sentimental order.

It was therefore necessary, at any price, for the cause of progress, that humans conserved a sovereign empire over the Earth.

Preservative measures were proposed. The one that would save the world consisted of treating the Whistlers as dangerous animals and killing them all. Their mothers, when they were of our race, would not oppose it, so much were they considered as monstrous products. Were not overly teratological newborns directly suppressed? Thus far, only the difficulty of distinguishing between *Homo priscus* and *Homo sibilans* in the cradle had saved the anthropoids born to humans. And thus, once the crisis of mutation was over, humans would be able to pursue in security their admirable work, which consists of putting ever more soul into matter.

The case was submitted to the World Delegation, the W.D., which governed what nations had in common: telephonophotography, money, gold deposits, weights and measures, astronomical observatories, meteorology, and intercommunication by air, water and land. It judged disputes between the various nations. It maintained, by its surveillance of vocabulary and education, the unity of "pidgin," the ancient Anglo-Chinese invention that had become the universal auxiliary language. Eventually, the study and operation of social forms had been entrusted to it. It had been remarked a long time before and by everyone that, by virtue of the economic solidarity of nations, none of them could consider itself in isolation in the legislation of labor; agreements were necessary. It had, however, taken a long time for that idea to enter into practice by the foundation of a section of the W.D. responsible for agreements. The W.D., therefore, took over the problem of the Whistlers, a problem that was eminently social and international.

After a serious examination, it set aside the option of general massacre. A question of sentiment opposed it. In addition, there were certain economic problems in suppressing a labor force as intelligent and considerable as that of the anthropoids. Several delegates suggested reducing them to slavery, in perfect conformity with the law, since all species other than human were human possessions. That solution was also rejected. It was feared, with good reason, that the cost of labor might be excessively depressed, which would plunge workers into poverty.

Finally enlightened by long debates, the W.D. promulgated a decree, of which the essential dispositions were as follows:

The anthropoids known as Whistlers, not being human, do not enjoy any human rights. With regard to legislation, they are neither citizens nor spouses. Nevertheless, grave social interests prevent them from being ranked among the animals, objects of private property and transactions between individuals. They must be considered as a labor force put at the disposal of the community. By exploiting them wisely, they can be made to serve the good of all, and, far from threatening progress, will contribute to it if they are submitted to statutes elaborated in their regard. These statutes will finally resolve the social question.

Henceforth, the anthropoids, whatever they may be, are assigned to the proletariat. They may not exercise the liberal professions, nor live idly, and not direct any commerce or industry, except in the cases indicated hereafter. They may only possess an essentially precarious usufruct. They may change residence according to the needs of labor, without being able to transport anything except personal effects. Outside of the journeys necessitated by labor, the various companies of communal transport will refuse to accommodate anthropoids in their vehicles, under penalty of heavy fines.

To begin, an exact census will be complied of all existing *Whistlers*, in order that they can be redistributed between nations in proportion to the human population. That done, the distribution of the labor force in question between the various exploitations will be left to the national *C.G.T.s*, which will obey the following principles: first supplying the industries where wages are minimal; not allowing the wages of purely human labor to become less than the wages of industries with a mixed labor force; and finally, in equivalent economic conditions, establishing in all similar establishments the same proportion between the number of human laborers and the number of anthropoid laborers.

The wages of an anthropoid will be one tenth that of a human, which is amply sufficient for a creature devoid of needs, which does not like wine or meat. But that reduced pay should never diminish the sum presently expended by employers for labor. Syndicates will see to that. To render their supervision easier, it will be given the force of the law, in almost universal usage today, of global pay. It is by that means that the happiness of laborious humanity, sought in vain thus far, at the cost of utopias and upheavals, by all socialisms, will finally be achieved.

Let us take an example: a trust employs a hundred men in its exploitation. It pays them the present minimum daily wage, which is two dollars a head. It therefore pays two hundred dollars daily to the syndicate of those hundred men. Now, that work is divided with an anthropoid workforce. Let us suppose a ratio of two anthropoids to one human, and that the production of two anthropoids is only equivalent to that of one human—which is a very pessimistic estimate, since at present, two anthropoids work as hard as three men. The exploitation in question will thus employ fifty humans and a hundred anthropoids. The employer will still pay the syndicate two hundred dollars. The latter will attribute twenty cents to each anthropoid, which is twenty dollars in all; 180 dollars will remain for the fifty men, which represents 3.60 dollars per head instead of two.

Urban anthropoids will live in special quarters analogous to compounds or the legendary ghettos. These ghettos, which ought to enclose a maximum of a thousand adult occupants, will be formed of the poorest houses. They will be closed by railings. A severe punishment awaits anthropoids that are found outside their ghetto between 9 p.m. and 6 a.m. They will be free within the quarters reserved for them. The administration will only intervene to take census or to displace them. It will hold them collectively responsible. Any unjustified absence from the workplace, and any fault in the work on their part, will be punished by the confiscation of furniture or other objects taken at random from their ghetto.

As far as possible, the regime of compounds will also be applied to Whistlers distributed among agricultural exploitations.

The death penalty, long erased from legal codes, is reestablished for anthropoids.

The immediate and total seizure of property owned by the anthropoids will provide the expenses of the new organization: the reassignment of present human habitations for future compounds or ghettos, the furnishing of houses constituting the ghettos, the division and census of anthropoids, indemnities, etc.

The anthropoids will thus commence the new regime by possessing nothing. Then they will have their wages, of which they can dispose at their complete liberty, and it will be permissible for them to engage in industry or commerce provided that it is restricted to their fellows, inside the ghetto, without any detriment to the labor they owe to humans. They will have no lack of leisure, because it is severely prohibited to employ them outside the seven legal hours. Human protection from competition is completed by prohibiting any exportation of any commodities whatsoever from ghettos.

If, in spite of all the precautions taken, the Whistlers come to constitute a menacing economic force, national authorities may take such urgent measures as they deem necessary, subject to subsequent referral to the World Delegation.

Such was the D.M. decree, reduced to a few lines, although it filled a large volume, so many are the mechanisms that have to be put in place when social reorganizations are undertaken.

During the W.D.'s long deliberations, there was considerable emotion, which justified in advance the statute elaborated with respect of the Whistlers.

The latter were not unaware that their fate was at stake. Their small groups communicated with one another in spite of the spontaneous brutality of humans.

An anthropoid boards an aerocar, followed by a human traveler, who seizes him by the shoulders and throws him out as the vehicle takes off. Everyone laughs. There is the same hilarity among telecommunications employees when a Whistler is thrown out without his being allowed to send his message, the price of which has been collected. An isolated anthropoid is beaten up—an easy task, as he is a coward.

That was what was reported every day. The authorities closed their eyes and blocked their ears, with the complicity of public opinion. But there was not enough determination in that persecution for it to be effective.

The phonophotogazettes of 23.7.211.II[37] published the following story:

Last night, on a road on the edge of a marshy plain in Hungary. The peasant Raczos, driving a locomotor, is towing to the nearest factory—which is still quite distant—a harvester-thresher-miller-baker that is in need of urgent repair. Suddenly, the tractor stops. A breakdown! Raczos gets down from his seat. He has scarcely begun to examine the components of the machine when he shudders. A murmur breaks the silence. What can it be? Night-birds? But their calls do not have that

---

[37] Author's note: "The 23rd day of the 7th month of the 211th year of the 2nd cycle."

surprising variety. As for humans, they do not produce a concert so discordant, nor at that hour, nor in that deserted spot.

Then Raczos thinks of anthropoids, and though he knows that they are despicable, his fear dissipates. Nevertheless, he remains anxious, anticipating nothing good for human peace in such a clearing. In order to gather more information, he tries to get closer to the Whistlers. He walks silently through the reeds, crouching down. Soon, the anthropoids appear. In spite of the obscurity, one might be able to estimate their number at a hundred. None of them seems to be fulfilling the function of chairman or leader. They voice their trills one after another, briefly. Sometimes a no-less-brief medley responds. Assent or jeering? Impossible to tell.

Raczos returns to his tractor. The breakdown, fortunately not serious, is quickly repaired. Half an hour later, Raczos finds on his route a wireless telegraph caller. The police, alerted and informed, mount aircraft and intercept twenty anthropoids at dawn, which are promptly arrested and put in prison. At least twice as many have escaped. They are actively sought.

24.7.211.II

Only one new arrest has been made among the anthropoid conspirators. The Hungarian authorities proceed with an initial interrogation. It is observed that none of the detainees understands Hungarian. On the other hand, none of them is ignorant of the international language. It is, therefore, pidgin that the police employ in communication. However, as the anthropoids are unintelligible when they try to speak, they are made to write their answers down.

Interrogated as to their origin, the detainees declare fifteen different nationalities.

Q. Were there Hungarians among you?

A. Yes. They escaped.

Q. Their names? Descriptions?

A. We could not distinguish their features in the darkness. We do not know their names.

Q. It is not plausible, however, that you held your meeting without knowing one another, without being able to prove your identities to one another or show some kind of mandate.

A. Why know one another? Why mandates? We met, two or three per nation, to discuss the interests of our entire species. Our fellows understood that our numbers were sufficient, and none of them would have gone to the trouble of increasing it needlessly.

Q. You were elected, though?

A. Not at all. We knew that a universal understanding was necessary. In every country, the first two or three who took the initiative of realizing it and possessed enough money to travel so far were naturally designated.

Q. Designated how?

A. Via the newspapers. Everything happens in each country as if there were a single newspaper for our species. You ought to know that. Universal and then national information is inserted therein. What would be the point of different versions?

Q. Do you all have the same opinion, then?

A. Certainly, since we form a single species. Each of us is mistaken occasionally. The others perceive it and correct it instantly, without there being the slightest inclination to persist. Among rational beings, only humans can persevere deliberately in error.

Q. We're not here to talk philosophy. Tell us instead how you understood one another, although belonging to different nationalities.

A. We have adopted one of our languages, which will henceforth be our only language.

Q. That's a new development, if I'm not mistaken?

A. Entirely new. Our conference was the first opportunity for us to employ that universal language, which was imposed by the necessity of our universal understanding.

Q. Explain the manner in which you were able to agree on the choice of that language and learn it so rapidly.

A. How can you not know? Or, if you don't know, guess? The agreement was made in advance in our minds. The language spoken by the greatest number was chosen, for two obvious reasons: the first was that the fewest possible people would be obliged to learn it, and the second that there would be the largest possible number of people capable of teaching it. After a year, there were people everywhere sufficiently educated to take part in our conference. In three years, no one will make use of particular dialects anywhere.

Q. National pride doesn't inhibit you?

A. All pride is foreign to us. We have a great deal of difficulty understanding the constitution of that sentiment among you.

Q. You are dangerous, then. You are not human. It is evident that your conference was preparing the destruction of our species.

A. For the moment, we are uniquely occupied in presenting our claims to the W.D.

The remainder of the interrogation is postponed until tomorrow.

This news spread surprise and, it must be confessed, almost fear among humans. The national languages of the anthropoids were known and, even quite often understood, but no one had been astonished by their appearance, even though it would have been a rare merit for disseminated beings to agree with one another on the symbols of thought. Explanations suppressed the excessively odious necessity of admiring the anthropoids. They had, it was said, imitated to the best of their ability the languages most commonly employed around them. Thus, their twitterings were born of human languages, as black men had once acquired the languages of whites.

Such might well, in fact, have been the origin of the means that the Whistlers had found to exchange their ideas. As for verifying it by linguistic studies, it was out of the question.

A sequence of musical notes—*do re*, for example—might have forty different significations among the anthropoids, according to whether the two were emitted as a crotchet followed by a quaver, a quaver followed by a crotchet, or two quavers, or two crochets, or depending on the octaves from which they were taken, or the timbre of the flute, the clarinet, the oboe or the ocarina that they were given or according to whether they were sounded as *ou, a, é, eu, u, in, an, on* or *i*. How could one disentangle from all that what had become of the articulations?

The annoying but evident truth was that the anthropoids did not lack creative power. Their ingenuity had endowed them, for the depiction of thought, with a sonorous palette much richer than that of humans. That had not seemed astonishing because the acquisition of the palette in question had seemed progressive, thanks to the penumbra of scorn in which the Whistlers lived. But now, suddenly, under the pressure of a perceived danger, they had adopted a universal language! What a facility of understanding! What ability!

In truth, those monsters formed only one single entity. By virtue of the spontaneous effect of a characteristic of their species, they had realized a common and universal action, at which humankind had only arrived after millennia of suffering, and very imperfectly. The tremulous already saw civilization annihilated.

Their fears were further augmented when a document was published that had been sent to the W.D. under the title *Claims of United Humanity against Divided Humanity*. It was known that the anthropoids called themselves "the United."

We belong to two different and incompatible species, said the document in question, in summary. *If we live together, we shall oppress you tomorrow as you oppress us today. It is therefore necessary for us to separate. We, the United, are forty millions, against four billions of Divided Humans. Give us, therefore, an amount of land that presently nourishes forty million inhabitants, in two or several territories. In equity, we ought to share the expenses of the operation proportionally to our respective numerical importance, but we consent to the United bearing half. Let us make an arrangement on that basis. Henceforth, every hundred years, the territory of each species will be augmented or diminished in accordance with the initial rule.*

Do this because it is the least disagreeable means of allowing natural selection to decide between us. You doubtless have your reasons for believing yourselves better adapted than us to the administration of the planet. These are ours for sustaining the contrary. Since it has existed, Divided Humanity has striven in vain to realize a good economy. It has never succeeded, by reason of its very nature, of which contradiction is the essence. It understands that there is a communality of interests that permits it to subsist, but all its energy is expended in a struggle of particular interests against the general interest. Its pretended solidarity has the sole effect of substituting collective hatreds for individual hatreds. When it calls itself socialist, it wants exception for all.

Whether it is socialist or something else, it condemns in wastage any attack on the satisfaction of its needs, and wastage follows as a necessary consequence of its most imperious needs. Thus, in Divided Humanity, women need to be dressed, but have even more need to follow fashion. Is it not necessary every year to devote much labor and money to a simple change of fabric and cut? That represents a quantity of obsolete garments. Many other examples show your ineptitude in putting actions in accord with ideas in the economic domain.

It follows from those same causes that you merit your name of Divided Humans. Every one of you is, in fact, divided against himself. There is a reason that shows him a goal, and impulses of activity that drive him in the opposite direction to that goal. Those impulses are vanity, his desire for adornment, honor, sexual jealousy and a thousand singular appetites, such as love of beauty, of meat, of alcohol and of glory.

We, the United, are, on the contrary, driven by our whole nature in the direction that intelligence recognizes as that of the common god. None of us experiences desires that a social organization devoid of utopia cannot easily satisfy for everyone. And this, in sum, is the respect in which we are far superior to you: we have no preference for individuals, as we only love, in reality, our species—all our children and all our women, not, as among you, a few children and two or three women. We are bees, but instead of having several hives, we only know one: our own humanity, the United. That is sufficient to ensure that the world will one day belong to us: after a peaceful evolution, if you consent to the arrangement we propose; by other means of selection, if you reject our request.

People were struck, in this document as in the recent interrogation of the anthropoid conspirators, by an audacious tone that contrasted so strongly with the cowardice of the isolated Whistler. Pessimists took the opportunity to say: "Annihilate the rival species while you still have the numbers, or satisfy it, for it is true that it is showing itself strong and courageous when it is threatened, in spite of the timidity of its members taken separately.

The W.D. did not listen to these Cassandras.

It did well, in the general opinion, insofar as the ghettoization was carried out peacefully. The anthropoids, momentarily so proud, did not resist when they were reduced to servitude for the good of humanity. All they gained from that adventure, therefore, was a reputation as bluffers.

The measures taken in their regard were, moreover, justified by the rise in the minimum wage by a third that followed almost immediately, for care was taken to apply the anthropoids initially to the least well-paid work, and their labor proved more productive than had been hoped.

They became increasingly abundant in factories, thanks to a rapid multiplication, soon bringing working humans the salaries of senior functionaries without it costing employers a penny. Poverty disappeared.

Everyone was happy, even the anthropoids, who seemed to adapt to their condition very well. Of their twenty cents a day, they spent ten on the primary necessities of life; they cooked communally, slept in vast dormitories formed of piles of straw on inclined plants, dressing like harlequins, sowing together all the sturdy rags they could find. The other ten cents went to hygiene, especially to a public bath they all frequented, as well as on education, on caring for the sick and on the purchase of raw materials that supplied the industries created in the ghettos—for the Whistlers, after having worked seven hours for humans, worked a further five hours for themselves. They thus had factories of all sorts, whose products were reserved for them, since no merchandise emerged from their quarters.

Humankind congratulated itself on its luck and its genius. It had finally resolved the seemingly insoluble problem of satisfying needs as they grew. Until then, the progress of industry and social organization had not been able to go quickly enough to follow the metamorphosis of petty luxury into primary necessity. Desire grew in geometric proportion, while their satiation dragged itself painfully up the slope of gradual progression. Now that too had wings. Anthropoid labor played the role of an intelligent technology possessed by human workers, who thus saw, in an unexpected and indirect fashion, the realization of their old dream of owning the means of production. At the same time, the employers did not lose anything.

Humans, therefore, lived the years of their earthly lives happily. And the happiness would increase incessantly. The Whistlers did not seem to pose any threat to security. They were docile. That is why no one feared employing them in industries of transportation and administration. People even went so far as to recruit several companies of them into the permanent army of mercenaries that was designed to form militias in case the W.D. had to employ force to put its decrees into effect among nations or classes. Observation proved, in fact, that if there were a hundred of them together, the anthropoids ceased to be so fainthearted.

Meanwhile, human families tended to restrict their number of offspring. Perhaps the crisis of mutation, which did indeed come to an end, left the older species weakened in its procreative power—but calculation soon added its effect. To diminish the number of humans was to increase the relative proportion of Whistlers, and, in consequence, wealth and leisure. The time arrived quite swiftly when the two species counted as many adults as one another.

The statistical bureau of the W.D. published that fact, which the press qualified as fortunate, and proposed to celebrate it with a grand fête. People were far from suspecting the frightful cataclysm that was about to replace it.

It was night in China. A rumor awoke the cities. People ran through the streets shouting: "The Whistlers! The Whistlers! Every man for himself! To arms!" The light of conflagrations could be seen, and people were especially frightened by a noise that no one had ever heard before; it was reminiscent of the vibrations of gongs combined with the appeal of trumpets, but also with echoes that seemed to be produced by human throats.

People ran to the automatic wireless telephone; the central transmitter was no longer functioning. They went to knock on neighbors' doors. What was happening? No one knew, exactly. Determined men, taking their fulgurators, mingled with the agitation of the city, which was that of an anthill overturned by the thrust of a spade.

"To the Tele!" said some—but they encountered running fugitives who said: "*They*'re there!"

They gradually learned in that fashion that all the places from which news might be transmitted, or orders, or force, or means of transportation, were in the hands of the Whistlers.

The unfortunate humans ran around in ever-decreasing circles. Driven back by the flames from a warehouse that was on fire, they ran into a dynamited house, only to fall thereafter into a storm of mortal lightning. And the noise of the gong, the clamor of the rallying cry uttered by the anthropoids, drew nearer. A great empty space was hollowed out between the two crowds, with rare blasts of fulgurators fired from one side, while sheaves of lightning replied from the other. Eventually, the United saw nothing else before them but the dead and the wounded.

Humans fled in aircraft, hoping to find salvation in another city. The light changed as the sun rose above the horizon, but there was no change from one city to the next; all of them had collapsed in the same catastrophe. By the afternoon, a noxious odor signaled them from afar; the anthropoids were beginning to burn cadavers doused in gasoline.

As the cataclysm had been unleashed everywhere at the same time, in order that no country would have time to put itself on guard after the alert produced by the interruption of international communications, it unfolded in broad daylight in Western Europe. That circumstance was unfavorable to the Whistlers. So, even though they had to contend with people less militaristic than the Chinese, they suffered a few setbacks. Here and there, in barracks—for it had been necessary to make numerous exceptions to the ghetto regime—human soldiers, better commanded, did not succumb to the unexpected aggression of their anthropoid comrades. They resisted and were able to preserve depots of arms and ammunition, and finally to annihilate the Whistlers, who, gripped by their hive instincts, had fought furiously and had died to the last man. A few human armies went on campaign, but were so inferior numerically that they quickly recognized the folly of their attempts.

They were even helped. "Surrender voluntarily," the United said to them. "If not, we shall shoot the Divided, who are almost all in our possession, in a ratio of one in a thousand to begin with, until the day when you comply with our ultimatum."

As this threat was made good, and for want of any equilibrium of reprisals, the last human champions were obliged to lay down their arms.

There was then no more devastation or killing. The Uniteds applied the regime of separation of the species that they had once proposed to the W.D., except that they applied it as victors. Humans found themselves assigned a host of small territories separated from one another, without sea coasts or large navigable rivers. They were free, on condition that they had neither arms nor aircraft, submit to a census, to surveillance and to searches, and only communicate with other human territories via the intermediary or with the permission of the Uniteds.

From that moment on, humankind declined very rapidly. It understood very well that its only chance of salvation lay in increasing its population, but everyone said to himself: "It's necessary that the mass of humans procreate, but as for me, I will follow my own inclinations; what does the conduct of one individual matter in the overall bearing of the group?" Thus persisted the old human contradiction between the intelligence of collective good and individual actions.

On the other hand, it confirmed that the sterility of the root species was an effect of the crisis of mutation. There was soon no more than one child per couple, then one per two couples. At each significant diminution of a population, the Uniteds restricted its territory. The circles of the human fatherland became dots on the world map, and the dots, one after another, disappeared.

What remains of it now? Perhaps nothing, except for me.

The history of humankind was told to me by my parents, who are dead. I could not have obtained it from the Uniteds. They only have statistical archives. Since humankind has become a negligible quantity, all the documents concerning it have been burned. What is the point of cluttering up the libraries?

The present masters of the world have no curiosity regarding the past. They have no historical monuments, nor anything that does not have a present utility. All the paintings, all the statues, all the works of art, all the vestiges of antiquity, all the old books, have disappeared, been destroyed or thrown into the filling material of earthworks. And that wealth, which was dear to us, has not been replaced.

No aesthetic need has emerged among the anthropoids. All they know about color is that it is cooler in summer to have houses with white walls and blue windows, and warmer in winter to have those same houses painted black and those same windows painted red. The unique genius of their painters consists of finding increasingly rapid and facile means of effecting those changes of coloration.

Nothing subsists of civilization except for what concerns material life, simplified by the absence of several needs that were once commonplace. Science alone preserves its importance, because it aids industry and hygiene, which never cease to progress. Even that science which only responded to curiosity has been abandoned. The origin of worlds and the constitution of matter are irrelevant to the anthropoids. They see the stars as a convenient reference point for the measurement of time, the estimation of longitudes and latitudes, but they do not care about how they are composed physically or chemically. Fossils only interest them insofar as they inform them about mineral deposits; they do not occupy themselves for an instant in considering the evolution of life.

Nevertheless, with such restricted reasons for living, the Uniteds are happy, as the expressions of their physiognomy, almost always cheerful, show. It is necessary for me, in spite of all the repugnance they inspire in me, to recognize the elements of happiness with which they are endowed.

First of all, they are marvelously healthy, perhaps because they are ignorant of the usage of meat and alcoholic beverages, and cultivate hygiene assiduously. The small number of their needs permits, thanks to industrial progress, that none of them is deprived of what they desire. Above all, the anthropoids have the good fortune to be, as they say, social beings, bee-men whose hive extends over the entire Earth. Their nature does not give them any instinct that is foreign to the instinct of the hive. From that followed their pitiful depression when they found themselves isolated, in the days when their species was born, and also their facility for acting in common, their triumph, and later, the absence of rivalries, jealousies, quarrels, without which the lack of competition or individual disinterest produces relaxed labor.

The Uniteds were once reproached for their amorous mores. They were considered to be unnatural because the family did not exist among them. That trait of their species has an aspect favorable to happiness. They are ignorant of the sufferings of love, although they do not know its superior joys, and it is certainly an advantage that they have no prostitution or shame.

The absolute lack of exclusivism in sexual relations is, moreover, without any inconvenience for the future of the United race, for, like those bees and ants that are preoccupied before anything else with their larvae, they reserve their greatest regard for pregnant women, surrounding them with solicitude. From the cradle onwards, children receive from the group better care than if they had a father and a mother. Although their nurses feed any infant, without distinction, born at the same time as their own, the maternal instinct is not lacking—or, to put it another way, it is replaced by a hive instinct just as powerful and just as marvelous.

That hive instinct still permits the regulation of population growth, in order that the number of consumers remains in proportion to resources, and wellbeing never diminishes. They do not procreate for themselves, but for the species. That interest alone is the motive that causes pregnancy to be desired or shunned. That is why they regulate themselves on the basis of daily statistics that indicate, on the one hand, the number of births necessary to a district in the current year, and on the other hand, the total of those that have occurred since the beginning of the year. As soon as the two numbers are equal, sterility is practiced until the following year.

The happiness of the Uniteds might seem to be negative. I feel led to believe that, with more leisure and fewer needs than humans, they ought to be bored. They are not. One never sees in them the dismal face of people who feel a confused emptiness and do not know how to fill it. The anthropoids practice a thousand athletic sports, and they study. Although the instinct of the species limits their intellectual effort to techniques, the field is still vast enough for none of them to know everything.

They are happy! And yet, I do not admire them, nor do I envy them. Their civilization is, for me, barbarity; it makes me sick, because I am human. Why did I not live a long time ago, even at the price of the calamities that desolated my fellows? Humankind has endured too long, since I am perpetuating it in a terrestrial paradise that is not its own. It is necessary not to live too long, whether one is an individual or a race. If one encounters misfortune, one suffers in consequence, and if one encounters happiness, one still suffers in consequence, for the people of the past have nothing in their nature that can adapt to the fetishes of the future.

But how have I been able to communicate with you, who are separated from me by so many millennia of elapsed time? That is a great mystery. I am however, in a position to....

Here the anonymous spirit stopped. Was he making fun of us or did he yield to the jealous spirit that watches over the inviolability of the arcane? The only certain thing is that he never returned.

Gaston de Pawlowski: *The Veridical Ascension Through History of James Stout Brighton*
(1909)

Without a doubt, Monsieur, you who seem so well-informed don't yet know the veritable circumstances of the strange adventure that turned the life of our friend James Stout Brighton upside-down last year, and led to his disappearance from our world for a time that neither you nor I can estimate at present.

You know, don't you, like everyone else, that James came to Yorick Garden by airplane every evening, and that that concession made to the mores of the time delighted all the regulars of the theater. Then again, everyone knew that James had a curious mind, infatuated with strangeness, always in search of singular adventures, and that his actions were never those of vulgar individuals.

Given that he had already spent ten years transforming the simple airplanes of which you and I still make use every day, one can imagine that the effects that he was able to obtain were out of the ordinary. Thus, no one was unduly astonished on the day when he was seen to arrive from Paris with his new machine, at least four hours before the doors of the theater opened.

James, you will remember, manifested some impatience that evening. No one was there yet, and the scenery had not even been set up. Four hours of waiting was, for James, something utterly impossible, and he resolved, as you know, to take a little trip in order to try out the new machine that he had just invented.

It was, you will doubtless recall, a redoubtable engine of ninety-two powers, directly fueled by the combustion of air, the speed of which could increase in an indefinite fashion, thanks to the pipe-cylinder, rifled turbine-fashion, which plunged in a spiral fashion into the air, bringing into the motor an ever-increasing provision of liquefied ozone.

When he left the square in front of the Yorick Theater, James, without any preconceived plan, set his flight compass in a westerly direction and bounded forward with such rapidity that he disappeared from sight like one of those soap bubbles that rises up and vanishes in a sunbeam.

With tranquilly maintained in the central cabin, James darted a glance behind him, but, to his great regret, could not see anything. Invigorated by his speed, chimneys, small cottages and entire sheepfolds, ripped from the ground, rose into the air in the wake of the aerovortex and obstructed his view. James amused himself for a moment contemplating a bleating ewe that was still suckling her lamb as she flew, and then set his turbines on full and looked toward the sun.

To his great astonishment, he observed that the coasts of England had already disappeared and that he was flying over the Ocean.

Feverishly, he consulted his chronograph; three minutes had gone by since his departure from London. The time in the Scilly Isles being twenty-eight minutes behind that of London, James had already gone back in time by twenty-five minutes. Having left London at four o'clock, James set out to sea at three thirty-five.

That initial success intoxicated him. He moved his lever directly to sixty-fourth gear, raised the firescreen against the inflammation of the air, and the airplane set off over the Ocean like a meteor.

Fifteen minutes later James passed over New York like a comet, at exactly eleven-eighteen in the morning, the time in New York being five hours behind Greenwich time.

From then on, there was a mad dash in pursuit of the past. Well before San Francisco, James caught up with the preceding night, and then the previous evening's sunset, and then the previous day, and then the preceding days of the past.

He saw England again, and the public queuing the day before at the doors of the Yorick Theater, as he was skidding over the clouds, still traveling at top speed and full ozone, with the magnetic currents behind him.

Sometimes, he checked the direction of his flight-compass, took a liquefied beef pill and a few grams of lead somnoline. Then, regenerated, he looked down again at what was happening on Earth.

As he caught up with the months and the years, James became more interested in people and things, and his eyes never quit the guiderope-telephone-amplifier.

Indignantly, he saw himself at the age of six, stealing gin from his poor grandmother, and furiously cut the ignition. He only stopped after two further tours of the Earth, and scolded himself rudely on the eve of the sin. The child laughed at him and called him an old madman. James understood then how many young people make the mistake of not believing in the predictions of old men, and set off again sadly. In addition, he could not understand why he did not remember meeting himself once at the age of six, and that anguishing question earned him a partial seizure of the second frontal circumvolution on the left.

Soon, James felt out of place. The execution of Charles I left him cold, and the discovery of America scarcely excited him anymore, having just discovered it so many times.

Once he stopped in order to have a chat with some Roman generals. He wanted to astonish his listeners, to predict their future; he bluffed, but gave himself away. He was taken for a simple fortuneteller and given a few drachms in exchange for a gold Napoléon, which was accepted without difficulty.

Ever more anxious, James went back through history furiously. He passed over ancient Greece like a shooting star, and disturbed the astronomical observations of Chaldea.

Soon, humans disappeared, volcanoes ignited and the ground was convulsed. James crossed the limits of history and carried on toward the origins of the world.

One day, when he was flying over a virgin forest, listening in amazement to the animals talking, as they still had the right to do before the creation of humans, James suddenly felt a sharp pain in the extremity of his vertebral column, while the aerovortex suddenly stopped, as if jammed by an unusual object.

Astonished, James tried to discover what had happened, and, feeling the injured spot, was utterly amazed to observe, behind his back, the presence of the commencement of a tail. James Stout Brighton was going back to the ape!

"My God," he said, "I believe that it's time to stop, or else I'll soon be in the skin of a zoophyte."

With difficulty, James then retraced his route eastwards, but in first gear this time, the engine having been seriously damaged, and he scarcely got back to history without breaking down.

Fittingly, he returned in time for the creation of man, and God used him as an anonymous worker to avoid incest.

Some say, my dear Monsieur, that he perished lamentably in prehistory, under the pseudonym of Prometheus, others that he returned to his own century on foot, under the name of the Wandering Jew, and yet others that he married the daughter of Seth, by whom he had Enos, who lived for seventy-five years and engendered Lamech, who lived for ninety-two years and engendered Noah, who lived for five hundred years and engendered the *Shamrock*, the first boat worthy of the name. But the future alone will inform us in a certain fashion of that which is true in the human past.

Michel Epuy: *Anthea; or, The Strange Planet*
(1918)

Prologue

Stories of adventure, particularly so-called "interplanetary" fiction, are fashionable. That is one of the reasons that has led the editors of the Bibliothèque de la Plume de Paon to introduce into this collection the short novel *Anthée*, which a master of the genre, J. H. Rosny aîné, greeted on its publication in a literary periodical with vigorous eulogies and a testimony of keen admiration.

The author of *Anthée*, the laureate of one of the most important prizes of the Societé des Gens de Lettres de France (the Prix Jean Revel) has published numerous works in another genre: *Le Sentiment de la Nature, Petite âme, Le Nouvel homme*, etc. Let us also mention his translations; *Oeuvres choisies de Rudyard Kipling*, *Anthologie des humoristes anglais et américains*, *Daphné* by Mrs. Humphry Ward, *Rien que David* by Eleanor H. Porter and ten other novels.

But where Michel Epuy seems to have obtained the greatest success is with his books for children, such as *Petite Princesse, Jacqueline Sylvestre*, etc.

The short novel *Anthée* allies the qualities of an adventure story—originality and fecundity of imagination—with those of the literary novel—a sentiment of beauty and descriptive artistry—and by virtue of that, it is destined to please young readers as well as adults.

To J. H. Rosny aîné,
with admiration and
respectful affection.

Now that my mind has gradually recovered its vigor, lucidity and tranquility after several years of meditation and reflection, I feel a strong urge to describe in detail all that I saw, felt and experienced during the few weeks that I spent on another world.

It was my ambition that was the manifest primary cause of the entire affair. I was an assistant astronomer at the Observatoire de Paris; I was twenty-seven years old; I was impatient to arrive, to make a name for myself—and in order to do that, I didn't spare myself, but until then, my observations and my work had only obtained a rather chilly welcome on the part of my superiors.

I remember very clearly the day on which the great scientist Lador announced that he had discovered a new comet, which was advancing toward the solar system, with a prodigious velocity. There was a tremendous excitement in our small society of young astronomers, infatuated with glory, and as soon as it was asserted that the unknown body would pass even closer to the Earth than Halley's Comet in 1910, everyone did his utmost to obtain some kind of mission, a particular detail to observe, photographs to take or calculations to make. The luckiest, in my view, were those who were appointed to go to a particular point on the equator, because it was from the equatorial line that the passage of Lador's Comet would probably be most clearly visible.

Personally, in spite of my previous work, in spite of the urgent steps I took and the solicitations of my friends, I obtained nothing…less than nothing, since I was obliged to surrender the ocular of my telescope to an aged Swedish scientist who was staying in Paris.

On the evening of the comet's passage, I was wandering sadly through the streets. Deeply affected by my bad luck, I decided to go to a cheerful theater and then to supper—in brief, to numb myself in order to forget my ennui—and not even to raise my eyes to perceive the milky tail of the astral voyager.

I held firm until one o'clock in the morning, but when I came out of the restaurant, all my chagrin returned, and all of a sudden, as if to reduce its force slightly, an idea occurred to me: why did I not go to see my old master Artemion at the Eiffel Tower? He had shown me so much sympathy once. He would certainly be sorry to hear about the injustice of which I was the victim, and would doubtless permit me to glance at the heavens with him.

I took a cab to the Eiffel Tower. I found Artemion beside the wireless telegraph apparatus. His eyesight was poor, as he was not observing himself. He was waiting for dispatches that one of his friends, an illustrious American astronomer, was going to send him from Quito. Because of the difference in longitude, it was scarcely six o'clock in Quito. It was at seven o'clock that the Comet was due to pass close to the Earth. Thus, assuming that the observations would take an hour and the telegraphic transmissions another hour, it would be necessary for us to wait three hours to obtain news. We spent that time pleasantly smoking cigarettes and remembering good times at the École Polytechnique, where Artemion had taught me the elements of the differential calculus.

The hours went by very quickly. I was no longer sad; it seemed to me that somewhere, in the shadow or the mystery of things that are yet to be, a triumph was in preparation for me. I was, at any rate, full of a new ardor and already planning to write a magazine article about my nocturnal conversation with the great scientist. He only incidentally talked to me about the Comet.

"It will probably be the same as it was with Halley's," he said. "All the threats of catastrophe and all the pessimistic anticipations are more or less fantastic. These comets are nothing but masses of very rarefied gases."

"But might we not find one that will impregnate us with deleterious gases?"

"Obviously," Artemion replied, "anything's possible, but these gases, even if they're deleterious, can hardly penetrate the terrestrial atmosphere, which is impermeable as marble to substances of such feeble density."

At this juncture I saw that the wireless telegraph apparatus was functioning. I signaled the fact to the master, and we leaned over the operator's shoulder. The man wrote: *From Quito (Ecuador) relayed via New York: Very good observations. Weather fine. Passage of Comet accompanied by high winds....*

At this point there was a brief interruption, but before I had time to resume my conversation with the scientist, the apparatus began to function again. I leaned over once more.

Very curious phenomenon, the dispatch continued. *Star of apparent diameter equal to the moon static overhead. Seems immobile in our telescopes....*

This time the communication stopped completely. The operator in Quito must have gone to look at the new star, because nothing more reached New York that night—or, in consequence, us.

Personally, I was exultant. Finally, I had my chance. I had no intention of going to bed. At daybreak, I ran to wake up my Aunt Adeline and explain to her precipitately that my glory was ensured if I could lay my hands on twenty thousand francs.

Still half-asleep, the dear old lady, frightened, did not believe a word of what I was saying, but, fearing some tragic story of gambling, signed a blank check for me.

On returning home I piled a few instruments and a few underclothes into a valise and leapt into a cab.

I departed for my conquest. I was going to see the new star, study it, explore it at the closest possible range, make it mine....

It really was a new star. The morning newspapers published the dispatch that I had been the first to see. Others had arrived during the morning, and at midday, special editions gave a few details of the marvelous event. Already, a few precise observations had been made by the astronomers in Quito, who reported that the star abandoned in their sky by the Comet was nowhere near as large as the moon, but that its apparent size was due to its excessive proximity to the Earth.

I didn't wait to find out any more. The same day I took the train to Le Havre, wanting to take advantage of the departure of a fast transatlantic liner. Seven days later I disembarked in New York. Just taking time to buy the last week's newspapers, I leapt aboard a steamer that would transport me to Panama. Four days of sailing, and then across in isthmus by railway; two more days aboard a very comfortable boat, and I found myself in Guayaquil, the port of Quito.

Already, since the second day I had spent on the Pacific waves, I had perceived an enormous round mass on the southern horizon, above the high summits of the Andes, milky white in color, which resembled the moon seen in daylight, and which grew larger the closer we came to the equator. That was the unknown star, the new world that Lador's Comet had been able to pick up in the unexplored regions of space and abandoned there, in close proximity to our Earth.

As I emerged from the railway station in Quito, with my nose in the air, looking for the star, I suddenly heard the jovial and encouraging "Hi there!" by which every good American announces his presence. It was my old friend Merryman, of Harvard University, whom I had met in Australia during the last transit of Venus over the solar disk. He greeted me warmly, and then, divining my intense curiosity, immediately cried: "Interrogate me, my friend. I can give you all the latest details while we go to the hotel."

"Bravo!" I replied. "And thanks. Well, what about this asteroid?"

"It's a tiny planet that has come from God knows where. It has become our satellite. Its name is Anthea…in accordance with the desire expressed by yours truly…."

"You were the first to see it?"

301

"Yes, and as one generally gives planets mythological names, I thought of the name Anthea, with which the Greeks labeled a number of goddesses.[38] It fits quite well, for our celestial Anthea certainly has the look of a big flower blossoming up there...."

"My felicitations," I replied. "So we've got a grip on an unknown world, and we're holding it firmly?"

"Exactly. Anthea is motionless above Quito—which is to say that it's orbiting around the Earth in precisely twenty-four hours, so that it doesn't move relative to us."

"Good—and its dimensions?"

He replied volubly: "Radius of fifty kilometers. Surface area eight hundred and twenty-seven square kilometers. Volume fourteen thousand one hundred and thirty cubic kilometers. Circumference at the equator ninety-four kilometers. Density considerably less than that of Earth, but about equal to that of the moon, about three grams per cubic centimeter."

I didn't flinch under that avalanche of figures, but said: "That gives us a very small planet. Less than a hundred kilometers around! And how far is it from the Earth?"

"Three hundred and eighty-one kilometers."

"But that's no distance at all. Are you sure?"

In fact, compared with the formidable distances that separate the nearest planets, that figure of three hundred and eighty-one kilometers appeared to me to be ridiculously small.

My interlocutor replied: "We're absolutely certain. The planet Anthea is no more than three hundred and eighty-one kilometers away; nevertheless, it hasn't fallen onto the Earth's surface because, compared to the moon, it has a mass a million times lighter...and I dare say that it needs to be, because, being a thousand times closer to us than the moon, it's subject to an attraction a million times greater. There is, therefore, an equilibrium."

Accustomed as I was to the mathematical precision of astronomical observations, I remained nonplussed momentarily

---

[38] Anthea [blossom] was an epithet of the Greek goddess Hera.

before all these certainties acquired in such a short time. Truly, science is a beautiful thing. But I began to question him again.

"You say that Anthea is orbiting the Earth above the equator?"

"Yes, in a plane parallel to the equator. Its orbit is forty-two thousand three hundred and ninety-two kilometers."

"Its velocity?"

"One thousand seven hundred and sixty-seven kilometers an hour. It also rotates on its axis in one hour.

I finally arrived at the palpitating question: "At such close range, your telescopes must have been able to search its surface…?"

"Oh, you old sea-dog!" exclaimed Merryman, rubbing his hands. "I can see where you're going! The figures don't amuse you. You're not a mathematical astronomer; you're a sentimental astronomer. Well, Anthea, which is a solid globe, offers various particularities…."

"Has it got an atmosphere?"

"Yes, and relative to the smallness of the planet, that atmosphere is heavy—by which I mean dense—and it constitutes an envelope several kilometers thick."

"It's a miniature Earth!"

"One never knows," said the American, calmly. "At any rate, no one has yet perceived bipeds there."

"What, nothing at all?"

"Yes, plants—or, at least, dark patches that the telescope resolves into foliage, branches, dendrites…or something similar. But you've brought, I believe, lenses more powerful than ours, so you're going to be the first one to discover whatever there is of interest on Anthea."

There were, indeed, magnificent perspectives for me. I could already see myself famous, in consequence of the works I would publish on the flora and fauna of Anthea. Then again, I thought, that minuscule planet might perhaps be carrying creatures analogous to us. What glory if I succeeded in discovering them, in attracting their attention, in communicating with them! Given the short distance that separated us, every supposition, every hope, and every great dream was possible.

I raised my head and looked at the asteroid. It was a large round patch, a slightly shiny gray-blue in color, suspended like a crystal cup in the pure and ardent equatorial sky. Without wasting any more time studying it with the naked eye, I hastened feverishly to set up the telescope that I had brought from France. The most propitious hours for observation were in the morning and evening, shortly before sunrise and shortly after sunset, because during the night, Anthea enters into the shadow of the Earth, and in the middle of the day it was too close to the sun to be usefully examined.

In spite of the relatively powerful magnification of my instrument, I perceived nothing more than what my friend Merryman had told me. The surface of our new satellite displayed areas as bright and shiny as those of telescopic planets, but what attracted my attention more particularly was the presence in a few relatively scarce places of bizarre patches reminiscent of the appearance of the entangled dendrites that sometimes form on the windows of our apartments after a frosty night. Were they forests? They were brightly colored and vivid in places, in which blue dominated, shiny raw and sparkling. Obviously, nothing similar had been observed on a planet, but my small telescope did not give me greatly magnified images of the patches, or tree-like masses.

After having rapidly repeated the calculations and checked the information furnished by my friend, I spent long hours studying Anthea. There were no mountains there, no rivers or streams; the ground seemed to be very uneven, but covered with rocks of various forms; the flat and shiny parts might have been standing water. I could not perceive any mist or cloud, however; the little planet's atmosphere seemed perfectly limpid and tranquil.

I studied that atmosphere for a long time. When the solar light was refracted through it, it made the asteroid a magnificent blonde halo. With my imperfect instruments, I could not think of discerning the presence of water vapor there, or any specific gas. The absence of clouds and ice caps at Anthea's poles did not please me, for that was strong evidence that the satellite was an entirely cold and dead world. However, the existence of an atmosphere and those singular vegetal forms permitted doubt.

A few days passed during which we did not perceive anything unusual on Anthea. I could not make observations in depth for lack of better—and most of all larger—instruments, and I was desolate. My American friend, seeing that I was irritated and overexcited, succeeded in drawing me away from my vain contemplation by proposing that we undertake a long excursion. He suggested that we attempt an ascension of Chimborazo, the famous volcano whose snowy summit rises to more than six thousand meters above sea level. Thinking that from that height I might be able to see more of Anthea, I agreed.

I won't relate the adventures of that picturesque journey in detail here. In any case, compared with those that befell me shortly afterwards, they would seem insignificant. The only important event, and the one that requires the mention I'm making here, happened at the moment when, exhausted by fatigue, we reached one of the summits neighboring the giant of the Andes.

My feet had scarcely landed on that narrow plateau when I turned toward the star, which was no longer directly overhead. Dusk was falling. The sun was setting in a scarlet atmosphere above the shiny waters of the Pacific, and in the sky, long pink and mauve streamers testified to the presence of a great quantity of water vapor in the normally dry and pure atmosphere of that side of the Andes. Anthea had not darkened yet, for at that height, the solar rays would illuminate it for some time after the disappearance of the sun below our horizon.

Between the violet-tinted mists of the setting sun, at one moment, the sun darted a long beam of light. Then, between my eyes and the green and red spaces flamboyant on the occidental horizon, an immense pink column was interposed, which appeared to link the Earth to Anthea.

Broadening out at each extremity, that long diaphanous stem was perfectly distinct throughout its span. One might have thought that a stalagmite and a stalactite of pure crystal were forming and meeting between the Earth and the asteroid.

My intelligence seemed paralyzed by incredulity before that miraculous apparition.

Merryman did not lose possession of his faculties. After half a minute, triumphantly, he gave me an explanation of the phenomenon.

"It's a column of air!" he said. "It's perceptible because it contains water vapor, which the light is striking very obliquely. From Quito it was always invisible because we were plunged into its base. Its presence proves to us that there's sufficient reciprocal attraction between Anthea and the Earth to provoke a protuberance in the atmospheric envelope on either side; those protuberances have met up, and there's the communication they've established!"

I understood then that something had occurred analogous to what happens at the surface of a liquid in which bubbles of air are floating; one sees the smallest bubbles grouping into a chaplet between two large bubbles. With Anthea remaining constantly above the same point on the terrestrial surface, a suction had been established between the two atmospheres, which, as each is attracted by the neighboring star, had elongated to the extent of meeting up.

In consequence, while returning to Quito, I examined the great problem of traveling to Anthea! The air offered me a route. But who could tell: perhaps the gases surrounding the satellite were deleterious?

No matter: it was necessary to go and see; the chance was too good to miss.

A little later, I revealed my plans to the scientists of the city. All of them, including my intrepid American, thought that I was mad. They kept up appearances and were very polite, but I could see that they had doubts about my mental state.

Once an idea has taken root in oneself, however, and when one has sworn to accomplish a striking feat no matter what the cost, one no longer listens to anything or anyone. I therefore resolved to reach my goal alone.

I shall not weary the reader with a description of my research nor the story of my preparations. This is simply what I did after having meditated my expedition for a long time and ripened my plan.

Secretly, I bought from the government of the little Ecuadorian republic its one and only—but immense—dirigible. The balloon was designed to take eight people up to three thousand meters, along with machinery, reserves of fuel, projectiles, and so on, the whole weighing several tens of thousands of kilos. I had all that scrap iron taken out and replaced by ballast. I had a light glass case fitted into the nacelle, which could be hermetically sealed. From within the case, without giving access to the exterior air, I could operate the valve and drop, by means of successive releases, any quantity of ballast I desired. I took water and food supplies for a week. I added to my provisions a few canisters of compressed oxygen, weapons and blankets.

All these preparations remained unknown to my colleagues and friends. Ten days after my return from Chimborazo my balloon was fully inflated in an enclosure situated in a remote quarter of the city. I was ready to attempt the great adventure.

It was on a tranquil blue night that I walked through the deserted streets of Quito toward the hangars where a few Indians in my service were watching over my balloon. I checked the hydrogen tension and the solidity of the nacelle's attachments. In spite of my ardent enthusiasm, I felt a little embarrassed then, and my bold project appeared to me to be a crazy escapade from which I would obviously not come back alive. Sinister thoughts assailed me at that moment, and I believe it would not have taken much to make me abandon the whole thing at the last moment. My workmen were there, however, waiting calmly for me to go aboard my nacelle.

I had not confided in them, but I assume that they had guessed what I planned to do, for they were looking at me with a sort of superstitious terror that frightfully contracted their grave features. I spared a thought for my friends, my masters....

Having no family, I could certainly risk my life to conquer the fame that is so slow to come nowadays to the most knowledgeable and hard working....

I shut myself in the glazed case of the nacelle. I switched on a little electric lamp, and made sure once again of the presence of my provisions, my implements and my oxygen canisters. Finally, I gave the agreed signal.

The muscular arms of the Indians rose and fell in unison; the axes that cut the mooring ropes gleamed in the night, and the balloon suddenly rose up with a prodigious bound to a thousand meters above the capital of Ecuador.

The die was cast! I was off!

I had deliberately chosen a night free of wind. The balloon therefore continued to rise, albeit more slowly, and to head directly toward the marvelous flower of the heavens, around which shone the pure equatorial stars.

I had calculated that with the reduced weight that it was carrying, my balloon ought to rise initially to a height of about ten kilometers without it being necessary to discard any ballast. I suspended my electric lamp from the ceiling of my glass case and, with my eyes fixed on the barometer, I waited.

The instrument lowered constantly, but much more slowly than I had thought. Knowing that in order to bring my reckless enterprise to a successful conclusion it was necessary to act quickly, and so I hastened to activate the hook that was retaining my ballast and to drop a considerable fraction of it.

The balloon must certainly have made an enormous bound, but, strangely enough, the barometric level hardly quivered. I remained perplexed for a moment, but then I reflected that I was inside the column of air extending between the Earth and the new star, and I realized that all along that column, the atmospheric pressure did not diminish as one drew away from the Earth, because I had air above me all the way to the other atmosphere.

I obtained precious encouragement from that: as a consequence of the constancy of the atmospheric pressure, my balloon would continue to rise indefinitely. I aided it by getting rid of almost all my ballast, and I waited....

Whatever the undoubtedly prodigious speed was at which I was drawing away from the Earth, a journey of three hundred and eighty kilometers could not be accomplished in two or three hours, and as one never has any sensation of displacement when in a balloon, I remained very anxious and impatient.

Beneath me, the Earth was plunged in shadow, and the last lights of Quito had faded away into the distance a long time ago. Above my head, the enormous mass of the balloon prevented me from seeing the star. I was afraid, most of all, of a sudden gust of wind that might have caused me to deviate from my route and driven me outside the column of air, but in that case the barometer would have warned me about my actual elevation.

Slowly—very slowly—the night went by. Day returned. I saw the Earth again. There was no longer anything below me but an enormous round surface around which the sky made a blue halo. I concluded that I was a long way away.

At that moment, an unexpected phenomenon occurred. I felt a great shock, as if my balloon, projected through the air, had suddenly stopped; then it appeared to me to deviate from the perpendicular. It was as if it were being pushed sideways by an invisible force, which my nacelle remained beneath the point that it had occupied a moment before.

For a second I saw Anthea, enormous and very close. I did not have time to cry "Hurrah!" The body of the balloon inclined further, sufficiently to reach the height of the nacelle, and then it performed a pirouette, changing its orientation completely, and, suspended once again immediately beneath the balloon, I perceived the unknown world beneath my feet.

I understood that the attraction of the star had just made itself felt, and that if I didn't do something, I would rise up again toward the Earth, or at least remain in suspense between the two attractive forces of our immense globe and its tiny satellite. I hastened to open the valve, and then saw the barometer rise progressively again as I descended slowly toward Anthea.

Having arrived a few hundred meters above the ground, I let a little air into a cage containing a canary. Before anything else, I wanted to make sure that the atmosphere that I had entered was breathable. The little animal did not appear to experience any inconvenience. This time, I did utter a resounding "Hurrah!" and I tugged the cord of the valve again.

My landing was easy; no wind hindered the operation. I descended slowly on to a fairly large rock surrounded on all sides by a shiny expanse that I took at a distance to be ice. Before jumping out of the nacelle I was able to hook my anchor onto a fissure in the stone. Once disembarked, I coiled my rope around a large block of granite, and was finally able to look around.

My rocky outcrop was a few meters square. Around that islet, a shiny substance was sparkling in the sunlight. I drew nearer to it; it was as hard and unified as glass; one might have thought it an immense sheet of mica. The extent was not very considerable, however; a few hundred meters away I perceived a line of rocks, and further away, entangled branching forms that looked something like gray trees, live olive trees.

I took a tentative step onto the shiny substance surrounding the islet. It was so smooth and polished that I nearly lost my footing. I returned to my nacelle, equipped myself with weapons and a sack of provisions and returned to the edge of the lake of glass. It was not ice, but a kind of rock analogous to hyaline quartz. I took off my shoes, and was able to venture on to the slippery surface carrying my shoes in my hand.

A strange arrival for a Terran on a new world! It made me think of a Muslim going into a mosque. And to be sure, a certain religious dread and apprehension of the unknown slipped into my sentiments.

Having reached the other shore, I put my shoes back on and climbed up onto the ridge.

The air was diaphanous, light and slightly chilly, akin to a frosty white morning in autumn. So far as I could see ahead of me, there was nothing but stony surfaces strew with stone blacks with clear-cut ridges, and in the marvelous light that bathed the rocks with rich and various colors there was a perpetual steaming of colored rays reflected by innumerable facets of crystals, gems and sparkling pebbles.

At first, I did not pause to examine those minerals, so brilliantly colored and illuminated, but searched avidly for traces of organic beings, for I had not yet perceived a blade of grass or a flying bird—nothing suggestive of active life. There was nothing in the vicinity but one of the patches of vegetation already glimpsed from the Earth. I ran toward it, so desirous was I of making contact with a living being, even a simple tree.

Alas, the dendrites were made of stone!

They offered such striking resemblances to real vegetables, however, being provided with leaves, thorns and even fruits in pods, that I wanted to examine them more closely. I broke a few branches and studied the interior material with the aid of a pocket magnifying glass. The cross-sections revealed a perfectly normal structure; within the thickness of the leaves the cells were perfectly recognizable, and in the center of the branches, the medullary sheath was also quite distinct. I had, therefore, petrified vegetables before my eyes.

Nothing can give an idea of the picturesque appearance of those forests of stone. They displayed their rigid lacework far and wide beneath the brilliant sky. The mineral substances that had been incorporated into the plant cells were all coated with delicate tints of opal and pearl. Here and there, entire branches seemed to have been penetrated by violet fluorine;

311

elsewhere, stems had been changed into wands or steles of amethyst quartz.

I observed that the mosses and lichens that grew in the cracks in the rocks, as well as the grasses and small plants in the fields had not escaped the disaster either. Even the nourishing soil seemed to have been metamorphosed into stone everywhere. It was only some time later that I discovered humus beneath the vitrified layers resembling glass or mica.

Saddened, I was about to continue the exploration of that globe, on which some frightful cataclysm had fallen in the course of the ages, when I perceived that the sun was declining toward the horizon. I was surprised, because I thought it was still the middle of the day. Had my chronometer stopped and then stated working again without my realizing it?

Disconcerted, I studied the dazzling occidental regions, where the sky was a gilded green. The sun was descending rapidly below the horizon. But then, to my great astonishment, the light did not diminish, and my body projected a huge shadow in front of me….

I turned around swiftly. In the direction opposite to the one in which the sun had just disappeared, an enormous and luminous star was rising rapidly. The ascent of the gigantic globe into a deeply tinted, almost violet sky dissipated the initial shadows of dusk, bathing the green and pink spaces, the red rocks and the blue and opaline petrifications with blonde light.

The star was immense; it had only partly emerged as yet from the horizon, but the edge of its circumference was already high in the sky. Once risen, it seemed to occupy about a quarter of the whole celestial expanse, but because of its vast surface area and its relative proximity, its illumination was equal to that of the sun. On considering the star very attentively, I perceived a number of large dark patches on the surface, and other greenish ones, bulges, and then, a little farther away, snowy peaks, and finally, an entire coastline and a huge shiny surface. It reminded me of a geographical map, and I immediately understood. It was the Earth, our Earth, rising in the sky of Anthea.

It did not require long reflection to grasp the reasons for all those phenomena. I knew that Anthea rotated on its axis in an hour. Thus, for half an hour it was the sun that illuminated me, and during the following half hour it was the Earth, which, entirely sunlit, was sending me a large quantity of light. When it was dark in South America, it was also dark over the entire surface of Anthea, since its rotatory movement was then accomplished in the Earth's conical shadow.

I resumed exploring the little planet. It was evident that in the wake of a terrible catastrophe—some contact with a sun—molten rocks or unknown gases had caused a total mineralization of Anthea. Trees, plants and flowers had existed there, but had there had ever been animals on its surface, or even humans?

I could not see any trace of them, and I thought that the asteroid had only ever known the vegetal realm. Even the vegetables had not belonged to any definite and known family. Insofar as could be judged after their petrifaction, they had had a radial structure reminiscent of that of an octopus. They possessed a globular body slightly larger than a human head, and from which departed relatively thin branches, abundantly supplied with leaves, cilia and thorns. The great central vesicle also bore spurs or rigid spines, which were planted in the ground. I could not determine anything with regard to their roots.

There were evidently several species of the vegetables in question, for I saw petrifactions that were very different from one another, either in size or in general morphology, but the basic form, with the central globule, was always retained.

When evening came—the true evening of the Earth—and our immense globe only reappeared over my horizon after sunset as a large pale azure star, I experienced an indescribable anguish. I walked slowly through the rocks, which seemed to take on strange and hostile attitudes in the shadow. At the feet of blocks of pink porphyry, basaltic prisms and trachyte obelisks, diamonds sparkle like the eyes of animals lying in ambush. Further away, large cliffs, painted in fresco fashion as if they were made of Australian opal, displayed their dream landscape beneath the unfamiliar sky. Everywhere, I trod on rubies, topazes and garnets, which rolled under my footsteps and shattered on the marble with sharp sounds like bursts of satanic laughter.

The magnificent evening exhaled an unknown sadness. The virginal air arrived from the confines of space, and instead of intoxicating me, weighed upon my chest. I was on a dead world, an earth buried forever beneath its garment of stone. I would never know what prodigious beings had lived there. There was nothing more for me to do but go away.

I spent the night aboard my nacelle. Exhausted by fatigue, I slept heavily and dreamlessly.

When I woke up, it was daylight.

During the final moments of my sleep I had seemed to hear soft music, like that of a distant choir of child-like voices. I rubbed my eyes and stood up in the nacelle.

I could no longer hear anything, but at the moment that I put my hands on the bulwark in order to jump down to the ground, the distant concert resumed. Yes, that was definitely what I had heard, and probably what had woken me up. It was a slow chant comparable to the one crickets produce on beautiful summer evenings, but in what I could hear there were more nuances, more harmony, more notes—more artistry, in a word.

It lasted for a few seconds, and then ceased completely.

I immediately thought of some chemical, physical or electrical phenomenon, and, my repose having restored my energy and my audacity, I resolved to elucidate the problem— and, in any case, to explore the dead planet as scientifically as possible. I equipped myself with a mineral box, a revolver, a sturdy knife and enough food for two days, and set out across the strangely colored rocks of Anthea.

The bizarre music did not make itself heard again. Only my footsteps resounded in that bleak and lifeless world. I

314

walked rapidly, with a view to reaching as quickly as possible a line of large rocks that I had perceived on the horizon the day before, like a crenellated wall. I recalled that my star, small as it was, nevertheless had a circumference of a hundred kilometers, and that it would require a certain time to study it thoroughly. On the other hand, I only had food for a week; I therefore had to hurry, for it was scarcely probable that other people would ever attempt to repeat my perilous voyage.

On the way I admired once again the splendor of the rocks. There were malachites, cinnabars, agates, onyxes, marbles and varicolored sandstones. In places, stones assembled in circles formed vast amphitheaters whose arenas were covered in fine soft sand where brilliant flecks of gold abounded.

Elsewhere, crenellated, excavated and sculpted, I was presented with the aspect of an old fortified city that had fallen into ruins thousands of years ago. Church steeples, towers, ramparts, houses and palaces were aggregated there. Magnificent porticos in pink tourmaline opened in smooth walls of Sarrancolin marble. Further away, minarets embroidered beryl lacework in the sky. Everywhere, streets and corridors zigzagged through the ruins. Spacious avenues were bordered by basalt steles, and here and there, the figures of sphinxes and monsters, winged chimeras and satyrs' faces were perceptible in the infinite heaps of rocks.

Apart from those fantastic cities, the surface of Anthea was as smooth as glass or rippled, like an abruptly frozen sea. I had not heard the distant music again, nor seen anything that might explain it.

In the middle of the day I was wandering in one of those mysterious deserted cities of feldspar and chrysoprase, in which several winding and intersecting corridors always brought me back to the center of the city. Weary and enervated, I renounced following my route for the moment and sat down in the shade of a large cornaline obelisk. I started eating lunch.

While I was thus occupied, I heard something like a feeble flutter of wings, which was almost immediately followed by a slight sound similar to the scraping of a cicada, which only lasted for a fraction of a second. All that seemed to come from the top of the pillar in the shade of which I was sitting. I looked up swiftly.

About twenty meters above me, at the summit of the red stele, a monstrous plant was looking at me....

I do mean a *plant*. It had a green body, a little larger than a human head, and from that globe protruded flexible leafy or flowery branches, with spikes, suckers, hair and moving tendrils, at the ends of which eyes were shining: veritable human eyes, which were staring at me.

Gripped with horror, I thought that I was about to be changed into stone in my turn, like all the living beings on the asteroid. But that reflection brought me back to a sentiment of reality: there were, in fact, living organisms that had survived the terrible cataclysm of old. I was about to enter into contact with them, and I understood that the interesting phase of my voyage had begun.

The vegetal creature was posed on three spines, and moving its eye-bearing tendrils very slowly, as if to modify the aspect and the angle from which it was able to look at me. I didn't move an inch, telling myself that if it suddenly extended its supple branches, equipped with claws analogous to those of ivy, I would surely be at its mercy. Better to play dead.

I was lucky, for after a few moments, after its tendrils had twisted considerably, a few of them stretched out horizontally, their leaves, which were conspicuously digitate, started striking the air like the feet of aquatic birds on the water; the being rose up, hovered momentarily around the obelisk, and finally disappeared behind a dome of viridian sandstone.

I was no longer hungry. My forehead was covered in sweat. After a brief hesitation, however, the scientific instinct got the upper hand over fear and I hastened to climb a kind of pyramid nearby, in the hope of following the flight of the strange being.

From up there, in fact, I perceived it again. It descended slowly to the ground and, having reached the bottom of a steep cliff, suddenly disappeared into a fissure that I had not seen at first, which seemed to be the entrance to a cavern.

Then, from that gaping dark hole, the same music emerged that had surprised me when I awoke. One might have thought it a chorus of crystalline cicadas. It was an exceedingly delicate symphony, very diversely modulated, and subtly nuanced.

There were evidently numerous performers, and it was their thin and various voices that were producing the singular sounds. That was soon confirmed for me; about ten plants immediately emerged from the cavern; they were all similar to the one on the obelisk, except for their flowers, which were various in color: reds, yellows and blues.

The creatures flew toward me; their eyes were wide open at the end of extended stems, and their spines were aimed in my direction. I wanted to run away but I didn't have time. They surrounded me; their crampons seized me; I was lifted up and carried away into the air....

I could scarcely struggle. In any case, if I had succeeded in freeing myself, I would have fallen onto the rocks from a height of several meters. I therefore waited for a propitious moment.

Soon, the flying vegetables descended. They settled, without letting go of me, on a flat surface covered with sand. Then I started struggling. I succeeded in getting my knife out of my pocket, and with one hand free, I slashed at the supple tendrils that were gripping me.

Moans emerged from the green globes; spines, which were two or three meters long and very sharp, were thrust toward me. I saw that they were about to transpierce me like a fly beneath a pin. With a desperate effort I seized my revolver and started firing at the monsters' globular bodies.

That saved me. The grip of the claws relaxed; I finished freeing myself with the aid of my knife, bounded out of the stone circle and ran like a madman into a long avenue.

I darted glances in all directions looking for a refuge. It took a long time to find one, and I expected at every moment to hear the quivering of propulsive leaves behind me, but I finally glimpsed a narrow fissure in the rocks, behind which a dark space appeared to me to suggest the existence of a little grotto.

I headed for it; indeed, beyond the fissure, the rock hollowed out into a kind of rounded pocket. It seemed like a useful shelter to me; it had no other opening than the one through which I could scarcely slide; the bodies of the vegetables could not, therefore, get through. Lying on the sand that covered the floor of the small cavern, I looked outside.

A few of the monsters had followed me. They were there, posed on their spurs. Their eye-bearing stalks were lowered, creeping along the ground, advancing as far as the corners of the fissure. Then they became still, staring at me. I was, in consequence, a prisoner, but probably safe so long as I remained in my hole. I recovered my composure and consoled myself slightly with the thought that I had food for two days and that in the meantime, I would doubtless find a means of getting rid of my singular jailers.

I considered them curiously.

They were creatures without any possible name. Simultaneously vegetables, by virtue of their leaves, flowers, coloring and general appearance, and animals by virtue of their eyes, their mobility and their voices, they must be part of an intermediate realm that had only developed on Anthea.

I thought about the petrified forests that had attracted my attention when I arrived. The forms immobilized by the mineralization of their tissues recalled those of the living beings that were watching me at present. Undoubtedly, these, better organized and not rooted, had been able to escape the cataclysmic petrifaction by taking shelter in deep caverns, but there was certainly an analogy between the two kinds.

I soon observed, joyfully, that the creatures were not attempting to get into my refuge. Although their globular bodies could not get through the entrance, I had feared that their spines or their long tendrils fitted with crampons might seek me there.

There was doubtless a mysterious reason for that reluctance on their part. Perhaps they were afraid of my knife. In any case, assuming a defensive stance, I used a few solid blocks of stone that I had found in my cave to wall up the entrance a little more securely.

I kept my revolver and my knife in hand until dusk. I hoped that the approach of night might incite my guards to relax their surveillance, and perhaps even to abandon it, but nothing of the sort. As soon as the sun had completed the last of its twelve daily journeys through the Anthean sky, vivid phosphorescences lit up on the creatures' ocular peduncles. In combination, those gleams illuminated the nearby rocks clearly, and I saw that my jailers had become more numerous.

They were greatly agitated. They were conferring with one another, talking—there is no other way to describe the modulated sounds that they were emitting. Thus, I saw two of them that were detached from the principal group, and obviously conversing with one another: responses followed questions and were spoken in a humble and evidently subaltern tone.

From time to time the eye-bearing branches rose up and came to apply their pupils to the gap that I had left in my defensive wall, the phosphorescent dots projecting a bright light into my grotto—and when the eyes had perceived me, they withdrew in order to settle on the sand again or some ledge in the rock.

From that moment on I judged that I was doomed. My cavern had no other exit. If, therefore, I was surrounded there for four or five days, I was certain to die of hunger. Could I attempt a sortie? Undoubtedly, before launching myself outside, I had a good chance of putting down several of the denizens of Anthea's *hors de combat* with revolver shots, but what about afterwards? Without ammunition, how would I get away from the others?

I shall not give an account here of the sufferings and tortures I endured during my long imprisonment in that narrow cavern. When hunger and thirst had weakened me, horrible hallucinations came to add to the anguish of the real...and always, through the fissure that gave me a little light and air, those eyes surrounded by leaves were spying on me.

During the early hours, I tried to allay my terror and egotistical cares by devoting myself to disinterested investigations: I observed the forms, the organs and the mores of the inhabitants of Anthea.

The Antheans were not ugly, but they defied comparison with any living creature known on the Earth. Cephalopods, corals, starfish, trees, butterflies, birds: they were all of those in one, and they were even human as well; it was impossible to be mistaken about the signs of intelligence, reflection and decision that they displayed. The sounds they emitted were, I believe, produced by small taut membranes at certain points in their spherical bodies. The same organ might have served their sense of hearing, which was evidently very keen, for as soon as I stirred in my hiding place, several eyes turned in my direction.

At any rate, they conversed between themselves by means of sounds they emitted at will. I saw them depart, stop, act and pause in response to modulations produced by others, doubtless their leaders.

I made all those observations during the first days, but when I had exhausted my food supplies, I no longer had the courage to study the curious beings. At the end of the fifth day, I was lying drowsily on the floor of the little grotto. I thought that death would be a long time coming, and I could not think of anything to do except to make use of my revolver to cut short my suffering.

I was still there when, in the evening, I was surprised to feel myself lightly stirred, as if the ground on which I was lying had shifted. I thought I was the victim of one of the frightful dreams that were haunting me, but a few seconds later, the same phenomenon was reproduced. At the same time a long muffled rumor seemed to come from the entrails of the little planet.

That died down, but then, a few moments later, the tremors and subterranean noises resumed, more loudly, It was definitely an earthquake. Finally, a shock more powerful than the preceding ones flipped me over like an omelet, and at the same time, a block of stone, detached from the vault, blocked the opening completely.

Thus, I was imprisoned alive. Nevertheless, I felt my strength returning as a new idea occurred to me. I had seen that block seal the entrance to the cave; it was therefore possible that a fissure had opened up somewhere in the walls, which might communicate with other caverns. In addition, a moment before, I had felt warm breath on my face, like that of an animal; I had an intuition that a shaft descending very deeply into the central core had opened up not far away from me.

I started crawling, very cautiously and with great difficulty, around the perimeter of my cavern. After a short while, I did indeed find a tunnel that descended almost vertically. I followed it.

It descended, and then rose up again. Over its course orifices opened, from which hot air was exhaled. It went through chambers of whose dimensions I had no indication, except for the distant echoes of my footfalls…but I always found an exit. I leapt over obstacles and gaping shafts with the precision of a somnambulist. It seemed to me that I was acting in a dream.

I don't know how long that terrible flight through the darkness went on. Instinct alone, the old animal instinct of self-preservation, kept driving me forward in the scarcely lucid hope of finding a way out.

Finally, I reached a terminus. There was no exit; it was a cul-de-sac.

Well, it was all over. It ended there. My adventure, my life—it was all finished. There was nothing more to do. No possibility remained to me. I would never be able to find my way back to the first cave through the maze of subterranean tunnels, and even if I did manage to return to that first grotto, it would be impossible for me to move the rock that had obstructed its entrance. In any case, what evidence did I have that the terrible Antheans were not still at their post back there?

I thought, therefore, that it was all over. After a time, I woke up again, recovering a little consciousness. In my despair, I grabbed hold of a projection of the rock, which I shook frantically, as if in the puerile hope of shifting it.

I only succeeded in provoking a slight rain of fine sand, which started trickling slowly over my hand.

Already weary, defeated and resigned, I fell unconscious again. I left my hand where it was, in the little stream of sand, which caressed it as it fell, slowly....

Again, time faded away, becoming an indeterminate notion. Pessimism weighed upon me in consequence. Hideous visions passed before my eyes. The passage of blood through my cerebral arteries metamorphosed into the sound of a drum, trumpets or cymbals, and then into choirs of angels, very soft and very distant....

I had closed my eyes....

Suddenly, the cessation of the drizzle of sand over my hand interrupted my lethargy. I opened my eyes again....

Then life flooded my veins with magnificent waves.

Daylight! I could see daylight!

Above me, in the hole hollowed out by the flight of the sand, light was filtering through a pane of dirty glass. I tapped on it with my fingertips. The pane was thin; it resonated. I struck it with a stone; it shattered, and a rush of pure air hit my face.

A few seconds later the opening had been enlarged and I emerged onto the surface of the shiny mica that surrounded, like a dazzling frozen pond, the islet on which my balloon was moored.

My poor balloon! Something terrible had happened to it as well. I saw that it was utterly deflated, lying limply over the rock like a rag. Even before thinking about digging into my reserves of food, I gazed at the envelope. It had large gashes all over it, all of the same nature and the same size, through which the gas must have escaped in a matter of seconds. By their pattern and the neatness of the lacerations, I had no difficulty deducing that they were due to the large spines of the Antheans.

That new catastrophe, arriving at the very moment that I had thought I was saved, floored me. I don't know what primitive and instinctive force prevented me from lying down beside my nacelle, prey to a mortal torpor.

After having pulled myself together somewhat, I examined the canvas and gutta-percha envelope for some time in order to take account of the exact extent of the disaster. I was already thinking about repairing the gashes, but I realized that they were too large, and I did not have the necessary materials.

No, it was no longer permissible for me to think about returning one day to the society of my fellows, to the gentle Earth on which wheat grows, where flowers are rooted in the soft ground amid silky grass, and where women's eyes cause one to dream in the evening....

I was condemned to live for a few more days on that mineral globe and then to die of hunger, even if the frightful Antheans left me in peace.

Perhaps I might escape them by taking refuge in the dark subterranean tunnels from which I had just emerged, but what was the point in running away from them?

Yielding completely to reflections of that sort, I gradually slipped into a heavy and reparative sleep.

I had doubtless been asleep for several hours when I was half-awakened by a light breath that passed over my face several times.

Still exhausted by fatigue, I paid no attention to that phenomenon, which would have been striking had I been awake, for no wind ever blew over the surface of Anthea.

I went back to sleep.

After an interval, the breath recommenced, and then there were slight touch sensations. Still drowsy, I tried to make a gesture with my hand to chase away the importunate contact—but my hand did not obey; it remained bound to something whose nature I could not discern. Suddenly, I woke up completely.

I had been recaptured!

Numerous Antheans were surrounding me, their vegetal claws holding me tightly everywhere. A second after I had opened my eyes, they all took off together, and I found myself suspended twenty meters above the ground. This time, it was impossible for me to defend myself; my feet, my hands and my head were tightly confined by mobile and vigorous tendrils; I could not move so much as my little finger.

It soon seemed to me, however, that the Antheans that had captured me were less well armed and less turbulent—less malevolent, if I might put it that way—than those from the rock city. They did not press their spines against my flesh; they did not squeeze me to the point of suffocation, and—most significant of all—in the keen blue eyes that their leafy tentacles parades around me, I thought I could discern a gentler, less savage gleam.

That aerial journey lasted a long time. We passed over huge masses of rocks, unfathomable precipices, formidable blocks of quartz, ruby obelisks, immense violet, yellow or pink petrified forests.

Finally, the flight of the Antheans slowed down and descended. They circled over a strange round area stranger and even more fantastic than everything I had so far seen on the little planet. It was constituted by a narrow circle of aquamarine blue cliffs. The cliffs, which narrowed in the form of a funnel, were translucent in all their sections; all around their perimeter, mineral concretions affected the forms of monstrous or gigantic flowers and animals. Beryl, lapis lazuli, agate and opal, and numerous unknown stones were blossoming there, under the influence of a mysterious force, in an unimaginable glittering flowering.

Between the marble stems and the delicate sculptures of calcium carbonate, among the calcite foliage, the Antheans took me down gently as far as the narrow opening of a corridor that plunged beneath the rocks. They drew me along that subterranean tunnel, which was faintly illuminated.

Finally, they set me down in an immense and more brightly illuminated grotto. They released me. I stretched myself, and massaged my stiff limbs while already searching with my eyes for an escape route. All the exits were, however, guarded by one or two Antheans, solidly planted on their crampons with their spikes advanced.

At any rate, they did not appear to wish me any harm. The numerous individuals who were in the immense cave paid little attention to me; they continued their fidgeting, their fluttering or their conversations. They seemed to me to belong to a different race from the savage inhabitants of the stone city. Their form and organization was similar, but their voices, still produced by membranes disposed around the perimeter of the globular body, were softer and more musical, their leaves more delicate and covered with a silky down instead of the glandulous cilia with which the other day's pirates had been barbed, and, finally, their flowers were pure marvels. Oh, if it had not been for the anguish of the moment, how I would have been able to admire them!

We think we know on Earth what a beautiful flower can be, evoking the corollas of lilies, the petals of poppies, the cups of buttercups, the bells of campanulas, the faces of pansies, and the strange splendor of orchids. Bah! That's nothing. It's necessary to have seen, as I have, those multicolored corollas, those dreamlike hues, those indescribable forms, all stroked by divine light.

I now regret not having looked more closely at those marvels, but at the time I saw nothing but presages of death everywhere. I was, however, able to walk freely about the caves, each of which must have been hundreds of meters in length and breadth, and which followed one another in sequence like the reception rooms of a palace. The light therein came from outside, through the vitrified layers that I had so often observed on the surface of Anthea.

The successive rooms contained marvels: stalagmites grouped into inextricable forests; colored concretions formed multitudes of frightening and monstrous figures; calcareous deposits formed fringes and lacework. Crystals sparkled everywhere. Shallow bowls superimposed in steps were made of opaline quartz as translucent as glass. Entire walls of columns, like huge organs, were ornamented with prisms of white, yellow or pink calcium carbonate, which sparkled with stony vegetation like gigantic polyps. Then there were the bas-reliefs, the fluted columns, the strange sculptures, the rounded bosses.

A well organized activity reigned throughout the home of that Anthean people, composed of ten or twelve thousand individuals. I could not discern at first the precise objective of their activity, but I recognized later that their organization was perfect; they went in search, outside or in distant caverns, of mineral substances that they brought back, manipulated and stored. Thus, they prepared reserves of nutrients, which they enclosed in geodes or hollow stones, which abounded everywhere in all the grottoes.

Having walked for a long time through the workshops and storerooms of the Antheans, and feeling hunger gnawing at me, I was obliged to taste that aliment, initially in small doses. It was a slightly sugary substance, apparently very rich in carbon and nitrogen. Several individuals, on seeing me consuming that nourishment, assembled around me and considered me with curiosity, but they made no attempt to stop me from eating. I suppose that, like bees, those creatures subject certain unknown substances to a kind of fermentation—or, rather, chemical transformation—from which that slightly insipid sustenance results, but in sum, nourishing.

After several fruitless attempts, I made no further attempt to escape. The Antheans were keeping me at their disposal with some mysterious objective that I could not fathom. Doubtless, for them, I was a monstrous and bizarre creature that they were studying. Several of them came to see me every day; they prodded me, considering me at length, and conversed between themselves. At length, I recognized that they were always the same individuals. They retired after each visit to a little gypsum grotto. They must have been that people's scientists.

Gradually, I took more interest in those laborious sages. Morning and evening they met up and sang in chorus hymns of a sort that surpassed in harmony, softness and magnificent sweetness the purest trills of nightingales and the most sonorous cantilenas of crickets.

I was often witness to the nuptials of those strange creatures: the males and females circled slowly beneath the high vaults of the caverns, and when their flowers, extended at the end of spiraloid peduncles finally came together for the sacred exchange of pollen, a formidable clamor of joy rose up from the entire city.

I spent several months there. I eventually began to aid the Antheans in their labors. I rolled before them the nodules of flint that they filled with their alimentary preparations, and replaced them afterwards. Was I their slave? Perhaps, but what does it matter? Activity is a law of life, and I could not get used to doing nothing.

I therefore rendered a few services to certain Anthean workers, who showed unmistakable signs of gratitude toward me. They gathered around me in the evening, during and after the songs that concluded the working day. By dint of repeating the same sounds and pointing to objects with the tips of their leafy tentacles, I began to understand a few of their words, and I was formulating the dream of learning their language, of writing it...what do I know?...when an event rich in consequences caused upheaval in the city of the Antheans and put my life in danger again.

It will be remembered that it was due to an earthquake that I was able to escape from the little cave where the malevolent Antheans of the surface were keeping me imprisoned. The subterranean rumblings that I had heard then were frequently reproduced, filling the grottos with loud rumors reverberated from wall to wall and followed by fearful cries from

327

the people. It even happened that fissures opened up in the rocks and cracks streaked the walls of the large rooms.

Evidently, the central fire of the little planet was not extinct. The entire globe probably being composed of caverns superimposed like a honeycomb, all the somersaults of the molten central nucleus had enormous effects. In any case, the very recent neighborhood of terrestrial mass sufficed to explain the increasingly numerous perturbations that were produced in the entrails of Anthea. Whatever the reason was, the quakes and subterranean rumbles increased progressively in frequency and intensity. I saw the Anthean scientists making several inspections of recent crevices, but the mass of the people remained calm.

Over several days, the volcanic agitation had increased considerably, when, all of a sudden, one morning, an intense shock shook the grottos and dislocated a part of the wall of the one in which I happened to be. Blocks of basalt fell and crushed several Antheans. A few seconds later another subterranean convulsion broke thousands of stalagmites and opened a large fissure in the vault of the cavern, through which air and light from outside entered in floods.

Then the people became excited. All work ceased. Leaders twirled their leaves turbulently and went to take up positions on the outer edges of the opening; guards launched themselves outside and occupied a number of elevated positions in the vicinity.

I soon found out what it was that the Antheans feared.

A few hours after the seismic upheaval, without any further quake having taken place, the Antheans uttered loud cries of fright. The strongest rushed outside, the others hid in cracks in the rock, hid behind stalagmites or enclosed themselves in small caves.

Personally, I climbed onto a sort of ledge that ran around the side wall, rising progressively toward the accidental opening in the vault. I was waiting for a propitious moment to slip outside when I perceived a furious flock of Antheans of the other race.

It was an assault of pillagers, the brigands of the rocks, against the good people of the caverns. The laborious individuals defended themselves valiantly but their enemies were better armed: their spikes were stronger, longer and sharper; their branches were covered with formidable spines or rigid, glandulous, poisoned tendrils. They pierced the bodies of the defenders and poured into the grottos like a whirlwind. One might have thought them a swarm of monstrous hornets raiding a fortunate hive. There was a terrible battle. Hundreds of workers fell, and the attackers soon set about savagely consuming the aliments heaped up in the storerooms. Their leaves were agitating frantically, the elongated flowers on their peduncles waving with proud satisfaction.

As for me, I could not flee. There were still ten meters of sheer wall between the surface and the narrow ledge on which I was crouched. I dared not budge, for fear of revealing my presence to the pirates, and I dreaded that after they had gorged themselves on nourishment, the terrible Antheans might return to the hunt.

This is what happened. They killed many more defenseless individuals, and then, finally, two of them perceived me and flew toward me. They did not strike me immediately, but limited themselves initially to carrying me up to the surface. There they assembled several of their fellows, and then, simultaneously recoiling slightly, as they had the habit of doing before plunging upon an adversary, they aimed their spikes and launched themselves forward.

Facing imminent death, I closed my eyes.

Then, as if the blink of my eyelids had been able to shake the little planet, the subterranean thunder resumed with formidable violence. At the same time, rocks as big as mountains shook, cubic kilometers of basalt rose into the air, and there was a universal chaotic upheaval.

The whole of Althea convulsed.

In a matter of seconds the little globe was dislocated; it broke apart and crumbled. Cracks hundreds of meters long zigzagged in all directions with lightning rapidity. One might have thought that they were running like cracks over breaking ice.

Finally, there was one last explosion, and the asteroid itself shattered into smithereens, its fragments radiating though space in all directions.

The mass of pumice stone on which I was standing was hurled into the sky with an incredible violence. After a few seconds, I saw that it was not falling backwards, as there was no longer a center of gravity behind it, since Anthea, pulverized, was no more.

I no longer had the sensation of being drawn along; my rock seemed to be motionless. It had the form of a pyramid; it might have amounted to a few dozen cubic meters. I reflected that it was bearing away, attached to its mass, a certain quantity of air—but for how long would I have it, and where was I going? Toward what solar system? Toward what constellation?

I hoisted myself up to the summit of the pyramid that now formed the entirety of my world, and had the surprise of seeing on the opposite face the old flattened envelope of my balloon.

I succeeded in crawling underneath the mass of rigging and fabric. It was only an inanimate thing, but in the circumstances in which I found myself, it was pleasant for me to rediscover that object, which had come with me from good old Earth.

Thinking that my minuscule asteroid was continuing to move rapidly through space, I looked around, anxious. I soon had the joy of perceiving a vast blue globe beneath me that appeared to be rapidly increasing in size. Ah! It was the Earth, finally, the Earth! My rock had therefore been hurled in the direction of the Earth, and its initial velocity had been sufficient to bring it into the field of terrestrial attraction—and now it was falling toward our globe with the velocity of a stone falling from the heavens.

I reflected that, after the fashion of shooting stars, it would doubtless catch fire and become incandescent under the friction of our atmosphere. I therefore hugged the punctured envelope of my balloon more violently, attached myself to it by the ends of the mooring ropes, and waited…but not for very long.

Soon, a wind of extreme violence swept the surface of my rock, and I felt it becoming hot. We were entering the terrestrial atmosphere at high speed. It was time to act. I raised myself up to my full height and tried to deploy against the wind the shreds of canvas to which I was attached. The air that was rushing passed with hurricane force inflated the envelope, lifted it up, detached it from the rock….and the fall that was beginning to cut off my breath stopped.

I remained suspended from my improvised parachute…which oscillated for several hours in more or less contrary atmospheric currents, and finally descended slowly, approached the ground and deposited me there, safe and sound…a good kilometer from the coast of Spain.

I thought that destiny wanted to add irony to cruelty by simply letting me perish after my miraculous return to our world, but no—that was only one more petty ordeal, for after a few minutes, I was spotted by the crew of a fishing boat, who picked me up and brought me back to France.

As I've said, several years have already passed since all these events took place, but I didn't feel strong enough until now and sufficiently recovered from my terrible emotions to attempt to recount my adventures. Now it's done.

I suspect that no one will believe me, but I can't help that. Everyone remembers Anthea, its arrival in the skies of Ecuador and its sudden disappearance…but I alone can say: I was there.

I have no witnesses that I can call. I can offer no other proof than my sincerity.

SF & FANTASY

Adolphe Alhaiza. *Cybele*

Alphonse Allais. *The Adventures of Captain Cap*

Henri Allorge. *The Great Cataclysm*

Guy d'Armen. *Doc Ardan: The City of Gold and Lepers*

G.-J. Arnaud. *The Ice Company*

Charles Asselineau. *The Double Life*

Henri Austruy. *The Eupantophone; The Olotelepan; The Petitpaon Era*

Cyprien Bérard. *The Vampire Lord Ruthwen*

S. Henry Berthoud. *Martyrs of Science*

Aloysius Bertrand. *Gaspard de la Nuit*

Richard Bessière. *The Gardens of the Apocalypse; The Masters of Silence*

Albert Bleunard. *Ever Smaller*

Félix Bodin. *The Novel of the Future*

Louis Boussenard. *Monsieur Synthesis*

Alphonse Brown. *City of Glass; The Conquest of the Air*

Emile Calvet. *In a Thousand Years*

André Caroff. *The Terror of Madame Atomos; Miss Atomos; The Return of Madame Atomos; The Mistake of Madame Atomos; The Monsters of Madame Atomos; The Revenge of Madame Atomos; The Resurrection of Madame Atomos; The Mark of Madame Atomos; The Spheres of Madame Atomos*

Félicien Champsaur. *The Human Arrow; Ouha, King of the Apes; Pharaoh's Wife*

Didier de Chousy. *Ignis*

Jules Clarétie. *Obsession*

Michel Corday. *The Eternal Flame*

André Couvreur. *The Necessary Evil*; *Caresco, Superman; The Exploits of Professor Tornada* (3 vols.)

Captain Danrit. *Undersea Odyssey*

C. I. Defontenay. *Star (Psi Cassiopeia)*

Charles Derennes. *The People of the Pole*

Georges Dodds (anthologist). *The Missing Link*

Charles Dodeman. *The Silent Bomb*

Harry Dickson. *The Heir of Dracula; Harry Dickson vs. The Spider*

Jules Dornay. *Lord Ruthven Begins*

Alfred Driou. *The Adventures of a Parisian Aeronaut*

Sâr Dubnotal *vs. Jack the Ripper*
Alexandre Dumas. *The Return of Lord Ruthven*
Renée Dunan. *Baal*
J.-C. Dunyach. *The Night Orchid; The Thieves of Silence*
Henri Duvernois. *The Man Who Found Himself*
Achille Eyraud. *Voyage to Venus*
Henri Falk. *The Age of Lead*
Paul Féval. *Anne of the Isles; Knightshade; Revenants; Vampire City; The Vampire Countess; The Wandering Jew's Daughter*
Paul Féval, *fils. Felifax, the Tiger-Man*
Charles de Fieux. *Lamékis*
Louis Forest. *Someone is Stealing Children in Paris*
Arnould Galopin. *Doctor Omega; Doctor Omega and the Shadowmen* (anthology)
Judith Gautier. *Isoline and the Serpent-Flower*
H. Gayar. *The Marvelous Adventures of Serge Myrandhal on Mars*
Léon Gozlan. *The Vampire of the Val-de-Grâce*
G.L. Gick. *Harry Dickson and the Werewolf of Rutherford Grange*
Edmond Haraucourt. *Illusions of Immortality*
Nathalie Henneberg. *The Green Gods*
V. Hugo, P. Foucher & P. Meurice. *The Hunchback of Notre-Dame*
Romain d'Huissier. *Hexagon: Dark Matter*
Jules Janin. *The Magnetized Corpse*
Michel Jeury. *Chronolysis*
Gustave Kahn. *The Tale of Gold and Silence*
Gérard Klein. *The Mote in Time's Eye*
Fernand Kolney. *Love in 5000 Years*
Paul Lacroix. *Danse Macabre*
Louis-Guillaume de La Follie. *The Unpretentious Philosopher*
Jean de La Hire. *Enter the Nyctalope; The Nyctalope on Mars; The Nyctalope vs. Lucifer; The Nyctalope Steps In; Night of the Nyctalope; Return of the Nyctalope; The Fiery Wheel*
Etienne-Léon de Lamothe-Langon. *The Virgin Vampire*
André Laurie. *Spiridon*
Gabriel de Lautrec. *The Vengeance of the Oval Portrait*
Alain le Drimeur. *The Future City*
Georges Le Faure & Henri de Graffigny. *The Extraordinary Adventures of a Russian Scientist Across the Solar System* (2 vols.)
Gustave Le Rouge. *The Mysterious Doctor Cornelius* (3 vols.); *The Vampires of Mars; The Dominion of the World* (w/Gustave Guitton) (4 vols.)

Jules Lermina. *Mysteryville; Panic in Paris; To-Ho and the Gold Destroyers; The Secret of Zippeliu; The Battle of Strasbourg*
André Lichtenberger. *The Centaurs; The Children of the Crab*
Jean-Marc & Randy Lofficier. *Edgar Allan Poe on Mars; The Katrina Protocol; Pacifica; Robonocchio; Return of the Nyctalope;* (anthologists) *Tales of the Shadowmen 1-10*
Xavier Mauméjean. *The League of Heroes*
Joseph Méry. *The Tower of Destiny*
Hippolyte Mettais. *The Year 5865; Paris Before the Deluge*
Louise Michel. *The Human Microbes; The New World*
Tony Moilin. *Paris in the Year 2000*
José Moselli. *Illa's End*
John-Antoine Nau. *Enemy Force*
Marie Nizet. *Captain Vampire*
C. Nodier, A. Beraud & Toussaint-Merle. *Frankenstein*
Henri de Parville. *An Inhabitant of the Planet Mars*
Gaston de Pawlowski. *Journey to the Land of the 4th Dimension*
Georges Pellerin. *The World in 2000 Years*
Ernest Pérochon. *The Frenetic People*
Pierre Pelot. *The Child Who Walked on the Sky*
J. Polidori, C. Nodier, E. Scribe. *Lord Ruthven the Vampire*
P.-A. Ponson du Terrail. *The Vampire and the Devil's Son; The Immortal Woman*
Edgar Quinet. *Ahasuerus; The Enchanter Merlin*
Henri de Régnier. *A Surfeit of Mirrors*
Maurice Renard. *The Blue Peril; Doctor Lerne; The Doctored Man; A Man Among the Microbes; The Master of Light*
Jean Richepin. *The Wing; The Crazy Corner*
Albert Robida. *The Adventures of Saturnin Farandoul; The Clock of the Centuries; Chalet in the Sky; The Electric Life*
J.-H. Rosny Aîné. *Helgvor of the Blue River; The Givreuse Enigma; The Mysterious Force; The Navigators of Space; Vamireh; The World of the Variants; The Young Vampire*
Marcel Rouff. *Journey to the Inverted World*
Han Ryner. *The Superhumans; The Human Ant*
Pierre de Selenes: *An Unknown World*
Angelo de Sorr. *The Vampires of London*
Brian Stableford. *The New Faust at the Tragicomique;The Empire of the Necromancers (The Shadow of Frankenstein; Frankenstein and the Vampire Countess; Frankenstein in London); Sherlock Holmes & The Vampires of Eternity; The Stones of Camelot; The Wayward*

Muse. (anthologist) *News from the Moon; The Germans on Venus; The Supreme Progress; The World Above the World; Nemoville; Investigations of the Future; The Conqueror of Death*

Jacques Spitz. *The Eye of Purgatory*

Kurt Steiner. *Ortog*

Eugène Thébault. *Radio-Terror*

C.-F. Tiphaigne de La Roche. *Amilec*

Louis Ulbach. *Prince Bonifacio*

Théo Varlet. *The Golden Rock. The Xenobiotic Invasion; The Castaways of Eros; Timeslip Troopers* (w/André Blandin); *The Martian Epic* (w/Octave Joncquel)

Paul Vibert. *The Mysterious Fluid*

Villiers de l'Isle-Adam. *The Scaffold; The Vampire Soul*

Philippe Ward. *Artahe ; The Song of Montségur* (w/Sylvie Miller) *Manhattan Ghost* (w/Mickael Laguerre)

MYSTERIES & THRILLERS

M. Allain & P. Souvestre. *The Daughter of Fantômas*

A. Anicet-Bourgeois, Lucien Dabril. *Rocambole*

A. Bernède. *Belphegor*; *Judex* (w/Louis Feuillade); *The Return of Judex* (w/Louis Feuillade); *The Shadow of Judex*

A. Bisson & G. Livet. *Nick Carter vs. Fantômas*

V. Darlay & H. de Gorsse. *Arsène Lupin vs. Sherlock Holmes: The Stage Play*

Séamas Duffy. *Sherlock Holmes in Paris*

Paul Féval. *Gentlemen of the Night; John Devil; The Black Coats ('Salem Street; The Invisible Weapon; The Parisian Jungle; The Companions of the Treasure; Heart of Steel; The Cadet Gang; The Sword-Swallower)*

Emile Gaboriau. *Monsieur Lecoq*

Goron & Emile Gautier. *Spawn of the Penitentiary*

Rick Lai. *Shadows of the Opera: Retribution in Blood; Sisters of the Shadows: The Curse of Cagliostro*

Steve Leadley. *Sherlock Holmes: The Circle of Blood*

Maurice Leblanc. *Arsène Lupin vs. Countess Cagliostro; Arsène Lupin vs. Sherlock Holmes (The Blonde Phantom; The Hollow Needle); The Many Faces of Arsène Lupin*

Gaston Leroux. *Chéri-Bibi; The Phantom of the Opera; Rouletabille & the Mystery of the Yellow Room; Rouletabille at Krupp's*

Richard Marsh. *The Complete Adventures of Judith Lee*

William Patrick Maynard. *The Terror of Fu Manchu; The Destiny of Fu Manchu*
Frank J. Morlock. *Sherlock Holmes: The Grand Horizontals; Sherlock Holmes vs Jack the Ripper*
Jean Petithuguenin. *The Adventures of Ethel King*
Antonin Reschal. *The Adventures of Miss Boston*
P. de Wattyne & Y. Walter. *Sherlock Holmes vs. Fantômas*
David White. *Fantômas in America*
Pierre Yrondy. *The Adventures of Thérèse Arnaud*

SCREENPLAYS

Mike Baron. *The Iron Triangle*
Emma Bull & Will Shetterly. *Nightspeeder; War for the Oaks*
Gerry Conway & Roy Thomas. *Doc Dynamo*
Steve Englehart. *Majorca*
James Hudnall. *The Devastator*
Jean-Marc & Randy Lofficier. *Royal Flush*
J.-M. & R. Lofficier & Marc Agapit. *Despair*
J.-M. & R. Lofficier & Joël Houssin. *City*
Andrew Paquette. *Peripheral Vision*
Robert L. Robinson, Jr. *Judex*
R. Thomas, J. Hendler & L. Sprague de Camp. *Rivers of Time*

NON-FICTION

Stephen R. Bissette. *Blur 1-5. Green Mountain Cinema 1; Teen Angels*
Win Scott Eckert. *Crossovers* (2 vols.)
Jean-Marc & Randy Lofficier. *Shadowmen* (2 vols.)
Randy Lofficier. *Over Here*

ART BOOKS

Jean-Pierre Normand. *Science Fiction Illustrations*
Raven Okeefe. *Raven's L'il Critters; Rave's Faves*
Randy Lofficier & Raven Okeefe. *If Your Possum Go Daylight...*
Daniele Serra. *Illusions*

HEXAGON COMICS

Franco Frescura & Luciano Bernasconi. *Wampus*
Franco Frescura & Giorgio Trevisan. *CLASH*
L. Bernasconi, J.-M. Lofficier & Juan Roncagliolo. *Phenix*
Claude Legrand, J.-M. Lofficier & L. Bernasconi. *Kabur*
Franco Oneta. *Zembla*
L. Buffolente, Lofficier & J.-J. Dzialowski. *Strangers: Homicron*
Danilo Grossi. *Strangers: Jaydee*
Claude Legrand & Luciano Bernasconi. *Strangers: Starlock*
Thierry Mornet & Juan Roncagliolo. *Guardian of the Republic*
J.-M. Lofficier, M. Garcia, F. Blanco & J. Pima. *Strangers in a Strange Land*